About

Stacy Connelly drea[...] was a kid writing ab[...] boys made it onto t[...] of romance and the [...] 2008, that dream came true when [...] *Wants for Christmas* to Mills & Boon. When she is not lost in the land of make-believe, Stacy lives in Arizona with her two spoiled dogs.

Teresa Southwick lives with her husband in Las Vegas, the city that reinvents itself every day. An avid fan of romance novels, she is delighted to be living out her dream of writing for Mills & Boon.

Despite a no-nonsense background as a West Point graduate, Army officer, and Fortune 100 sales executive, **Caro Carson** has always treasured the happily-ever-after of a good romance novel. As a *RITA*®-winning Mills & Boon author, Caro is delighted to be living her own happily-ever-after with her husband and children in Florida, a location which has saved the coaster-loving theme park fanatic a fortune on plane tickets.

A Christmas Romance

STACY CONNELLY

TERESA SOUTHWICK

CARO CARSON

MILLS & BOON

First Published in Great Britain 2022
By Mills & Boon, an imprint of HarperCollins*Publishers*
1 London Bridge Street, London, SE1 9GF

www.harpercollins.co.uk

HarperCollins*Publishers*
1st Floor, Watermarque Building,
Ringsend Road, Dublin 4, Ireland

A CHRISTMAS ROMANCE © 2022 Harlequin Enterprises ULC

Once Upon a Wedding © 2009 Stacy Cornell
The Maverick's Christmas Homecoming © 2012 Harlequin Enterprises ULC
The Maverick's Holiday Masquerade © 2015 Caro Carson

Special thanks and acknowledgement to Teresa Southwick for her contribution to the *Montana Mavericks: Back in the Saddle* continuity and Caro Carson for her contribution to the *Montana Mavericks: What Happened at the Wedding?* continuity.

ISBN: 978-0-263-31779-4

ONCE UPON A WEDDING

STACY CONNELLY

To all my friends –
Thanks for being as excited about my dream
coming true as I have been.

Chapter One

I can't believe I'm doing this, Kelsey Wilson thought as she hurried through the airport as fast as possible in her straight skirt and low-heeled pumps. Her oversized purse thudded against her side with every step. The shoulder strap caught a lock of red hair that had escaped her sensible bun, and she felt as though someone had reached out and grabbed her. Holding her back from the job she had to do.

The family is counting on you, Kelsey. Her aunt's voice rang in her mind. *You know what can happen when a woman falls for the wrong kind of man.*

Kelsey hadn't needed Aunt Charlene's reminder. She had her mother as an example. Olivia Wilson had thrown away everything for a man who left her with nothing. Olivia had been eighteen when she met Donnie Mardell—Kelsey's father, though she never thought of him in those terms. Donnie had promised Olivia a love of a lifetime, as well as freedom from her too-strict parents, and she fell for every word. When her father made her choose between Donnie and her family, Olivia chose Donnie. But while Olivia may have had stars in her eyes, Donnie had dollar signs in his. When the Wilsons offered him money to leave town, he took it without a glance back at his girlfriend or unborn child.

But Kelsey's cousin Emily hadn't fallen for the wrong man. She was engaged to Todd Dunworthy. The only son of a wealthy Chicago family, he'd come to Scottsdale to start his own company and add to his already considerable fortune. Todd was handsome, charming, and Charlene couldn't have handpicked a better son-in-law.

Kelsey had worked nonstop for the past two months to put together the perfect wedding. The dress, the flowers, the music, the cake, everything wove together like the hand-stitched Irish lace in Emily's veil. But Kelsey knew how delicate that lace was. One wrong pull, and it could all fall apart.

She refused to let that happen.

She *needed* this wedding to be amazing. She'd staked her reputation on the success of the ceremony, certain her cousin's wedding was the spotlight that would make her business shine. She'd been so sure of that she'd put most of her savings into a down payment for a small shop in Glendale. Kelsey had felt confident making the huge step. After all, her aunt and uncle were wealthy, influential people with wealthy, influential friends. Once the guests saw the job she'd done, Wedding Amour would flourish.

Even more important, her aunt and uncle would see that she, too, could succeed, that she was more than the poor relation they'd taken into their home. She'd been sixteen when her mother died, sixteen when Olivia finally admitted she was not an only child as she'd led Kelsey to believe. Oliv had an older brother, a sister-in-law and two nieces...total strangers who became Kelsey's only family.

Hold your head high, Olivia had whispered to Kelsey only days before passing away. Her face pale and gaunt, her blond hair long gone, her mother's eyes still blazed with the pride that empowered her to walk away from her family when she'd been pregnant at eighteen. *You may not have been raised as one of the wealthy Wilsons, but you're going to show them what an amazing young woman you are.*

Tears scalding her throat like acid, Kelsey had promised. She'd had no idea how difficult—how *impossible*—keeping that promise would be.

Finally, though, after eight years, she would have her chance to make good on her word. As a wedding planner, Kelsey had found her niche. She was organized, efficient, detail-oriented. Lessons learned as she scheduled her mother's doctor appointments, oversaw her medications and dealt with the insurance company served her well as she juggled caterers, musicians, photographers and the occasional Bridezilla.

Every wedding that ended in *I do* was a tribute to her mother's memory, and Emily's walk down the aisle would mean more than all the previous weddings. But before Emily could say her vows, Kelsey had to deal with one serious snag.

A sudden attack of nerves cartwheeling through her stomach, Kelsey swung her purse off her shoulder. She unzipped the center pocket and pulled out her day planner where, along with every detail of the wedding, she'd written the flight information. According to the listed arrivals, the plane from Los Angeles was on time.

Connor McClane was back in town.

Kelsey flipped to the front of the day planner and pulled out a photograph. Her aunt had said the picture was ten years old, which could account for the worn edges and creased

corner. Kelsey feared there might be another reason. How
many times had Emily stared at this photograph and wondered
what might have been?

Kelsey had never met her cousin's ex-boyfriend, the bad
boy from the wrong side of the tracks, but the snapshot said
it all. Connor McClane leaned against a motorcycle, dressed
head-to-toe in black—from his boots, to the jeans that clung
to his long legs, to the T-shirt that hugged his muscular chest.
His arms were crossed, and he glared into the camera. A
shock of shaggy dark hair, a shadow of stubble on his stubborn
jaw and mirrored sunglasses completed the look.

Kelsey could tell everything she needed to know from that
picture except the color of Connor McClane's eyes. The man
was trouble, as bad a boy as Donnie Mardell had ever been.
Kelsey knew it, just like she knew Connor was better looking
in a two-dimensional photo than any living, breathing man
she'd ever meet.

Stuffing the picture and her day planner back in her purse,
she hurried to the waiting area, where she focused on every
man headed her way. He'd be twenty-nine by now, she
reminded herself, four years her senior. Kelsey didn't suppose
she was lucky enough that he'd aged badly or gone prema-
turely bald.

A beer belly, she thought, mentally crossing her fingers.
beer belly would be good.

But at the first glimpse of the dark-haired man sauntering
down the corridor, her heart flipped within her chest and h
hopes crashed. No signs of age, baldness or overhanging
waistline…just pure masculine perfection. Her mouth we
as dry as the surrounding desert.

Connor McClane had stepped to life from the photograp
From his form-hugging T-shirt, to his worn jeans and boo
to the sunglasses covering his eyes, every detail remained t

same. A plane took off from a nearby runway, and the low rumble reverberating in her chest could have easily come from a motorcycle.

Kelsey tried to swallow. Once, twice. Finally she gave up and croaked out, "Mr. McClane?"

"Yes?" He stopped to look at her, and Kelsey's only thought was that she still didn't know the color of his eyes. Brown, maybe? To match the mahogany of his hair and tanned skin. Or blue? A bright, vivid contrast to his coloring.

A dark eyebrow rose above his mirrored sunglasses, a reminder that she had yet to answer him. A rush of heat flooded her cheeks. "Uh, Mr. McClane—"

"We've already established who I am. Question is, who are you?"

"My name's Kelsey Wilson."

He flashed a smile that revved her pulse. His head dipped, and she sensed him taking in the red hair she struggled to control, the freckled skin she tried to cover, and the extra pounds she sought to hide beneath the khaki skirt and boxy shirt. She saw her reflection in his mirrored glasses, a much shorter, much wider version of herself, like a carnival funhouse distortion.

Kelsey didn't feel much like laughing.

Had she known her aunt was going to assign her this mission, she would have worn something different—like full body armor. The image of what Emily might have worn to meet her former boyfriend flashed in Kelsey's mind. She shoved the pointless comparison away. Too much like trying to force Strawberry Shortcake into Barbie's wardrobe.

"Well, what do you know?" Connor stood in the middle of the corridor, mindless of the sea of people parting around him. "The Wilsons sent out a welcoming party. Heck, if I'd known I'd get this kind of reception, I might have come back sooner."

"I doubt that," Kelsey muttered.

Connor McClane had planned his return perfectly, coming back to ruin Emily's wedding. Aunt Charlene was certain of it. Kelsey knew only one thing. Her cousin had nearly thrown her future away once for this man, and she could see how Emily might be tempted to do it again.

"Don't underestimate your appeal," he told her, and though she couldn't see beyond the reflective sunglasses, she had the distinct impression he'd winked at her.

Kelsey straightened her spine to the shattering point. "My appeal isn't in question. I'm here to—"

Keep him away from Emily, Kelsey. I don't care how you do it, but keep that man away from my daughter!

"To do what, Kelsey Wilson?"

His deep voice made her name sound like a seduction, and suddenly she could think of all kinds of things to do that had nothing to do with her aunt's wishes. Or did they? How far would Aunt Charlene expect her to go to keep Connor away from Emily?

"To give you a ride from the airport," she answered with saccharine smile. "Baggage claim is this way."

Connor patted the duffel bag slung over one shoulder. "Got everything with me."

Eyeing the lumpy bag, Kelsey wondered how dress clothes could survive such careless packing. Maybe he planned to ride his motorcycle up to the church in leather and denim, the same way he'd ridden out of town ten years ago? Unless—

"You didn't bring much with you. You must not plan to stay long."

Something in her voice must have given away her hope, because Connor chuckled. He adjusted the duffel bag and headed down the corridor, his strides so long Kelsey nearly had to jog to keep up.

"Oh, I'll be here as long as it takes," he told her with a sideways glance, "but I won't need more than a few days."

A few days. Did she really want to know? Did she really want to throw down the verbal gauntlet? Kelsey took a deep breath, partly to gather some courage, partly to gather some much needed oxygen. "A few days to what?"

"To stop Emily from marrying the wrong man."

Connor hadn't known what to expect when he stepped off the plane. He'd given Emily his flight information with the hope she might meet him at the airport. He'd wanted a chance to talk to her away from her family and her fiancé. He was realistic enough to know the whole Wilson brigade might be lined up at the gate like some kind of high-fashion firing squad. But he hadn't expected a petite redhead. He'd never imagined the Wilson genes could produce a petite redhead.

"So who are you anyway?" he asked, only to realize the woman was no longer at his side.

He glanced back over his shoulder. Kelsey Wilson stood in the middle of the corridor, her brown eyes wide, her lips adorably parted in shock. She didn't look anything like the other Wilsons, and curiosity stirred inside him. He couldn't picture her at the elegant country-club settings the status-conscious family enjoyed any more than he'd imagined himself there.

A Wilson misfit, he thought, *on the outside looking in.* Their gazes locked, and the momentary connection rocked him. Shaking off the feeling, he circled back around and asked, "You coming?"

The flush of color on her cheeks nearly blotted out her freckles. "You don't actually think you can come back here after ten years and expect to take up where you left off? You weren't right for Emily back then, and you aren't right for her now!"

As far as insults went, the words were pretty tame, especially coming from a Wilson. And it wasn't as if he had any intention of taking up where he and Emily had left off. He'd made his share of mistakes, and some—like thinking he and Emily had a chance—didn't bear repeating. Emily had been looking for someone to rescue her from the life her parents had planned for her, and he'd been young enough to think of himself as a hero.

Connor knew better now. He was nobody's hero.

Still, Kelsey's reminder stirred long-buried resentment. *Worthless. Good for nothing. Troublemaker.* Gordon Wilson had shouted them all when he'd discovered his younger daughter sneaking out to meet Connor. After being knocked around by his old man during his childhood, he knew a thing or two about male aggression and had arrogantly faced down the older man.

But Charlene Wilson's clipped, controlled words had managed to pierce his cocky facade. "From the moment Emily was born, she has had nothing but the best," Charlene told him with ice practically hanging from her words. "We have given her the world. What could *you* possibly give her?"

He'd tried to give her her freedom, the chance to live her life without bowing to her family's expectations. If someone had given his mother that same chance, things would have been different, and maybe, just maybe, she would still be alive. But when Emily made her choice, she didn't choose him. She took the easy way out—and in the end, so did he, Connor thought, guilt from the past and present mixing. But he wasn't going to fail this time. He was here to help Emily, no matter what the redhead standing in front of him like a curvaceous barricade thought.

"Look, whoever you are," he said, since she'd never explained her relationship to the Wilsons, "you didn't know me then, and you don't know me now. You don't have a clue what I'm good for."

He ducked his head and lowered his voice, not wanting to attract attention, but the words came out like a seductive challenge. He stood close enough to catch a hint of cinnamon coming from her skin. The color faded from her complexion, and her freckles stood out clearly enough to play a game of connect-the-dots. He shoved his hands into his pockets rather than give into the urge to trace a five-point star over one cheek. He tried to imagine Kelsey's reaction if he touched her. Would she recoil in shock? Or would he see an answering awareness in her chocolate eyes?

Right now, sparks of annoyance lit her gaze. "I know all I need to know. You're no good for Emily. You never were— What are you doing?" she demanded when Connor leaned around to look over her shoulder.

"Amazing. You can't even see the strings."

"What strings?"

"The ones Charlene Wilson uses to control you."

"Aunt Charlene does not control me."

Aunt Charlene, was it? He didn't remember Emily talking about a cousin, but they hadn't spent time discussing genealogy. "Funny, 'cause you sure sound like her."

"That's because we both want to protect Emily."

Protecting Emily was exactly why he was there. Adjusting the duffel bag on his shoulder, he started toward the parking garage. "So do I."

"Right." Kelsey struggled to keep up with him, and Connor shortened his stride. "Who do you think you have to protect her from?"

"From Charlene. From you." Before Kelsey could voice the protest he read in her stubborn expression, he added, "Mostly from Todd."

"From *Todd?* That's ridiculous. Todd loves Emily."

Yeah, well, Connor had seen what a man could do to a woman in the name of love. Seen it and had been helpless to stop it from happening… Shoving the dark memories of his mother and Cara Mitchell aside, Connor said, "Todd's not the golden boy the Wilsons think he is. The guy's bad news."

"How would you know?" Kelsey challenged as they stepped out the automatic doors and into the midday sunshine. Exhaust and honking horns rode the waves of heat. "My car's this way."

Connor followed Kelsey across the street to the short-term parking, where the fumes and noise faded slightly in the dimly lit garage. "I could tell from the second we met."

She stopped so suddenly he almost crashed into her back. When she turned, he was close enough that her shoulder brushed his chest, and the inane thought that she would fit perfectly in his arms crossed his mind.

Her eyes narrowed in suspicion. "You've never met Todd."

"How do you know?"

"Be-because," she sputtered. "Emily would have told me."

Despite her words, Connor saw the doubt written in her furrowed brow as she walked over to a gray sedan. The car nearly blended into the concrete floor and pylons. Between her plain vehicle and sedate clothes, he had the feeling Kelsey Wilson was a woman who liked to fade into the background.

But he was trained to notice details. He'd bet the brilliant hair she kept coiled at the back of her neck was longer and wilder than it looked, and try as they might, the shapeless clothes did little to hide some amazing curves.

"If Emily tells you everything, then you know she and Dunworthy spent a weekend in San Diego a few weeks ago, right?" At Kelsey's nod, Connor added, "Well, I drove there to meet them, and we had dinner." Keeping his voice deceptively innocent, he asked, "Emily didn't mention that?"

"Um, no," Kelsey grudgingly confessed.

"I wonder why. Don't you?" he pressed.

Not that there was much to tell, although he wasn't about to admit that to Kelsey. When he left town, he never thought he'd see Emily again. But after hearing through the long-distance grapevine that she was getting married, calling to congratulate her seemed like a good way to put the past behind him. The last thing he expected was Emily's invitation to have dinner with her and her fiancé while they were vacationing in California. But he'd agreed, thinking the meeting might ease his guilt. After all, if Emily had found Mr. Right, maybe that would finally justify his reasons for leaving Scottsdale.

But when Connor went to dinner with Emily, he didn't see a woman who'd grown and matured and found her place in life. Instead, he saw in Emily's eyes the same trapped look as when they'd first met—a look he could not, would not ignore.

Kelsey kept both hands on the wheel and her gaze focused on the road, but she was far too aware of Connor McClane to pay much attention to the buildings, billboards and exit signs speeding by. The air-conditioning blew his aftershave toward her heated face, a scent reminiscent of surf, sand and sea. His big body barely fit in the passenger seat. Twice now, his arm brushed against hers, sending her pulse racing, and she nearly swerved out of her lane.

She'd been right in thinking the man was dangerous, and not just to Emily's future or her own peace of mind, but to passing motorists, as well.

"I can't believe how much the city has grown. All these new freeways and houses…" He leaned forward to study a sign. "Hey, take this next exit."

Kelsey followed his directions, wishing she could drop him off at a hotel and call her familial duty done. Unfortunately, playing chauffeur wasn't her real purpose. Connor had flat-out told her he planned to ruin Emily's wedding. If she didn't stop him, her own business would be destroyed in the fallout. Who would trust a wedding planner who couldn't pull off her own cousin's wedding?

Panic tightened her hands on the wheel. "Where are we going?" she asked.

"My friend Javy's family owns a restaurant around here. Best Mexican food you've ever tasted."

"I don't like Mexican food."

He shook his head. "Poor Kelsey. Can't take the heat, huh?"

They stopped at a red light, and she risked a glance at him. He still wore those darn sunglasses, but she didn't need to look into his eyes to read his thoughts. He was here to win back Emily and show the Wilsons and the rest of the world they'd underestimated him all those years ago. But until then, he'd kill some time by flirting with her.

Kelsey didn't know why the thought hurt so much. After all, it wasn't the first time a man had used her to try and get to her beautiful, desirable cousin.

The light turned green, and she hit the gas harder than necessary. "Let's just say I've been burned before."

A heartbeat's silence passed. When Connor spoke again, his voice was friendly, casual and missing the seductive undertone. "You'll like this place." He chuckled. "I can't tell you how many meals I've had there. If it hadn't been for Señora Delgado…"

Kelsey wondered at the warmth and gratitude in his words. Something told her Connor wasn't simply reminiscing about tacos and burritos. An undeniable curiosity built as she pulled into the parking lot. The restaurant looked like an old-time hacienda with its flat roof and arched entryway. The stucco had been painted a welcoming terra-cotta. Strings of outdoor lights scalloped the front porch, and large clay pots housed a variety of heat-tolerant plants: pink and white vinca, yellow gazanias, and clusters of cacti.

Still checking out the exterior, Kelsey remained behind the wheel until Connor circled the car and opened the door for her. Startled by the chivalry, she grabbed her purse and took his hand. As she slid out of the seat, she hoped Connor didn't guess how rare or surprising she found the gesture.

She thought he'd let go, but he kept hold of her hand as he led her along red, green and yellow mosaic stepping stones that cut through the gravel landscape. His palm felt hard and masculine against her own, but without the calluses she'd somehow expected.

When he opened the carved door, he let go of her hand to lay claim to the small of her back. A shiver rocked her entire body. His solicitous touch shouldn't have the power to turn on every nerve ending. And it certainly shouldn't have the inexplicable ability to send her mind reeling with images of his hand stroking down her naked spine…

Full body armor, Kelsey thought once again, uncertain even that extreme could shield her from her own reactions.

Desperate to change her focus, she looked around the restaurant. A dozen round tables stood in the center of the Saltillo-tiled room, and booths lined each wall. The scent of grilled peppers and mouthwatering spices filled the air.

"Man, would you look at this place?" Connor waved a hand at the brightly colored walls, the piñatas dangling from the ceiling and the woven-blanket wall hangings.

He removed his sunglasses to take in the dimly lit restaurant, but Kelsey couldn't see beyond his eyes. Not brown, not blue, but gorgeous, glorious green. A reminder of spring, the short burst of cool days, the promise of dew-kissed grass. Without the glasses to shield his eyes, Connor McClane looked younger, more approachable, a little less badass.

"Has it changed?"

"No, everything's exactly the same. Just like it should be," he added with a determination that made Kelsey wonder. Had someone once threatened to change the restaurant that was so important to his friends?

A young woman wearing a red peasant-style blouse and white three-tiered skirt approached, menus in hand. "*Buenas tardes.* Two for lunch?"

"*Sí. Dónde está Señora Delgado?*"

Startled, Kelsey listened to Connor converse in fluent Spanish. She couldn't understand a word, so why did his deep voice pour like hot fudge through her veins?

Get a grip! Connor McClane is in town for one reason and one reason only. And that reason was not her.

The hostess led them to a corner booth. Kelsey barely had a chance to slide across the red Naugahyde and glance at the menu when a masculine voice called out, "Look what the cat dragged in!"

A good-looking Hispanic man dressed in a white button-down shirt and khakis walked over. Connor stood and slapped him on the back in a moment of male bonding. "Javy! Good to see you, man!"

"How's life in L.A.?"

"Not bad. How's your mother? The hostess says she's not here today?"

"She's semiretired, which means she's only here to kick my butt half the time," Javy laughed.

"I didn't think you'd ever get Maria to slow down."

"This place means the world to her. I still don't know how to thank you."

"Forget it, man," Connor quickly interrupted. "It was nothing compared to what your family's done for me over the years."

Modesty? Kelsey wondered, though Connor didn't seem

the type. And yet she didn't read even an ounce of pride in his expression. If anything, he looked...guilty.

"I'm not about to forget it, and I *will* find a way to pay you back," Javy insisted. "Hey, do you want to crash at my place while you're here?"

"No, thanks. I've got a hotel room."

Finally Connor turned back to Kelsey. "Javy, there's someone I'd like you to meet. Javier Delgado, Kelsey Wilson."

Javy did a double take at Kelsey's last name, then slanted Connor a warning look. "Man, some people never learn."

Still, his dark eyes glittered and a dimple flashed in one cheek as he said, "Pleasure to meet you, *señorita*. Take care of this one, will you? He's not as tough as he thinks he is."

"Get outta here." Connor shoved his friend's shoulder before sliding into the booth across from Kelsey. "And bring us some food. I've been dying for your mother's enchiladas." He handed back the menu without opening it. "What about you, Kelsey?"

"I'm, um, not sure." The menu was written in Spanish on the right and English on the left, but even with the translation, she didn't know what to order.

"She'll have a chicken quesadilla with the guacamole and sour cream on the side. And we'll both have margaritas."

"I'll take mine without alcohol," Kelsey insisted. Bad enough he'd ordered her lunch. She didn't need him ordering a drink for her, especially not one laden with tequila and guaranteed to go right to her head.

"Two margaritas, one virgin," Connor said with a wink that sent a rush of heat to Kelsey's cheeks. With her fair complexion, she figured she could give the red pepper garland strung across the ceiling a run for its money.

"I'll get those orders right up."

As his friend walked toward the kitchen, Connor leaned

back in the booth and gazed around the restaurant. Nostalgia lifted the corners of his mouth in a genuine smile. "Man, I've missed this place."

"So why haven't you come back before now?" Kelsey asked, curious despite sensible warnings to keep her distance.

He shrugged. "Never had reason to, I guess."

"Until now," she added flatly, "when you've come to crash Emily's wedding."

Losing his relaxed pose, he braced his muscled forearms on the table and erased the separation between them. His smile disappeared, nostalgia burned away by determination. "First of all, there isn't going to be a wedding. And second, even if there was a wedding, I wouldn't be crashing. I'd be an invited guest."

"Invited!" Surprise and something she didn't want to label had her pulling back, hoping to create some sanity-saving distance. "Who…" She groaned at the obvious answer, and the confident spark in Connor's emerald eyes. "What on earth was Emily thinking?"

"Actually, she summed up her thoughts pretty well."

Connor reached into his back pocket and pulled out an invitation. He offered it up like a challenge, holding a corner between his first and second fingers. She snatched it away, almost afraid to read what her cousin had written. Emily's girlish script flowered across the cream-colored vellum.

Please say you'll come. I can't imagine my wedding day without you.

Good Lord, it was worse than she'd thought! The words practically sounded like a proposal. Was Emily hoping Connor would stop her wedding? That he'd speak now rather than hold his peace?

"Okay," she said with the hope of defusing the situation, "so Emily invited you."

"That's not an invitation. It's a cry for help."

"It's—it's closure," she said, knowing she was grasping at straws. "Emily has moved on with her life, and she's hoping you'll do the same."

He frowned. "What makes you think I haven't?"

"Are you married? Engaged? In a serious relationship?" Kelsey pressed. Each shake of his head proved Kelsey's point. He wasn't over Emily.

Kelsey couldn't blame him. Her cousin was beautiful, inside and out. And experience had taught Kelsey how far a man would go to be a part of Emily's life.

Connor slid the invitation from her hand in what felt like a caress. "There's no reason for me not to be here, Kelsey."

Here, in Arizona, to stop the wedding, she had to remind herself as she snatched her hand back and laced her fingers together beneath the table. Not *here* with her.

The waitress's arrival with their drinks spared Kelsey from having to come up with a response. Connor lifted his margarita. "To new friends."

Rising to the challenge this time, she tapped her glass against his. "And old lovers?"

If she'd hoped to somehow put him in his place, she failed miserably. With a low chuckle, he amended, "Let's make that old friends…and new lovers."

His vibrant gaze held her captive as he raised his glass. Ignoring the straw, he took a drink. A hum of pleasure escaped him. The sound seemed to vibrate straight from his body and into hers, a low-frequency awareness that shook her to the core.

He lowered the glass and licked the tequila, salt and lime from his upper lip. "You don't know what you're missing."

Oh, she knew. The taste of a man's kiss, the scent of his aftershave on her clothes, the feel of his hard body moving against her own. How long had it been since a man had stolen her breath, her sanity? How many weeks, months? She'd probably be better converting the time into years—fewer numbers to count.

Odd how Kelsey hadn't missed any of those things until the moment Connor McClane walked down the airport corridor. No, she had to admit, she'd suffered the first twinge of— loneliness? Lust? She didn't know exactly *what* it was, but she'd first felt it the moment she'd looked at Connor's picture.

"Aren't you having any?"

Her gaze dropped to his mouth, and for one second, she imagined leaning over the table and tasting the tequila straight from Connor's lips.

"Kelsey, your drink?" he all but growled. The heat in his gaze made it clear he knew her sudden thirst had nothing to do with margaritas.

Maybe if she downed the whole thing in one swallow, the brain freeze might be enough to cool her body. She sucked in a quick strawful of the tart, icy mixture with little effect. Frozen nonalcoholic drinks had nothing on Connor McClane.

Still, she set the glass down with a decisive clunk. "You can't come back here and decide what's best for Emily. It doesn't matter if *you* don't like Todd. You're not the one marrying him. Emily is, and her opinion is the only one that matters."

Connor let out a bark of laughter. "Right! How much weight do you think her *opinion* carried when we were dating?"

"That was different."

"Yeah, because I was a nobody from the wrong side of the tracks instead of some old-money entrepreneur with the Wilson stamp of approval on my backside."

A nobody from the wrong side of the tracks. Kelsey schooled her expression not to reveal how closely those words struck home. What would Connor McClane think if he learned she had more in common with *him* than with her wealthy cousins?

Kelsey shook off the feeling. It didn't matter what they did or didn't have in common; they were on opposite sides.

"Did you ever consider that Emily's parents thought she was too young? She was barely out of high school, and all she could talk about was running away with you."

"Exactly."

Expecting a vehement denial, Kelsey shook her head. "Huh?"

One corner of his mouth tilted in a smile. "I might have been blind back then, but I've learned a thing or two. Emily was always a good girl, never caused her parents any trouble. She didn't smoke, didn't drink, didn't do drugs. No tattoos or piercings for her."

"Of course not."

From the time Kelsey had moved in with her aunt and uncle, she'd lived in her cousin's shadow. She knew all about how perfect Emily was—her fling with Connor the sole imperfection that proved she was actually human.

"Emily didn't have to do those things. She had me. I was her ultimate act of rebellion."

Kelsey listened for the arrogant ring in his words, but the cocky tone was absent. In its place, she heard a faint bitterness. "No one likes being used," she murmured, thoughts of her ex-boyfriend coming to mind.

Matt Moran had her completely fooled during the six months they dated. With his shy personality and awkward social skills, she couldn't say he swept her off her feet. But he'd seemed sweet, caring, and truly interested in her.

And she'd never once suspected he was secretly in love with her cousin or that he'd been using her to get closer to Emily. So Kelsey knew how Connor felt, and somehow knowing that was like knowing *him*. Her gaze locked with his in a moment of emotional recognition she didn't dare acknowledge.

The question was written in his eyes, but she didn't want

to answer, didn't want him seeing inside her soul. "What was Emily rebelling against?"

Connor hesitated, and for a second Kelsey feared he might not let the change of subject slide. Finally, though, he responded, "It had to do with her choice of college. She hated that exclusive prep school, but Charlene insisted on only the best. I suppose that's where you went, too."

"Not me," she protested. "I had the finest education taxpayers could provide." One of Connor's dark eyebrows rose, and Kelsey hurried on before he could ask why her childhood had differed from her cousins'. "So after Emily survived prep school…"

He picked up where she left off, but Kelsey had the feeling he'd filed away her evasion for another time. "After graduation, Gordon wanted Emily to enroll at an Ivy League school. She didn't want to, but her parents held all the cards—until I came along. I was the ace up her sleeve. Guess I still am."

The bad-boy grin and teasing light were absent from his expression, and Kelsey felt a flicker of unease tumbling helplessly through her stomach. Did Connor know something about Todd that would stop the wedding? Something that would tear apart all Kelsey's dreams for success and her chance to prove herself in her family's eyes?

"Emily invited me because her parents are pushing her into this marriage. She's pushing back the only way she knows how. She *wants* me to stop the wedding."

"That's crazy! Do you realize Emily is having her dress fitting right now? And we're going to the hotel tomorrow evening to make final arrangements for the reception? She loves Todd and wants to spend the rest of her life with him."

Leaning forward, he challenged, "If you're right, if Emily's so crazy about this guy, then why are you worried I'm here?"

A knowing light glowed in his green eyes, and history told

Kelsey she had every reason to worry. After all, on the night of her senior prom, after spending the day having her hair artfully styled and her makeup expertly applied, and wearing the perfect dress, Emily had stood up her parents' handpicked date...to ride off with Connor on the back of his motorcycle.

Having met Connor, Kelsey could see how easily he must have seduced her cousin. With his looks, charm, his flat-out masculine appeal, how was a woman supposed to resist?

And Kelsey wondered if maybe Emily wasn't the only one she should be worried about.

Chapter Two

"Honestly, Kelsey, why are you ringing the doorbell like some stranger?" Aileen Wilson-Kirkland demanded as she opened the front door. She latched on to Kelsey's arm and nearly dragged her inside her aunt and uncle's travertine-tiled foyer.

"Well, it's not like I still live here," Kelsey reminded her cousin.

Aileen rolled her eyes. "You probably rang the doorbell even when this *was* your home."

"I did not," Kelsey protested, even as heat bloomed in her cheeks. Her cousin might have been teasing, but the comment wasn't far off. She'd never felt comfortable living in her aunt and uncle's gorgeous Scottsdale house, with its country-club lifestyle and golf-course views. Before moving in with her relatives, *home* had been a series of low-rent apartments. And, oh, how she'd missed those small, cozy places she'd shared with her mother.

"I didn't want to barge in," she added.

"You're kidding, right? Like I haven't been dying to hear how things went! Did you pick up Connor? Does he look the same? Do you think—"

Ignoring the rapid-fire questions, Kelsey asked, "Where are Emily and Aunt Charlene?"

"Emily's still having her dress fitted."

"Oh, I'd love to see it." A designer friend of Kelsey's had made the dress for her cousin, but so far Kelsey had seen only drawings and fabric swatches.

For such a gorgeous woman, Aileen gave a decidedly inelegant snort as they walked down the hall. "Nice try. Do you really think you can escape without going over every detail from the first second you saw Connor right up to when you left him—" Emily's older sister frowned. "Where *did* you leave him?"

"At a restaurant."

"By himself?"

"What else could I do, Aileen? Follow him to his hotel and ask for an invitation inside?"

"Well, that would make it easier to keep an eye on him."

"Aileen!"

Waving aside Kelsey's indignation, Aileen said, "I'm just kidding. Besides, he doesn't have a car, right?"

"Like that's going to slow him down! Don't you remember the time Connor got busted for joyriding in a 'borrowed' car?" She hadn't been around then, but her aunt had remarked on Connor's misdeeds long after he'd left town. In fact, Connor's name had come up any time Emily threatened to disobey her parents. Like some kind of bogeyman Aunt Charlene evoked to keep her younger daughter in line.

Her cousin's perfectly shaped brows rose. "You don't think he's still involved in illegal activities, do you?"

"I have no idea," Kelsey said, ignoring the internal voice yelling *no*. Her automatic desire to rush to Connor's defense worried her. She was supposed to stop him, not champion him.

"You should find out," Aileen said as she led the way into the study. The bookshelf-lined room, with its leather and mahogany furniture, was her uncle's masculine domain, but even this room had been taken over by wedding preparations. Stacks of photo albums cluttered the coffee table.

"Why me?" Kelsey groaned.

"You want to help Emily, don't you?"

"Of course I do!" she insisted, even if she had to admit her motives weren't completely altruistic.

"And you want the wedding to be perfect, right?" Her cousin already knew the answer and didn't wait for Kelsey's response.

"I know Mother exaggerates, but not when it comes to Connor McClane. I wouldn't be surprised if he tried kidnapping Emily again," Aileen added.

Kelsey fought to keep from rolling her eyes. "She took off with Connor on prom night and didn't come back until the next day. I think your parents overreacted."

"Maybe, but I guarantee he'll try to stop the wedding somehow." Aileen pointed an older-therefore-wiser finger in Kelsey's direction. "But don't let him fool you."

He hadn't bothered to try to fool her. Was Connor so confident he could stop the wedding that he didn't care who knew about his plan?

Walking over to the coffee table, Aileen picked up a stack of photos. "Here are the pictures Mother wants to show during the reception."

"Thanks." Kelsey flipped through images of her cousin's life. Not a bad-hair day or an acne breakout in the bunch. Even in pigtails and braces Emily had been adorable. As

Kelsey tucked them into her purse, she noticed a stray photo had fallen to the Oriental area rug. "Did you want to include this one?"

Her voice trailed off as she had a better look at the picture. At first glance, the young woman could have been Emily, but the feathered hair and ruffled prom dress were wrong. "Oh, wow."

From the time Kelsey had come to live with her aunt and uncle, she'd heard how much Emily looked like Kelsey's mother, Olivia. Kelsey had seen similarities in the blond hair and blue eyes, but from this picture of a teenage Olivia dressed for a high school dance, she and Emily could have passed for sisters.

Reading her thoughts, Aileen said, "Amazing, isn't it?"

"It is. Everyone always said—" Kelsey shook her head. "I never noticed."

"Really? But they look so much alike!"

"My mother, she didn't—" Laugh? Smile? Ever look as *alive* as she looked in that photo? Uncertain what to say, Kelsey weakly finished, "I don't remember her looking like this."

"Oh, Kelse. I'm sorry." Concern darkened Aileen's eyes. "I should have realized with your mother being so sick and having to go through chemo. Of course, she didn't look the same."

Accepting her cousin's condolences with a touch of guilt, Kelsey silently admitted Olivia Wilson had lost any resemblance to the girl in the picture long before being diagnosed with cancer. What would it have been like had her mother retained some of that carefree, joyful spirit? Kelsey immediately thrust the disloyal thought aside.

Olivia had given up everything—including the wealth and family that now surrounded Kelsey—to raise her daughter. Emily's wedding was Kelsey's chance to live up to her promise. To hold her head high and finally show the Wilsons how amazing she could be.

With a final look at the picture, Kelsey slid the photo of her mother back into one of the albums. "It's okay," she told Aileen. "Let's go see if Emily's done with the fitting."

"All right. But be warned," Aileen said as she led the way down the hall toward Emily's bedroom. "The photographer's in there."

"Really?" Kelsey frowned. "I don't remember pictures of the fitting being included. Was that something Emily requested?"

She had long accepted that her ideas and her cousins' differed greatly, but a seamstress fretting over her measurements would have been a nightmare for Kelsey, not a photo op.

Aileen shrugged and opened the door just a crack. "The photographer said it was all part of the package."

A quick glance inside, and Kelsey immediately saw what "package" the photographer was interested in. Emily stood in the middle of the bedroom, with its girlish four-poster bed and French provincial furniture. Her sheer, lace-covered arms were held out straight at her sides while the seamstress pinned the beaded bodice to fit her willowy curves. Dewy makeup highlighted her wide blue eyes, flawless cheekbones and smiling lips.

"What do you think, Mother? Will Todd like it?" Emily leaned forward to examine the skirt, testing the limits of a dozen stickpins.

The photographer, a man in his midtwenties, started snapping shots as fast as his index finger could fly. It wasn't the first time Kelsey had seen slack-jawed amazement on a man's face. Too bad she saw the expression only when her cousin was around.

"Of course he will. Audra is an amazing designer, and she created that dress just for you. It's perfect," Aunt Charlene insisted, keeping a narrow-eyed glare on the photographer.

Charlene Wilson didn't share her daughters' beauty, but she

was a tall, striking woman. She could instantly command a room with her timeless sense of style and demand for perfection from herself and those around her. Today she wore a beige silk suit that wouldn't dare wrinkle and her brown hair in an elegant twist at the nape of her neck.

Glancing down at her own clothes, a map of creases that spelled fashion disaster, Kelsey knew her aunt would be horrified by the sight. Fortunately, Charlene was far too busy to notice. Kelsey slid the door shut and walked back down the hallway with Aileen.

"I know all brides are supposed to be beautiful," Aileen said with a mixture of sisterly affection and envy, "but that's ridiculous."

"Please, I've seen pictures of your wedding. You were just as gorgeous."

Aileen gave a theatrical sigh. "True. Of course, I wasn't lucky enough to have you to plan everything. I ran myself ragged, and you make it look so easy."

Kelsey laughed even as her cheeks heated with embarrassed pleasure. "That's because I'm only planning the wedding. It's far more stressful to be the bride."

"Still, you're doing an amazing job. Mother thinks so, too, even if she hasn't told you. This wedding will make your company."

That was just what she was counting on, Kelsey thought, excitement filling her once again. "I know." Taking a deep breath, she confessed, "I put down first and last month's rent on that shop in Glendale."

Aileen made a sound of delight and threw her arms around Kelsey in a hug that ended before she could lift her stiff arms in response. After eight years, Kelsey should have anticipated the enthusiastic embrace, but somehow, both her cousins' easy affection always caught her off guard.

"That is so exciting, and it's about time! You should have opened a shop a long time ago instead of working out of your home."

"I couldn't afford it until now."

"You could have if you'd taken my father up on his loan," Aileen said.

Kelsey swallowed. "I couldn't," she said, knowing Aileen wouldn't understand any more than her uncle Gordon had. Starting her business was something she had to do for herself and for her mother's memory.

Wilson women against the world... Her mother's voice rang in her head. Opening the shop wouldn't have the same meaning with her uncle's money behind the success.

Aileen shook her head. "Honestly, Kelsey, you are so stubborn." A slight frown pulled her eyebrows together. "But something tells me you're going to need every bit of that determination—"

Kelsey jumped in. "To keep Connor McClane away from Emily. I know, Aileen. But if Emily's so crazy about Todd, what difference does it make that Connor's in town?"

Ever since he'd posed that question, Kelsey couldn't get his words out of her mind. Okay, so in her opinion, Todd Dunworthy didn't hold even a teeny, tiny, flickering match to Connor McClane. But if her cousin truly loved Todd, shouldn't he outshine every other man—including an old flame like Connor?

"Kelsey, we're talking about Connor McClane. I know you've sworn off men since Matt, but please tell me that idiot didn't rob you of every female hormone in your body!"

Even after two years, the thought of her ex-boyfriend made Kelsey cringe. Not because of the heartbreak but because of the humiliation. Still, she argued, "I'm not discounting Connor's appeal." If anything, she'd been mentally recounting every attractive feature, from his quick wit to his sexy smile and killer bod. "But if I were a week away from getting married and madly in love with my fiancé, none of that would matter."

Aileen sighed and slanted Kelsey a look filled with worldly wisdom. "It's cold feet. Every engaged woman goes through it. I called things off with Tom three times before we finally made it to the altar. You'll see what I mean when you get engaged."

The idea of Kelsey getting engaged was in serious question, but if that time ever did come, she was sure she'd be so in love she'd never harbor any doubts. "Okay, so you called off your engagement. Did you run off with another man?"

"You know I didn't."

"Well, that's my point. If Emily and Todd are right for each other, Connor's presence shouldn't matter."

"It shouldn't, but it does. You weren't here when Emily and Connor were together. He's the kind of man who makes a woman want to live for the moment and never think of tomorrow. When Emily was around him, she'd get completely caught up in the here and now of Connor McClane. But her relationship with Todd is something that can last." Aileen flashed a bright smile. "Look, you've handled prewedding problems before. All you have to do is keep Connor away. You can do that, can't you, Kelsey?"

What else could she do but say yes?

Connor scrolled through his laptop's files, going over the information he'd compiled on Todd Dunworthy. He had to have missed something.

Swearing, he rolled away from the desk in his hotel suite and pushed out of the chair. He paced the length of the room, but even with the extra money he'd paid for a suite, he couldn't go far. From the closet, past the bathroom, between the desk and footboard, to the window and back. He supposed he should consider himself lucky not to have

Kelsey Wilson shadowing his every step. An unwanted smile tugged at his lips at the thought of the woman he'd met the day before.

He'd finally convinced her to leave him at the restaurant, telling her he had years to catch up with his friend, Javy. The words were true enough, but he'd seen the suspicion in her brown eyes. He chuckled at the thought of the atypical Wilson relative. She was nothing like Emily, that was for sure. Compared to Kelsey's fiery red hair, deep brown eyes, and womanly curves, Emily suddenly seemed like a blond-haired, blue-eyed paper doll.

But no matter how much curiosity Kelsey Wilson provoked, Connor couldn't let himself be distracted.

After his relationship with Emily ended, Connor had drifted around Southern California. Different state, but he'd hung out with the same crowd. Busting up a fight in a club had gotten him his first job as a bouncer. He'd worked security for several years before taking a chance and opening a P.I. business.

Up until three months ago, he would have said he was good at his job, one of the best. That he had a feel for people, an instinct that told him when someone was lying. Listening to his gut had saved his skin more than once. Not listening had nearly gotten a woman killed.

From the first moment he'd met Todd Dunworthy, Connor had that same hit-below-the-belt feeling. And this time he was damn sure gonna listen. So far, though, his background check had merely revealed Dunworthy was the youngest son of a wealthy Chicago family. Numerous newspaper photos showed him at the opera, a benefit for the symphony, a gallery opening. And while the events and locales changed, he always had a different woman—tall, blond and beautiful—on his arm.

No doubt about it, Emily was definitely Todd's type.

"You sure you don't hate the guy just 'cause the Wilsons

love him?" Javy had pressed on the ride from the restaurant to the hotel.

Connor couldn't blame his friend for asking. And, okay, so maybe he would dislike anyone who met with the Wilsons' approval, but that didn't change his opinion. Todd Dunworthy was not the man they thought he was.

He'd spoken to several of the Dunworthy family employees and none of them were talking. It wasn't that they wouldn't say anything bad about their employers; Connor expected that. But these people refused to say a word, which told him one important thing. As well paid as they might be to do their jobs, they were even better compensated to keep quiet.

Most were lifers—employees who had been with the family for decades. But there was one woman he hadn't been able to reach. A former maid named Sophia Pirelli. She'd worked for the family for two years before suddenly quitting or getting fired—no one would say—two months ago. The silence alone made Connor suspicious, and figuring an ex-employee might be willing to talk, Connor wanted to find her.

A few days ago he'd found a lead on Sophia's whereabouts. As much as he longed to follow that trail and see where it ended, he couldn't be in two places at once. He wanted to stay focused on Todd, so he'd asked his friend and fellow P.I., Jake Cameron, to see if the former maid was staying with friends in St. Louis.

Grabbing his cell phone, he dialed Jake's number. His friend didn't bother with pleasantries. "You were right. She's here."

Finally! A lead that might pan out. "Have you found anything?"

"Not yet. This one's going take some time."

Frustration built inside Connor. Although he trusted Jake and knew the man was a good P.I., Connor wasn't used to relying on someone else. "We don't have a lot of time here."

"Hey, I've got this," Jake said with typical confidence. "I'm just telling you, she's not the type to spill all her secrets on a first date."

Connor shook his head. He shouldn't have worried. His friend had been in St. Louis for all of two days, and he already had a date with the former maid. "Call me when you've got anything."

"Will do."

Snapping the cell phone shut, Connor hoped Jake worked his cases as quickly as he worked with women. But he wasn't going to sit around waiting for Jake; he wanted to find something on Dunworthy, irrefutable proof that the guy wasn't the loving husband-to-be he pretended.

Scowling, he resumed pacing, lengthening his stride to cross the room in four steps instead of eight. Connor had never been one to back down from a fight, but some battles were lost before they'd even begun. Gordon and Charlene Wilson would never take the word of the kid from the wrong side of the tracks over their handpicked golden boy.

Dammit, he needed an insider. He needed someone the Wilsons trusted to break the bad news. He needed one of their own. He needed…Kelsey.

Connor laughed out loud at the idea, but damned if he didn't think it might work. Kelsey hadn't played a part in his past relationship with Emily. She was as unbiased a witness as he could hope to find. She had nothing at stake with Emily's wedding, nothing riding on her cousin saying "I do."

No doubt about it, Kelsey was his best shot.

The following evening, Emily twirled around the hotel's atrium, her arms outspread like Sleeping Beauty. "You were right, Kelsey. This is the perfect place for the reception. Don't you think so, Mother?"

She looked so beautiful and happy Kelsey half-expected cartoon animals to surround her at any moment. Smiling at her cousin's unfettered happiness, she breathed a sigh of relief. Connor McClane was wrong, dead wrong. Emily and Todd were meant to be.

"It's lovely," Aunt Charlene commented without looking up from her mother-of-the-bride notebook. "I knew we could count on Kelsey to find the perfect place."

"Um, thank you, Aunt Charlene," Kelsey said, surprised and pleased by the compliment. Even after eight years, Kelsey and Charlene had a tentative, tightrope relationship that had yet to get past a disastrous beginning.

When Kelsey had first come to live with the Wilsons, she'd been overwhelmed by their obvious wealth, and her cousins' beauty and grace had left her feeling outclassed. Especially when Charlene took one look at her and declared, "Someone must take this girl shopping."

Looking back now, Kelsey realized her aunt had been trying to relate to her the same way she did to her own daughters, who loved nothing more than a day spent raiding Scottsdale boutiques. But back then, as an intimidated, awkward teenager, Kelsey had suffered the pain of being seen as an embarrassment by her new family.

She'd survived the multiple fittings and outfit changes—a living, breathing, *silent* mannequin—as her aunt and a shopkeeper went back and forth over which colors, styles and accessories best suited Kelsey. But when she stood with her aunt at the register, when she saw the *hundreds* of dollars a single item cost, a sick sense of disbelief hit her stomach.

How many weeks' rent would that pair of shoes have paid for when she and her mother were living in tiny one-room apartments? How many months of food? How much better might her mother's medical have been with that kind of money?

In a quiet, cold voice, Kelsey had told the saleswoman to put every item back, before marching out of the store.

Later, once Kelsey had calmed down and realized how ungrateful her actions must have seemed, she tried to apologize to her aunt. Charlene had declared the matter over and forgotten, but never again did she offer to take Kelsey shopping.

Their relationship had yet to recover from that day. By asking Kelsey to coordinate the wedding, Charlene had helped breach the gap, but Kelsey knew this opportunity didn't come with second chances. This was her one shot.

"I've always thought this was an amazing place for a reception," Kelsey said, hearing the dreamy wistfulness in her own voice. The glass ceiling and towering plants gave the illusion of being in a tropical paradise, and from the first time she'd seen the hotel, Kelsey had known it was perfect.

Perfect for Emily, she reminded herself.

Although between having so many of her friends working the wedding and Emily's willingness to let Kelsey make so many of the decisions, the entire event was feeling more like *Kelsey's* dream wedding.

Except the choice of groom...

The insidious thought wove through her mind along with images of Connor McClane... His rebellious saunter, his too confident grin, his...*everything.*

"I hope Todd likes it." Emily lowered her arms, a small frown tugging at her eyebrows. "Do you think he will?"

"It's a five-star hotel, one of the finest in the state," Charlene said imperiously.

"I know, but Todd's family is from Chicago. They have all those historic buildings and...Todd can be particular."

Kelsey's hand tightened on her day planner at her cousin's hesitant tone. Suspicions planted by Connor's too-pointed comments threatened to sprout into tangled choking weeds, but

Kelsey ground them down. Finger by finger, she eased her grip before she left permanent indentations on the leather book.

Her cousin was a people pleaser. Of course she worried what Todd would think. "He agreed to let you make all the decisions about the wedding," Kelsey reminded Emily, who had in turn, left most of the decisions up to her. "So he must trust your choices."

"I know, but…" Emily took a look around the atrium without the excitement she'd shown moments ago. Trying to see it through Todd's particular eyes?

"But what?" Kelsey prompted gently.

"It's—it's nothing." Emily shook her head with a laugh. "I just want everything to be perfect. You understand, don't you, Kelsey?"

Yes, she knew all about trying and failing again and again. But not this time—not with Emily's wedding. "Of course I do. And your wedding will be perfect," she insisted, before an already familiar masculine voice filled the atrium and sent shivers up and down her spine.

"Hey, Em! How's the blushing bride?"

"Oh, my gosh! Connor!" Emily squealed her former boyfriend's name and ran to meet him. A broad smile on his handsome face, he caught her in his arms and spun her around. "What are you doing here?" she asked.

Keeping an arm around Emily's shoulders, Connor glanced at Kelsey. "When Kelsey said you'd be here, I had to see you."

Heat rushed to Kelsey's face. Bad enough Connor had out-maneuvered her. Did he have to rub it in in front of her aunt?

Connor McClane had been in town less than twenty-four hours, and she could already feel the familiar undertow of failure dragging her under.

"You told him we'd be here?" The words barely escaped the frozen smile on her aunt's face. Charlene would never make a scene in public. Even if it meant smiling at the man out to ruin her daughter's future.

"No! I didn't." Except she *had* told Connor Emily was making final arrangements for the reception that evening, and he would know where the reception was being held. After all, he'd been invited. "I didn't mean to," she almost groaned.

Charlene straightened her razor-sharp shoulders, taking charge of a situation that had gotten out of control. Out of *Kelsey*'s control. Interrupting Emily and Connor's conversation, she said, "Mr. McClane, you'll have to excuse us. Emily has a wedding to plan."

"Mother!" her daughter protested. "Connor's come all this way to see me. We have so much to talk about. Can't this wait?"

"This is *your* wedding we're talking about, Emily! The most important day of your life."

The most important day of your life. Kelsey understood the sentiment. Every bride wanted her wedding day to be perfect, and she was doing everything in her power to see that this affair was the type every girl dreamed about, but Emily was only twenty-eight years old. Shouldn't she have something to look forward to?

Why Kelsey chose that moment to meet Connor's glance, she didn't know. He flashed her a half smile as if he could not only read her thoughts but agreed one hundred percent.

"You're right, of course, Mother." Emily turned to Connor with a smile. "I'm sorry, Connor. We don't have much time before the wedding, and there's still so much to do."

"Don't worry, Em. We'll have plenty of time to talk before then. I'm in Room 415."

"You're staying here?" Kelsey blurted the words in horror. At the hotel where not only the reception was taking place, but also the rehearsal dinner.

Connor's grin was maddening—and disturbingly enticing. "Thought it would be convenient."

"Convenient. Right." That way he could *conveniently* intrude on every event she had planned for the location and drive her insane!

"Kelsey, Emily and I can take things from here. You have...other matters to attend to now."

Her aunt's pointed look spoke volumes. Charlene could handle the final wedding details. Kelsey's job was to handle Connor McClane. She desperately clutched her day planner to her chest like a leather-bound shield. There were some things in life she could not control, but everything else made it onto a list. A methodical, point-by-point inventory of what she needed to accomplish, making even the impossible seem manageable. Nothing beat the satisfaction of marking off a completed task.

And although Kelsey certainly hadn't counted on Connor when she prioritized her checklist for Emily's wedding, as long as she kept him occupied for the next week and a half, Kelsey would be able to cross him off once and for all.

Catching a touch of her aunt's righteous indignation, she straightened her own shoulders and nodded imperceptibly. Satisfied, Charlene marched Emily out of the atrium.

Emily cast a last, longing glance over her shoulder, and the uncertainty Kelsey saw in her cousin's gaze strengthened her resolve. Aileen was right. Emily was suffering from cold feet. Her worries about her future as a wife and eventually a mother had her looking back to simpler times. Back when she could lose herself in Connor's live-for-the-day attitude.

But her cousin would only regret it if she threw away her future for a man of the moment like Connor McClane. And Kelsey could not allow Emily to make the same mistake her own mother had.

Chapter Three

"**Y**ou know, Kelsey, I've never been *attended to* before."

Even with her back turned, as she watched Emily and Charlene walk away, Connor sensed the determination rolling off Kelsey in waves. Shoulders straight and head held high, she looked ready for battle. And yet when he took a closer step, his gaze locked on a curl of hair that had escaped the confining bun. The urge to tuck that curl behind her ear and taste her creamy skin nearly overwhelmed him. He sucked in what was supposed to be a steadying breath, but the air—scented with cinnamon and spice and *Kelsey*—only added to the desire burning through his veins.

Struggling to hide behind the cocky facade that had served him so well in his youth, Connor murmured, "Gotta say I'm looking forward to it."

"I don't know what you mean," she said stiffly.

"You think I don't know I'm those 'other matters' your aunt was talking about?"

Kelsey opened her mouth, looking ready to spout another unbelievable denial, only to do them both the favor of telling the truth. "You're right, Connor. My aunt wants me to keep you away from Emily."

"Charlene wants me gone and Emily happily married. There's just one problem."

"That would be you," Kelsey pointed out. "A problem easily solved if you were actually gone."

"If I leave, Emily's problems will have just begun."

"That's your unbiased opinion?"

"Yeah, it is," he agreed. "And not one your aunt and uncle are gonna listen to."

"Can you blame them?" Kelsey demanded.

No, and that was the hell of it. Connor knew *he* was the only one to blame. He knew what the Wilsons thought of him and he knew why. He could still see the look in Gordon Wilson's eyes when he offered Connor money to break up with Emily. Not a hint of doubt flashed in the older man's gaze. He'd been so sure Connor—a dirt-poor loser from the wrong side of town—would take the money.

Connor had longed to shove the money and his fist into the smug SOB's face. But he hadn't. He *couldn't.* And the pride he'd had to swallow that day still lingered, a bitter taste on his tongue.

He'd let Emily down, although from what he'd gathered during their recent conversations, she didn't know anything about the payoff. She thought their breakup had been her idea…just as she thought marrying Todd Dunworthy was her idea. But Connor knew better, and this time he wasn't going to be bought off.

"The Wilsons aren't going to listen to anything I have to say," he acknowledged. "That's where you come in."

Kelsey frowned. "I *am* a Wilson."

He hadn't forgotten...exactly. "You're different."

Drawing herself up to her five-foot-nothing height, shoulders so straight Connor thought they just might snap, Kelsey said, "Right. Different." Hurt flashed in her chocolate-brown eyes as if he'd just insulted her, when nothing could be further from the truth.

"Hey, wait a minute." Pulling her into a nearby alcove, out of the way of nearby guests, Connor insisted, "That was *not* a put-down. Your aunt and uncle turned their noses up so high when they met me, if it rained, they would have drowned. I was trailer trash, and no way was I good enough for their little girl. So when I say you're nothing like them, you can say 'thank you,' because it's a compliment."

There were a dozen words he could have said, compliments he could have used, but the stubborn tilt of Kelsey's chin told him she wouldn't have listened to a single one. Someone—her family, some guy from her past—had done a number on her.

No, words wouldn't do it, but actions... How far would he have to go to show Kelsey how attractive he found her? A touch? A kiss? The undeniable proof of his body pressed tight to hers?

"In case you've forgotten," Kelsey pointed out, her voice husky enough to let him know she'd picked up on some of his thoughts and wasn't as immune as she'd like him to believe, "according to my aunt and uncle you *kidnapped* their daughter."

"It was not kidnapping," he argued, though he'd had a hell of a time convincing the police. Fortunately Emily had backed his story, insisting that she'd left willingly. Eventually the charges had been dropped; Emily had been eighteen and legally an adult, able to make her own choices. Not that her parents had seen it that way. "But that's my point. Your aunt and uncle won't listen to anything I have to say. Which is where you come in."

"Me?"

"Right. We'll be partners."

"Partners?"

"Sure. After all, we're on the same side."

"Are you crazy? We are not on the same side!" Kelsey argued.

"I want Emily to be happy," he interjected, shaking her thoughts as easily as his sexy grin weakened her composure. "What do *you* want?"

Challenge rose in the lift of his eyebrow, but Kelsey couldn't see a way out. The trap was set, and all she could do was jump in with both feet. "Of course I want her to be happy."

"That's what I thought. Kelsey, this guy won't make her happy. He's not what he seems, and I want to prove it. The Wilsons won't believe *me,* but with you to back me up, they'll have to at least listen."

Kelsey longed to refuse. She didn't trust him. Not for a second. Oh, sure, his story sounded good, but finding dirt on Todd wasn't just a matter of looking out for Emily—it played perfectly into Connor's interests, as well.

If Connor did find some deep, dark secret to convince Emily to call off the wedding, not only would he be the hero who saved her from a horrible marriage, he'd also be there to help pick up the pieces. But if Connor couldn't find anything in Todd's past, what was to keep him from making something up? Working together, he wouldn't be able to lie. Not to mention, he'd given her a way to keep an eye on him.

Connor held out his hand. "Deal?"

Sighing, she reached out. "Deal."

Connor's lean fingers closed around her hand. Heat shot up her arm, and a warm shiver shook her whole body. Like stepping from ice-cold air-conditioning into the warmth of a sunny day.

"All right, partner."

"Not so fast." She hadn't lived with her businessman uncle for as long as she had without learning a thing or two about negotiation. "You might want to hear my terms first."

"Terms?"

Kelsey nodded. As long as Connor thought he needed her, maybe she could get a few concessions.

Instead of balking, Connor grinned. "Let's hear 'em."

"First, we're equal partners. I want to be in on this every step of the way. No hearing about anything you've found on Todd after the fact."

"No problem. From this point on, we're joined at the hip. 'Course, that will make for some interesting sleeping arrangements."

"Second, this is strictly business," Kelsey interrupted, as if cutting off his words might somehow short-circuit the thoughts in her head. But they were already there: sexy, seductive images of hot kisses and naked limbs slipping through satin sheets in her mind. She could only hope Connor couldn't read them so clearly by the heat coloring her face.

"And third?"

"Thi-third," she said, clearing her throat, "you stay away from Emily. *If* we get any dirt on Todd, *I'll* break the news to her. Until then, I don't want you filling her head with your 'bad feelings.'"

Expecting an argument, Kelsey was surprised when Connor nodded. "I'll keep my distance."

"Okay, then, we're partners." She should have experienced a moment of triumph, but all Kelsey could think was that she'd just made a deal with the devil.

Certainly, when Connor smiled, he looked like sheer temptation.

"Got to hand it to you, Kelsey, you're one hell of a negotiator. Two outta three ain't bad."

It wasn't until Connor strode away that Kelsey realized he'd never agreed to her second condition.

As Kelsey stepped into the florist shop the next morning, cool, floral-scented air washed over her. She breathed deeply, enjoying the feeling of a refreshing spa treatment without the outrageous prices. She wasn't a big believer in aromatherapy, but the stress of dealing with Connor might drive her to alternative measures. Anything to stop her pulse from jumping each time she saw him—and to keep her hormones under wraps and in control for the next ten days.

Why couldn't life be easy? Why couldn't she plan an elegant, trouble-free wedding? The kind where the biggest worry was the ice sculpture melting too quickly in the summer heat. Instead, she got Connor McClane, a man guaranteed to make women melt with nothing more than a look.

"Kelsey! Thanks so much for coming!" Lisa Remming, Kelsey's friend and the owner of In Bloom, circled the checkout counter to greet her with a hug. As always, Lisa dressed in clothes inspired by her favorite flower—bird of paradise. Her long brown hair and blue eyes were complemented by a sleeveless fiery-orange blouse and swirling olive-green skirt. "I feel so bad for calling you."

"Don't be silly." Kelsey waved off her friend's apology and pulled out her checkbook from her purse. "It's no problem."

"I still can't believe I'm doing flowers for Emily Wilson's wedding! There isn't a florist around who wouldn't kill for this job."

Hiding a smile, Kelsey teased, "Wow, who knew florists were so bloodthirsty?"

Lisa made a face, then gave Kelsey another hug. "I totally have you to thank for this."

The two women had gone to high school together, and

Lisa was one of the few people in whom Kelsey confided. By the time she'd moved in with her aunt and uncle, Kelsey had gotten accustomed to blending in and going through her teen years unnoticed. Telling her fellow students she was a long-lost member of the wealthy Wilson family would have shoved her under a microscope.

The only worse fate would have been the exclusive prep school her aunt had suggested she attend.

"I really hate asking you to do this," Lisa said as she reached behind the counter for an invoice.

"A deposit is standard practice."

"I know, but— We're talking about the Wilsons. It's not like they're going to leave me holding the bill. But with the flowers for the church and the bouquets and the boutonnieres, I have to pay my suppliers and—"

"And that's why you need the money up front." Kelsey tore off a check. The amount for the deposit alone would have depleted her own meager bank account, but Aunt Charlene had given her access to the special account established for Emily's wedding.

"Thanks." Lisa breathed a sigh of relief as she noted the deposit on the invoice. "This wedding is going to mean the world to my business." She laughed as she pressed a button on the cash register and slid the check inside. "Like I need to tell *you* that, right? You'll be flooded with calls after Emily's friends see the amazing job you're doing. Have you thought anymore about getting your own place?"

Excitement pulsing through her veins, Kelsey nodded. "I've put down first and last month's rent on the space in downtown Glendale, near the antique shops."

Lisa gave a squeal. "And you didn't even say anything! When are you moving in?"

"As soon as the current renters move out. The landlord's supposed to give me a call."

"You must be so excited! I know I was when I first opened this place. Do you have all the furniture and office equipment you'll need? Have you thought about hiring a support staff and—"

"Whoa, Lisa! Don't get carried away," Kelsey said with a laugh that sounded far too shaky.

"I'm not. Don't tell me you of all people—with your day planner and your endless lists—haven't thought of these things."

In fact, she *had,* and only days ago she'd been riding high on her plans. Now, with Connor back in town, she feared she'd put the honeymoon before the wedding, and her stomach roiled at the thought of losing control. "I don't want to get too far ahead of myself."

"What are you talking about?" Lisa challenged. "Emily's wedding is only a week and half away. You aren't too far ahead. If anything, you're behind!"

"Well, thank you for giving me that combination vote of confidence and total panic attack."

"I'm sorry. But I know how much effort you've put into this, and I want to see it pay off for you."

I want Emily to be happy. What do you *want?*

With Connor's words ringing in her head, Kelsey insisted, "Emily's happiness comes first."

"Honey, Emily's happiness *always* come first," Lisa deadpanned.

"That's not fair, Lisa," Kelsey insisted quietly.

Emily and Aileen could have turned their backs when their unknown and potentially unwanted cousin showed up to live with them. Instead, they'd done everything possible to include Kelsey. It certainly wasn't their fault she'd never fit in.

"I know." Lisa's sigh expressed an unspoken apology. "But

I also know you've played second fiddle to both your cousins for as long as I've known you. I don't want you to be so focused on Emily's wedding that you lose track of your dream."

"I haven't and I won't."

Despite her determined vow, a touch of guilt squirmed through Kelsey. She'd kept silent about renting the shop for exactly the reasons Lisa mentioned. Her aunt wouldn't want her attention on anything other than the wedding. But the shop was nothing compared to Connor McClane. The man was a living, breathing distraction.

"Emily's wedding *is* my dream," Kelsey added. "A high-profile event with an extravagant budget and built-in publicity thanks to my uncle's business contacts and my aunt's country-club friends—it's guaranteed to put my business on the map."

"I agree, and I can't believe you pulled it off in only two months!"

"It *was* short notice, wasn't it?" Kelsey asked, fiddling with the zipper on her purse.

"Yes, but you did it!"

Kelsey nodded. Thanks to working almost nonstop, she'd pulled off planning the event in a fraction of the time it normally took, but Emily had insisted on a June wedding... hadn't she?

Sudden doubts buzzed through her mind like annoying insects, unrelenting and unavoidable. Had Emily pushed for the summer wedding? Or was the idea Charlene's...or Todd's? Kelsey had been so focused on getting everything done on time, she hadn't stopped to wonder about the short engagement. Until now...until Connor had stirred up the hornet's nest of doubt.

Connor hung up the phone after ordering breakfast and ran his hands over his face. He hoped the distraction of food would wipe the nightmare from his memory. It wasn't the first time disturbing images had invaded his sleep.

The beginning of the dream was always the same. Connor watched his client, Doug Mitchell, arrive at his wife's apartment through the tunnel-eye view of a telephoto lens; only when he tried to stop the man from attacking his estranged wife, did the dream shift and alter, keeping him off balance, unsure, helpless. Sometimes he froze in place, unable to move a muscle, unable to shout a warning. Other times, he ran through air thick as quicksand, each move bogged down by guilt and regret.

But no matter how the dream changed, one thing remained the same: Connor never arrived in time to stop Doug.

A sudden knock at the door jarred the memories from Connor's thoughts. Undoubtedly the Wilsons had picked the best hotel around for Emily's reception, but no one's room service was *that* fast. Besides, he had an idea who might be on the other side of the door, and it wasn't the maid with fresh towels.

Opening the door, he summoned a smile for the woman standing in the corridor. "Morning."

Emily Wilson beamed at him, looking like a Hollywood fashion plate of old in a yellow sundress layered beneath a light-weight sweater and a scarf knotted at her neck. "Connor! I'm so glad you're here. I know I should have called first, but—"

He waved off her not-quite-an-apology and held the door open. "Come on in."

As she breezed into the hotel room and set her handbag next to his laptop, Connor was glad to see the computer logo flashing across the screen. Last thing he needed was for Emily to see the dossier on her fiancé.

Emily took her time looking around the suite's miniature living area: a cluster of armchairs and end tables encircling the entertainment center. The added touches of a stone fireplace, balcony overlooking the pool and hot tub spoke of the hotel's five-star accommodations, but Connor doubted she was impressed. After all, she'd grown up surrounded by luxury and wealth.

"What are you doing here, Em?"

"I wanted to see you." She blushed as prettily now as she had at eighteen, but somehow for Connor the effect wasn't the same.

An image of Kelsey flashed in his mind, and he couldn't help making the comparison between Emily and her cousin. It was the difference between a sepia photograph—all soft, dreamy hues—and a full-color, HD image that instantly caught the eye.

As a hotheaded teen, Emily had been his unattainable fantasy. But now it was Kelsey and her down-to-earth reality who kept intruding into his thoughts.

Like yesterday evening, when he'd stood on the balcony and watched to see if the Arizona sunsets were still as amazing as he remembered. As he watched the blazing light slowly fade on the horizon, it wasn't past evenings that came to mind. Instead he thought of the way sunshine caught the fire in Kelsey's auburn curls…

"I snuck out like when we were kids."

Emily's words jarred Kelsey from his mind. He told himself the swift kick in the gut was remembered pain and not anything current or life threatening. But, dammit, he didn't need the reminder that as far as the Wilsons were concerned, he'd never be good enough. And while Kelsey might not look like her blond-haired, blue-eyed cousins, she was still a Wilson, and some things never changed.

Judging by Emily's impish grin, she'd enjoyed reliving her youthful rebellion and the walk down memory lane. Too bad the trip wasn't so pleasant for him. Feeling his smile take a sardonic twist, he asked, "Still can't risk being seen with me in public, huh, Em?"

Her eyes widened in what looked like genuine dismay. "No, Connor! It's not like that." She reached out and grasped his arm, and the frantic expression did take him back in time, filling his thoughts with memories of the girl so desperate to make everyone else happy, she'd made herself miserable.

Relenting slightly, he leaned one hip against the arm of the sofa and reminded her, "We're not kids anymore, and we're too old to be sneaking around."

"I know." Fidgeting with her engagement ring, she added, "But I wanted to see you, and I didn't want...anyone to get upset."

"You mean Todd?" Connor asked pointedly.

"You have to understand, he's very protective of me. I'm sorry the two of you didn't hit it off when we met for dinner in San Diego last month."

Connor held back a snort of derisive laughter at the irony. No, he and Todd hadn't hit it off. In fact, at the end of the night they'd nearly come to blows. Connor could admit he hadn't walked into the restaurant with a totally open mind. It was entirely possible Connor would dislike any man who met with the Wilsons' approval on principle alone. But within fifteen minutes of meeting Todd Dunworthy, Connor had stopped thinking about the past and started worrying about Emily.

In that short span of time, Dunworthy bragged about his Scottsdale loft apartment, his top-of-the-line SUV, his various summer homes in exotic ports of call, all of which would have been little more than annoying except for one thing.

He talked about Emily the same way. She was new and bright and shiny just like the fancy Lexus he drove, and Connor hadn't been able to shake the feeling that Dunworthy wouldn't have thought twice about tossing her aside for a newer model.

And the bad feeling roiling through Connor's gut like acid

ever since he'd been hired by Doug Mitchell got so much worse. Outwardly, Doug and Todd Dunworthy had as little in common as, well, as Connor and Todd did. But from the moment he met Doug, the cold look in the man's eyes and the way he spoke about his wife set Connor's teeth on edge, too reminiscent of the way his father had talked about his mother, the bitter blame he'd placed on her for dying and saddling him with an unwanted kid to raise.

But Connor had set aside his personal feelings and taken the job. *Taken the money,* his conscience accused. If only he'd listened to his gut then...

Taking a deep breath, Connor looked out the window, hoping the daylight might dispel his dark thoughts. Only, it wasn't the sunshine that broke through the shadows, but memories of the sunset, memories of Kelsey, that eased the weight on his chest.

The spark in her dark eyes, the stubborn jut of her chin, her determination to stand up to him...even if she barely stood up to the height of his shoulder. He didn't doubt for one second she'd be a formidable opponent, and he was glad to have her on his side.

Turning his focus back to Emily, he said, "I'm sorry, too, Em." And he was. He wanted her to be happy, and he was sorry Dunworthy wasn't the man she—or more important, he suspected, her parents—thought him to be.

Something in his tone must have given his suspicions away, because Emily's already perfect posture straightened to a regal, Charlene-like stature. "Todd is a wonderful man," she insisted. "I love him. I really do, and I can't wait to be his wife."

How many times had Emily repeated that statement before she started believing it was true? The words had a mantralike sound to them. Or maybe more like the punishment meted out by a second-grade teacher: *I will not chew gum in class. I will not chew gum in class.*

"I should go," she murmured.

"Emily, wait." A knock on the door broke the tension. "Look, that's room service. I ordered way too much food. Stay and have breakfast with me."

Without waiting for her response, he stepped around her and opened the door. The waiter wheeled in the cart, filling the room with the scent of bacon and eggs. He pulled the covers off the steaming plates and revealed a meal large enough for two.

"I shouldn't," she protested, eyeing the food with a look of longing. "I need to watch what I eat or I won't be able to fit into my dress."

Connor tried to smile; dieting before a big occasion was undoubtedly a prerequisite for most women, but he didn't think it was the dress Emily had in mind. He'd shared only a single meal with Dunworthy, but he could still see the smug smile on the bastard's face as he waved the waiter and the dessert tray away with a laugh. "Gotta keep my bride-to-be looking as beautiful as ever!"

"Come on," Connor cajoled. "You're not going to make me eat alone, are you?"

Sighing, she slid onto the chair and confessed, "This smells amazing."

"Dig in," he encouraged. "Nothing like carbs and choles-terol to start the day right."

The spark in her eyes reminded him of the old Emily, and she grabbed a fork with an almost defiant toss to her head. "Thank you, Connor."

"Anytime, Em," he vowed, knowing her gratitude was for much more than a simple offer to share breakfast.

He picked up his own fork, ready to dig into the eggs,

when a hint of spice seemed to sneak into his senses. Normally sides like toast or muffins were an afterthought, something to eat only if the main meal wasn't filling enough. But the powder-sprinkled muffin on the edge of his plate suddenly had his mouth watering.

He broke off an edge and popped it into his mouth. The moist confection melted on his tongue, tempting his senses with sugar, cinnamon and...*Kelsey*.

The hint of sweet and spicy had filled his head when he stood close to her, urging him to discover if the cinnamon scent was thanks to a shampoo she used on the red-gold curls she tried to tame or a lotion she smoothed over her pale skin.

If he kissed her, was that how she'd taste?

"What's Kelsey doing today?"

The question popped out before Connor ever thought to ask it, revealing a curiosity he couldn't deny yet didn't want to admit. He set the muffin aside and shoved a forkful of eggs into his mouth in case any other questions decided to circumvent his thought process.

After taking a drink of juice, Emily said, "Oh, she's likely running herself ragged with wedding preparations, making sure everything's going to go according to plan."

Her words sent suspicion slithering down his spine. At a small, low-key wedding, the bride's cousin might be the one behind the scenes, making sure everything went *according to plan*. But not at the Wilson-Dunworthy wedding, where professionals would handle those kind of details.

"What, exactly," he asked, "does Kelsey have to do with the wedding preparations?"

Emily frowned. "Didn't she tell you she's my wedding coordinator?"

"No," he said, setting his fork aside and leaning back in the chair, "no, she didn't."

"I'm lucky to have her working on the wedding. She's amazing when it comes to organization, and she's taking care of everything."

Everything, Connor thought wryly, including him.

Chapter Four

So much for unbiased. So much for impartial. So much for finding his insider in the Wilson camp, Connor thought. Kelsey was involved in this wedding right up to her gorgeous red head.

"She started her business over a year ago," Emily was saying. "My father offered to finance the company, but she wouldn't take the loan. She's always been weird about money."

Ignoring his grudging respect for Kelsey's decision and the curiosity about her *weirdness* when it came to her family's money, Connor focused on what she was getting from the Wilson family name. "So this wedding's a big deal to Kelsey, huh?"

"Oh, it's huge! She's counting on my wedding being the launching pad for Weddings Amour. The business is totally her baby, and she loves it. Says it makes her feel like a fairy god-mother, starting couples out on their own happily-ever-after."

Connor let out a snort of disbelief. He hadn't read any

fairy tales since he was six and figured it had been nearly as long since he'd believed in happily-ever-after.

"What?" Emily demanded.

"It's—nothing." He stabbed at his eggs. "The whole thing is crazy. Fairy godmothers, everlasting love, all of it—"

It was impossible. He'd seen far too many marriage vows broken from behind the telescopic lens of his camera. Those couples had likely had dream weddings, too, but the dream couldn't survive reality. And sometimes—like with Cara Mitchell—happily-ever-after turned into a living nightmare.

"Well, don't tell Kelsey her business is a joke. She takes it very seriously."

"I bet she does."

Seriously enough that Charlene Wilson had put Kelsey in charge of "attending to him." He'd overheard the comment yesterday but hadn't realized he'd be in the hands of a professional.

"Why all the questions about Kelsey?"

"Just curious." When Emily's eyes narrowed thoughtfully, he added, "I don't remember you talking about her when we were going out, that's all."

She shrugged. "I didn't know her then."

"Didn't *know* her? She's your cousin, right?"

"I, uh, I meant I didn't know her well."

"Uh-huh." Emily was a horrible liar and not much better at keeping secrets. He could have pressed. A few pointed questions, and Emily would have told him everything.

Connor refused to ask. Even as curiosity stacked one row of questions upon the next, he wouldn't ask. Not about why Emily hadn't known her own relative, not about why Kelsey had gone to public school instead of the exclusive prep schools her cousins had attended, not about why she was *weird* when it came to the family fortune.

He wasn't back in Arizona to find out about Kelsey Wilson.

Returning his focus to that goal, he asked, "What's Todd up to today? He must have a lot of free time on his hands while you and your mother and Kelsey take care of all the wedding details."

"Oh, no. He has a meeting this morning. He'll be at his office most of the day."

"Really?" Now, this could be something. Connor forced himself to take a few bites of waffle before he asked, "What kind of meeting?"

"I'm not sure." A tiny frown tugged her eyebrows. "Todd doesn't tell me much about his work." Laughter chased the frown away. "Just as well. I'd be bored silly."

"I doubt that. You're smart, Emily. Smarter than you give yourself credit for."

"Thank you, Connor," she said softly.

"How'd you two meet anyway? I don't think you've said."

"At a department store." She smiled. "We were both shopping for Christmas presents for our mothers, but he didn't have a clue. Finally he asked me for help. It was really cute."

"Hmm. Almost as cute as when we met."

"Oh, you mean in that sleazy bar where you had to fight off those bikers who were hitting on me?"

"A bar you weren't old enough to be at in the first place," Connor pointed out.

"Luckily you were there to rescue me," she said, lifting her glass in a teasing toast.

"Yeah, lucky," Connor agreed as he tapped his own glass against hers.

Emily might not know it, but he was here to save her again.

The tiny butterflies taking flight in Kelsey's stomach as she drove toward the hotel turned into radioactive monsters by the time she stepped into the lobby. She'd been crazy to make a deal with Connor McClane. Somewhere along the way she was going to lose her soul.

Although they hadn't made plans to meet this morning, the best way to keep an eye on Connor was to embrace their partnership. As she walked by the three-tiered fountain toward the elevators, the doors slid open. Kelsey gasped and ducked into an alcove—the same alcove to which Connor had pulled her aside the day before—and watched in disbelief as her cousin walked by.

What was Emily doing at Connor's hotel?

Her cousin rarely left the house before noon, and it was barely nine o'clock. What was Emily doing up so early? Or had she stayed out too late? Kelsey's stomach churned at the thought. She hated to think her cousin would be so susceptible to Connor's charms. *And what about you?* her conscience mocked. *How easily did you agree to work with Connor in this very spot?*

But that was different! That was about business and keeping an eye on Connor and keeping him away from Emily...not that Kelsey had done a bang-up job at either so far.

Emily slipped on a pair of sunglasses and smiled at a bellboy, who nearly tripped over his feet as she walked by. She didn't look as if she'd rolled out of bed with her ex-lover, but then again, Kelsey had never seen Emily look less than perfect. Ever.

Kelsey stayed hidden as her cousin sashayed across the lobby and out the automatic doors, then made a beeline for the elevator. "So much for his promises," she muttered as she jabbed the Up button.

"But why am I even surprised?"

She stomped out of the elevator on the fourth floor. Had she really believed Connor would keep his word?

Maybe she had. Which only went to prove how some

people never learned. Rapping on Connor's door hard enough to bruise her knuckles, she thought she'd be better off banging her head against the wood.

"Kelsey." Opening the door, Connor greeted her with an assessing look and not an ounce of shame. Bracing one arm on the doorjamb, he said, "I'm surprised to see you here."

"Are you?" Determined to ignore the masculine pose that could have come straight from some sexy man-of-the-month calendar, she ducked beneath his arm and made her way inside. She refused to have an argument in the hall where any guest, bellhop or room-service waiter might walk by. "If I'd shown up a few minutes earlier, it would have been a regular family reunion."

"You saw Emily?"

"So much for your promise to keep your distance!"

Connor frowned. "I said I'd stay away. I can't help it if she comes to see me."

"Right. And I'm sure she forced her way inside your hotel room. Probably tied you up and had her way with you, too."

Connor pushed away from the door and stalked toward her with that challenging expression still in his eyes. "That would really mess up your plans, wouldn't it?"

"She's engaged, Connor. Doesn't that mean anything to you?"

"Yeah. It means she's about to make a mistake."

Connor stepped closer, and the only mistake Kelsey could concentrate on was her own in thinking she could confront Connor face-to-face and not be overwhelmed by his masculine sensuality. He hadn't shaved and the morning stubble only made him that much more appealing. Worse, she could practically feel the erotic scrape of whisker-rough skin against her cheeks, her neck, her breasts—

Afraid he could read her every thought by the glow in her cheeks, Kelsey ducked her head. Her gaze landed on the nearby breakfast tray, on a white coffee cup and a pink bow-shaped smudge left by Emily's lipstick. The mark may have been left on Connor's cup, not on the man himself, but the reminder that Emily had been there first doused Kelsey like a bucket of ice water. "Emily's only mistake was inviting *you*."

"Yeah, I bet that's tough on you, isn't it? When you told me yesterday working together would be strictly business, I didn't realize that meant you were getting paid."

"So I'm coordinating Emily's wedding. Don't act all offended like it was some big secret. I thought you already knew."

"Yeah, well, I didn't. If I had—"

"You would have what?"

Scowling at her, he said, "Look, if you want to work together, I need to know you care more about your cousin than you do about your business."

If she wanted to work together! Just yesterday, she thought agreeing to work with Connor was possibly the most foolish thing she'd ever done. And now she had to fight to keep the opportunity?

Yes! a voice inside her head argued. *Because it's the only one you'll get. How else will you keep an eye on him? How else will you keep him from stopping the wedding?*

"Of course I care about Emily."

A sardonic twist of a smile lifted one corner of Connor's mouth. Darn him for making even sarcasm look sexy! "I know you care about her. The question is, do you care enough to put her first over everything else you want?"

The intensity in his eyes transformed the question from a challenge about her loyalty to Emily into something more personal. Something dark and revealing about his past. *Prove that you care...*

It was a test Emily had failed. She hadn't cared enough, or

she'd cared about her family's approval more. Was Emily the only woman who hadn't passed, Kelsey wondered, or were there other women who hadn't given Connor the proof he needed?

"You can't prove you care about someone," she stated flatly. "Not in words. Actions show how you truly feel."

Like Connor showing up for Emily's wedding...and Emily showing up at Connor's hotel room. Trying not to think what those actions meant, Kelsey continued, "I'm here. That alone should prove—"

"That you're a clever businesswoman? I already knew that."

Tightening her grip on her purse strap, Kelsey fought for control. She couldn't pretend she didn't have a lot riding on Emily's wedding.

As she racked her brain for a way to prove her loyalty, Kelsey realized nothing she said would be enough. Meeting his gaze, she stated, "I can't prove it to you, Connor. Because love and caring aren't about proof. They're about faith. So, if I'm supposed to trust your gut when you tell me Todd isn't right for Emily, you're going to have to trust me when I tell you Emily's happiness matters most."

With his gaze locked on hers, Connor stayed silent long enough for Kelsey to anticipate half a dozen responses. Would he laugh in her face? Turn away in cynical disgust?

Seconds ticked by, and she held her ground by pulling off a decent imitation of her aunt. She kept her back straight, her head held high, and still managed to look down her nose at a much taller Connor.

He ruined the hard-won effect with a single touch, tracing a finger over her cheek. The steel in her spine melted into a puddle of desire.

"Good to have you back on the team," he said softly. "We have work to do."

* * *

Connor knew he'd crossed the line when Kelsey's eyes widened to a deer-caught-in-the-headlights look. He needed to back off. If he pushed, she'd bolt. But it was the urge to ignore his own boundaries that had him pulling back even further.

If anyone could make him *want* to trust again, Kelsey might. And that sure as hell wasn't the kind of thought a man wanted to have while sober. Especially not a man like him about a woman like her.

Kelsey was a Wilson, and he'd already learned his lesson when it came to how Wilson-McClane relationships ended. He knew better than to make the same mistake twice... Didn't he? Just because he'd indulged in a minor fantasy—discovering the five freckles on Kelsey's cheek *did* combine to make a perfect star—didn't mean he was losing his grip on the situation. He had everything under control, even if that star-shaped outline made him wonder what other patterns he might find on Kelsey's body....

Far too aware of the bed only a few feet away and Kelsey's teasing scent, that alluring combination of cinnamon and spice, Connor redirected his focus. "Are you hungry? I could order more room service."

"No, thank you." Her words were too polite, bordering on stiff, and they matched her posture.

"All right," he said, thinking it just as well they get out of the hotel room before he ended up doing something as stupid as touching Kelsey...and not stopping. "But you really don't want to go on a stakeout on an empty stomach." Connor didn't know if his sudden announcement loosened anything, but Kelsey definitely looked shaken.

"Stakeout?" Echoing the word, her brown eyes widened.

"Don't worry. We'll stop for staples along the way." He grabbed her hand, pulled her from the room and out into the hall.

She protested every step of the way and all throughout the elevator ride down to the lobby. "Are you insane? I am *not* going on a stakeout."

Her voice dropped to a hiss as the elevator door opened, and she even managed a smile at the elderly couple waiting in the lobby.

"You agreed to this, remember? Equal partners?"

As he strode across the lobby, Connor realized Kelsey was practically running to keep up with his long strides, and he slowed his steps.

Jeez, it'd be faster if he picked her up and carried her. A corner of his mouth lifted at the thought of Kelsey's reaction if he tried. "You really are tiny, aren't you?"

"I— What?"

She bumped into him when Connor paused for the automatic doors to open. He had the quick impression of soft breasts against his back before Kelsey jumped away.

Tiny, he decided as he looked over his shoulder with an appreciative glance, but curved in all the right places.

Something in his expression must have given his thoughts away. Kelsey glared at him. "I am not going on a stakeout."

"How are we going to find anything out about Todd if we don't watch him?"

"I thought you'd hire someone!"

"Right. Because the Wilsons would believe whatever some guy I *paid* has to say about their golden boy."

Score one for the away team, Connor thought, when Kelsey stopped arguing. Pressing his advantage, he guided her outside. "Besides," he added, "staking people out is what I do."

"You—you're a cop?"

He couldn't blame her for the shock in her voice and gave a scoffing laugh. "No. I'm a private investigator. Turns out we're both professionals," he said. "And if it makes you feel any better, I do have a friend working another lead. But he's in St. Louis."

"What's in St. Louis?"

"A maid who used to work for the Dunworthy family. She either quit or was let go a few months ago."

"So?"

"She pretty much disappeared after that, and I want to hear what she has to say about her former employers."

Midmorning sunlight glinted off the line of luxury cars brought around by the valets: Lexus, BMW, Mercedes. He'd come a long way from his bike days. Too bad. He would have enjoyed getting Kelsey on a Harley. Once she loosened up a bit, she'd love the freedom of hugging the curves, wind whipping through her hair, speed pouring through her veins. He could almost feel her arms around his waist…

Kelsey waved toward the visitor's lot. "We can take my car."

It didn't look like loosening up would happen anytime soon. "Sorry, sweetheart, but I'll bet Dunworthy has already seen your car."

Connor signaled a valet, and within minutes a vintage black Mustang pulled up to the curb. Seeing the question in Kelsey's eyes, he explained, "It's Javy's. Something less flashy would be better for surveillance, but borrowers can't be choosers."

He tipped the valet and opened the passenger door for Kelsey. When she looked ready to argue, he said, "Todd has a big meeting at his office." He'd looked up the address after Emily left. "I'm curious to find out who it's with. How 'bout you?"

As she slid into the passenger seat, Kelsey muttered something he couldn't quite make out.

Connor figured it was just as well.

* * *

"I cannot believe I'm doing this," Kelsey muttered from her slumped-down position in the passenger seat.

"You've mentioned that," Connor replied.

They were parked in a lot across the street from Todd's office. The row of two-story suites lined a busy side street off Scottsdale Road, the black glass and concrete a sharp contrast to the gold and russet rock landscape, with its clusters of purple sage, flowering bougainvillea and cacti. Connor had circled the building when they first arrived, noting all the building's entrances and confirming Todd's car wasn't in the lot.

"What if someone sees us?"

"What are they going to see?" he retorted.

She supposed from a distance the car did blend in. Thanks to heavily tinted windows, it was unlikely anyone could see inside. Tilting the vents to try to get a bit more air to blow in her direction, Kelsey admitted, "This is a bit more boring than I expected."

"Boring is good," Connor insisted. Despite his words, he drummed his fingers against the steering wheel in an impatient rhythm, clearly ready for action.

"I'm surprised Emily didn't tell me more about your job."

"Why would she?"

"Because to anyone not sitting in this car, being a P.I. sounds exciting." When Connor stayed silent, she asked, "Do you like it?"

"Yeah. Most of the time."

The tapping on the steering wheel increased like the sudden peaks on a lie detector, and Kelsey sensed he was telling her not what he thought she wanted to hear, but what he *wanted* to believe. Something had happened to change his mind about the job she suspected he'd once loved. "It must be difficult. Seeing so much of the darker side of life."

"It can be. Sometimes human nature is dark, but at least my job is about discovering the truth."

Was it only her imagination, or had he emphasized that pronoun? Subtly saying that while he pursued truth and justice, she— "You think *my* job is about telling lies?"

"Selling lies," he clarified.

"I promise a beautiful wedding and give the bride and groom what they're looking for. That's not a lie."

"Okay," he conceded, "maybe not the beautiful wedding part, but the sentiment behind it? Happily-ever-after? Love of a lifetime? Till death do us part? Come on!"

"Not every marriage ends with the bride and groom riding off into the sunset. Real life comes with real problems, but if two people love each other, they work it out."

He snorted. "Not from my side of the video camera, they don't."

Irritation crackled inside her like radio static—annoying, incessant and almost loud enough to drown out a vague and misplaced feeling of disillusionment. All these years, she'd heard about Connor and Emily as a modern-day Romeo and Juliet, but the story of star-crossed lovers lost all meaning if one of the players didn't believe in love.

And while Kelsey's faith might have been shaken by what happened with Matt, she still longed for those happily-ever-after and love-of-a-lifetime dreams Connor cynically mocked.

"My aunt and uncle never believed you loved Emily," she said, disappointed. "Everything you've said proves them right."

"Your aunt and uncle weren't right about me—no matter what they think."

Dead certainty ricocheted in his voice, and Kelsey regretted the tack she'd taken. Too late to back down and far too curious about what made Connor tick, she pressed, "Either you believe in love or you don't. You can't have it both ways."

"I just don't want to see Emily get hurt. That's why I'm here."

She opened her mouth, ready to push further, when Connor pulled the handle on the driver's-side door. "I'll be right back."

Kelsey grabbed his arm. "Wait! Where are you going?"

"To check the rear lot. Todd might have pulled in back there while we've been watching the front." With one foot already on the asphalt and refusing to meet her gaze, Connor seemed more interested in escaping her questions.

"I'm coming with you." She scrambled to unlock the passenger door. When she sensed an oncoming protest, she said, "Partners, remember? You're the one who dragged me along. You aren't leaving me now."

"Forget it! He'll recognize you."

"Todd knows what you look like, too," she argued as she turned back toward him.

"Fine," he bit out as he dropped back into the seat, "but there's something you have to do first."

Thanks to her questions, a noticeable tension vibrated through Connor, evident in his clenched jaw and the taut muscles in the arm he'd braced against the wheel. But the tension gradually changed, not easing, but instead focusing to a fine, definitive point—one that seemed wholly centered on her.

His intense gaze traveled over her hair, her face, her mouth... The gold flecks in his green eyes glowed, and Kelsey's skin tingled as if warmed by his touch. Surely he wouldn't try to kiss her. Not here, not now! Time raced by with each rapid beat of her heart, a single question echoing in her veins.

Why *didn't* he kiss her? Right here, right now—

Her pulse pounded in her ears, drowning out the sound of passing traffic. The heat shimmering on her skin could put the mirage hovering above the asphalt to shame. Shifting his body in the driver's seat, Connor eased closer. The scent of his aftershave, a clean fragrance that called to mind ocean breezes and sun-kissed sand, drew her in. Like waves rushing to the shore, helpless to resist the undeniable pull, she reached for him….

But instead of a roll on the beach, Kelsey crashed against the shoals, her pride battered against the rocks when Connor suddenly turned away. He twisted his upper body between the seats and reached into the back. "Here, take this."

Kelsey stared dumbly at the baseball hat he held.

"See if you can cover your hair."

Her hand was still raised in an attempt to reach out and capture a passion obviously only she felt. An admission of her willingness to make a fool of herself.

Kelsey jerked the hat from Connor, eager to grab hold of anything to save face. "Do you really think this will make a difference?"

"A huge one." Almost reluctantly he added, "Your hair is unforgettable."

But he'd forget all about her and her hair once Emily was a free woman again. Unforgettable. Yeah, right.

Kelsey didn't realize she'd spoken the words until Connor murmured, "It's the kind of hair a man fantasizes about. Trust me."

But she couldn't. She'd nearly made a fool of herself seconds ago, and in case she ever forgot, she had the living, breathing epitome of Connor's perfect woman as her cousin. Kelsey couldn't compare; she never had.

Jerking back toward the door to put as much room as possible between them, she shook back her hair and pulled it away from her face with sharp, almost painful movements. Unable to hide behind her long locks, she felt exposed, vulnerable. Even more so when Connor's gaze remained locked on her features.

"How's that?" she asked, as she twisted her hair into a bun and shoved the bright red Diamondbacks cap into place. When

Connor continued to stare, Kelsey fisted her hands in her lap to keep from yanking off the ridiculous hat. Finally, she demanded, "What?"

Shaking his head, Connor seemed to snap out of his stupor. "I hadn't realized how much you look like Emily."

His words hit like a punch in the stomach. Look like Emily? Not a chance. She'd seen the disappointment in the Wilsons' faces when they first saw her. If Emily and Aileen were beautiful Barbie dolls, then Kelsey was clearly supposed to be Skipper, a younger, blonder version. But she looked *nothing* like her cousins, a point driven home at every Wilson function, with every meeting of their friends and associates. The surprise—if not flat-out disbelief—when Kelsey was introduced as one of the Wilsons.

I hope they had her DNA tested, Kelsey had heard one uninformed, high-society snob whisper. *It wouldn't surprise me if that girl ended up being a con artist out for the family fortune.*

Kelsey had struggled to hold her head high and hold back the tears when she wanted to lash out at the woman. She was every bit her mother's daughter, *not* her father's, and inside she was as much a Wilson as Gordon, Aileen and Emily. But outside—where it counted—she couldn't be more different.

"Give me a break!" She tried to laugh off the remark, but the fake sound stuck in her throat. "Emily and I look nothing alike! She's tall and thin and blond and—beautiful!"

Her voice broke on the last word, and Kelsey had never been so close to hitting anyone. Giving in to the impulse, she socked Connor in the shoulder. She had a quick impression of dense muscle and bone, but he caught her hand before she could fool herself into thinking she could do more damage.

"Hey!" A quick tug of her arm had her falling against him. "So are you!"

"Tall? Blond?" Kelsey shot back sarcastically.

"Beautiful!" he retorted.

"But I'm not—"

"Not Emily?" he interjected softly. He brushed an escaping strand of hair—her unforgettable hair—back from her face, and the touch she'd only imagined became reality as he traced his index finger over her eyebrow, across her cheekbone, and skimmed the corner of her mouth. Heat and hunger combined with a tenderness that snuck beneath her defenses. "There's more than one ideal for beauty, Kelsey."

Still pressed against his muscular chest, she knew Connor was the epitome of masculine beauty for her, and she had the devastating feeling that would never change, even years from now. He was the best of the best, and she was a long shot, the dark horse.

"Stop it," she whispered furiously.

"You don't have to be Emily. You can just be yourself."

The deep murmur of his voice reached inside and touched that vulnerable place, but this time instead of opening old wounds, his words offered a healing balm. And meeting his gaze, Kelsey realized he understood her vulnerability in a way no one else could because he'd felt the same way. He'd never been good enough to date the daughter of the wealthy Wilsons, and she had never felt good enough to *be* one of the wealthy Wilsons.

"Connor…" Just one word, his name spoken in a hushed whisper, broke the connection. He blinked, or maybe Kelsey did, because when she looked again, his sexy smile was back in place, all sense of vulnerability gone. "Except for right now. Right now you have to be someone Todd won't recognize."

"Right." Kelsey pulled back, and Connor let her go. She might not have a sexy smile to hide behind, but she could be businesslike and professional…or as businesslike and professional as a wedding coordinator spying on a future groom could be.

"Come on," she muttered as she tugged the brim lower. She didn't know if she'd need the hat to hide her identity from Todd, but maybe she could use it to hide her emotions from Connor. "Let's do this."

She climbed from the car and was headed straight for the building by the time Connor caught up with her. Grabbing her hand, he said, "This way."

With Connor leading the way, they walked half a block before crossing the street and doubling back behind Todd's building. But the lot was empty except for some abandoned crates and an overflowing Dumpster.

"Let's go. Todd's meeting must have been canceled," Kelsey said. She walked around to the front of the building without bothering to take the circular route that got them there, her low heels striking the steaming pavement.

Connor caught up to her as she reached the front of the building. "Look, I admit this was a dud, but—" He cut off with a curse.

Kelsey didn't have time to take a breath before he shoved her into a recessed doorway and nearly smothered her with his body. Her vehement protest came out a puny squeak.

"Don't move." The husky whisper and warm breath against her ear guaranteed she couldn't take a single step without falling flat on her face. "Todd's pulling into the parking lot."

No, no, no! This could not be happening! Swallowing against a lump of horror, Kelsey fisted her hands in his T-shirt and tugged. "Let's go," she hissed.

"Can't. He'll see us if we move. Just…relax."

Despite the advice, every muscle in his body was tense, primed and ready for action. But it was Kelsey who jumped when the car door slammed. "He'll see us."

"No, he won't. He's heading for his office."

She had to take Connor's word for it. With his body

blocking every bit of daylight, she couldn't see beyond his broad shoulders. Too bad the rest of her senses weren't so completely cut off. Instead, the scent of his sea-breeze aftershave combined with potent warm male, and the masculine heat of Connor's chest burned into her skin where he made contact with her. Kelsey locked her knees to keep from sinking right into him.

Heart pounding in her ears, she whispered, "Where is he now?"

"Unlocking the door."

She felt as much as heard his low murmur and hissed, "We should go." Right now, before the heat went straight to her head and she did something unforgivably stupid, like melt into a puddle of desire at Connor's feet.

Chapter Five

"I am not meant for a life of crime."

Seated in a restaurant not far from Dunworthy's business, Connor pressed a beer into Kelsey's hand. That she took it without complaint told him how much the incident at Todd's office had shaken her.

Their near miss had lasted only seconds. Connor had pulled Kelsey toward the car immediately after Todd entered the suite; she'd barely ducked inside the Mustang's ovenlike interior when he came back outside. Connor might have suspected the other man sensed something wrong if not for the way he sauntered out to his top-of-the-line SUV without checking his surroundings. If he had, it was a good bet he would have caught sight of Connor sliding into the driver's seat only a few yards away.

Connor had wanted to follow him, but with Kelsey along, the risk wasn't worth it. Not that it was her fault they'd nearly been spotted. No, Connor took full blame. He'd let Kelsey distract him. He could have driven her back to the hotel and her waiting car but had instead veered off to the restaurant, which had a bar. He figured she could use a drink. After standing in the doorway with the Arizona sun roasting his back, Connor could use a cold shower, but a cold beer was the next best thing.

Liar, a mocking voice jeered. The hundred-plus temperature was a killer, but it was the feeling of Kelsey's body pressed to his that heated his blood.

"Hate to tell you, but we didn't break any laws."

She took a long pull on the bottle, then set it back on the bar with an audible clunk. "We were trespassing."

Hiding his smile behind the beer bottle, he bit back a burst of laughter. "The parking lot is public property. We had every right to be there."

"Oh." Kelsey stared thoughtfully at the bottle. He couldn't tell if she was relieved or disappointed. Finally, she looked up, her expression resolute. "Okay, so maybe what we did wasn't illegal, but—but it was unethical. It isn't right to go around spying on people. Especially when they aren't doing anything wrong. And I don't have time to waste chasing Todd or any of your ghosts around town." She slid out of the booth.

Connor frowned. "Hey, this doesn't have anything to do with me."

"Bull. You're out to prove to Aunt Charlene and Uncle Gordon you're much better for Emily than their handpicked golden boy."

Connor recoiled against the padded booth. Was Kelsey right? Did coming back to Arizona have more to do with salvaging his ego than protecting Emily?

No. No way. He wasn't nearly that pathetic. Unfortunately,

Kelsey had almost reached the door by the time he came to that conclusion. "Kelsey, wait!"

"Hey!" The bartender called after him. "Those beers weren't free, you know."

Swearing, Connor dug out his wallet, threw a handful of bills on the bar, and raced after Kelsey. The sunlight threatened to sear his corneas after the dimly lit bar, and he shaded his eyes against the glare. "Kelsey!"

The rush of nearby traffic nearly drowned out his voice, but Connor doubted that was why she didn't stop. Jogging after her, he caught her as she reached the car. It took a second longer to realize he had the keys, and she couldn't go anywhere without him.

Dammit, what was it about Kelsey that made him so crazy? He hadn't felt like this since—since Emily.

You're a fool, boy. Just like your old man. His father's voice rang in his head. *The both of us always want to hold on to what we can't have.*

Thrusting the comparisons aside, he said, "Look, I know this afternoon was a bust, but this isn't about me."

"Really?" Disbelief colored her words, and Connor fought a flare of irritation mixed with admiration. Had to respect a woman who wasn't easily snowed.

Taking a deep breath, he forced the irritation aside. He couldn't risk losing Kelsey as a partner. That was the reason he didn't want her to leave. It had nothing to do with wanting to spend more time with the woman who had him so fascinated.

Yeah, right, his conscience mocked. Back at Todd's office, he'd been tempted to forget all about the other man and prove to Kelsey just how beautiful she was. But he refused to make out with a woman in a parked car. Especially *not* Javy's car, the same vintage automobile he'd borrowed to take Emily out on dates all those years ago.

He wasn't that same punk kid anymore, even if he was once again lusting after one of the wealthy Wilsons.

"Let me buy you lunch, and I'll tell you what I *do* know about Todd."

Back in the restaurant, under the bartender's watchful eye, Connor and Kelsey placed their orders. As soon as the waitress walked away, Kelsey leaned forward and prompted, "Okay, let's hear it."

"First, did Emily ever tell you how we met?"

Kelsey's gaze dropped as she fiddled with her napkin. "She might have."

"Well, just so you have the whole story, Emily went to a bar. She was underage and in over her head. Some guys started hitting on her. She tried to shrug it off, but she was afraid to tell them to go take a hike. Because that wouldn't have been *nice*. But I could see the panic in her eyes. She was waiting for someone to step in and save her."

"And so you did."

"And so I did." Leaning across the table, he covered Kelsey's hand, intent on claiming her complete attention. Only when her eyes widened perceptibly did Connor realize he'd nearly erased the two-foot distance separating them. He was close enough to count the freckles dotting her upturned nose, to catch hold of her cinnamon scent. Her startled gaze flew to meet his, and as the spark of attraction he saw in her brown eyes flared to life inside him, Connor was the one having a hard time staying focused.

"The, uh, thing is—when I look at Emily now, I see that same panic. She's in over her head, letting herself get pushed along because she's too *nice* to stand up for herself."

"So you rode back into town, ready to play the hero."

"I'm no hero," Connor stated flatly, leaning back in the booth and pulling his hands from Kelsey's. The softness of her skin threatened to slip beneath his defenses, making him weak. The passion in her eyes when she spoke about everlasting love and dreams coming true made him want to believe though he knew better.

Even if he didn't have countless professional examples of love gone wrong to draw from, he also had his parents' as proof of love's fallibility. During their short-lived marriage, his parents drifted so far apart that in the end, neither his father nor Connor had been able to pull his mother back to safety.

If only she'd listened— Helplessness roiled in his gut, but he'd learned his lesson.

It would take more than words to keep Emily safe; he had to have proof. But right now, words were all he had to convince Kelsey. The only way to do that would be to open up and be completely honest. "I didn't expect to like Todd when I met him. I walked into that restaurant in San Diego knowing he's the Wilsons' golden boy and everything I'm not."

"Now who needs the lesson about being himself?" Kelsey murmured.

"Nothing like having my own words shoved back in my face," he said with a smile, which fell away as he realized how much they did have in common, how easily Kelsey understood him. Their gazes caught and held, the spark of desire running on a supercharged emotional current.

A touch of pink—sunset pink—highlighted Kelsey's cheeks, and she dropped her gaze. "Not shoving, exactly. More like gently tossing."

The waitress arrived with their food, breaking the moment and giving Connor a chance to refocus on what he wanted to say. "This is about more than disliking Dunworthy on sight. It's about the way he treats people he thinks are beneath him."

"Like who?"

"Like the valet he was pushing around after we left the restaurant."

"What?"

"I was pulling out of the lot when I saw Todd grab the kid and shove his face an inch from the bumper to show where he'd *dented* the car." Leaning forward, Connor added, "It was a rental, Kelsey. You can't tell me he had any clue whether that scratch was there before or not. But he's the type of guy who likes to intimidate people, especially people who can't or won't fight back."

"What did you do?"

"Jumped out of my car and pulled him off."

"And Todd actually grabbed this kid in front of Emily?"

Connor snorted. "No. She'd left her sweater in the restaurant and had gone back for it. By the time she came out, Todd was wearing a crocodile grin and the valet had pocketed a tip the size of his monthly paycheck."

Something else Dunworthy had in common with the Wilsons—thinking money could make anything or anyone disappear. Not that he blamed the kid for taking the cash. How could he when he'd done the same thing ten years ago?

"You don't think Todd would hurt Emily, do you?" Kelsey asked, disbelief and worry mingling in her expression.

"I don't know," he said. "All I know is that he thinks he can do whatever he damn well wants as long as he pays for the privilege."

"Kelsey! Where have you been all day?" Emily rose from the table in the middle of the Italian restaurant. "I've been calling you since first thing this morning."

Kelsey braced herself against Emily's exuberant greeting, hesitantly patting her cousin's slender shoulder blades. First thing this morning, Emily had been with Connor. Kelsey seriously doubted she'd been on her cousin's mind. "I've, um, been busy."

"What have you been doing?" Emily demanded as Kelsey slipped into a seat next to her and across from Aileen and her husband.

"I was—" Kelsey's mind blanked as she met her cousin's curious gaze, and she couldn't think of a single excuse.

I was with Connor. We spent the day spying on your fiancé, which was possibly the craziest thing I've ever done, right up to the time I thought Connor might kiss me.

"Kelsey!"

She jumped at the sound of her aunt's voice, terrified for a split second that she'd said the unbelievable words out loud. "What?"

Charlene frowned with a question in her eyes. "You paid the florist, didn't you?"

"Yes! Yes, I did." As if the forty-minute errand explained her absence during most of the day.

"Good. I hope it wasn't a mistake going with such a small shop. As worried as that woman sounded, you'd think she was down to her last dollar."

Irritation buzzed like a rash under Kelsey's skin. "Her name is Lisa Remming, and she's an amazing florist. A deposit is standard policy. We signed a contract stating she could cancel the order if it wasn't paid on time," she added, knowing her friend would never have considered canceling such an important order.

"All right, Kelsey. You've made your point," Charlene said. Kelsey thought she might have caught a hint of respect in her aunt's expression.

But Emily's eyes widened, and she grabbed Kelsey's hand. "Lisa wouldn't do that, would she?"

"No, of course not," she reassured her cousin, feeling like

a jerk for worrying her cousin just to make a point with Charlene. "The flowers are going to be beautiful."

Emily smiled, relieved someone else had solved the problem. "Thank goodness. I can't imagine getting married without the right bouquet."

Kelsey, personally, couldn't imagine getting married without the right groom. She *wanted* to believe Todd was that man for her cousin, but ever since Connor had rolled into town, doubts had swirled through her mind like a desert dust devil.

"Emily, darling!" a masculine voice called out. Dressed in designer slacks and a slate-blue silk shirt, Todd Dunworthy approached, his perfectly groomed blond hair glinting, and his teeth flashing in a blinding smile.

Sheep's clothing, Kelsey thought suddenly. Expensive, designer-crafted sheep's clothing…if she believed Connor. But that was the question. *Did* she believe him?

"Sorry I'm late," Todd apologized without looking away from his fiancée. "My meeting ran late."

"Your meeting?" Kelsey didn't realize she'd spoken the words out loud until all eyes turned her way. Tempted to blurt out that he'd spent less than five minutes at the office, she choked back the words. She couldn't say that without revealing her own presence. And, as she'd told Connor, Todd's meeting could have changed locations. Hoping Todd would reveal that was the case, she pressed, "I mean, what meeting, Todd?"

He waved his hand carelessly, and his sleeve pulled back to show a hint of the gold watch he wore. "Just business. You wouldn't be interested," he said, flashing a wink that was more condescending than charming.

"Oh, but I am," Kelsey interjected, when Todd would have changed the subject. He shot her a look clearly meant to back her down—*to put her in her place*—but Kelsey stood her ground. She could almost feel Connor at her back, giving her the strength to do the right thing. "You'll be family soon, and I hardly know anything about what you do."

"Honestly, Kelsey, enough about work," Emily interrupted, despite the fact that Todd had remained completely—suspiciously?—silent. "We have more important things to discuss."

Ever the peacemaker, Emily turned the conversation to the wedding and her honeymoon. She smoothed over the tension like a pro until, on the outside at least, everything *looked* perfect.

But as the conversation moved on to drinks and appetizers and who wanted to try the chef's special, Kelsey couldn't help noticing how her cousin's gaze would occasionally drift off in the distance. And she wondered if maybe, just maybe, Emily was waiting for Connor—or *anyone*—to rescue her again.

Connor drummed his fingers against the steering wheel, his gaze locked on the Italian restaurant. Candlelight flickered in the antique sconces, illuminating the rustic red brick, aged pergola, and carved wooden doors.

After taking Kelsey back to the hotel and her car, Connor called Jake Cameron, eager to hear what the man had found. But the conversation hadn't gone as he'd hoped.

"I told you this would take some time," Jake had said, sounding more frustrated and less confident than during the last call.

"Yeah, I know. You also told me you had a date with Sophia Pirelli. You had to have found *something*."

Silence filled the line, and Connor might have thought the call was disconnected, except he could still sense his friend's tension coming across loud and clear. "Jake—"

"Look, I'm seeing her again. I'll call you later."

He'd hung up after that, leaving Connor to battle his own tension and frustration. Unwilling to sit in his hotel room and go over the same information on Dunworthy again, he'd headed for Todd's condo, planning to talk with some of the man's neighbors, when he spotted the familiar SUV leaving the parking garage.

As Connor followed Dunworthy from his Scottsdale loft, careful to stay two car lengths behind, he had plenty of time to make some calls, and discovered the studio-sized units cost well over two million dollars. Knowing the man would pay such an outrageous price for an exclusive address to call home, Connor should have expected what was to come.

He'd already trailed Emily's fiancé from one expensive store to another, growing more and more disgusted as Dunworthy racked up a small fortune in purchases. Wine shops, jewelers, tailors. Connor had held back far enough to keep Dunworthy from spotting him, but not so far that he couldn't see the dollar signs in the salespeople's eyes.

The afternoon had proved a dud just like the meeting that morning, and Connor wished Kelsey had come along. He missed her company—an odd admission for a man who worked alone. He missed her wry comments and witty comebacks, not to mention the tempting thought of kissing her. It was no longer a question of if, but when…

He did have one lead, thanks to a call he'd overheard Todd make on his cell phone, but he would have to wait to follow up.

He sat up straight in the driver's seat as the restaurant's carved doors opened. "'Bout time," he muttered as the elder Wilsons stepped outside along with Aileen and her husband. Todd and Emily followed, and even though Connor had his gaze locked on the other man, it didn't take much to distract him. Just Kelsey.

She stood apart from the rest of the group—not so far she couldn't hear the conversation, just far enough she couldn't be easily drawn in. He'd noticed her do that at the hotel when he'd crashed their little reception planning session. She'd trailed a step or two behind her aunt and cousin, hiding behind the copious notes she took in her day planner. Observing, but not really joining.

Just the way he did. He never would have thought his job as a private eye and Kelsey's job as a wedding coordinator would give them something else in common, but there it was. Still, the Wilsons were more than Kelsey's clients; they were her family. So what was the reason for that distance?

Now wasn't the time to worry about it. Connor jerked his gaze away from Kelsey. He didn't let his attention stray back to her, not even once, surprised by how hard that was.

Todd slapped his future father-in-law on the back, then kissed Charlene's cheek and said something to make the older woman laugh.

I'll be damned, Connor thought, his respect for Dunworthy as an adversary rising a few notches. He'd never seen the woman crack a smile, yet Todd had Emily's mother eating out of his hand.

The group, a silent film of family togetherness, said their goodbyes amid hugs and kisses, with Kelsey drifting just outside the happy circle. They broke into pairs, the elder Wilsons off to the left with Aileen and her husband, Emily and Dunworthy to his car—illegally parked, Connor noted—alongside the restaurant. Kelsey, the odd woman out, headed toward the back of the restaurant, crossing the parking lot…alone.

Todd's SUV engine roared. He should follow, Connor knew. His hand went to the ignition, but he didn't turn the key. A gut feeling, the kind Kelsey had sardonically discounted, held him in place even as Todd backed his vehicle away from the restaurant.

He had to go now if he had any hope of following. Instead, he leaned forward. Kelsey had nearly disappeared around the building. That side of the restaurant wasn't as well lit. Her hair looked brown in the meager light, the shadows dousing its fiery color. Dressed in a denim skirt and lace-trimmed green T-shirt, she looked smaller than usual…younger and more vulnerable.

Connor had already pushed the car door open before he caught sight of the dark shape of a man cutting across the parking lot and heading her way. Surprise drew Kelsey up short. Connor was still too far away to hear what she said, but he was close enough to see the guy reach out to grab her.

It was his nightmare brought to life. Close enough to see, too far away to help… For a split second, Connor froze until he realized this was no dream and the woman in danger wasn't Cara Mitchell. It was *Kelsey*.

Adrenaline pounded through his veins. A short burst of speed, the rhythmic thumping of feet against pavement, and he was there. Muscles flexing, he had the guy's arm twisted behind his back, his face shoved against the side of the restaurant.

"You okay?" he demanded of Kelsey, surprised by the breathless gasp fueling the words. His heart pounded like he'd run half a mile instead of thirty yards. Trying to outrun the past…

"Kelsey?" He could feel her behind him but didn't risk looking over his shoulder. "Are you okay?"

"Connor, what—" Too stunned by his sudden appearance to get the words out, Kelsey pressed a hand to her pounding heart, surprised the organ was still where it was supposed to be. For a second, she thought it had jumped right out of her chest.

"Did he hurt you?"

She blinked, the question not quite registering, and stared at her ex-boyfriend, who was pressed like a pancake against the restaurant's brick wall. Matt Moran had hurt her. He'd wounded her pride, trashed her self-confidence, hitting her where she was most vulnerable with the reminder she could never compare to her oh-so-beautiful cousin.

Matt made a strangled, high-pitched sound that might have been her name. "Kelsey! Tell him I wouldn't hurt you."

Connor shot her a quick glance. "You know this guy?"

The tension eased from his shoulders, but Kelsey knew he could be back in battle mode in a split second. The masculine display shouldn't have impressed her. She'd never advocated violence as a way to problem-solve. But seeing her former boyfriend pinned to a wall, well, it did her heart some good.

"Yes. You can let him go. He just wanted to talk to me."

Only, Kelsey hadn't wanted to hear anything Matt had to say. She'd already heard it all, ironically enough, from Connor.

He let go of the other man's arm and spun him around. "I take it you don't want to talk to him," Connor said. "Can't blame you there." He gave the other man a hard, intense look, then seemed to sum up Matt's entire character with a single shake of his head. Too bad Connor hadn't been around when Kelsey first met Matt.

Oh, who are you kidding? a mocking inner voice asked. She would never have noticed Matt if Connor had been around. But for all their differences, Connor and Matt had one glaring similarity.

"Kelsey, please," her ex-boyfriend practically whimpered. "You've gotta talk to Emily and tell her she can't marry that guy!"

Even without glancing in Connor's direction, she could feel his gaze. Heat rose to her face. She wanted to ignore both men at the moment, but she focused on Matt who was suddenly, oddly enough, the lesser of two humiliations.

"Emily's in love with Todd, and their wedding is going to be perfect." Determination rang in her voice, but Kelsey wondered who she was hoping to convince.

"You don't understand!" Matt took a single step in her direction, but froze when Connor uncrossed his arms. Keeping a nervous eye on the other man, Matt weakly finished, "I love her."

"Believe me. That is one thing I *do* understand."

He'd offered the same pitiful excuse as an explanation for using her, for taking advantage of her feelings, for making love to her and imagining Emily in her place.

Her ex-boyfriend had the grace to hang his head in shame but not enough sense to know when to give up. "Maybe if I could talk to her—" Matt pressed.

"Oh, for Pete's sake, get over it!"

His eyes widened in surprise, but Kelsey felt a shock when the words sank into her soul, and she realized the real object of her anger. She was tired of feeling like a fool for believing his lies. Of accepting his unacceptable behavior. Of shouldering the blame for the failure of their relationship when Matt was at fault.

"Let it go, Matt, and move on. I have."

Maybe that wasn't entirely true. As far as love was concerned, she certainly wasn't ready to take the plunge again, but might it be worthwhile to test the water?

"The lady asked you to leave." Connor crossed his arms over his broad chest, suddenly seeming to take up twice as much space and ready to literally enforce her advice for Matt to move on.

With a single, pitiful glance at Kelsey, Matt shrank back into the shadows. She didn't know if he'd heard a single word she said, but it didn't matter. *She'd* listened.

"Man, you've had your work cut out for you, haven't you?" Connor asked, once Matt had left. "How many of Emily's exes have you had to deal with?"

Emily's exes. Kelsey crossed her arms over her stomach, some of her earlier pleasure fading. The toe she'd stuck in the deep end felt chilled by frigid water. "So far, you're the only one. Matt isn't one of Emily's ex-boyfriends. He's mine."

Kelsey didn't know why she spilled that bit of information.

It wasn't as if she wanted Connor to feel sorry for her. She didn't know *what* she wanted from him.

He kicked at the asphalt and glanced in the direction the other man had disappeared. "Hell, Kelsey, you shoulda told me that before. I wouldn't have been so gentle."

The unexpected comment startled a laugh from her. It bubbled inside, shaky at first but growing stronger until she felt lighter, buoyed by the emotion and perhaps the chance to let go of the past. "How exactly do you throw a man *gently* against a wall?"

"*Gently* means he gets to slink off under his own power. *Not so gently* requires an ambulance."

"I guess Matt doesn't know how lucky he was."

"You're right, Kelsey. Something tells me he has no idea."

Certainty filled Connor's deep voice. Just listening to him made her feel free from the shame and embarrassment that had held her down for so long. Stepping closer, he crooked a finger beneath her chin. "You okay?"

She nodded, feeling his finger slide along the sensitive skin beneath her jaw. "Yes."

Concern gave way to relief and then anger. "You should have had someone walk you to your car. You have no idea what could happen—"

"Connor, I'm okay," Kelsey interrupted, worried by the tension that was evident in the set of his shoulders. A tension that seemed rooted in a different incident from a different time. "I wasn't in any danger."

Exhaling a breath, Connor seemed to release the pressure building inside and shake off whatever memories had caught him in their grasp. "You still need to be more careful."

True, Matt had startled her, coming out of the shadows the way he had, but he'd lost the power to hurt her long ago. And despite Connor's warning that she should be more careful, *he* was the most dangerous threat around. His lethal charm tore through her defenses, and a question that should have come to her much, much sooner sprang to mind. "What are *you* doing here, anyway? How did you even know we'd be having dinner tonight?"

Connor glanced at the front of the restaurant. A frown darkened his expression before he shook his head and blew out a breath. "Well, I *was* following Todd."

"What!"

"That's how I knew he was at the restaurant," he explained slowly, as if she had trouble keeping up. "So, tell me about dinner."

"Not so fast. You first."

"Okay," he said agreeably. "I haven't had dinner yet, and I'm starving!"

"I meant, tell me what you found following Todd."

"I will, but I really am starving. Come on." With a last look at the now-empty spot in front of the restaurant, he caught Kelsey's hand and said, "Let's go."

"Go where?" she demanded even as she followed alongside, far too aware of the tingle that raced up her spine as his fingers entwined with hers. The innocent touch certainly shouldn't have weakened her knees, but Kelsey could barely concentrate beyond the heat of his skin pressed to hers.

"To find someplace to eat."

Despite the extreme heat during the day, the temperature had lowered with the sunset. A gentle breeze carried the scents and sounds of nearby shops: gourmet coffee, decadent chocolate, the rise and fall of laughter and the faint strains of jazz music.

A group of girls walked toward Kelsey and Connor, heading in the other direction. Tall and beautiful, long limbs left bare by short skirts and tank tops, their not-so-subtle glances at Connor quickly turned to confusion as they shifted to Kelsey.

She didn't need a thought bubble over their heads to know what they were thinking: *What is* he *doing with* her? And after the run-in with Matt, Kelsey couldn't stop that question from digging deeper and deeper.

"Hey." Connor tugged at her hand. "You still with me?" he asked, as if he had somehow lost *her* interest.

"I'm here," she said. Now if she could only focus on *why* she was there. "Did you find anything on Todd?"

Connor took his time answering, waiting until he'd found a casual dining restaurant with outdoor seating. Cooling misters hissed overhead, the sound blending with the distant strains of an acoustic guitar being played on an outdoor stage. After giving the waiter his order, Connor leaned back in his chair and said, "If I'd found anything, you'd be the first to know. Unfortunately, all he did was shop."

"All afternoon?"

He laughed at her startled response. "I thought you'd be impressed."

"Surprised is more like it," she muttered, thinking of Todd's excuse. Still, she hesitated before confessing, "Todd was late for dinner. He said it was because of a business meeting."

"What? That five-second trip to his office this morning?" Connor scoffed.

"Maybe he didn't want to tell Emily he'd gone shopping for her."

"Except he was shopping for himself—unless Emily's taken up imported cigars."

"Um, no."

After a waiter dropped off glasses of ice water and Connor's steak sandwich, he said, "What else?"

"It was dinner, Connor, not an inquisition," she said as Connor dug in with both hands.

Truthfully, Kelsey hadn't *wanted* to find anything. She

wanted to believe Todd and Emily would have a beautiful wedding followed by a happy marriage. "It's probably nothing but—" she paused, not believing her own words "—none of Todd's family are coming to the wedding."

"Did he say why?" he asked, sliding his plate of fries her way.

Kelsey shook her head at the offer and said, "His parents already had a trip to Europe planned, and his sister is pregnant and didn't want to travel."

Connor shrugged. "So it could be nothing."

She blinked. Connor had jumped on even the slightest inconsistency in Todd's behavior. She couldn't believe he was letting this one go. "Are you serious? Can you imagine my aunt and uncle *not* showing up to Emily's wedding?"

"Not every family is like yours."

"Okay, fine. Forget the Wilsons. You might be the P.I. expert, but I'm the wedding expert, remember? And families *always* come to weddings!"

Connor's gaze cut away from her as he balled a paper napkin between his fists, and Kelsey knew. This wasn't about Todd's family or her family or families in general. It was about Connor's. A family she knew nothing about, one she couldn't recall Emily ever mentioning.

"You know, I don't think Emily's ever talked about your family."

"Why would she?"

Because, at one time or another, Emily had told Kelsey nearly everything about Connor. So much that Kelsey felt she'd known him long before she first caught sight of him at the airport. But she certainly couldn't tell Connor how she'd listened to those stories the same way a teenager might pore over celebrity magazines for the latest gossip on the current Hollywood heartthrob.

"I don't know. Maybe because if things had worked out like you'd planned, they would have been *her* family, too."

Connor gave a rough bark of laughter. "Emily had enough family to deal with without adding mine to the mix. Besides, my parents died before I met Emily."

The abrupt comment hit Kelsey in the chest, and she felt ashamed for pushing. She ached for his loss, an echo to the pain she still felt over the death of her own mother.

"Oh, Connor." Her defenses crumbled to dust, and with her heart already reaching out, her hands immediately followed. The heat of his hands—strong, rawboned, and masculine—sent an instant jolt up her arms. Her heart skipped a beat at the simple contact, but it was the emotional connection that had her pulse picking up an even greater speed. For a second, as their eyes met, Connor looked as startled as she felt.

Taking a breath deep enough to force her heart back into place, she focused on the reason she'd dared touch him in the first place. "I'm so sorry. I lost my mom when I was sixteen. Do you want—"

"It was a long time ago," he interrupted, jerking his hands out from hers in a pretense of reaching for his wallet to pull out a few bills. "I should get going. I'll walk you back to your car."

Stung by his abrupt withdrawal, Kelsey ducked her head before he could see the embarrassed color burning in her cheeks. Focusing on her purse, she searched for the keys she knew perfectly well were in the outside pocket.

"No need. I'll be fine," she insisted, and started walking. But if she thought she could out-stubborn Connor, he quickly proved her wrong.

"You will be fine," he agreed, his light touch against her lower back a complete contrast to the steely determination in his voice. "Because I'm walking you to your car."

Kelsey didn't argue, even though Matt was probably long gone. Thanks to Connor, he'd learned his lesson. Too bad she had yet to learn hers. Because no matter what Connor said about how beautiful she was, actions spoke louder than words, and all the compliments in the world couldn't erase the hurt of reaching out to Connor only to have him pull away.

Chapter Six

Early the next morning Kelsey stood outside her shop, gripping the key tightly enough to dig grooves into her palm. The unexpected phone call from her landlord couldn't have come at a better time. She still had plenty left to do for Emily's wedding, but she couldn't think of Emily without thinking of Connor. And Kelsey definitely did *not* want to think of him. Last night, she'd felt a connection—that loss and difficult childhoods gave them something in common. But Connor didn't want common.

He didn't want *her*.

With the morning sunlight glinting off the windows, she couldn't see inside, but in her mind's eye she pictured *her* shop. The subtle green and pink colors, the faded rose wallpaper, the shabby-chic-style parlor where she would meet with clients. Romantic without being overblown; classy while still being casual.

It was going to be perfect. Excitement jazzing her veins, Kelsey stuck the key in the lock, opened the door and blinked. With her dream office so firm in her thoughts she could practically smell her favorite peach potpourri, reality hit like a slap to the forehead.

No soft colors, no floral wallpaper... Shabby, yes, but chic?

"Not even close," Kelsey muttered as she flicked on the lights and stepped inside.

The landlord had shown her the space a few weeks ago, when it had been a struggling craft store. Shelves and bins had lined every wall, filled with yarn and cloth, paints and silk flowers. She'd focused on the space, knowing everything else would go when the other store closed. But she never stopped to think about the mess left behind.

Holes from the now-absent shelves marred the walls with peg-board consistency. The carpet had a two-tone hue thanks to the areas exposed to foot traffic, and the bare fluorescent bulbs overhead buzzed like bug zappers in August. No wonder the landlord had left the key hidden outside instead of meeting Kelsey.

But Kelsey hadn't spent her childhood living in sub-par apartments without learning a thing or two from her mother. "Wilson women against the world," she murmured as she pulled the phone from her purse and called the landlord.

If there was one thing Connor hated, it was being wrong. The only thing worse was being wrong and knowing he had to apologize. Meeting his own gaze in the mirror, he knew he owed Kelsey a big apology. He'd seen the hurt in her chocolate eyes at his abrupt withdrawal and he felt like a jerk. She'd reached out to him—physically and emotionally—and he'd pulled away.

He could justify his actions with the same excuse he always used when thoughts of the past intruded. That time was over

and done, enough said. And yet, the sympathy and understanding in Kelsey's expression made him *want* to talk about
the past. He'd wanted to turn his wrist, take her hand into his
and hold on tight. That completely foreign desire had so
rattled him, that he'd locked his jaw and put an early end to
the evening.

After showering and throwing on some clothes, Connor
called Kelsey's cell. The phone rang four times before she
answered, sounding breathless and sexy and— "Where the
hell are you?" he demanded before he could keep the words
from bursting out.

And what was she *doing* to give her voice that husky,
bedroom quality?

"I'm...working."

She was *lying.* Before he could remind himself what
Kelsey did or who she did it with was none of his business,
he heard a loud clatter followed by an abbreviated scream and
a thump that sent his heart racing. "Kelsey!" Silence filled the
line, giving Connor plenty of time to imagine half a dozen
dangerous possibilities. "Kelsey!"

"I'm here. I'm fine," she said after what sounded like a
scramble for the phone. "I knocked over a ladder and a bucket
of spackle went flying."

Ladder? "Spackle?"

"You know," she said, her voice sounding slightly muffled,
and he imagined the phone held against her shoulder. "That
compound stuff you use to patch walls."

"I know what spackle is. The big question is, why do *you*
know what it is?"

"I'm just handy that way," she said a little too brightly,
and Connor flashed back to the hurt in her eyes. Her answer
might have been different if he hadn't pulled away the night
before. "Kelsey—"

"I've found an office space to rent. That way I'll have more room to sell my lies about happily-ever-after to unsuspecting brides and grooms."

Connor flinched despite her light-hearted tone. Seemed as if he might have even more to apologize for than he'd thought. "What's the address?"

"Why?" she asked, as if she thought he planned to come by and torch the place.

"Because," he said after a deep breath and a ten count for patience, "I owe you an apology." Kelsey didn't respond, and in the silence, Connor knew she wanted more. That need rose up again, pressure building inside him as words he'd held back for years struggled to get out. "I owe you an apology," he repeated, "and an explanation."

"I'm an idiot," Kelsey muttered as she washed spackle from her hands in the tiny bathroom. She would have liked to look herself in the eye as she spoke those words, but the bathroom was missing a mirror, had no hot water, and a questionable-at-best toilet.

Why had she given Connor the address? Why had she invited him to invade her place? The dream office that filled her thoughts so strongly that morning had faded over the past several hours of hard work. The last thing she needed was Connor's presence to overwhelm what was left of her lace-and-roses dream in a deluge of cotton and denim.

Not to mention his cynicism.

Yet she'd been unable to resist the demand in his voice or his promised apology.

The ring of the bell above the front door alerted her to her first visitor and saved her from her own thoughts. "Kelsey?" a familiar female voice called out.

She banged on the faucet handle a few times to turn off the

water and hurried out, shaking her hands to get them dry. "Lisa? What are you doing here?"

Walking through the shop with a bouquet of gerbera daisies in one hand and a bottle of wine in the other, her friend cast a dubious look around. "Not quite what I expected," she said as she met Kelsey at the back of the shop.

"It needs work," Kelsey admitted. "But I called the landlord and talked him into reducing the first month's rent if I handle the repairs."

"And that's why I'm here," her friend announced as she set the wine and flowers on the ladder. "I know you too well. You're always willing to help your friends, but you never ask for help. Of course, I had no idea you'd need this much help, but it's a good thing I called Trey, too." Trey Jamison was another good friend, and she frequently hired him as a DJ for her weddings.

"You didn't have to do that," Kelsey told Lisa.

"Yes, I did because you wouldn't. I knew you'd be here all alone with no one to help you and…"

Lisa turned as the bell announced another arrival, her words trailing away. Kelsey couldn't blame her friend. She felt pretty speechless as Connor stripped off his reflective glasses and locked that green gaze on her from across the shop. "Hey."

"Hey," Kelsey responded, the word far more breathless than she wanted to admit. Her stomach did a slow roll at the sight of him. Just as she'd feared, he shrank the space until it encompassed only the two of them. Thoughts of lace and roses fell away, overwhelmed by Connor's masculine presence. Her senses took in every bit of him—the faded gray T-shirt that stretched across his chest, the jeans that clung to his muscular legs, the low murmur of his voice.

Lisa's silence didn't last nearly as long as Kelsey's. Her friend gripped her arm and whispered, "Who *is* that?"

"Connor McClane," Kelsey murmured back.

"Connor—" Lisa's eyebrows rose. "Emily's ex? What is he doing here?"

Emily's ex. Kelsey's heart cringed at the description. "Good question," she muttered as his promised apology and explanation rang in her mind.

Before she had the chance to ask, Trey pushed through the doorway. With his long hair caught back in a ponytail, and wearing an oversize T-shirt and raggedy cutoffs, he looked ready to work. But after gazing around, he said, "Way to go, Kelse!" Walking over, he spun her in an exuberant hug. "This place is great."

"You think?" she asked, with a laugh at her friend's enthusiasm.

"Well, it will be when you're done with it, right?" He glanced at Lisa and Connor for confirmation, and only then did Kelsey realize she had yet to introduce them.

"Oh, I'm sorry. Trey, Lisa, this is Connor…"

The introduction faded away as she caught sight of the scowl on Connor's face. Instinctively she stepped out of Trey's embrace, which was *crazy.* Because Trey was just a friend and crazier still because Connor could *not* be jealous.

Could he?

Still, Connor was less than friendly as he crossed the shop to greet Trey. The handshake the two men exchanged seemed more like a prelude to battle than a customary introduction. "Good to meet you," Trey said, his smile growing wide even though Kelsey thought she saw him subtly flexing his hand once Connor released it.

"Pleasure," Connor said, the word sounding anything but.

"Okay, let's put all this testosterone to use," Lisa said, bringing a heated blush to Kelsey's face. "Where do we start?"

"Yeah, give us the list," Trey said, holding out his hand.

"You guys don't have to do this. You can't give up your weekend to help me out."

"Like the time you filled in for me when I got snowed in back East and didn't have anyone to open up the flower shop?" Lisa challenged before glancing at Trey expectantly.

Immediately he picked up where she'd left off. "Or the time you shoved chicken soup and hot tea down my throat to get my voice back in time to DJ that last wedding?"

"That's different," Kelsey protested.

"Why? Why are you the only one allowed to help?" Lisa demanded. "When do we get to return the favor? And hey, we're not dummies. We all know helping you helps us."

"Yeah, as long as she doesn't forget her friends when she's off coordinating weddings for the rich and famous," Trey whispered in an aside to Lisa.

Overwhelmed by their generosity, Kelsey blinked back tears. Growing up, it had always been Kelsey and her mom— Wilson women against the world. But maybe that was only because Olivia hadn't had friends as amazing as Lisa and Trey.

"All right! All right! I give in. And I promise to remember all the little people," Kelsey laughed before grabbing the list as well as a handful of paint swatches, wallpaper samples and various store ads from her day planner.

"Trey, here are the paint colors and wallpaper. If you could pick them up from the hardware store along with a carpet steamer, that would be great. Lisa, here's a picture of the drapes I want for the front window. Could you see if they have a large area rug to match? Anything to hide this carpet."

Even as Kelsey split the shopping between her friends, she was aware of Connor's speculative gaze focused on her. What was he thinking? she wondered. That her romantic trappings were literally that—traps for couples foolish enough to believe in love?

"Got it, boss," Trey said, saluting her with the green and pink paint samples. "Want me to pick up lunch while I'm out?"

"No need. Sara's catering our workday. Her word, not mine," Lisa laughed as she grabbed Trey's arm and led him toward the door.

"Man, I wanted pizza and beer. Sara'll probably bring mini quiches and crudités." As the two of them walked outside, the laughter and casual camaraderie went with them, leaving behind a tension that for Kelsey buzzed as loudly as the fluorescent light overhead.

Ready to take the offensive, she turned to Connor. What apology did he want to give? What explanation? Her lips parted on those questions, but he beat her to the punch.

"How many of your friends are working Emily's wedding?"

Just like that, momentum changed, and Connor had her backpedaling and on the defensive. "Lisa and I went to high school together, and I've made friends with some of the other people I've worked with. But I never would have hired them if I didn't think they'd do an awesome job."

She lifted her chin, ready to battle for her friends the same way she had when she hired them for Emily's wedding. But if this was a fight, Connor didn't play fair.

Reaching up, he tucked a loose curl behind one ear. His eyes glowing with a warmth that stole the fight from her spirit and the breath from her lungs, he murmured, "It wasn't a criticism. Only an observation. Your friends obviously care a lot about you. Just like you care about them."

Intensity lit his emerald eyes, and Kelsey could almost believe he wanted her to look out for him, to care about him—but that had to be a delusion due to lack of oxygen from the breath he'd stolen with his nearness. "I do," she managed to murmur.

"So why was it so hard for you to accept their help?"

She started to deny it, but when Connor's eyebrows rose

in challenge, she knew he wouldn't believe anything but the truth. And maybe if she told him, he would understand why Emily's wedding was so important. "Fixing things is what I do. It's what I'm good at. I wasn't brought up as one of the wealthy Wilsons. I was raised by my mother. We didn't have much, but growing up I didn't know that. All I knew was that I had an amazing mother who taught me how to cook delicious meals without spending more than a few dollars and how to clip coupons to make the most of what little money we had."

A memory came to mind, and Kelsey smiled. "Our favorite day was Black Friday, but we didn't just shop for Christmas. We bargain-hunted for the whole year. My mom taught me how to look at secondhand furniture and see beyond the layers of flaking paint or rust. She showed me how to strip away the exterior to the natural beauty beneath."

Her smile faded away. "But then she died, and I came to live with my aunt and uncle. None of the things I knew how to do mattered anymore. Coupons and discount stores and secondhand furniture were as foreign to them as paying hundreds of dollars for a pair of shoes was to me. They had people to shop and clean and fix things." Kelsey gave a short, sad laugh. "The only thing broken in their house was me. I know they cared about me, but…I just didn't fit, no matter how hard I tried."

"Kelsey." The low murmur of Connor's voice mirrored the tenderness in his gaze. This time it was Kelsey's turn to pull away, to try to escape.

"That's why the wedding is so important. It's my chance—" her *only* chance, because if she screwed this up, why would the Wilsons or anyone trust her again? "—to prove that I can do this, that I'm good at *something*. So I really hope your gut's wrong, Connor, and that Todd is everything my family thinks he is. Or all this hard work is going to be for nothing."

"It won't be for nothing because you're going to be a

success with or without Emily's wedding. Maybe if you *were* more like Emily or Aileen, more used to everything going your way, you'd be more likely to give up. But a single setback won't stop you. You're stronger than that." Catching her hands and smiling at the streaks of spackle marring her skin, he said, "You aren't afraid of hard work."

Strong…unafraid… Kelsey liked the sound of that, but she wasn't feeling the least bit of either as Connor stroked his thumbs across the palm of her hands. She felt downright weak and terrified by the desire coursing through her at such a simple touch.

Her fingertips tingled, tempted to chart the planes and angles of his face, the strong column of his throat. The broad shoulders and wide chest covered by cotton as soft as Connor's body was strong. But she curled her hands into fists. She wouldn't—couldn't—reach out to him again. The embarrassment of Connor pulling away was too painfully fresh in her mind, and her heart was too vulnerable to risk rejection a second time.

In the end, she didn't have to reach out; she didn't even have to move. It was Connor who pulled her closer, Connor who lowered his head, Connor who brushed his mouth against hers. Any thought of him pulling away disappeared as he deepened the kiss. He buried one hand in her hair and wrapped the other around her waist, holding her body tight to his, as if she were the one who might back away.

But escape was the last thing Kelsey wanted.

Instead she wanted to capture this moment, bottle it up, save it for a time when memories were all she would have left of Connor. But even that proved impossible, as he slanted his mouth over hers, his lips and tongue stealing her breath, robbing her of her ability to think, and leaving her with no choice but to feel….

Her breasts against the hard wall of his chest, her heart pounding desperately enough to match the rapid beat of his, the firm press of his fingers against her hip. She splayed her fingers across his back, searching out as much contact as possible, the material thin enough, soft enough, heated enough, that she could imagine his naked skin and the play of muscles beneath her hands.

"Connor." His name escaped her on a breathless sigh as he trailed a kiss across her cheek to her jaw, his warm breath setting off a chain reaction of shivers down her spine. She swayed closer, her hips brushing against his solid thigh. The heated contact weakened her knees, and all she wanted was to sink to the floor, pull Connor down with her and feel the weight of his body on top of hers.

She might have done just that if not for the ring of the bell and an embarrassed "Oops. Pretend I was never here."

Kelsey tore away from Connor in time to see her friend Sara backing out of the door with a platter of food in her hands. She wanted to call Sara back, but it was too late, leaving Kelsey with little choice but to face Connor. With his eyes dark with passion, his chest rising and falling, it was all she could do not to dive back into his arms.

Two seconds ago an interruption was the last thing she wanted. But now with passion clearing, she realized it was exactly what she needed. Already Connor was going to her head; it wouldn't take much for him to go straight to her heart. "That, um, was Sara. I should ask her to come back inside."

Her friends were waiting, her dreams were waiting and she didn't dare push them aside. Not even for Connor. No matter how much she wanted to.

Hours later, Connor looked around Kelsey's shop, amazed by the transformation. The scent of paint filled the shop, and the soft pink and green colors highlighted the walls. The carpets had been shampooed, and the new rug and drapes stored in the back would soon complete the new look. Kelsey's self-proclaimed talent for stripping away the layers and revealing the beauty beneath was on magnificent display in all the work she'd done.

How could she possibly doubt her own worth, her own ability? Connor wondered...until he tried to imagine Emily—or heaven forbid, Charlene—dressed in a T-shirt and cutoffs, with their hair covered by a bandana, a streak of pale pink war paint on one cheek and spackle on the other. None of the other Wilson women would be caught dead looking the way Kelsey did right then. Yet seeing her eyes sparkle as she laughed with her friends, celebrated every small success and worked her *ass* off, Connor didn't think he'd ever seen a woman look as vibrant, as alive, as *sexy,* as Kelsey.

As if feeling the heat of his gaze, Kelsey glanced his way. Heat flared in her cheeks, and she ducked her head, taking a sudden interest in flipping through the phone directory, cell phone in hand as she searched for a plumber.

A phone call to her uncle, and her plumbing problems would have been solved. Hell, a single call to Gordon Wilson and *all* her problems would have been solved. Gordon could have easily set up Kelsey in a furnished, upscale Scottsdale or Paradise Valley suite instead of a work-in-progress strip mall in downtown Glendale.

He'd meant every word when he called Kelsey strong and fearless. She'd been only sixteen when she went to live with her aunt and uncle, an age when most kids would have lost themselves in a world filled with wealth and privilege. But not Kelsey. She'd stayed true to herself, to the lessons her mother had taught her. Even now, when her family's money could make her dream an instant success, Kelsey refused to take the easy way out...not like he had.

He'd had his reasons for taking the money Gordon Wilson had offered him to leave town all those years ago, reasons he believed justified his actions, but he couldn't help thinking that had Kelsey faced the same choice, she would have found another way.

She flat-out amazed him. He would have liked to ignore the emotion spilling through him, but Connor had learned his lesson when it came to ignoring feelings...even if this one wasn't hitting his gut as much as it was pulling at his heart.

"Place looks great, doesn't it?"

The sudden question jerked Connor from his thoughts, and he turned to face Lisa. Judging by the woman's sharp gaze, he doubted Kelsey's shop was on the woman's mind. "It does. You, Trey and Sara were a huge help," he added.

Kelsey's friends had thrown themselves into helping, Trey especially. But despite the close eye Connor kept on the other man, he hadn't seen any proof Trey and Kelsey were anything other than friends. And yet Trey's touchy-feely familiarity had set Connor's teeth on edge. A reaction as unfamiliar as it was uncomfortable.

He rarely felt possessive over a woman, and certainly not after a kiss or two. But then again, what a kiss! He could still taste her, could smell the cinnamon and spice he'd come to associate with Kelsey. No too-sweet floral scents for her. Nothing expensive, nothing fancy, just...Kelsey.

"You weren't too bad yourself," Lisa said with enough tongue-in-cheek attitude to make Connor wonder if she'd noticed how he strove to outlift, outwork, out*do* Trey. Turning serious, she said, "We're all glad to help Kelsey. She's the kind of friend who always takes care of everyone else. This is the first chance we've had to pay her back."

"I doubt she expects payment."

"She doesn't. It's in her nature to help." The brunette paused, and Connor sensed her debating over her next words. "I think a lot of it comes from taking care of her mom."

"Kelsey told me her mother died when she was sixteen." But despite what she'd told him, Connor knew he had only part of the story. Why had Kelsey's mother—Gordon Wilson's sister—raised Kelsey on her own? Single mom or not, she should have had the family fortune at her disposal, and yet that clearly hadn't been the case.

What had caused the rift between Kelsey's mother and her family? And what about the father Kelsey never mentioned? Connor didn't ask Lisa those questions. It was up to Kelsey to offer answers...if he asked her.

With a glance at her watch, Lisa told him she had to go, but she left with a few final words he translated into a warning. "Kelsey's a great girl. She deserves the best."

Connor waited for the woman to add that Kelsey deserved better than him, but when she merely gazed at him in expectation, he realized Lisa wasn't telling him Kelsey deserved better *than him;* she was telling him Kelsey deserved the best *from him.*

"Well, I finally found a plumber who can come this week..." Kelsey's voice trailed off as she walked from the back room, cell phone in hand.

Connor stood alone in the middle of the shop. Even with the progress they'd made, bringing her dream closer to reality, he overwhelmed the place. If anything, the shop's increasingly feminine decor only served as a larger reminder of Connor's masculinity. And after that kiss, Kelsey didn't have any doubt whatsoever about his undeniable and—she was beginning to fear—irresistible masculinity.

"Lisa had to take off," he explained.

"Oh. She was probably afraid I'd put her to work again if she didn't sneak away."

"I don't think so. Your friends will obviously do anything for you."

Uncomfortable with the praise, Kelsey countered, "Like Javy would for you."

Connor frowned. "Yeah. He thinks he owes me, but the truth is, his family bailed me out when I was a kid. Nothing I've done would be enough to repay them."

Despite the explanation he'd promised earlier, Connor's voluntary statement caught Kelsey off guard, surprising her almost as much as his kiss. She shook her head and protested, "Just because I spilled my guts doesn't mean you have to—"

"I want to," he interrupted. "I should have told you about my past last night, but I haven't told anyone since Señora Delgado pried it out of me as a kid."

"You—you didn't tell *anyone?*" Kelsey prodded.

You didn't tell Emily?

His penetrating gaze read into the heart of her question, hearing what she *hadn't* asked, and he vowed, "I didn't tell anyone."

And suddenly Kelsey wasn't sure she wanted to know. Listening to what he had to say seemed to take on a greater significance because Connor wanted to tell *her,* to confide in her, something he'd never told Emily.

Without saying another word, Connor stepped forward, his long strides erasing the distance between them. He caught her hand and led her over to the love seat her friends had surprised her with. She'd been overwhelmed by their generosity. The sofa would be the perfect place for her soon-to-be-married couples to sit side by side and decide floral arrangements, wedding invitations, dinner menus.

But as soon as Connor sank down onto the love seat, she

decided it would be the perfect place for her to curl up in his arms, the perfect place to kiss him and never stop. The masculine-feminine contrast sent a slow roll of awareness through her stomach as he settled back against the rose-covered cushions. In faded cotton and rough worn denim, he should have looked out of place; instead, his broad shoulders and wide chest looked far more comfortable and inviting than the floral chintz ever could.

Swallowing, she folded onto the couch beside him, one leg bent and angled toward Connor. He stared straight ahead, keeping his silence, and Kelsey sensed his thoughts drifting back to a past he'd purposely chosen not to face…until now.

Taking a deep breath, he said, "My father was a truck driver. Eighteen-wheeler. He worked hard, drank hard. He was…strict."

The tension in Connor's shoulders and the way his hands tightened into fists gave a clear definition of the word. Her heart ached for the boy he'd been, a boy she could picture so easily. Dark hair that was too long, a body that was too skinny, and a gaze that was too old. She could see him in her mind as if, somehow, he'd been there all along.

Crazy, she thought, but she felt she knew him so well. And now that Connor was willing to give out answers, did she dare ask more questions? Could she risk getting to know him even better?

In the end, no matter the potential danger to her heart, Kelsey had to ask. Not because she needed to hear the story… but because Connor needed to tell it. "And your mother?" she asked softly.

One by one his fingers unclenched then slowly laced together as if cradling something precious. "She was a dreamer. She was always…looking for something. Always hoping for a better life, only she never found it. I was eight when she died.

She'd been taking art lessons, or maybe it was a dance class. I can't remember."

Connor cleared his throat. "Anyway, this place wasn't in the best part of town. I begged her not to go. I knew something bad was going to happen. But she went anyway. No one knows exactly what happened," he added, the tension pulling at his shoulders revealing how much not knowing still troubled him, "but the police figured a mugging went wrong. Either my mom fought back or the guy panicked, and the gun went off."

"Oh, Connor, I'm so sorry." Just as she feared, her heart ached a little more at the telling, and she longed to reach out to him, to comfort him. But she didn't. This time it was her turn to twist her fingers together, strangling the desire to touch him.

Because—despite his kiss—she still feared her touch wasn't the one Connor wanted.

But he never told Emily about his family. He's telling you! Aching or not, her heart had the strength to argue, and Kelsey felt her resistance crumbling.

"The guy stole her purse and wallet," Connor went on as if she hadn't spoken. "It took three days before the police figured out who she was."

"Didn't your dad report her missing?"

"He was on a long-distance drive. He didn't know anything was wrong."

"But when your mother didn't come home, someone must have tried to get hold of him. The people you were staying with—" As soon as she said the words, realization flooded Kelsey and her breath caught. "You were alone, weren't you?"

"My mom thought I was old enough to take care of myself, and it should have only been for a few hours."

Hours that had stretched into days.

"Wasn't there anyone you could call? A friend of the family?"

"Probably, but hell, I was eight. My mom had told me she

was going to be right back. Calling someone would have been like admitting something was wrong, admitting she wasn't coming back. Ever."

Kelsey felt heartsick at the thought of the frightened, abandoned boy Connor had been. "You were so young. How did you get on without her?"

"My dad and I stumbled along, but he always blamed my mom for dying. If she'd been happy with her life, if she hadn't always been out looking for more and expecting something better, she'd still be alive. If she'd just *listened* to me. I could have—"

Saved her. Connor didn't say the words, but they rang in the silence and underscored everything he did. "It's not your fault, Connor," she insisted, and this time she couldn't keep from reaching out and grasping his hands as if she could somehow heal the pain and guilt with her touch. "People make their own decisions, and you aren't responsible for their choices."

"No, only for my own," he agreed darkly, but tension tightened his hands into rock-hard fists.

Her family was so wrong about Connor. He wasn't out to ruin Emily's wedding—he was trying to save her from a past he couldn't possibly change. But Kelsey still wasn't convinced Todd was the threat Connor thought him to be. After all, Connor's *gut reaction* had pinned Matt to the restaurant, mistakenly seeing her ex-boyfriend as a physical threat. Wasn't it possible Todd was as harmless as Matt, and Connor was looking through the eyes of the past and seeing a danger that wasn't there?

"I can't imagine what that must have been like to lose your mother so suddenly." *So violently.* "But don't you think maybe that's colored the way you see people?"

"People like Dunworthy?" he asked with a wry twist to his lips. He pulled his hands out from beneath hers in the pretense of shifting to face her on the love seat. "I know you think I'm wrong about him, but it's because of my past that I'm sure I'm right." As if sensing her doubt, he asked, "Haven't you ever met someone and instantly known the kind of person they are?"

Thoughts of her first impression of Connor assailed Kelsey. The bad boy. The troublemaker. The man out to ruin Emily's wedding and destroy Kelsey's chance to prove herself to her family, to make her mother proud... But he was so much more than that.

"Maybe once or twice."

"Like when you met me?"

One corner of his mouth kicked up with the teasing comment, but the smile lacked full-force charm, his heart not in it. The emotional waters had gotten too deep, and Connor was clearly pulling back to shallower depths. And Kelsey almost wished she had stayed on the surface, wished she could still see Connor the way he wanted to be seen—cocky, self-confident, unbreakable. But she felt herself going under, caught by the pull of this man who was so much more than the rebel he played.

Struggling to break free, she focused on the easy out Connor had taken and followed him to more solid ground. "I knew you were going to be trouble the moment I met you. Does that count?"

"Talk about biased," he murmured. "How many Connor McClane stories have you heard over the years?"

"More than a few."

"More than a few hundred, if your aunt and uncle had anything to say about it." The teasing tone stayed in his voice, but Kelsey could tell her family's poor opinion of him still rankled. He was clearly out to prove the Wilsons wrong, but Kelsey suspected he had as much to prove to himself. "And here I've been a perfect gentleman."

"Well, not perfect," she argued. But who wanted perfect? Perfect was for women like her cousins; Kelsey much preferred the real thing to Ken-like perfection.

"I'm crushed. Señora Delgado will be so disappointed."

"Señora Delgado?"

"Javy's mother."

"How did you and Javy meet?"

"We went to school together. Mrs. Brown's sixth-grade glass."

"And you two became fast friends?"

"Nah, we hated each other. I can't even remember why. Oh, wait, it had something to do with a girl. We thought we were pretty hot stuff on the playground. Both trying to impress Alicia Martin. Unfortunately for us, she had a thing for older men."

"Eighth grader?" Kelsey guessed, playing along to maintain the teasing mood.

"Worse. P.E. teacher. And man, the guy was old. Like twenty-five. Anyway, we bonded over a couple of cafeteria juice boxes, and I started hanging out with him at his mother's restaurant. Before long, I was washing dishes and bussing tables. If the Delgados hadn't fed me through most of junior high and high school, I don't know what I would have done. Probably would have dropped out to work full-time if Maria hadn't stopped me."

Kelsey knew the drop-out rate was horrible, especially in Arizona, but as much as she'd hated school, she never once considered not finishing. "How did she stop you?"

"By telling me I *should*," Connor said wryly. "She said anyone foolish enough to give up a free education didn't deserve one."

Smiling at the woman's use of reverse psychology, Kelsey said, "I think I'd like to meet her. Not every woman has enough influence to keep a boy in school *and* teach him to clear dishes off a table."

"You're on. Let's go to the Delgados' restaurant. Maybe Maria will be there."

Kelsey swallowed. Was Connor asking her out? On a *date?* She waited for the little voice in her head to tell her this was a bad idea, but she didn't hear it. Possibly because it was drowned out by the *big* voice screaming, "Go for it!"

She knew the voice of reason would be back, loud and clear, and ready to say "I told you so" if she let herself fall for Connor. But that worry, like the voice, seemed far off, and she couldn't resist the chance to spend more time with Connor.

"I'm a mess," she said in weak protest. "I can't go anywhere looking like this."

As Connor's gaze swept over her, Kelsey felt her face heat. She could only imagine what he saw. She had spackle under her nails, drywall dust in her hair, and more splotches of paint than freckles covering her arms. She was sweaty and disheveled, and even though Connor had worked as hard as anyone, he looked—

Gorgeous, she thought with a sigh, taking in the lock of dark hair he'd constantly pushed back from his paint-streaked forehead, the hint of five o'clock shadow shading his jaw, the damp T-shirt that molded to his shoulders and chest.

"I'll pick you up at your place in half an hour," he said as he stood and reached down to pull her to her feet.

Kelsey shook her head, ready to refuse, and yet when she opened her mouth she said, "An hour."

"Forty-five minutes."

"An hour." She laughed as she shoved him toward the door. "And not a minute sooner."

Chapter Seven

Mariachi music greeted Connor as he opened the car door. Judging by the nearly full parking lot, the restaurant was packed. The lunch hour tended to draw patrons from nearby businesses; at night, the place had more of a party atmosphere. The music would play, tables would be pushed aside to create a dance floor, and he was *definitely* looking forward to slow dancing with Kelsey.

He was looking forward to the entire evening with an anticipation that caught him off guard. After spilling his guts the way he had, escape should have been the only thing on his mind. He never talked about his past—*never*—and as little as two days ago, the thought of opening up about a time that still left him feeling lost and vulnerable would have tied his stomach into barbed-wire knots. And the thought of confiding in a Wilson!

Connor shook his head in disbelief, even as he admitted

Kelsey was no ordinary Wilson. She might not fit the Wilsons' model of perfection, but she fit his.

He rounded the car to open Kelsey's door, a split second too late, as it turned out. She already had one shapely leg extended, but he was in time to reach out a hand to help her out. Surprise lit her gaze, as if she hadn't considered his invitation to dinner a *real* date.

And despite the casual, last-minute offer, Connor realized he very much wanted this to be a real date. The kind of date where everyone in the restaurant would know Kelsey was with him. The kind where he never wanted the night to end and where, when the evening finally *did* end, a good-night kiss was not only expected, but breathlessly anticipated.

And when that time came, Connor vowed, he'd make sure there was no doubt in Kelsey's mind.

"You look amazing," he murmured, placing a hand at the small of her back.

Pleasure brightened her eyes and put color in her cheeks despite the less-than-original compliment. But hell, it was more than her looks. It was Kelsey. *She* amazed him.

"Thank you." She smoothed her hands over the embroidered skirt she wore. "I was hoping it wouldn't be too dressy."

"It's perfect." The flared skirt and off-the-shoulder blouse had a Spanish touch that emphasized her curves, and he wondered again how she could be so oblivious to how good she looked.

But that mix of confidence and insecurity was so much a part of Kelsey. He'd watched her divide the workload and make decisions without hesitation this afternoon, giving him an idea of how good a wedding coordinator she must be. Yet that confidence completely deserted her when it came to her personal life.

Living with the Wilsons had done that to her, Connor was

certain of it. They'd stripped her of her confidence, of her faith in her abilities, which they deemed worthless and beneath them.

Same way they'd declared *him* worthless and beneath them.

Connor shook off the dark thoughts as they stepped inside the restaurant. The scent of sizzling fajitas and salsa reminded him Trey hadn't been too far off about Sara's lunch. The caterer had brought delicate sandwiches and a fruit salad that looked more like a table centerpiece than something to eat.

"Man, I'm starving. I had a total slave driver nearly work me to death and only feed me bread and water."

"It was sandwiches, not just bread. And sparkling water, if that makes you feel any better." Kelsey laughed. "Besides, *you* volunteered, remember?"

"Yeah, I did." And he'd gladly do it again. Just looking into her excited brown eyes, listening to her laughter, made him feel—Connor thought for a moment, searching for the right word—happy. At peace. With nothing to prove, nothing to make up for. For the first time in his life, despite spilling the story of his sorry, less-than-sterling past, Connor felt he could be himself and that alone would be enough.

Except you didn't tell Kelsey the whole *story,* his conscience argued, dimming his contentment.

He hadn't told her about the money he'd taken, money he'd given to the Delgados to save the restaurant that pulsed with life around them. The business meant the world to Maria, especially following the dark days after her husband passed away. But Miguel's medical bills and the damage caused by an accidental grease fire had almost ruined the restaurant financially. In an effort to save it, Connor had taken the money from Gordon Wilson instead of throwing the check back in the smug SOB's face.

He knew what the older man thought. That he was nothing more than a gold-digging opportunist. But he was starting to think Kelsey might be the one Wilson, the one woman, to understand.

Was that why he'd invited her here? So she could meet Maria Delgado and see how important the woman was to him? So she could see for herself why he'd taken the money?

"Kelsey—"

"How about this? I'll pay for dinner tonight, compensation for all that slave labor?" she suggested as she stepped forward to talk to the hostess.

"Kelsey, wait." He caught her hand, wanting, *needing* to tell her the whole truth.

The seriousness in his tone made her eyes widen. "Hey, if you want to pay—"

"It's not that. I need to tell you—"

"Connor! *Mijo!*"

Hearing the familiar voice, Connor turned toward the sound with a large dose of relief and only the smallest amount of disappointment. The moment was gone, and he focused on Maria Delgado as she moved among the crowded tables toward him. She hadn't changed from the woman he remembered. Sure, she had a touch more gray in her waist-length hair and a few more wrinkles, but her dark eyes were as warm and welcoming as ever.

"Señora!" Connor bent to wrap his arms around the diminutive woman.

"My son told me you had come home! It is so good for you to be back!"

"It's good to see you, too." Seeing the undisguised interest in the older woman's eyes, he added, "Maria Delgado, this is Kelsey Wilson."

"Pleasure to meet you, Mrs. Delgado. Connor has told me a lot about you and how much your family means to him."

Maria beamed at him like a proud mother. "Connor, he is

family," she said to Kelsey. "And for him to bring you here, you must be very special. Never has he brought a young lady to the restaurant."

The implication that he'd brought Kelsey "home" to meet his family should have sent panic shooting like warning flares through his system, and yet seeing the two women talking and laughing together felt...*right*.

Kelsey also ignored the too-telling observation, but an adorable blush lit her cheeks as she added, "Your restaurant is amazing. I have to admit, I've never cared for Mexican food, but the quesadilla I had the other day was delicious."

"I always say, people who do not like Mexican food have not had *my* food." Maria pressed a hand against her bosom, pride shining in her dark eyes.

As Maria led them through a maze of crowded tables, Connor asked, "Where is Javy tonight?"

The *señora* waved a dismissive hand. "Ah, that boy. He is out with some girl. I tell him he needs to settle down, but does he listen? No. My son, he is too handsome for his own good. He does not have to work to get these girls' attention. Too often he chooses the easy way. He does not realize some things you must work for." She turned to Kelsey in a shared feminine confidence, a twinkle in her dark eyes. "But Connor, he is just handsome enough, no?"

"No. I mean, yes," Kelsey stuttered, flustered by the question. Connor was ready to jump in and rescue her from having to answer when she made her own save. "I think Connor is more than handsome enough," she said in a whisper plenty loud enough for him to overhear, "but he still has his work cut out for him."

Señora Delgado chortled and gave what sounded like a quick prayer beneath her breath. "Come, I will give you the best table in the house."

"I thought all the tables were the best tables," he teased with a wink at Kelsey as he placed his hand on the small of her back.

"*Sí,*" the older woman agreed, "they are all the best."

Kelsey grinned, sharing his humor in the *señora's* unflappable logic.

After showing them to a secluded table in the back, Maria kissed Connor's cheek and went back to work. Kelsey's hand touched the ladder-back chair, but Connor beat her to it. As he pulled it out for her, he leaned close. Close enough to catch the cinnamon scent of her skin. Close enough to see the freckles she'd tried to hide beneath makeup. Close enough to hear her breath catch in reaction to his nearness. "You should know by now, Kelsey," he murmured, "I'm not afraid of a little hard work."

Her eyes widened, but just like she had with Señora Delgado, Kelsey found her own footing and knocked him for a loop when she said, "I'm counting on it."

Time froze as the moment held them in its grip. The restaurant, with its loud music and bright lights, faded away, leaving behind only Kelsey's gorgeous brown eyes and softly parted lips. A burst of laughter from a nearby table broke the moment, and Kelsey sank into the chair he held for her. Connor had little choice but to take his own seat and curse the table separating them.

A waiter came by with menus, but Connor could tell by the frequent glances she sent his way Kelsey's mind wasn't on dinner. Finally she set the menu aside and said, "Is it true what Señora Delgado said before? You never brought anyone here?"

He'd let her get away with the unasked question before, but not this time. "Come on, Kelsey. Are you interested in *anybody* or in Emily?"

At first she looked ready to protest, only to square her

shoulders and meet his gaze head-on. "Okay. Did you ever bring Emily here?"

"No. The Delgados are like family to me, and I wasn't sure Emily would get that." He hadn't been able to picture Emily at the rustic, homey restaurant. He still couldn't...and yet Kelsey fit in so perfectly. He'd never had a doubt about bringing *her*.

Not waiting for her to ask why—or wanting to look too closely for a reason himself—Connor pushed back from the table. Kelsey's eyes widened in surprise as he held out his hand and said, "Come on. Let's dance."

As Kelsey took Connor's hand, it occurred to her that she had no idea how to dance to the Latin-flavored beat pulsing from the speakers. But that didn't stop her from following him onto the tiny dance floor, where the music instantly switched to a ballad.

Connor's smile flashed as he pulled her into his arms. "Couldn't have planned it better myself."

"I'm not so sure you didn't."

"This wasn't me. It must be fate."

Kelsey didn't know about fate, but being held in Connor's arms certainly felt like a dream. She wasn't the only one who had dressed up for the evening. Connor had showered and shaved, brushed his dark hair back from his forehead. A touch of sexy sophistication replaced a bit of his bad-boy image thanks to the white button-down shirt and black slacks he wore instead of his usual T-shirt and jeans. No matter what Maria Delgado said about her son, it was Connor who took Kelsey's breath away. He was the most gorgeous man she'd ever met, and the sheer look of masculine appreciation in his eyes made her feel beautiful. But even as the physical connection robbed her of her breath, the emotional connection threatened to steal her heart.

Listening to him talk about his past and seeing his love for
Señora Delgado revealed a different side of Connor. A fiercely
loyal and caring side that would be as easy to fall for as his
cocky grin and killer body.

Right, her conscience told her. *And the fact that Connor
never shared that side of himself with Emily, never told her
about his childhood, never brought her to the restaurant, that
has* nothing *to do with it.*

Kelsey wanted to shove the goading voice aside, but it was
impossible to ignore. Connor had trusted her with the heartbreak of his past and a happier part of his present, and it was
almost impossible not to think of the future. Not a forever
future, of course, but the immediate future—and how she'd
gladly spend what time she and Connor had left in his arms.

For the first time in years, Kelsey didn't feel like she'd
come in a distant second to her too-beautiful cousin, an irony
her disapproving conscience couldn't overlook, as Connor
was the one man in a position to best make comparisons...

"You're too quiet," Connor murmured in her ear. "It makes
me nervous."

Kelsey laughed at the thought of *anything* making Connor
nervous. "Don't be. I was just thinking."

"Hmm. Those might be the most nerve-racking words a
man ever hears. Should I ask *what* you've been thinking?"

Not brave enough to admit the whole truth, Kelsey said,
"Only that we don't have much time left."

Connor cocked an eyebrow. "Until the wedding?"

"Until you leave."

"Ready to see me go, huh?"

"Surprisingly, no," Kelsey said, although Connor didn't
seem surprised by her admission.

Because it was so obvious how her heart slammed into her
chest every time he came near? How her knees turned to jelly

with a single look? It wasn't something she wanted to admit to herself, forget giving Connor that kind of ammunition. Because even though telling her about his past and bringing her to meet his surrogate mother might have melted the walls around her heart, nothing said Connor felt the same.

"Good," he said. "Since I'm not ready to leave."

"Because you haven't figured Todd out yet?"

Connor scoffed. "I did that a long time ago. No, it's you I'm still trying to figure out."

This time it was Kelsey's turn to laugh. "I'm no mystery. I've already spilled all my secrets."

"I think there's more to discover. But I've already figured out a few things on my own. Like how you feel in my arms…how you taste when I kiss you…how I can make you blush without even trying."

Feeling her face heat, Kelsey protested, "Like you aren't trying right now."

"Naw," he said with a grin that did more than make her face heat as he lifted a hand and traced a pattern on her cheek. "If I was really trying to make you blush, I'd tell you how much this star on your cheek turns me on—especially when I think about all the other shapes I might find…and where I might find them."

Kelsey swallowed. She'd spent her whole life hating the freckles that marked her pale skin, but in a split second, in a single sentence, Connor had made her forget every teasing comment, every self-conscious thought.

"Connor." The lone word was all she could manage, but every bit of the emotion she felt echoed in her voice.

Making a sound deep in his throat that could have been a groan, he protested, "Don't look at me like that or I'll end up doing something not meant to be done in public."

Kelsey did lower her gaze, from the hunger in his eyes and

past his too-tempting lips, to stare at his throat. Not because of what he'd said, but because she didn't have the courage to look him in the face and say what she wanted to say. "There are…more private places."

Connor's arms flexed, pulling her closer, and his voice was a deep rumble in her ear as he said, "My hotel room."

Seemingly without conscious thought, an image flashed in Kelsey's mind—Emily leaving Connor's room—and she blurted out, "My house."

Bringing their dance to a halt, Connor stepped back slightly and nudged her chin up. "Are you sure?"

Even though he was asking about so much more than a simple destination, Kelsey met his gaze and repeated, "My house."

She felt slightly guilty as Connor pulled her through the restaurant. "Shouldn't we say goodbye?"

"Maria'll understand," Connor insisted without breaking stride.

Deciding she'd rather not think about how much the woman might understand, Kelsey focused on keeping up with Connor's long strides. Her heart pounded wildly in her chest, but the crazed rhythm had less to do with how fast they were going and so much more to do with what would happen once they got back to her place. And Kelsey didn't think Connor could walk fast enough….

And he must have felt the same, she realized when they reached the car. Instead of unlocking the door, Connor turned and pulled her into his arms.

"I've wanted to do this from the moment I saw you."

The husky words would have been easier to believe had Kelsey spoken them, but coming from Connor, they sent a thrill rushing through her as enticing as his kiss. "You wanted to do this at the airport?"

"At the airport. In your car on the way from the airport. The first time we came to the restaurant." His voice dropped to a husky murmur. "My hotel room."

Kelsey shivered, her thoughts instantly turning to the king-size bed where she wouldn't have to imagine the press of Connor's body against her own. His green eyes glowed as if he'd read her thoughts and was right there...in his hotel bed...with her.

Ducking his head, he caught her lips in a kiss that picked up right where the last had left off. The hunger and intensity didn't have to build; passion and desire had shimmered between them all evening like desert heat. Kelsey sank her hands into his dark hair, her fingers sifting through the silky strands. With Connor leaning against the side of the car, Kelsey didn't have to stretch to reach his mouth; they were perfectly aligned—lips to lips, chest to chest, thigh to thigh.

Connor slid his hands down her back, his fingers claiming the soft flesh of her hips as he pulled her tighter into the vee of his body. Kelsey thought if it were possible to pass out from pure pleasure, she might sink to the ground on the spot.

Instead, she broke away from his kiss. Hiding her face against his neck, she murmured, "My house, remember?" And then she gave in to temptation and pressed her mouth to the strong column of his throat, right where his pulse pounded in time with the pulsing Latin beat coming from the restaurant.

His throat jerked as he swallowed, and he pushed away from the car door without breaking their embrace. He reached back for the door handle and fumbled for a second before he broke away with a muffled curse and twisted around to get a better grip. But instead of pulling the door open, Connor paused, hand in the air as if he'd forgotten what he was doing. Seeming to shake off the hesitation, he opened the door for her.

But in that split-second hesitation, the intensity dissipated like smoke from a doused fire. Her heart still pounded from the kiss, and her breath was far from steady, but the mood had definitely changed. He wouldn't meet her gaze, and Kelsey couldn't help wondering… "Connor, what's wrong? Did I do something—"

"No," he bit out. His fierce expression lessened when he saw her flinch, but frustration filled his movements as he ran a hand through his hair. "No, you didn't do anything wrong. It's just—this is crazy. *You* make me crazy! I haven't made out with a girl in a car since Emily, and now here I am with another Wilson—"

His words cut off abruptly, but not before the small thrill Kelsey experienced at the thought of driving Connor McClane crazy was buried by a wave of doubt and insecurity as she imagined Connor and Emily making out in a car.

And—could this really *get* any worse—not just any car. The vintage Mustang belonged to Javy, who'd undoubtedly owned it for years. Back when Connor would have borrowed the hot car to pick up Emily…

Humiliation burning in her cheeks, Kelsey wanted nothing more than to go home, but she dreaded getting in that car. It didn't matter that she and Connor had already driven all over town in it; now, all she could see was Emily in the passenger seat, wind whipping through her blond hair. Emily, searching for a favorite song on the radio. Emily, slipping into the back seat where Connor waited…

"This was a mistake."

"Kelsey—"

"Can we go?" she interrupted. Maybe if she closed her eyes, she could picture herself somewhere else.

"No."

"What?"

Connor's dark frown told her she'd definitely heard right the first time. "No. I'm not gonna let you run off."

"There's nothing else to talk about, Connor. You and Emily—"

"All right. Fine. Let's talk about how there hasn't been a 'me and Emily' for *years*. I can't change my past, and I can't change yours."

"*My* past?"

"How much of this is about me and Emily? And how much of it is about *you* and Emily? How many times have you felt you couldn't live up to your cousins? How many times have the Wilsons made you feel second best?"

How many? Kelsey couldn't count the numerous times she'd tried walking in her cousins' footsteps only to fall in disgrace again and again. "Uncle Gordon and Aunt Charlene treated me *exactly* like they treated Aileen and Emily. But that was the problem. I'm—not like those girls."

"You don't have to be, Kelsey. You're you. That's more than enough."

Honesty and desire glowed in Connor's eyes. But as much as she longed to believe him, as she slid into the passenger seat Kelsey couldn't help feeling like she was trying yet again to fill Emily's place.

Shoving the key into the ignition, Connor started the car, and they were silent throughout the ride back to Kelsey's; the rumble of the engine was the only sound. Only as they pulled into her driveway did she find the courage to ask the question shouting through her thoughts the whole time.

"Why did you stop? If it wasn't about Emily—"

Connor sighed. "We were in the middle of a public parking lot where anyone could walk by. I should have the self-control to keep my hands to myself. But being back here has me acting like a hotheaded kid again. *You* make me feel like a hotheaded kid," he practically growled, not sounding the least bit happy about the idea. "Not Emily. *You*."

"I want to believe you. But this is all happening so fast, and it isn't easy to change how I feel after a matter of days!"

"I know. But I'm gonna keep trying."

Connor walked her to the front door, where he leaned close, giving her ample time to pull away. If his earlier kiss had struck like a flash of lightning, this was like the slow promise of a sunrise. Kelsey felt the gentle rays first, the touch of warmth against her cheeks as his fingers slid into her hair. And then light blazed behind her eyelids as he kissed her.

Heat poured through her, starting where his mouth brushed against hers then spreading out to all parts of her body, all the way down to her tingling fingertips and toes. Just when he'd left her knees weak and her willpower completely shaken, he eased away, ending the kiss slowly, reluctantly. "I want to see you tomorrow."

"I can't—"

"Kelsey."

"Not because of, well, anything. I'm busy tomorrow."

"With your shop?"

Kelsey shook her head regretfully. "The shop will have to wait a few days. I'm meeting Emily for brunch, and then we're going shopping for bridesmaids' gifts. Assuming that doesn't take all day, I have to meet with a friend who's putting together an audiovisual presentation for the reception."

"What time?"

"In the afternoon."

"Dunworthy has a meeting set up for tomorrow at six. Interested in another stakeout?"

Kelsey forced herself not to look over at the Mustang. The vehicle had somehow turned into so much more than a simple car. It was a physical reminder of Connor's past with Emily. A past Kelsey wasn't sure she could ignore. "Do I even want to know how you came across the information?"

"Nothing illegal. I got it the old-fashioned way. I overheard a conversation he was having on his cell phone." Connor frowned. "Well, I guess the cell phone part isn't old-fashioned, but the eavesdropping was."

"It could be nothing. A dead end like the other day."

"Could be. Wanna find out?" His eyebrows rose in exaggerated challenge, and Kelsey couldn't say no.

"See you tomorrow."

Kelsey knew she should open the door and step inside instead of gazing after Connor like a lovesick teenager, but she couldn't tear her gaze away as he walked down her driveway to the car.

He turned back before she had the chance to duck indoors, seeming unsurprised to find her staring after him. "There's something you should know, Kelsey. I might have kissed your cousin in this car. But I never slept with her."

"In the car?"

His lips kicked up in a smile, but the look in his eyes was completely serious. "Or anywhere else."

Chapter Eight

The next afternoon, standing in her sun-filled kitchen, Kelsey poured steaming black coffee into a thermal mug. She'd tossed and turned most of the night, her sleep plagued by dreams. Even now, she was haunted by images of gliding down an endless, rose-strewn runner toward her groom—toward Connor—only to watch, helpless, as he smiled his devastating smile and walked away with Emily.

"It's just a stupid dream," she muttered, as if speaking the words aloud might give them more strength. "I'm not marrying Connor. I'm not *falling* for Connor."

So she'd had temporary a lapse of judgment, of sanity. She'd been caught in the moment—the restaurant's party atmosphere, the sexy rhythm of the music that had seeped into her soul and pulsed in her veins...

Oh, who are you kidding? an all-too-knowing voice

demanded. She hadn't been caught up in the moment; she'd been caught up in the man.

Maybe she should ask Emily how she'd dated Connor for months *without* sleeping with him. Although Emily never divulged intimate details, Kelsey assumed they had made love. Now that she'd met Connor, it seemed even harder to believe Emily—or any woman—could resist.

Knowing now that Emily *had* resisted made Kelsey wonder if her cousin's feelings for Connor were as strong as she'd once believed, or if Connor was right and Emily had only been using him. What was it he'd said—he was Emily's lone act of rebellion? But even if that were true, it didn't necessarily change his feelings. Maybe coming back wasn't about picking up where they'd left off, but about finally taking that relationship further.

Her stomach felt more than a little sick at the thought, and she thrust the glass pot back into the machine, grabbed the to-go lid and slapped it onto the mug. But her aim must have been slightly off, and the cup tipped, splashing coffee over the countertop.

Gasping, Kelsey dove for a manila envelope lying nearby, snatching it out of the way of the java flood. She clutched the package to her chest with a relieved sigh. Emily's life in pictures filled the envelope, most dating back to the days prior to digital CDs.

Kelsey shuddered at the thought of telling her aunt she'd ruined the photos of Emily's first piano recital, first ballet, first play. She had to get back in control. Her near destruction of the photographs was a small symptom of a larger problem.

She was letting Connor get under her skin.

She'd taken possession of her own shop the day before, the realization of a dream that sometimes seemed as old as she was. Her thoughts should have been consumed by plans for polish-

ing the place until it shined, expanding her nonexistent advertising budget, hiring the support staff Lisa had mentioned.

Instead Connor filled her thoughts and her dreams, and was
far too close to edging his way into her heart. Was this how her
mother felt when she met her father? Kelsey wondered. Had
Donnie Mardell become more important to Olivia than her own
hopes and dreams? More important than her own family?

Kelsey forced herself not to panic. Surely she wouldn't
make that big a mistake, not with her mother's life as an
example. How many times had Olivia warned Kelsey to rely
on herself and not to risk leaning on someone who would let
her down in the end?

"Wilson women against the world," Kelsey murmured, the
familiar motto calming her as she set the envelope safely
aside and unrolled a swath of paper towels.

The sudden sound of the doorbell caught her off guard. She
didn't have time for unexpected guests any more than she had
time for unexpected doubts. Dropping the paper towels over
the spilled coffee, she headed toward the front door as the bell
pealed again. After a quick glance through the peephole,
Kelsey pulled the door open.

As if her thoughts had somehow conjured him out of thin
air, Connor leaned against the doorway. How was it that he
looked better every time she saw him? Was it because she now
knew his shoulders were as strong as they looked? How solid
his chest had felt beneath her hands? How his hair had felt
like warm silk against her fingers? And how his mouth had
worked magic against her own?

"Hey, Kelsey," he said before striding inside.

Trailing after him as if *he* owned the place and she was the
uninvited guest, she asked, "What are you doing here?"

He stopped to face her, a frown replacing his cocky smile. "I
thought you were coming with me. Todd's meeting, remember?"

"That's not until six," she protested as she walked into the kitchen to the mess she'd left behind.

"What happened in here?"

As much as she would have liked to lay the blame at Connor's feet, she said, "Don't ask." She balled up the soggy paper towels, groaning at the coffee-colored stain left behind on her beige Formica, and tossed them into the trash. She grabbed the envelope of photographs and her purse and brushed by Connor on the way to the door.

"I have to meet my friend about the audio-video presentation for the reception, remember?"

Connor shrugged. "So we go there first and stake out the meeting after."

She should say no. She should keep him far, far away, and not just because of the havoc he might wreak on Emily's wedding. "I'm already running late." As a flat-out denial, the words fell short.

"So let's go."

"Okay, but—" Kelsey straightened her shoulders. "I'll drive." She should have known it wouldn't make any difference how matter-of-factly she made that statement, Connor would see through it.

Judging by the look in his dark eyes, he did see—straight through to her heart. "Sounds like I need to work even harder."

"Connor—"

"It's okay," he interrupted. He stepped closer, and Kelsey tensed, half in preparation to defend her decision and half in anticipation of his approach. But nothing could have readied her for Connor cupping the back of her neck and pulling her into a kiss.

To her dismay, it ended before it even began. A quick press of lips again her own, and then it was over. And Kelsey had to clench her hands into fists to keep from grabbing the front of Connor's T-shirt and demand that he do it again. That he do it *right*.

As he pulled away, he gazed at her flustered—heated—face and smiled. "I never could resist a challenge."

"Are you sure this is right?" Kelsey asked.

Connor's directions to Todd's meeting had brought them to a Scottsdale neighborhood that rivaled her aunt and uncle's when it came to exclusivity, opulence and sheer expense. The winding roads led them past multileveled mansions surrounded by artfully arranged desert landscapes, sparkling water fountains and wrought-iron gates.

They were practically the first words she'd spoken since they'd dropped off Emily's pictures earlier. Kelsey had been grateful to focus on the straightforward directions of right, left, north and south rather than try to traverse the dangerous path her heart was traveling down.

Catching a street sign carved into a boulder, Connor said, "Turn here. This is it."

"Nice place." Irony filled Kelsey's voice at the understated description. The two-story home had a circular entryway, decorative columns, and floor-to-ceiling windows.

When she tapped on the brake, Connor insisted, "Don't stop." With a glance out the back, he said, "Okay. We should be good here. Go ahead and turn around."

Kelsey glanced in the rearview mirror. Thanks to a neighboring oleander hedge, she could barely see the house. Hopefully Todd wouldn't notice the two of them lurking in her car a block away. After turning the car to face the house, she asked, "Now what?"

"Now we wait."

Kelsey sighed. "I don't think I have the patience for being a private eye."

Connor's lips quirked into a smile. "That's okay. I'm not planning on changing careers and becoming a wedding coordinator, either. Besides, it's almost six."

"Todd will be late," Kelsey predicted. "He's always late." Tardiness was one of her aunt's pet peeves. A sign, according to Charlene Wilson, that showed a person believed his time more important than those around him. Somehow, though, she smothered her annoyance when it came to Todd.

"So he isn't perfect after all."

"I never said he was."

Connor made a thoughtful sound but hardly embraced her words. No surprise. *She* wasn't the one Connor wanted to impress. He was determined to prove her aunt and uncle wrong about Todd. But would that really be enough to make Connor let go of the past? Would Connor ever believe he was good enough, or would it take being good enough for Emily for him to see his own worth?

She sighed and sank lower in the seat, not wanting to think too hard on the answer to that question. Seconds later a car rounded the corner, and Kelsey impulsively grabbed Connor's arm. "Look!"

Her heart skipped a beat at the feel of his warm skin and muscle beneath her palm. When he leaned closer for a better look, her pulse quickened.

A woman sat behind the wheel of the luxury car, and Kelsey wondered if Connor might get his proof. Neither of them spoke as they waited for Todd's arrival and the meeting to unfold. Ten minutes later, Todd's SUV pulled up. When he climbed from the vehicle and casually glanced in their direction, Kelsey gasped.

"Relax," Connor advised. "He can't see us."

As she focused on the scene outside, Kelsey frowned in confusion. Todd flashed a smile at the woman as he walked up the driveway, but when he reached out to shake the woman's hand, the gesture was not only platonic but professional.

Connor swore. "I don't believe it. That woman's a Realtor. There's a lockbox on the front door."

Sure enough, the brunette led Todd to the front door, where she opened the small box and pulled out a key. With a flourish she turned the handle and waved Todd inside. Since Emily hadn't mentioned a new home, Kelsey wondered if the place was a wedding gift. Despite her questionable opinion of the man, she couldn't help feeling impressed by the romantic and extravagant gesture.

"We should go."

"Just—wait," Connor ground out.

A few minutes later Todd and the Realtor exited the house. Judging by the smile on the woman's face, Kelsey assumed the meeting had gone well. She shook Todd's hand again, nodded enthusiastically over whatever he said, and waved as he drove off.

"That's that," Kelsey said as she reached for the ignition. Connor stopped her with a touch, closing his hand over hers and slipping the keys out of her grasp before she ever realized his intention. "Connor, what—"

"Come on."

Connor kept a firm grip on Kelsey's hand as they walked toward the house despite her repeated tugs and her sharply whispered protests. As long as he had the keys, she couldn't go anywhere without him. So why exactly was she trying to pull away? The better question: why was he still hanging on?

"Connor! Stop! We're going to get caught!"

"Doing what? You know, I'm really starting to wonder about this guilty conscience of yours."

"You should," she muttered, "considering I didn't *have* one until you came along."

The front door opened, and Kelsey dug in her heels deep enough to leave divots in the grass. The Realtor looked surprised, but only for a moment. Professional smile in place, she asked, "Are you two interested in the property?"

Kelsey's grip tightened on Connor's hand. A quick glance in her direction revealed a panicked look that screamed *busted*. Fortunately, he had a bit more experience when it came to covering his butt, as well as any curvaceous female backside he dragged along for the ride.

Flashing a smile, he said, "My fiancée and I were driving through the neighborhood and noticed the lockbox. We don't have an appointment, but—"

"Oh, I'd love to show you around."

The inside of the house lived up to the exterior's elegant promise. Gorgeous views, a wide-open floor plan and every upgrade imaginable—travertine floors, granite countertops, stainless-steel appliances. The decor matched the surrounding desert with golds and browns and a hint of green.

"The house is beautiful," Kelsey said, once she'd realized the Realtor wasn't going to accuse them of trespassing.

"It's only been on the market a few days," the Realtor said as she concluded the six-bedroom, four-bath, media-room tour back at the front entry. "Another couple is interested in the property for their first place."

"Right. 'Cause this is the perfect starter home," Connor muttered.

Kelsey opened her mouth, ready to insist she didn't need a mansion, only to remember she and Connor weren't engaged. They wouldn't need a starter home or any other kind.

"Out of curiosity," he said, "can you tell how much the other couple is offering?"

The woman's smile was both sympathetic and hopeful. "I don't think money was an issue, but I have several other properties I'd be more than willing to show you." She pulled a card from her pocket and held it out to Connor. "Give me a call, and I can give you a list of houses that might fit your lifestyle."

Connor managed a nod, but as they walked out of the house, he crushed her card in his hand. *"Fit my lifestyle,"* he bit out. "Not to mention my budget."

His body thrummed with frustration, and Kelsey expected him to chuck the card into the street. Finally he shoved it into his pocket and stalked toward her car.

Kelsey didn't bother to ask for her keys back when Connor automatically went to the driver's-side door. Instead, she slid into the passenger seat. Trying for a practical tone, she said, "We already knew Todd has money."

"Yeah, we did," he said with a grim twist to his lips. "I'm starting to think the guy might be perfect after all."

"No one's perfect," Kelsey insisted. "Everyone has their faults and—"

"And the Wilsons certainly saw mine."

"You were a kid," she argued. "You can't believe what happened back then has anything to do with the man you are now."

Muttering what sounded suspiciously like "Don't be so sure," he cranked the engine and peeled away from the house.

Kelsey slapped a hand down on the armrest, but her tight grip slowly loosened. Despite his obvious frustration, Connor kept the car under perfect control. Within minutes they were on the freeway, but the turn he took wouldn't lead to her house.

Streetlights flickered on as daylight faded, marking the way toward an older part of Phoenix. They passed an abandoned drive-in, a boarded-up gas station and liquor store, the only business likely to thrive in such a depressing neighborhood. She could have asked where they were going, but as they drove by houses with peeling paint and duct-taped windows, lawns choked by weeds and neglect, she already knew.

A few minutes later Connor braked to a halt, gravel crunching beneath the wheels. He didn't say anything or make a move to get out of the car. With both hands still gripping the wheel, he stared at the trailer park across the street.

Kelsey had seen plenty of mobile home communities before. Manufactured homes, they were called now. Houses laid out in neat rows, with flower beds and swimming pools like any other nice, little neighborhood.

This was not that kind of place. The dirt lot, with its haphazard trailers and junkyard of vehicles, made the use of the term *park* an irony. The murmur of the engine was the only sound until Connor gave a sudden, harsh bark of laughter. "This is it. Where I came from. Who I am."

"No, it isn't." Unlocking her seat belt, Kelsey shifted on the seat to face him. The fading sunset glowed in the distance, casting his profile in bronze. "This isn't you any more than where I grew up makes me who I am."

"You're a Wilson. You're—"

Connor cut himself off, giving Kelsey the chance to interject, "I *am* a Wilson. But I'm not Emily. I'm not Aileen. And I wasn't raised like them."

"I know. On the outside looking in," he said, as he turned to look at her. Face-to-face, Kelsey could see the gold flecks in his green eyes. "That's what I thought when I first met you. The Wilson outsider."

That insight, pointing how she'd always felt—a part of and yet apart from her family—made Kelsey feel as if Connor knew her better than anyone. His words and the tenderness in his gaze crept inside her chest and wrapped around her heart. Somehow, being on the outside didn't matter so much when he was there with her. "You were right," she said softly.

But if he could somehow see inside her, Kelsey felt she was starting to do the same and getting to know the real Connor. His coming back to Arizona had to do with more than simply disliking Todd or even with proving her family wrong. His return had to do with a guilt *inside* him. As if by stopping the wedding, he could somehow make up for a past he could not change.

"And maybe that's why I can see you so clearly. This isn't who you are, Connor," she repeated. "Maybe it's who you were, but that's all. I've seen who you are now. You're a good friend, a good man—"

A sound rose in Connor's throat, part denial, part despair, and he jerked open the car door as if desperate for escape. Kelsey winced as he slammed it behind him, but she didn't hesitate to follow. He couldn't shut her out that easily!

"Connor, wait!" She scrambled out of the car after him, trying to keep up with the long strides that carried him across the weed-and-trash-strewn lot. She gasped as her foot hit an uneven spot on the heaved asphalt. She took a tottering step, arms windmilling for balance, but gravity won the battle, and she hit the ground.

"Kelsey!" Connor swore beneath his breath. "Are you okay?"

With a close-up view of the weeds and trash littering the trailer lot, Kelsey felt a moment's relief that she hadn't landed in a black, greasy puddle inches from her face.

"I'm fine," she insisted, even as Connor leaned down to help her up. Flames of heat licked at her. Some from the heel of her hand that had scraped across the pavement, some from the blazing heat bouncing off the black surface, but mostly from the sheer embarrassment of Connor witnessing her utter clumsiness. "Really, I—" She sucked in a quick breath as he took her hand to pull her to her feet.

Beneath his tanned skin, Connor went pale. "You're hurt."

Taking a hesitant glance down, she breathed out a sigh of

relief. "It's nothing. Only a scratch." A few thin lines of blood showed through the abraded skin on her palm, but other than the slight sting, she was fine.

Running his thumb gently across the scrape as if he could heal by touch alone, Connor said, "I never should have brought you here. It's my fault."

"It was an accident that could have happened in front of my own shop! It is *not* your fault." Gentling her voice, she added, "You're not responsible for every bad thing that happens. I don't know why you feel that way, but Connor, looking for dirt on Todd won't change things. Especially when—" she took a deep breath, reluctant to say the words but knowing she had to "—when it doesn't seem like there's anything to find."

"There is," he said flatly, refusing to consider failure. "Jake's still following a lead in St. Louis, and I'm not giving up here. I know guys like Dunworthy. He can only keep up this golden boy B.S. for so long. He's gonna slip. The closer it gets to the wedding, the more pressure there's gonna be, and he'll slip. I know it—"

"In your gut," Kelsey finished with a sigh. She turned her hand within his. Even through that light touch, she could feel the tension tightening his shoulders and arms and radiating down to the fingers she linked with hers. As gently as she could, she suggested, "Maybe it's time to stop listening to your gut."

"I can't." He gritted the words out of clenched teeth.

"Why not?"

"Because the last time I didn't listen, a woman was nearly killed."

Connor reached over and cranked the car's air conditioner to full blast, even though he doubted the frigid air would help. Sweat soaked the back of his neck, but it had little to do with the outside temperature despite the hundred-plus heat. The relentless sun, which bounced off every shiny surface to pinpoint on him as if he were a bug trapped beneath a kid's magnifying glass, had nothing on Kelsey's questioning glances.

He felt as if he was burning up from the inside out...all thanks to four little words.

You're a good man.

Kelsey had looked him straight in the eye with those words, her soft voice packing the same punch as a sonic boom. He didn't deserve that kind of faith. He'd disappointed too many women in the past: his mother, Emily, Cara Mitchell...

The more Kelsey trusted in him, the more he longed to believe in that trust, the worse it would be when he finally, irrevocably, let her down.

He sucked in a lungful of air, the heat threatening to suffocate him. He needed space—space to breathe, space to run, space that wasn't filled with Kelsey's cinnamon scent, her concerned glances, her soft voice...

"Connor..."

She was going to ask him what happened with Cara. His grip tightened on the passenger armrest, inches from the door handle and escape...even if escape meant paying the price for hitting the ground running at forty miles an hour.

No, telling truth was better. More painful, maybe, but at least Kelsey would realize he wasn't the man she thought he was.

"One of the first things I learned after opening my business was that you don't turn down work. You might not like the job, you might not like the client, but if it pays the bills, you take the job."

Kelsey slowed for a red light. Freedom beckoned, but Connor kept his hand on the armrest. "I didn't like Doug Mitchell. I didn't like the job, even though catching cheating spouses has always been part of the P.I. business. My gut told me he was bad news, but I didn't listen."

Silence filled the car, and Kelsey's gaze was as tangible as the trickle of sweat running from his temple. "What happened?" she murmured.

"I did what I was paid to do. I followed Cara Mitchell. To the grocery store, the salon, the gym… It was tedious, boring," he added, reminded of the conversation they'd had waiting for Dunworthy's meeting. "And I thought maybe Doug was wrong. That he was worried about nothing and his marriage was one of the few that would make it."

His hand cramped, and try as he might, he couldn't loosen his grip. His fingers seemed to have melded into the padded vinyl. "But then, one Tuesday, Cara drove south on the freeway. And I kept thinking it was Tuesday, and Tuesday was art class. So why was she going in the wrong direction? Before long, she ended up at a motel and when this guy opened the door, I thought here we go. I was wrong, and Doug was right."

"So she was having an affair?"

"Sure seemed that way," he said with a grimace. "Meeting some guy, staying behind closed shades, and leaving an hour later with her hair mussed and her makeup smudged… What else would you think?"

"What did *you* think?"

"I—I didn't know. It was suspicious, sure. But it wasn't proof, you know? Not one hundred percent take-it-to-the-bank proof. And in my gut I didn't believe it. Maybe I'd gotten too close. It happens, P.I.s falling for their marks, but that wasn't it. I wasn't attracted to Cara Mitchell. But I guess I—*liked* her. Respected her. She smiled at kids in the store, took the time to talk to little old ladies. She told cashiers when they gave her back too much change! I just didn't believe she was having an affair. But her husband wanted an update. He was the client, and he paid to know what I'd seen."

"But…you didn't actually *see* anything."

Connor winced at her logical protest. "And that's exactly what I told Doug. Only it didn't matter. Far as he was concerned, I'd seen enough and was off the job."

If only it had ended there...

"I couldn't get over my gut feeling that I was wrong. Wrong about Cara, wrong about what I'd seen. I thought if I followed her a few more days, I'd know for sure." Kelsey hit the gas as another red light turned green, and Connor desperately wished he was still the one driving. He'd go from zero to sixty in a split second if pure speed would give him the chance to outrun his memories.

"I was across the street watching when Doug came home from work in the middle of the day. I don't know if he hoped to catch Cara in the act, or if his rage and jealousy got to be too much. I heard her scream. I rushed into the house."

"But you stopped Doug, right?"

"Not soon enough. Cara was badly beaten and nearly unconscious by the time I got into the house and pulled Doug off her."

He could still see her, bloody and bruised, lying on the floor because of him. "The guy she went to see was a counselor. He'd rented the motel room to give her a safe place to stay, but he couldn't convince her to leave Doug, even though he'd been abusing her for years. If I'd listened to my gut—"

"But you *did* listen. You listened when you knew you didn't have the whole story. Cara Mitchell would likely be dead if not for you. You saved her life, Connor."

"If I hadn't taken the job—"

"Someone else would have. Someone who wouldn't have *cared* about a gut feeling. Once the job was over, that would have been it. They wouldn't have given Cara Mitchell a second thought."

Connor opened his mouth, ready to argue, but Kelsey's words ran deeper into his soul, soothing some of his guilt. Not that he believed he was any kind of hero. But he'd witnessed Doug's determination. He wasn't the type of guy to give up easily. Had Connor turned down the job, Doug *would* have found another P.I.

"Maybe—maybe you're right."

As Kelsey stopped for another red light, she turned to meet his gaze straight on. "I know I am," she said with the same certainty as when she'd vowed he was a good man.

Would she still think so when he told her about the money her uncle had paid him to leave town? No one had ever put the kind of faith and trust in him that Kelsey did, and every ounce of self-preservation inside him resisted the thought of telling her the truth.

Even if she gave him the chance to explain, even if she understood his reasons, the truth would change things. And yet he had to tell her. If he wanted her to believe he truly was a good man, if *he* wanted to believe that, he had to tell her.

But not tonight. There'd already been enough revelations about the past. And in case finding out about the money did change things, well, Connor selfishly wanted to hold on to Kelsey's faith in him for a little while longer.

"You know, this isn't necessary." Side by side on her couch, Kelsey watched as Connor placed the last piece of tape over the bandage on her hand. As far as a protest went, her words were pretty weak. Just like the rest of her, she thought.

Connor smoothed his thumb across her palm, his gaze intent on his task. A lock of dark hair had fallen across his forehead, shadowing his eyes and adding the slightest touch of softness to the hard planes and angles of his features.

Little shocks zapped up her arm, but it had nothing to do with pain. If she hadn't been sitting next to Connor, she probably would have melted into a puddle at his feet.

"It would have been tricky to do this on your own. Besides, it was the least I could do," he said, guilt and concern filling his expression as his hand rose to brush her hair back from her cheek.

And Kelsey couldn't resist his caring side any more than she'd been able to resist the other facets of his personality: the bad boy, the loyal friend, the protective warrior. They all combined to make up the man Connor was—the man Kelsey loved.

Her every instinct shouted in denial, but it was a useless protest. She'd been falling for him since the moment they met, a slow-motion tumble that landed her in this place, in this time, in his arms...

The intimacy of the moment pulled her closer. Her job, her family, even Connor's relationship with Emily seemed like distant, insignificant concerns. His fingers tunneled into her hair. Her amazing hair, Kelsey thought, recalling the words he'd spoken outside of Todd's office. She hadn't believed him then, but she did now. On the day she confronted him in his hotel room, he'd demanded she prove her loyalty to Emily, and she'd told him actions, not words, proved how a person truly felt. And Connor was a man of action, and he proved his feelings by trusting *her*—with his past, with his close friendship with the Delgados. How could she do anything but trust him in return?

"The last thing I'd ever want to do is hurt you, Kelsey," he vowed, that sense of responsibility carving a groove between his eyebrows.

"You didn't," she promised. "You won't."

Despite her words, doubt lingered in his gaze. Leaning forward, she brushed her lips against his, actions once again backing up words. Because whether Connor knew it or not, she *was* his. Body and soul. She shifted closer but couldn't get close enough.

Her hands charted a course her body longed to make, following a path from his shoulders to his chest, where she could feel his heart pounding a wild rhythm, and to his flat stomach and muscled thighs, which tensed beneath her hands.

Connor's hands stayed buried in her hair, but like the emotional connection moments before, the physical connection was so deep that with her every touch her own body responded. She felt the brush of his fingers trailing from her collarbones down to her breasts, to her stomach, ticklish enough to tremble at the imaginary contact.

Connor ended the kiss for a much needed breath but kept his mouth pressed to her cheek, her jaw, her throat...

A shrill buzz started them both. After the first few bars, Connor recognized his phone's ring tone, but the electronic device—one he never went anywhere without—was the last thing on his mind. He nearly groaned in frustration at the very thought of ending the kiss, of pulling away from Kelsey's embrace.

Maybe his battery would die. Maybe the signal would cut out.

His wishes went unheard as the phone rang again. Desire gradually clearing from her eyes as her breathing slowed, Kelsey pushed at his shoulders, and he had no choice but to back away.

"It's not important," he vowed, hoping his words were true as he fumbled with the phone. "I'll turn it off." He actually had his thumb on the button when he saw the number glowing on the small screen, and hesitated.

Just a split second, but the slight pause didn't get by Kelsey. "Who is it?"

The husky, passion-filled sound of her voice sent another shaft of desire straight to his gut. He could still turn the phone off. Turn it off and pretend the interruption had never taken place. The lie hovered in his thoughts, but meeting her gaze, he couldn't take the easy way out. "It's Emily."

Kelsey's eyes widened, and the warmth in them chilled even as the fire in her cheeks suddenly blazed. "Well, then, you should answer it."

"Kelsey—"

"Answer the phone, Connor."

Biting back a curse, he nearly barked into the phone, "Yeah?"

"Connor...is that you?"

"It's me. What's up?" Silence followed the brusque demand, and wouldn't it figure if the damn signal cut out *now*. "Em? You still there?"

"Yes. I'm here. What are you— Never mind. You sound like you're busy."

Forcing the slang definition of *busy* from his thoughts, he cleared his throat and asked, "What's wrong?"

"Nothing, really. Can't I call without you assuming something's wrong?"

A note of desperation had entered her voice, telling Connor it was more than an assumption. "Yeah, sure you can. So, what's up?"

"I guess I wanted to talk," she offered, uncertainty filling her voice.

Connor couldn't help glancing over at Kelsey. Her face turned away from him, she was determinedly ignoring the conversation going on only a cushion away.

Hesitation cost him for the second time in a matter of minutes when Emily said, "This was a bad idea. I shouldn't have called."

"Em—" The line went silent before he could come up with even a halfhearted protest. Flipping the phone closed, he slid the tiny device back in his pocket.

"What did she say?"

"Not much."

"She didn't say why she called?"

"No." And he didn't care. At least, not nearly as much as he cared about what was going through Kelsey's mind. "Kelsey—"

"It's okay."

"Really?" Connor asked, doubt lacing the word.

But when Kelsey met his gaze, a smile teased her lips. A little shaky around the edges, but a smile just the same. And Connor felt something in his heart catch at her remarkable strength and resiliency. He knew the call had to bring up reminders of his relationship with Emily as well as Kelsey's long-ingrained feelings of inferiority.

"Really," she insisted. "Like you said, we can't change the past, and I think it's time we both moved on."

Chapter Nine

"Kelsey, this is a surprise." Emily rose from the large oak table in her parents' kitchen, where she'd been flipping through a bridal magazine, and gave her a hug.

"I had a free morning and wanted to come by and invite you to breakfast." Kelsey mentally cringed at the half-truth. She *did* have a free morning, but the invitation was an excuse to find out what that phone call to Connor meant.

Emily wrinkled her nose. "I can't. I'll never fit into my wedding dress if I stuff myself with waffles."

So Emily was still dieting. Almost every bride thought about dieting before the big day even if they didn't stick with it. Or need to lose a single pound, Kelsey thought, as Emily walked over to the pantry—slender, graceful, and gorgeous. A powder-blue silk robe wrapped her body, and her hair was pulled back in a simple ponytail.

"You can keep me company while I have some tea and toast," her cousin suggested, a hopeful note coming to her voice.

"I'd love to. It'll give us a chance to talk."

After setting a kettle on the stove, Emily popped a piece of what looked like whole-wheat cardboard into the toaster. "What did you want to talk about?" she asked, once Kelsey declined her offer of toast in favor of fresh strawberries.

About that phone call last night, Kelsey thought. *The one you placed an hour after your oh-so-perfect fiancé met a Realtor at your dream house.*

"Uh…" Unable to jump into the conversation, her mind blanked and the last thing she expected popped out of her mouth. "I saw Matt the other night."

"No!" Looking appropriately horrified and curious, Emily sank back against the tan-and-gold-flecked granite countertops. "What happened?" Before Kelsey could answer, Emily waved off the question. "No, don't start yet."

She plopped a tea bag in a mug the size of a cereal bowl, poured the hot water and dropped her hot toast—sans butter— onto a plate. Settling eagerly onto the chair next to Kelsey, she said, "Okay, tell me everything. Did he beg you to take him back? Has he come to his senses and realized that other woman can't compare to you?"

Kelsey managed a small smile, knowing Emily didn't realize the irony of her words. Kelsey had never told her cousin *she* was the woman Matt was in love with. As blind as Kelsey had been to her ex's infatuation, Emily had missed the signs, as well. Of course, she was used to attracting male attention. Matt's shy and awkward behavior had been nothing new.

"No, he didn't beg me to come back." Though some begging had been involved, she recalled with satisfaction, thinking of Matt pleading with her to call Connor off.

But it was the look in Connor's eyes when he'd touched

her cheek that stayed in her mind, replaying like the romantic comedies she enjoyed. Last night's kiss was another memory that played over and over, and unfortunately her mind didn't come with a handy remote. The images had flickered across her eyelids for hours.

She'd talked a good game last night, declaring the past over and done for both of them, but could it be that easy? Facing Emily on a day when her cousin looked gorgeous—as usual— and Kelsey felt tired and cranky and worn by comparison, could she really believe Connor was over Emily?

Waving the desert-dry toast, Emily decreed, "You're better off without Matt."

"Yeah, that's what—that's what I think, too."

"You're an amazing woman, Kelsey. You're sweet, successful. You own your own business, and you're so totally organized."

Rolling her eyes, Kelsey ignored the heat rising in her cheeks. "I don't know about amazing."

"Do you know how impressed Daddy was when you didn't take money from him to start your business?"

"I couldn't. Your parents have already done so much for me." And Kelsey had never forgotten that her father had gotten her mother pregnant—with her—in the hope of getting his hands on the Wilson fortune. She was *not* her father's daughter, and she flat-out refused to step anywhere near the tracks he'd left behind. "I couldn't take money from them. Your mother's referrals have been the real boost the business needed."

Referrals that hinged on Emily's wedding going off without a hitch.

You're going to be a success with or without Emily's wedding. Connor's words echoed in her mind. *A single setback won't stop you.*

He was right, Kelsey realized. Weddings Amour was her

calling, her dream, one she would fight for. One wedding was not going to make or break her business.

Just like her family's approval or disapproval would not make or break *her*. She was stronger than her cousin, and if Connor was right about Todd, Kelsey needed to do what she could to look out for Emily.

With the reminder in mind, Kelsey said, "Enough about me. What's Todd up to this morning? Why aren't you two lovebirds hanging out?"

"He and Daddy went golfing."

Golf. Kelsey had never understood the sport. Especially not during the summer when tee-off times were at the break of dawn. "I'm surprised you didn't go with them."

Emily, along with looking chic in linen capris and argyle print polo shirts, was an amazing golfer. She gave a soft laugh. "You know. Gentlemen only, ladies forbidden."

"Hmm." That long-ago restriction, the acronym that gave golf its name, might have something to do with Kelsey's aversion to the sport. "You probably would have beaten them. Which might be why they didn't invite you."

"Oh, I wouldn't have—" A soft blush lit Emily's cheeks, and she turned her attention to peeling the crust from her toast.

"Wouldn't what, Em? Play to win?" Between the abbreviation of her cousin's name and the challenge she'd issued, Kelsey felt like a ventriloquist's dummy with Connor pulling the strings and his words coming out of her mouth. But as worried as she might be by his influence, her cousin's possible answer worried her more.

"Come on, Kelsey," Emily said, "you know how fragile the male ego can be."

"I can understand why you wouldn't want to show Todd up, but do you really want to live your life playing second best?"

"It's only a silly game of golf, Kelsey."

"I think it's more than that."

Emily's smile faded away, and Kelsey felt like she'd caught a glimpse of the real woman lost behind the beautiful facade. "Todd is a wonderful man. I love him. Really, I do, and I can't wait until we're married."

Kelsey had heard the words before, but this was the first time she sensed a touch of desperation underscoring the refrain. "Emily—" she began, but the opening of the kitchen door interrupted what she might have said.

"Kelsey, good morning," Charlene greeted Kelsey with raised eyebrows that seemed to ask why she wasn't keeping an eye on Connor as she'd been told. "I didn't expect to see you here."

Emily flashed a smile she'd perfected years ago, during her beautiful baby and pageant days. The slight tilt of her head, the perfect curve to her lips, the flash of white teeth. The smile was camera ready, but like an image captured on photo paper, it wasn't real. The moment and whatever else they might have said was gone.

"Kelsey came by to talk about the shower tomorrow and go over a few last-minute wedding details," she filled in, but the excuse only made Charlene frown.

"What details?"

"We're, um, we're going over the items Emily will carry down the aisle. You know, the something borrowed, something blue…"

"That's already decided, remember?" Charlene filled her own teacup and set the pot back on the stove. "You'll wear my pearls as something borrowed. I wore them at my wedding, and Aileen wore them at hers. It's tradition."

"Oh, right," Emily agreed. Kelsey knew her cousin thought pearls old-fashioned. Instead of making a fuss, though, Emily bowed to her mother's wishes. An argument built inside Kelsey like the steam building in the teapot, but what good would it do to stand up for her cousin when Emily wouldn't stand up for herself? "My bouquet will be tied with a blue ribbon, and my ring is new. So that leaves something old."

"I have a lace handkerchief that belonged to your great-grandmother." Adding a tea bag to the water, Charlene said, "Kelsey, run upstairs, would you? The handkerchief is in the bottom drawer of my dresser."

Charlene turned back to the counter to add sugar to her tea, and Kelsey wondered if her aunt was sending her on the errand because she didn't want to leave Emily and Kelsey alone. Still, she agreed. "I'll go get it."

During the years Kelsey had lived with her aunt and uncle, she rarely intruded on their sanctuary. Once she stepped inside, she saw the dresser had three bottom drawers. Which one would hold the handkerchief Charlene mentioned?

Kelsey started at the nearest drawer and found a collection of family mementos. Glancing through the items, she realized these were her uncle's belongings, not her aunt's. A packet of envelopes nestled among a worn-out glove and baseball cap. She slid the drawer halfway closed before she noticed the address on the top envelope. A Nevada location that had once been her home.

Hesitating, she reached for the letters. Kelsey flipped through one after the other, noting the changing addresses and postmark dates as well as the undeniable "return to sender" printed across the fronts.

"You can open them if you want."

Kelsey jumped at the sound of her uncle's voice. Gordon stood framed by the doorway. Dressed in tan slacks and a blue polo shirt, he looked more casual than usual. The hint of sunburn above his close-cropped beard told of the morning hours spent on the golf course, and his silver-blond hair had recently lost some of its structured style. But regardless of what he wore, her uncle was a tall, handsome man whose presence demanded attention and respect.

Clutching the letters to her chest, she said, "Aunt Charlene sent me to look for Great-grandmother's handkerchief. For the wedding. You know, something old—"

Gordon waved a hand. "The middle drawer is your aunt's."

Ignoring the errand that had sent her to the room, Kelsey held out the letters. "You wrote to my mother?"

Gordon nodded. "More times than I can count. But it was all too little, too late."

Too little. Kelsey flipped through the envelopes—years' worth of envelopes, years' worth of effort—seeing nothing little about it. "I don't understand."

"Your grandfather was a hard man. He wouldn't stand for any sign of defiance, and your mother—" Gordon shook his head with a bittersweet smile. "Your mother challenged him from the day she was born. They butted heads constantly, but when she refused to stop seeing your father, that was an impasse neither of them could cross."

Kelsey's hands tightened on the letters at the mention of her father. "Maybe she should have listened."

"She made a bad choice, and at the time I thought your grandfather handled the situation very poorly. Years later I realized how desperate he must have felt to make the ultimatum he did—forcing your mother to choose between her family and your father."

And her mother chose Donnie Mardell. She'd never talked about him, and not until her illness reached a point where there was no hope did she tell Kelsey the whole story. How she had defied her father to leave home with Donnie. How her father refused to accept that decision and paid Donnie to leave town, thinking that would force Olivia to come to heel.

But that plan backfired. Donnie left town, money burning

a hole in his pocket, but Olivia hadn't returned home. Instead, she fled even farther, cutting all contact with her family...to the point where Kelsey hadn't known she *had* any family.

Regret furrowed his forehead. "I'd hoped your mother could forgive me for what she saw as my decision to side with our father." Gordon shook his head. "So stubborn, the both of them. So unwilling to bend."

Instant denial rose up inside Kelsey. "My mother was brave and strong. She took care of herself and me without help from *anyone.*"

"And she raised you to do the same, didn't she?"

Kelsey opened her mouth to respond, only to be silenced by her mother's voice echoing in her mind. *You may not have been raised as one of the wealthy Wilsons, but you're better than they are. Hold your head high and prove to them what an amazing young woman I've raised.*

She'd done her best, trying to prove herself instead of simply *being* herself. All the judgments, all the expectations, had her aunt and uncle put them on Kelsey...or had Olivia with her dying words?

Lifting a hand, Gordon brushed his fingertips against the edges of the envelopes, flipping through fifteen years of unanswered pleas. "She was my only sibling. The last link to my childhood and my parents. I never stopped hoping we'd have the chance to overcome the differences of the past. But she was so determined to prove she didn't need anybody." He met Kelsey's gaze with a melancholy grin. "There's no doubt *you* are your mother's daughter."

She'd spent eight years trying to be exactly that. Struggling to prove herself by trying to follow step by humiliating step in her cousins' footprints rather than simply *telling* her aunt and uncle she wasn't cut out for ballet or dressage or the lead role in the school play. Insisting on taking summer jobs to pay for her clothes and books and CDs; refusing to accept her uncle's loan to get her business going.

How many other times had she pushed her aunt and uncle away in her desperation to live up to her mother's stubborn independence? Unlike Olivia, Kelsey hadn't been totally alone, but she *had* followed her mother's footsteps when it came to protecting her heart. She'd kept people at a distance, never letting anyone—even family—too close, so she could never be let down, never be disappointed. Even with Matt…Kelsey saw now she'd purposely picked someone she liked but could never love.

And what about Connor? Had she resisted because she was afraid of his lingering feelings for Emily…or simply because she was afraid? Was she using his past as an excuse the same way her mother had held Gordon's past decisions against him? A reason not to give him—not to give *anyone*—a second chance?

Wilson women against the world. The motto that had once been a battle cry of strength and independence now seemed a cowardly whimper. And an excuse not to trust, not to fall in love…

Swallowing the lump in her throat, she asked, "Why didn't you tell me? Why let me think you'd cut my mother out of your life like your father did?"

Sorrow for the sister he'd lost pulled at Gordon's features. "Olivia was gone, and I didn't want to make you choose between your memory of her—your *good* memories of her—and the truth I could have told you."

Kelsey wondered if she might have been better off knowing the truth, but how could she fault her uncle when he'd made such an unselfish decision? "I'm so sorry, Uncle Gordon."

"Don't be. I know how much your mother meant to you, and I'd never want to take that away. Besides, I'm proud of you, Kelsey. Of your determination and drive. I'm sure your mother would be, as well."

Kelsey tried to answer, but the words were blocked by the lump in her throat. Swallowing, she said, "Uncle Gordon—"

"Kelsey, can't you find the handkerchief?" Charlene entered the bedroom and stepped around her husband. She frowned at the drawer Kelsey had left open. Her heart skipped a beat as her aunt crossed the room. But Charlene merely pushed the drawer shut, opened the correct one and lifted the handkerchief without sparing the envelopes in Kelsey's hand a single glance.

"Here it is," she said with an exasperated sigh. "I might as well hold on to it."

Kelsey blinked, the past falling away as she refocused on the present. "Isn't Emily downstairs?"

"Todd invited her to brunch."

She'd missed her chance to talk to Emily about her feelings for Todd and about the wedding, but Kelsey couldn't think about anything but the letters in her hands.

"Speaking of brunch," Gordon said, "I'm starved. You wouldn't believe the calories I burned beating that future son-in-law of mine. Although I do think he might have let me win."

"Nonsense," Charlene said briskly. "Experience trumps youth every time."

"I, um, should go," Kelsey said, ducking past her aunt. She tried to slip her uncle the letters, but he squeezed her hands and mouthed, "Keep them."

After giving a brief nod, Kelsey jogged down the stairs with her uncle's written words in her hands and his voice in her head.

You are your mother's daughter.

Connor stepped out of the shower, dropped the damp towel onto the marble floor in a limp heap and seriously considered following suit himself. He couldn't remember the last time he'd done enough reps to leave his arms and legs flopping like fish out of water.

His cell phone beeped as he pulled on a pair of well-worn jeans. The sound immediately took him back to the evening before and the reason he'd needed the killer workout. Memories of Kelsey's kiss, the feel of her curves beneath his hands, and the untimely interruption had tortured him through the night.

Only, the sound wasn't alerting him to an incoming call, but to a new message. Seeing Jake's number on the screen, he quickly dialed his voice mail.

"Come on, Jake. Tell me Sophia Pirelli gave you something on Dunworthy," he muttered while he waited for the message to play.

"Whatever happened to Sophia in Chicago still has her feeling vulnerable," Jake's message announced without preamble. "I'm getting close, though. She—she's starting to trust me. It won't be long now."

His friend said the words with an almost grim sense of finality. Once Jake found out what had made Sophia quit her job and whether or not it had anything to do with Dunworthy, Jake would be on the next plane back to L.A.

Just as Connor would be leaving Scottsdale…leaving Kelsey…

Leaving Kelsey to pick up the pieces, he thought as he snapped the phone shut and tossed it back on the dresser. If Emily called off the wedding, would it ruin Kelsey's business? He'd told her she had the strength and determination to succeed no matter what, and while he'd meant every word, he really didn't know what the hell he was talking about, did he? Could her dreams end up buried beneath a landslide of bad publicity for a wedding gone wrong?

And what about her family? The Wilsons were counting

on Kelsey. Would she see her failure as yet another time when she hadn't lived up to expectations?

But what was he supposed to do? Connor wondered. Step back and let Emily marry a guy with a narcissistic streak running like a fault line beneath his charming, sophisticated facade? Raise a glass of champagne and hope for the best?

Cara Mitchell would likely be dead if not for you. You saved her life, Connor.

He still wasn't sure he could take credit instead of blame for what happened to Cara, but he did know he couldn't have walked away. Just like he couldn't walk away from Emily.

But maybe he needed to walk away from Kelsey...

Bad enough that he'd be leaving her to deal with the professional fallout. The last thing he wanted was to leave her personal life in shambles after an affair that wouldn't—couldn't—go anywhere. It would be best to end things now, before someone got hurt.

Are you so sure it's Kelsey *you're trying to protect?* his sarcastic inner voice questioned, mocking his noble intentions for what they were—the act of a coward.

When it came right down to it, he had his own heart to protect, too. And Kelsey—with her caring, her concern, her willingness to see the best in everyone, including him—was already way too close to working her way inside.

A quiet knock on the door broke into his thoughts. He didn't bother to check the keyhole, accustomed to being able to handle anything, only to open the door and realize he could still be caught off guard.

Kelsey stood in the hallway, a lost look on her face.

"What are you doing here?" The question bordered on rude, but as he took in the uncertainty in her wide brown eyes, the sexier-than-hell freckles on her pale face, the plump lower lip she held caught between her teeth, his earlier intentions blew up in his face.

Walk away? As he caught the cinnamon scent of her skin, he couldn't even *move*.

"I went to see Emily this morning," she said as she ducked through the doorway. "I wanted to find out why she called you last night."

Last night.

The two simple words had the power to turn back time. His flesh still burned in the aftermath of her touch. He grabbed a clean T-shirt from the dresser and jerked it over his head as if he could smother the memories. Not likely. It would take much stronger fabric than simple cotton, especially with Kelsey standing mere feet from his bed.

Pushing his damp hair back with both hands, he caught Kelsey staring at him, desire and awareness swirling in her chocolate eyes. Slowly lowering his arms, he shoved his hands into the back pockets of his jeans rather than pull her into his arms. As if sensing his thoughts, Kelsey broke eye contact, her gaze skittering away as soft color lit her cheeks.

In a voice that sounded dry as the desert, he asked, "Did you?"

Blinking like waking from a dream, Kelsey asked, "Did I what?"

"Find out why Em called?"

"No. Well, maybe. It sounds like Uncle Gordon and Todd are getting pretty close. Emily says she's happy about it, but I'm not so sure."

Connor nodded. "Makes sense. Emily's always wanted her father's approval, and she's never known how to get it."

Silence followed his statement. He wasn't sure when he lost Kelsey. Her gaze was focused on the far wall, and he doubted she was captivated by the desertscape watercolor.

"Kelsey? You okay?"

"All this time, I thought I knew, but it was a lie, and I can't ask her why."

He frowned. "Ask who what?"

Shaking her head, she came back from whatever place or time had her spellbound. "Sorry. You don't even know what I'm talking about." She clutched at the oversize purse hanging from her shoulder, the lost, almost haunted look coming back.

Concern accomplished what little else could—pushing desire to the back burner. He stepped closer and watched her throat move as she swallowed—thanks to whatever she must have seen in his eyes—but he merely took her hand and led her to the couch.

"Tell me," he urged. "Maybe I can figure it out."

"If you can, you're one up on me," she said with a sound that could have been a laugh but wasn't. Still, she took a deep breath as she sank against one of the cushions and said, "Aunt Charlene walked in when I was with Emily. We told her we'd been discussing what Emily would carry down the aisle. Something old, something new…"

Kelsey seemed to expect him to fill in the rest, so Connor ventured, "Roses are red, violets are blue?"

A slight smile tweaked her lips, and she said, "Close. Something borrowed, something blue." Her smile faded as she pulled a rubber-banded stack of envelopes out of her purse. "I went looking for something old."

"And you found those?" he asked, nodding at the bundle in her hands.

"These are letters my uncle wrote to my mother. Letters I never knew about. From an uncle I never knew existed until I was sixteen."

Slowly Kelsey filled Connor in about her wrong-side-of-the-tracks father, about the demand her grandfather had made of her mother, and the money he'd paid her father to leave.

The words were a sucker punch to Connor's soul. "Your grandfather paid your father off?"

Damned if he didn't have to give the family credit. They were consistent if not original. Clearly payoffs were standard practice when it came to getting rid of unwanted boyfriends. He still remembered the look on Gordon Wilson's face when the older man handed *him* a check to stay away from Emily.

Money he still hadn't told Kelsey about...

"He took the money and never looked back. He didn't care that my mother gave up everything for him. Didn't even care that she was pregnant with me."

An old bitterness, stale and rusty, cut into Kelsey's words, and panic started to grow inside Connor. "But if he never contacted your mother, then you don't know his reasons. You don't know why he took the money—"

Kelsey gave a scoffing laugh. "Oh, believe me. I know *why*. He took the money because he was a selfish bastard. It was all he was interested in, all he wanted, and as soon as it was his, he was gone. Nothing he could say would matter, nothing he could do would ever make up for taking the money."

She might as well be talking about him, Connor thought, guilt churning inside him. There was nothing he could do to change the past. He'd known when he took the money, Emily would never understand why he'd done it, why it was so vital that he help the Delgados. Would Kelsey really be any different?

She is *different,* his conscience argued.

And, yeah, okay, he'd taken her to meet Maria with the thought that he could somehow explain. But with her past and her father's bought-and-paid-for desertion, well, she'd it said herself, hadn't she?

Nothing he could say would matter...

"I'm sorry, Kelsey," he bit out. Sorry for reasons he couldn't even tell her.

"So am I," she said as she placed the letters on the coffee table. Taking a deep breath, she seemed to come to a decision as she turned on the couch cushion to face him. "I'm sorry my mother couldn't see another choice—to let go of the past. But I've been just as guilty."

"Kelsey—"

"It's true," she insisted. "I've always kept my aunt and uncle at a distance. You saw that. I was afraid to trust them, to count on them, in case they turned their backs on me the same way I thought they'd turned their backs on my mom."

"And Gordon never told you the whole story until now?"

Kelsey shook her head. "He said he didn't want to make me choose between my loyalty to my mom and them." She caught sight of Connor's surprised look and added, "See? He's not all bad."

Surprising her, Connor said, "Yeah, I'm starting to see that." His jaw clenched. "I mean, talk about the past repeating. He looked at me and saw a guy like your father—"

"You're nothing like him," Kelsey insisted fiercely.

"Kelsey, you don't know—"

"I do. I know you're a good man."

A pained expression crossed his face. "No."

"You are," she insisted.

She thought of the way he'd taken responsibility for the women in his life: his mother, Emily, Cara Mitchell. He'd saved the woman's life, yet he held himself accountable for putting her in a dangerous situation. Then, there was the love and gratitude he showed the Delgados. And yet none of those things compared to how he made her feel. She didn't want to be a responsibility. She certainly didn't want to be family. She wanted to be the woman Connor thought she was—strong, beautiful, sexy…

She did not want to be her mother's daughter, refusing to give or take second chances. And while Connor had never actually *told* her she was sexy, he gave her the confidence to believe she was. Taking a deep breath, the emotions that had been swirling through her calmed, settled, focused on the present, on this moment, and what she wanted. "And I might be my mother's daughter, but I don't have to live my life like she did."

The confusion clouding Connor's expression dispersed as Kelsey rose to her knees and leaned closer. Crystal-clear desire and equally obvious denial filled the void. "Kelsey, wait."

Determined to wipe that denial from his eyes, Kelsey swung her knee over Connor's thighs. He caught her around the waist, the heat in his gaze burning brighter as his fingers flexed into her hips. Instead of pulling her closer, he held her steady. "Kelsey, you don't know—"

His hesitation only pushed Kelsey forward. "I know I want you to kiss me."

One kiss was all it would take to bury her doubts in a flood of need. She should have known Connor wouldn't make it that easy on her. Or on himself. A war seemed to rage inside him, the frown between his eyebrows and the lines cutting grooves in his cheeks telling the tale of the battle.

One she thought she might win when his gaze dropped to her mouth. His voice a husky rasp, he asked, "That's all you want? A kiss?"

Almost unconsciously she licked her lips, a feminine thrill rushing through her when she saw his eyes darken with desire. "It's a good place to start, don't you think?"

And she could think of only one place she wanted to finish—in Connor's arms and in his bed, with no phone calls or memories of the past to interfere. Reaching up to trace the planes and angles of his face, from the doubt still pulling at his eyebrows to the tension locking his jaw, her cousin Aileen's words rang in her head.

Connor's the kind of man who makes a woman want to live for the moment.

Maybe that was true, but all she wanted was this man, in this moment, Kelsey insisted, ignoring the greedy voice demanding more...demanding forever.

"Now," she argued with that voice, "I just want now."

"Want what?" Connor demanded, his voice a rough scrape that sent shivers down her nerve endings.

"This," she whispered as she brushed her fingertips over his mouth. "You."

Her pulse pounded so wildly in her ears, Kelsey barely heard the words, but to Connor, her response must have been loud and clear. The one word broke through his hesitation. Leaning forward, he pulled her tighter and caught her lips in the kiss she'd waited for. Just like she'd hoped, the sheer pleasure of his mouth on hers banished all doubt, erasing any worries about anything...or anyone.

His hands still on her hips, he twisted to the side, lowering her to the couch without breaking the mind-spinning kiss. She sank into the cushions, Connor's weight pressing her deeper, but even the full-body contact wasn't enough. She ran her hands down his back, breathing in his fresh-from-the-shower scent. Breaking the kiss, she trailed her lips down the column of his throat. His skin was still slightly damp, and she sipped tiny droplets of water from his skin like a woman dying of thirst in the desert.

And maybe she was, Kelsey thought, vaguely surprised by the need and desire spurring her on. After all, it had been a *long* time...

Rising on an elbow, Connor levered away from her. For a split second, Kelsey worried that something—the hotel room, the couch, *something*—had reminded him of the past, of Emily, and that he was going to pull away and leave her wanting. But neither the past nor, heaven forbid, Emily were reflected in his eyes. Instead, Kelsey saw herself as he saw her, and for the first time in her life, she felt beautiful.

"Connor." His name broke from her in a shaky whisper. She didn't think she could speak another word if she tried, but he said everything she wanted to say...everything she wanted to hear.

"A kiss is never going to be enough. I want more. I want everything."

"Okay," she breathed.

Connor's lips quirked in a half smile. "Okay?"

Nodding fiercely, she repeated, "Okay."

Taking her at her word, as limited as it might have been, Connor reclaimed her lips in a teasing, tantalizing kiss even as his fingers toyed with the buttons on her shirt. But after his determined comment, Kelsey should have known Connor wasn't playing.

Before she was even aware of what happened, Connor's hot palm laid claim to the bare skin of her stomach, stealing her breath from the outside in as Kelsey realized he'd completely unbuttoned her shirt.

"Amazing," he murmured, his eyes taking the curves rising and falling with every rapid breath.

Glancing at the off-white, no-frills bra, she gave a short laugh. She hadn't gone to Connor's hotel with seduction in mind and it showed. "Boring," she argued.

"Are you kidding?" Tracing a path across the freckles on her chest, a focused, concentrated frown on his face, Connor vowed, "I think I just found a map to the Lost Dutchman's mine."

The silly comment startled a laugh from Kelsey, and Connor's touch veered closer to hitting a different kind of gold mine. His fingers followed the map work of freckles, and her laughter faded away. Breathless anticipation took over, and she arched into his touch.

The plain material proved no match for Connor. He reached inside to cup her breast, and her nipple instantly tightened against his palm. The sheer pleasure of his touch sent her head spinning, and each gasp for breath only pressed her flesh tighter into his hand. He kissed her again, and Kelsey welcomed the exploring quest of his tongue. Her hands searched for the hem of his shirt, seeking out hidden treasure for herself. She followed the plain of his back, the valley of his spine, the rise of his shoulder blades, but none of it was enough.

Pulling her mouth away from his, she gasped, "Connor, wait."

"What's wrong?" Despite the desire pinpointing his pupils and turning his voice to gravel, Connor followed her command. Other than the rapid rise and fall of his chest, he didn't move a muscle.

And Kelsey couldn't help smiling. "You didn't want to make out in a car, and I don't want to make love on a couch. Not when the bed is only a few feet away."

Eyes dark with desire, he accused, "I told you, you make me crazy."

"The feeling's mutual."

Connor pushed off the couch and held out a hand. She linked her fingers through his and clung tight, desperate to hold onto the moment. But unlike previous interruptions that broke the mood, the walk to the bedroom, amid heated kisses and arousing touches, heightened the intensity. Her fingers clumsy with haste, Kelsey tugged at Connor's T-shirt. She stopped kissing him only long enough to push the shirt over his head and toss it aside.

In the back of her mind, she was still slightly amazed by her own actions. For the first time, need overwhelmed nerves. She could have blamed the previous interruptions or her own personal dry spell for the undeniable hunger. But the real reason was Connor. All Connor…

He pushed her shirt from her shoulders, then stripped away her bra, and Kelsey let the garments fall, too fascinated by the sheer perfection of his broad shoulders, muscular chest and flat stomach to care about the imperfection of freckles dotting her skin. Especially not when Connor seemed so fascinated by connecting the random marks and turning them into shapes: stars, triangles, hearts…

But the arousing touch was nothing compared to the intensity of his lips as they charted that same course. The damp heat of his breath against her skin was like a promise, and when his mouth made good on that promise, Kelsey's knees went weak. Connor followed her down to the mattress and reached for the waistband of her skirt. She expected him to whisk it away as quickly as he had her shirt, but instead her skirt and panties made a slow slide down the length of her legs. Inch by inch, and by the time he slipped them off, Kelsey had never been so glad to be so short.

"Connor." His name broke from her in a plea, and his green eyes glittered as he ran his hand up the inside of her thigh.

"Definitely not boring," he murmured. He stroked her skin, and waves of pleasure washed over her. She cried out his name a second time, even as he shoved aside his jeans. The well-worn denim did not make the same slow journey as her skirt. He kicked the jeans aside in a split second, then braced his body above hers.

He claimed her mouth in a kiss, his tongue plunging deep in the same moment he buried himself between her thighs. Her back arched, her body rising to meet his, and his low groan of desire escaped their kiss. And this time it was her name that broke the silence as Connor caught her hips in his hands.

That first thrust was like the striptease with her skirt: slow, seductive, measured. But then urgency took over, reckless and wild, and Kelsey had the instant thought that this must be what it was like to ride on the back of a bike—amazed, exhilarated and desperate to hold on. But unlike on a bike, the real ride began when she lost control, careening riotously, hurtling down a path that ended in a fiery explosion as she shuddered in ecstasy a second time, bringing Connor with her.

They collapsed in a heap together, both trying to catch their breath. "Definitely not boring," Connor repeated, as he brushed the hair away from her face. The look of tenderness in his gaze brought an ache to her throat, and Kelsey was glad when Connor eased away and tucked her against his side before he saw the tears burning her eyes.

With her head on his chest, Kelsey listened to his heartbeat gradually slow. But even without the weight of his body on hers, she couldn't breathe. A relentless pressure squeezed her heart, like she'd dived too deep and realized too late how far she was in over her head.

Her first impression had been wrong. Connor wasn't the type of man who made a woman want to live for the moment. He was the type of man, the *only* man, who'd made Kelsey long for forever.

Chapter Ten

Connor woke slowly, aware of two things. First it was way too early, and second, Kelsey was no longer in bed. The low murmur of her voice pulled him the rest of the way from sleep. "Everything's all set, and I'll be there to oversee the decorations and food." A slight pause followed. "Must be a bad connection. I'm—outside. I'll run out and get the cake right before the guests arrive. Yes, I'll make sure to leave plenty of time. Can I talk to Emily for a second? Oh, right. Of course. She needs her beauty sleep. I'll see you in an hour. Okay. Forty-five minutes. Bye."

A narrow shaft of light sliced through the curtains, and in the muted glow he watched Kelsey slip on her shoes. He didn't move or make a sound, but something must have given him away. She stiffened slightly and glanced his way as she straightened. "Hey," she said softly. "I was trying not to wake you."

She pushed her hair behind her ear in a nervous gesture,

and Connor felt a flicker of annoyance. What was she going to do? Slip away while he was still sleeping? And why the hell would that bother him? It wasn't as if he hadn't done the same thing before. But that was before, and those women weren't Kelsey, and he didn't want her to go.

A knot twisted in his stomach at the thought of asking her to stay. The memory of his mother's sad smile as she walked away time and time again flashed in his mind, and the words jammed in his throat. He fisted his hands against the mattress and pushed into a sitting position with a glance at the clock. "It's not even seven."

Her gaze fell from his to land on his naked chest and then cut away to search out the purse she'd left on the couch, but not before he'd seen something in her eyes that made the knot in his stomach tighten.

"I know it's early, but Emily's shower is this morning, and I have to oversee the decorations and the food and— I'm sorry."

Connor wasn't sure why she was apologizing—for the early hour, for leaving, for Emily's shower…or for the regret he'd seen in her eyes.

He'd known Kelsey would regret sleeping with him, but he'd taken her at her word when she said she wanted him. He'd believed her because—hell, because he'd wanted to believe her. But that was last night. Now, in the full light of day, with the Charlene Wilson calling the shots, everything changed.

Or, he thought grimly, everything was the same. Only this time it was Kelsey lying to the Wilsons, sneaking behind their backs to see him. It was Kelsey who pretended her relationship with him didn't exist. Familiar ground, but it hurt a hell of a lot more the second time around. And not because she'd torn open old wounds. Emily had damaged his pride, but this—this felt like something else entirely.

Tossing aside the sheet in an obvious reminder that last

night *had* happened, Connor swung his legs over the edge of the mattress and stood. Some other time, he might have teased Kelsey about the blush blooming in her face. But not this morning. Not when the heat signaled a different kind of embarrassment. He jerked on his jeans as quickly as he'd stripped them off the night before, annoyed by his body's reaction to the mere thought.

"I'm going to talk to Emily about the wedding—"

"I don't give a damn about the wedding," he said, surprised by the truth of the words. He was still worried about Emily, but as far as proving the Wilsons wrong about Dunworthy, proving them wrong about *him,* Connor no longer cared. Only Kelsey's opinion mattered, an opinion suddenly in doubt.

"I'm sorry," she repeated, before lifting distraught eyes to his.

Yeah, he got that part. She was sorry they'd slept together.

"Last night was…"

Connor's jaw clenched, waiting for the word he *knew* was coming.

"…amazing, and I'd give anything to stay in bed with you—"

"Wait? What?"

"Last night was amazing." Color flared brighter, nearly blotting out her freckles as she ducked her head. "At least I thought it was, but I'm not—"

Swallowing a curse, Connor pulled her into his arms as realization hit him like the slap upside the head he deserved. Kelsey's reactions hadn't been fueled by regret or embarrassment but by a vulnerability that played against his own insecurities. "Last night *was* amazing."

The memory combined with Kelsey's soft curves pressed against him, her warm breath feathering across his chest, was enough to remind him just *how* amazing.

"It was," Kelsey whispered. He heard the relief in her voice, felt her smile against his skin.

"This morning could be even more amazing."

"I know." Despite the apparent agreement in her words, her smile fell away, and this time, he knew he wasn't imagining the regret in her voice. Pulling out of his arms, she said, "And that's why I have to go. Because whether you give a damn or not, Emily's wedding is a week away and then you'll be going home."

She was talking about L.A., but home didn't bring to mind images of his sterile apartment. Instead, he thought of Señora Delgado's restaurant, he thought of his friendship with Javy, and he thought of every moment he'd spent with Kelsey...and he wondered what might happen if he didn't go back to L.A.

"Kelsey—"

"So, see? I have to leave," she continued despite his interruption. "Last night was an amazing moment, but it wasn't meant to last, right?"

The hope in her eyes waited for him to contradict every word she'd said, to tell her sometimes amazing moments added up to a lifetime, but he couldn't make himself say the words.

Ducking her head, Kelsey grabbed her purse off the couch and left. And even though the sound of the closing door slammed into his chest like a blow, Connor let her go. Because when it came right down to it, he was the one too afraid to ask her to stay.

Connor didn't have a destination in mind when he climbed behind the Mustang's wheel, but he couldn't stay in the hotel room any longer. Fortunately, Javy's car seemed to have a mind of its own, and he soon turned into the Delgado parking lot.

The restaurant wouldn't open for hours yet, but Connor knew Maria would already be in the kitchen, stirring giant pots of tortilla soup and prepping food. He pulled around back, the crunch of gravel beneath the tires the only sound, a sharp contrast to the night he'd brought Kelsey here when music and laughter filled the sultry air.

A metallic glint caught his eye as he climbed from the car, and he spotted a motionless wind chime made from silverware. Despite his mood, Connor smiled as a memory came to him. Furious with Javy over some scrape he'd gotten into, Maria whacked the counter with a carved spoon. The aged wood splintered on contact, adding to his mother's anger, and she'd threatened Javy with the dire prediction that if the restaurant closed, it would be all his fault; after all, how could she cook without her favorite spoon?

The statement was a meaningless heat-of-the-moment comment that had come far too close to coming true years later. Not because of a broken spoon, but due to the expenses that followed Javy's father's illness and the fire that had nearly destroyed the kitchen.

A faint humming broke into his memories, and he found Maria standing at the counter, vegetables piled high in front of her, the quick, continuous motion of the knife a steady rhythm to the song she sang beneath her breath. The rustic Delgado family recipes went back for decades, but the remodeled kitchen was completely modern with its stainless-steel counters and appliances.

Maria's face lit as he stepped inside the kitchen. "Connor! This is a surprise."

"I wanted to apologize for taking off without saying goodbye the other night."

She waved aside his apology with a flick of her knife before starting in on a jalapeno pepper, but curiosity lit her eyes as she said, "You and your Kelsey were in a hurry, no?"

Her words wiggled like bait on a hook, but Connor didn't bite. His silence wasn't enough to make the *señora* pull in her line. Watching him from the corner of her eye, she added, "That is how it is when you are in love."

Love. The word sent a flare of panic scorching through him like the grease fire that nearly destroyed the restaurant years ago. "Kelsey and I aren't in love."

Maria glared at him like she might toss him back into the water. "I was married to my Miguel for over twenty years. I know love."

Connor knew love, too. He knew the pain of losing a mother who loved him yet left him no matter how many times he asked her to stay. He knew the heartache of losing Emily, who claimed to love him but not enough to defy her parents. And Kelsey...would loving her be any different? If he told her the truth about the money he'd taken, money he'd used to save the restaurant, would love be enough to make her understand? Would it be enough for her to stand up to the family who'd taken her in when she was sixteen and scared with nowhere else to go?

"You don't understand, Maria. Kelsey's a Wilson. She's Emily's cousin—"

"And you think Kelsey is a foolish girl like Emily? Unable to think or do for herself?"

"No, she's not like that at all. She's used to taking care of herself and the people around her." He'd seen that at her shop, in her concern for her friends. Friends who had Kelsey's complete loyalty. Friends who *deserved* that loyalty.

Connor tried to picture Lisa or Trey fitting in at a Wilson family gathering and couldn't. Just as he couldn't imagine Kelsey caring what the Wilsons thought or ever, *ever* turning her back on her friends. Kelsey might not have wanted to follow in her mother's footsteps, but the path had led Kelsey to be a strong, independent woman. A woman who knew her own mind and knew what she wanted.

Suddenly it didn't matter if the Wilsons admitted they've been wrong about Dunworthy. It didn't even matter if they admitted they'd been wrong about *him*. All he cared about now was proving Kelsey *right*. She believed in him, and last night she'd wanted *him*. Now it was up to Connor to tell her the truth about the money he'd taken from her family and convince her she wanted more than a moment, that he could give her more. It was up to him to convince her that, together, they could have forever.

Kelsey struggled through the front door of her aunt and uncle's house, a huge bouquet of pink and silver helium-filled balloons trailing behind her. The carved wooden doors swung shut, catching one of the balloons in the jamb. She jumped as the loud-as-a-gunshot *pop* guaranteed her arrival wouldn't go unannounced.

"Kelsey. I expected you half an hour ago."

Okay, so she wouldn't have snuck in unnoticed anyway. "Sorry, Aunt Charlene."

"Where have you been?"

"With Connor." The truth popped out before the words even formed in her head, and she couldn't imagine what possessed her to tell the truth.

His image flashed in her mind, and she knew exactly what possessed her. She'd seen the look in his eyes when he'd caught her on the phone with her aunt. When he caught her *lying* to her aunt. If she wasn't such a coward, she would have told the truth when it mattered.

Just like she would have stayed with Connor that morning, in his hotel room, in his bed, with the courage to believe they could turn one night into something more.

Disapproval cut into Charlene's features, and Kelsey knew her aunt didn't think Connor was good enough for a Wilson—

any Wilson—but she knew the truth. She didn't deserve Connor.

"You're wrong about him," she announced, certainty backing ever word. "Connor's a good man. He isn't here to ruin Emily's life. He's here because he's worried she's marrying a man she doesn't love to please *you*."

Her aunt didn't speak. Kelsey thought maybe her words had made a difference, at least given her aunt pause. But Charlene's gaze never wavered, and as the silence grew, Kelsey knew her aunt wasn't using the silence to consider what Kelsey said. She was using the silence to make Kelsey *reconsider* what she'd said.

But she wasn't going to back down.

It was time for both her aunt and uncle to realize Connor was a good man, not some troubled kid out to steal their daughter. And they needed to let Emily go. To let her live her own life and to stop using one youthful indiscretion to keep her in line.

"Do you really think I can't see what's going on?" her aunt questioned on a sigh. "Connor McClane is out to stop Emily's wedding, and he's using you to do it! Honestly, Kelsey, I expected you to know better."

"Connor isn't using me. He wouldn't do that. I understand why you'd have a hard time believing he cares for me after how crazy he was about Emily—"

"Oh, for goodness' sake, follow me." Without checking to see if Kelsey would obey, Charlene turned on a heel and strode down the hall into Gordon's study. Kelsey reluctantly followed. "Connor wasn't in love with Emily any more than he's…"

In love with you. Her aunt's unspoken words bounced off the darkly paneled walls, hanging in the room like the scent of Gordon's cigars.

"The only thing that man has ever worried about is

himself." Crossing the room to open a desk drawer, she pulled out a manila folder. "When your uncle kept this for proof, I always thought Emily would be the one we'd show it to."

"Proof of what?" Kelsey asked uneasily as Charlene fingered a small rectangle of paper. The letters her uncle had written her mother had been shock enough. What else did her aunt and uncle have stashed away in desks and dressers?

"Proof of the kind of man Connor McClane really is." Charlene gazed at Kelsey across the polished mahogany surface, her gaze reflecting a hint of sympathy. "He must be very convincing. Emily was sure he loved her."

Kelsey didn't have her cousin's certainty. Connor had never mentioned the word *love.* But then again, neither had she, and Kelsey could no longer deny her feelings. She was in love with Connor. For a moment, she imagined saying the words out loud and punctuating them with a bold exit. Not needing any proof of the man Connor was aside from the truth written in her heart. But she wasn't that strong.

"What is it?" she whispered.

"See for yourself." Charlene slid the paper across the table. Kelsey stepped closer. It was a check. She recognized her uncle's signature, his name and address printed on the top left, the zeros following the number in the small box off to the right. But it was the person the check had been made out to that froze her gaze. Her stomach, which had been tossing back and forth, sank.

"Why do you think Connor left all those years ago? He might not have had Emily, but believe me, he got what he wanted."

Her hand shaking, Kelsey reached out and turned the check over. Connor's name was sprawled across the endorsement line. She stared at the signature rather than meet her aunt's knowing gaze. "That was a long time ago. Connor isn't the same person anymore."

Ten thousand dollars. A lot of money, but not enough to make a dent in the family fortune. Had her father held out for more? Kelsey wondered. Even twenty-four years ago, ten thousand dollars didn't go far. Ten years ago, it wouldn't have bought a new car.

"Is that what he told you? That he's changed?" Her aunt's cultured voice didn't reflect even a hint of disparagement, but Kelsey heard it all the same.

"He was a kid back when he was seeing Emily." An orphaned kid from the wrong side of the tracks. Could she blame him for taking the money? He'd told her how he'd struggled after his mother died.

But he didn't tell you about the check, a worried voice protested. She'd told him about the money her father took to abandon her and her mother, and Connor never said a word.

"Let's look at the way he's changed. Ten years ago, he nearly ruined Emily's life by convincing her to run away from her family with him. Now he's back, and this time he's out to ruin her life by convincing her to run away from her fiancé with him."

"That's not true," Kelsey argued against the ache in her chest. "He's concerned about Emily. Just like I am. She's making a mistake by marrying Todd."

"If I were you, I wouldn't be worried about Emily *or* Todd. I'd be worried about Connor McClane."

Kelsey wasn't sure how she made it through the shower. Probably thanks to her aunt's attention to detail. By following Charlene's every instruction, Kelsey moved by rote. She arranged the flowers and decorations; she picked up the cake and double-checked the catered finger food. She walked the guests through the games—silly, irreverent, last-days-as-a-free-woman tributes—followed by opening gifts.

Even in her dazed state, Kelsey could guess what each package contained. After all, she'd helped with the bridal registry, and no one would dare step outside the approved gift list. No surprises, just as her aunt demanded.

Charlene planned for every contingency. Even Connor McClane, Kelsey thought, her heart catching as his signature seemed to flash in front of her eyes, written by an unseen hand.

"Thank you, Kelsey! It's beautiful." Emily held up a snow globe. Strains of the wedding march filled the room as sparkling "snow" fell on the bride and groom waltzing through a wedding wonderland.

Kelsey offered a weak smile. She'd bought the gift B.C.— Before Connor. She couldn't *not* give her cousin a gift, but she felt as uncertain about Emily and Todd as she now did about Connor.

Kelsey had started to believe him, to trust his gut, as he called it, but now she didn't know what to believe, and her own gut was pitifully silent. "You're welcome, Emily. I just want you to be happy."

Emily masked the flicker of doubt with a wedding-portrait smile. "I am happy, Kelsey. I'm getting married!"

A half an hour later, as the guests were leaving, Kelsey started collecting the plates and utensils, her movements automatic and unthinking. She blinked in surprise when her aunt laid a hand on her arm.

"The maid can get that, Kelsey."

"It's my job—"

"And we're your family." Her expression softened to a degree Kelsey had never witnessed. "You're a beautiful woman in your own right, Kelsey, and I'm sorry if I've made you feel less than my own daughters. But there's only one thing Connor McClane is interested in, and it's not true love."

* * *

Kelsey debated calling Connor, but the conversation wasn't one she wanted to have over the phone. Stopping by his hotel room was out of the question. She'd come alive in Connor's arms the night before, letting go of the past and all her insecurities. But seeing proof of the money he'd taken, the past was in painful jeopardy of repeating. The insecurities Connor lifted with his seductive words and intoxicating touch crashed back down, hitting harder than ever. Making her question if last night had been as amazing as she'd thought...

Kelsey hit the brakes a good twenty feet shy of her driveway. The black Mustang was parked at the sidewalk, the right front tire bumped up on the curb. Mirrored glasses shielding his eyes, Connor leaned against the hood.

Ready or not, she was going to have to confront him about the money he'd taken. It wasn't something *she* could pretend hadn't happened. Nerves jerked in her stomach, and she carefully eased her foot back on the gas, her car crawling the last block.

Connor grinned as she stepped out of the car, and aching or not, her heart still sped up as he approached. Maybe he had a reason, an explanation for taking the money.

And a reason for keeping the truth from her?

Kelsey could forgive something that happened ten years ago, but why hadn't he told her? Why did she have to face the shock of another family secret?

"Hey, I went by to see Señora Delgado. You have an open invitation, and she made me promise that next time, I'd actually let you stay and eat." Connor stuck his hands in the pockets of his jeans, a hint of uncertainty in his stride weakening her resolve as she wondered what else he'd talked to the older woman about.

"Connor—"

"She likes you," he added with a crooked smile, "but then, who wouldn't?" His smile fell away when she didn't respond, and he stripped off his glasses. Worry shone in his emerald eyes. "What's wrong?"

"Wrong?" Kelsey echoed with a broken laugh, the word far too simple to describe everything that had happened. Her decision to trust him, to *sleep* with him, to defend him to her aunt…only to find out he was just like her father.

It was a long time ago, her heart argued. *Maybe he had a good reason. Maybe—*

"Why didn't you tell me?"

"Tell you what?"

"The real reason you left all those years ago. Why didn't you tell me about the money?"

A muscle in Connor's jaw flinched as if she'd slapped him. Kelsey wasn't sure what she'd expected—excuses, denials—but she hadn't counted on the dead silence that followed her words. The sun beat down on them, magnifying the pain in her head. Cicadas in a neighbor's tree started to buzz, a low pitch that soon revved louder and louder, building like the hurt and anger inside Kelsey until she couldn't keep from lashing out.

"I *told* you about my father—about the money he took to leave my mother, and you never said a word! I trusted you, I believed in you, I—"

Love you, she thought, her heart breaking as Connor stoically withstood her verbal attack. If not for that very first flinch, she wouldn't have even known he was listening.

Surely if he had some reason, some justification for taking the money beyond pure and simple greed, he would tell her. He would say…*something, anything!* But silence—*guilty* silence—was Connor's only response.

"My aunt and uncle were right about you all along," she

whispered. Just as her grandfather had been right about her father. "They were right about everything."

At her words, Connor finally reacted. A cruel, calculating smile curved his mouth, and though Kelsey never would have thought green eyes could be cold, a chill touched her as his gaze iced over. He looked every inch the bad boy her aunt had warned her about less than two weeks ago. If only she'd listened.

"Congratulations, Kelsey. Your family must be so proud. Seems like you're a real Wilson after all."

Muttering a curse beneath his breath, Connor stalked over to the car. Despite the weight of restrained sobs pressing on her chest, Kelsey let him go. She might have lived her life under the misconception of her and her mom against the world, but Connor was just as deluded, believing it was always him against the Wilsons. This wasn't about her family; it was all on Connor and the secret he'd kept.

"Mama's right. You look like hell."

Ignoring his friend's voice, Connor didn't look away from the production of sliced limes, saltshaker and shot glass he'd filled with tequila. He'd taken over the small outdoor bar at the back of the Delgados' restaurant, where they'd installed patio seating for times when the weather was nice. In the middle of June, even at eight o'clock at night, it wasn't.

He barely noticed the oppressive heat, the way his T-shirt clung damply to his skin, or the bugs that hovered around the string of multicolored lights. After shaking out salt on the back of his hand like it was rocket science, he reached for the shot glass.

Catching Connor's wrist, Javy asked, "How many of those have you had?"

Connor glared at his friend from the corner of his eye. "Counting this one? Two."

His friend barked out a laugh that ended in a curse as he let go. "You're in worse shape than I thought. Wanna tell me what happened?"

Wincing at the strong burn of the tequila, Connor replied, "You said it yourself when I brought Kelsey here. Some people never learn."

"Sorry, man."

Javy didn't say more, and the two of them sat without speaking. Mariachi music, the din of the diners, and the occasional shout from the kitchen were the only sounds.

Finally Connor shoved the shot glass aside. "It was Emily all over again. I was stupid enough to think things would be different this time. But when push came to shove, she sided with her family."

He'd seen the disappointment in Kelsey's eyes. Forget all she'd said about how he'd changed. Forget all they'd shared. She'd been waiting all along for him to show his true colors, and she'd jumped back to her own side of the tracks the minute his character came into question.

You should have told her sooner, his conscience berated him. If she hadn't found out the truth from Charlene... But would that have made a difference? Or would Kelsey's reaction have been the same?

He should have known he and Kelsey didn't have any chance at a future. Her family's disapproval would eat like acid, weakening Kelsey's feelings until they were worn clean away. He was lucky it had happened sooner rather than later. He couldn't stand to live life with Kelsey the way he had with his mother, always knowing she had one foot out the door and it was only a matter of time before she left and didn't come back.

"Wanna tell me what happened?"

"Her aunt told her I took money to leave town, to leave Emily."

"And she believed it?" his friend demanded, slumping back against the bar stool in disbelief. "Just like that? With no proof, no—"

"The Wilsons had all the proof they needed. I took the ten thousand dollars."

Shock straightened his friend's spine. "You what? But why would you—" Realization slowly spread across his features, along with a large dose of guilt. Javy swore. "Is that where you got the money you gave my mother for the restaurant?"

"Like you said, this place means everything to Maria. I couldn't let her lose it." Eyeing his friend closely, Connor said, "You never asked where I got the money."

"No, I never did." Javy let out a deep breath, reached for the bottle of tequila and poured himself a shot. For a long moment he stared into the glass before looking Connor in the eye. "I didn't want to know."

"What? In case I'd broken the law? Done something illegal?" Connor pressed. Well, why wouldn't Javy believe that? It was just the kind of thing Connor McClane would have done.

Once.

"You think *I* didn't consider it?" Javy shot back. "It's *my* restaurant! My responsibility. My family—"

"Mine, too."

"Yeah," his friend agreed, frustration and anger draining away. "But I should have been the one to come up with a solution. And you shouldn't be the one paying for it now."

"I made my choice, and I would do the same thing again. In a heartbeat. So, tell me, you gonna drink that?" Connor asked, pointing at the shot glass sitting untouched between them.

Javy slid it across the bar without spilling a drop. "Look, man, I've been trying to pay you back for years. You've gotta let me—"

"Forget it. After all your family did for me, it was the least I could do."

"Then we'll draw something up. Make you a partner in the restaurant. And I'll talk to Kelsey."

Connor shook his head. "No."

"What do you mean 'no'?" Javy demanded. "Why don't you want to tell her the truth?"

"She knows the truth. I took the money."

"Oh, come on, Connor! That's not the whole truth, and you damn well know it! If you told her *why*, Kelsey would understand."

Yeah, maybe she would…this time. But what about the next time she had to choose between him and her family?

Chapter Eleven

It had been three days since Kelsey had seen Connor. Three heartbreaking, regret-filled, uneventful days.

At first she'd been too hurt to do more than curl up on her sofa and cry. But Kelsey never believed self-pity helped anyone, so by the second day she had thrown herself into working on her shop, finishing up the details that transformed the place from a simple suite into the office of her dreams.

She'd had photographs from previous weddings enlarged and wrapped in gilded frames: an elegant wedding cake with a single piece missing; a bridal bouquet in midair with ribbons streaming; a close-up of an unseen couple's hands, fingers entwined, showing off sparkling wedding rings.

She'd hung sheer curtains and floral drapes at the windows and found a bargain on a secondhand wicker coffee table, which displayed a crystal vase and fresh flowers from Lisa's shop. She'd brought a CD player from home to fill the air with soft, lilting music.

And if her heart broke a little more with every romantic touch she added, not once did Kelsey let that slow her down.

If she had any doubts about her hard work paying off, she'd received encouragement from an unlikely source. When Charlene called earlier, the talk had centered around the rehearsal dinner that night, but nearing the end of the conversation, Charlene had fallen silent before saying, "If I haven't told you before now, Kelsey, I appreciate all you've done for Emily's wedding. We never would have been able to pull this off so quickly if not for you."

After saying goodbye to her aunt, Kelsey hung up the phone and looked around her shop. She had everything she wanted: her shop was up and running, Emily's wedding was only days away and her hard work had gained her aunt's approval.

Congratulations, Kelsey. Your family must be so proud. Seems like you're a real Wilson after all.

Guilt wormed its way through her stomach, but Kelsey pushed it away with a burst of anger as she grabbed her purse and keys. She had no cause to feel guilty, she decided as she locked the front door behind her with a definitive twist of the key. None at all. Connor was the one who'd kept secrets, told lies of omission.

And yet maybe he had a reason. After all, hadn't he encouraged her to consider that her father might have had his reasons for taking the money? At the time, Kelsey thought Connor was talking only about her father. But could Connor have been talking about himself? Hoping that she might understand why he'd taken the ten thousand dollars? And what had she told him?

Nothing he could say would matter, nothing he could do would ever make up for taking the money.

Little wonder, then, that he hadn't bothered with explanations!

She had to talk to Connor, Kelsey decided as she climbed into her car and turned the air on full blast. If she expected him to tell her the truth, she owed it to him to listen without making judgments based on her own past.

Her phone rang, reminding Kelsey that she couldn't drop everything to go see Connor. After the rehearsal, she vowed as she pulled out her cell and flipped it open.

"Kelsey?"

Startled by the unexpected male voice, Kelsey asked, "Yes?"

"It's Javy Delgado. Connor's friend."

"Javy?" She couldn't imagine why he'd call her unless… "Is Connor okay? Has something happened?"

He paused long enough to strip a few years off Kelsey's life before he said, "Do you still care about him?"

"Of course I care about him! I—" *Love him,* Kelsey thought.

"I wasn't sure after the way you treated him."

"The way *I* treated *him?* I know you're Connor's friend, but—"

"Not as good a friend as he's been to me," he interrupted. "And that's why I called even though he asked me not to."

So Connor didn't want to talk to her. He didn't even want his friend talking to her. That didn't give her much hope. "Why wouldn't he want you to talk to me?"

"He doesn't want me to tell you the truth. He's afraid it won't matter. I hope he's wrong about that. About you. Just like you've been wrong about him." Javy sighed. "The money he took, the money your uncle paid him—Connor gave it to my family. He used it to save our restaurant."

* * *

"I have what you need."

Even though Connor had been waiting for the damn call for days, it took him a moment to recognize the voice on the other end. He pushed away from the small table in his hotel room, pent-up energy surging through his veins.

"Jake, it's about time you called. Tell me what you've got is good. I can't wait to get out of this town."

The words were the biggest lie he'd told in the past five minutes. Which was about how long it'd been since he'd last tried to convince himself Kelsey Wilson wasn't worth the effort, and he'd forget all about her the second he got back to California.

"Good? No, I wouldn't call it good," Jake ground out.

Jake sounded nothing like his normal self, and although he and Connor were close, their relationship didn't include a lot of heart-to-heart talks. Still, he had to say, "You sound like hell, man."

"Doesn't matter. I got the job done. I found what I was looking for."

A garbled voice over a loudspeaker sounded in the background. "I have to go. They're calling my flight. I'm e-mailing everything you need right now. Just do me one favor."

"What is it?"

"Use it to nail that guy."

"I will."

"Good. It's about time he gets what he deserves."

As Connor flipped the cell phone closed, his friend's voice rang in his ears. Connor supposed most people would say he was getting what he deserved, too. That Kelsey turning her back on him was just desserts for the way he had taken the money and left Emily years ago.

Except maybe Kelsey's anger wasn't about his relationship

with Emily or the past he couldn't change. Maybe it was about *their* relationship right now, and the truth he'd kept from her.

Okay, yeah, she'd told him nothing could excuse what her father had done when he'd taken money to leave her mother, but maybe if Connor had explained about the Delgados' restaurant…maybe if he'd told her about the money up front so she wouldn't have had to hear about it from *Charlene,* of all people…

Could he really blame Kelsey for reacting the way she had? Between the money her father had taken and the secrets her mother had kept, she had every right to be wary.

Sure, it would have been nice if she'd learned about the money and had still been willing to believe the best about him. But he hadn't placed all his faith in Kelsey, either. He'd been afraid to tell her about the money because he'd feared his reasons—his love and loyalty to the Delgados—wouldn't matter. He'd been holding on to his own past and his own fears that *he* wouldn't matter. He should have trusted her more than that.

His computer e-mail alert sounded, letting him know Jake's report had arrived. A few taps on the keyboard, and Connor understood his friend's anger. "Don't worry, Jake. We've nailed the guy."

After Javy's call, Kelsey longed to turn the car around to go immediately to Connor's hotel, but she couldn't skip the rehearsal, not as Emily's wedding coordinator and not as a member of the Wilson family.

When her phone rang again, her heart skipped a beat as Connor's number flashed across the screen. Still, she hesitated a split second. She wanted to be able to look into his eyes when she apologized. To see that he believed her when she told him she understood why he took the money and she wouldn't expect any less of him than the sacrifice he'd made for his friends.

But after the way she'd treated him, she offered a quick whisper of thanks that he wanted to talk to her at all. Flipping the cell open with one hand, she turned into a nearby parking lot. She immediately sucked in a quick breath, but Connor interrupted any greeting or apology she might have made. "Kelsey, it's Connor. Don't hang up."

She pressed the phone tighter to her ear as if that might somehow bring her closer to Connor. "I'm not. I won't."

"Look, I can explain about the money, I swear—"

"You don't have to—"

"But not now—"

"I talked to Javy—"

"Jake called—"

"What?"

"Jake called. He found Sophia, the Dunworthy's former maid."

Trying to switch gears while her thoughts were going one hundred miles at hour, Kelsey said, "Did he find out why she quit?"

"Turns out she was fired after Dunworthy Senior caught her and Junior together."

"Caught them?"

"From what Sophia says, he'd been hitting on her for months before she finally gave in. Only to lose her job because of it."

"But didn't you say she stopped working for the Dunworthys only a few months ago?" Kelsey asked, mentally going over the timing and coming to an unbelievable conclusion. "Todd and Emily started dating six months ago. They were *engaged* two months ago!"

"Yeah, they were. Evidently sleeping with the maid was the last straw. The way I figure it, Todd proposed to Emily as a way to try to win back his family's approval."

"I can't believe he would do that to Emily!" Anger for her

cousin's sake started to boil inside Kelsey, along with a disgust at the way Todd had smiled and charmed his way into her aunt and uncle's good graces.

"It gets worse."

"Worse! How can it possibly get any worse! Is there someone else?"

"In a way." Connor paused. "Sophia's pregnant."

"Preg— Are you sure the child is Todd's? Considering the money his family has, and after the way Sophia lost her job—"

"Jake is sure of it. He believes her, and I believe him. Judging from his family's reactions, I'd say that the Dunworthys believe it, too. The family doesn't want anything to do with Todd. That's why they aren't here for the wedding." He hesitated. "You were right, Kelsey, and I should have listened to you."

"It doesn't matter now. You did it, Connor. You found the proof you needed."

"Yeah, I've got everything I need," he agreed, his voice sounding hollow. "Look, Kelsey—"

She waited, her heart pounding for everything she wanted to hear, everything she wanted to say. But the silence stretched on, the words unspoken. Finally she said, "The wedding rehearsal is tonight. I'm already on my way to the chapel."

"I'm at the hotel now. I can be there in fifteen minutes."

"Fifteen minutes," Kelsey echoed quietly, before hanging up the phone.

She had fallen in love with the small chapel the first time she saw the cottage-style building, with its cobblestone walls and stained-glass windows. The close proximity to the hotel made it an ideal location. Right now Kelsey wished the chapel were a world away, anything to delay the inevitable end. Once Connor stopped the wedding, he'd have no reason to stick around…and if he did, Kelsey feared it wouldn't be for her.

* * *

Minutes later Kelsey stood inside the empty chapel. It was as beautiful now as when she'd first laid eyes on it. She'd immediately known the perfect arrangement of flowers and candles for alongside the carved pews. Just the right placement of the wedding party on the steps leading to the altar. Exactly where the video and photographer should stand to best capture the light streaming through the windows. She'd known all of that months before Emily had gotten engaged. When Emily had bowed so easily to her suggestions, Kelsey had set in motion the wedding of her own dreams.

She was as guilty as Charlene in pushing her own ideas on Emily. It was *her* dream location for the wedding and reception. All of *her* friends were working side by side to make the day memorable. Maybe if she hadn't been so focused on what she wanted, she would have stopped a long time ago to ask if any of it was what *Emily* wanted.

But she hadn't, and now all their dreams were going down the drain—the perfect wedding to make her business, Emily's dream of marrying the perfect man, Gordon and Charlene's perfect son-in-law. Only Connor had succeeded. He was stopping the wedding as he'd said he would.

He was a man of his word, a good man, and she should have trusted him. Kelsey knew how much it must have hurt when she turned her back on him, just as much as regret and heartache were hurting her now.

A door squeaked behind her, letting in a rush of summer air, and Kelsey took a deep breath. Turning to face her aunt and uncle, she said, "Aunt Charlene, Uncle Gordon, I need to talk to you…" Her voice trailed away when she saw Emily and Todd following a few steps behind.

The one time Kelsey had counted on them being late.

"What is it, Kelsey?" Gordon asked.

"I—" She'd hoped to have a chance to talk to her aunt and uncle alone, to prepare them for what Connor had discovered, so together they could find a way to tell Emily. "I was wondering if I could speak to the two of you in private."

She tried to make the suggestion as casually as possible, but there was nothing casual about the way Charlene's eyebrows arched toward her hairline. "What's wrong? Is it the flowers? The music?"

"Relax, Char," Gordon interjected. "Weren't you saying this morning that Kelsey has everything under control?"

Her uncle's reminder and confident smile sent a sick feeling through Kelsey's stomach. How was she supposed to tell them about Todd?

Taking note of her watching him, Todd crossed his arms over his chest, a not-so-subtle challenge in his expression. "You have something to say, Kelsey?"

She took a deep breath, but before she had chance to speak, the chapel door swung open again. She heard Connor's voice a second before he stepped through the doorway. "Actually, I'm the one with something to say."

"McClane! What are you doing here?" Gordon demanded, a lightning bolt of wrinkles cutting across his thunderous expression.

Todd draped a proprietary arm over Emily's shoulders. "I told Emily inviting him was a mistake. He's still in love with her, and he's probably here because he thinks he can stop the wedding."

"I'm not in love with Emily," Connor insisted.

I'm in love with Kelsey. His heart pounded out the words he never thought he'd say, but damned if he'd say them for the first time with the Wilsons and Todd Dunworthy as witnesses.

He felt the irresistible pull of Kelsey's gaze and he couldn't help meeting her gaze any more than he could resist the earth's gravity. *Not now. Not like this,* he mentally pleaded as he looked into her eyes, willing her to understand.

"Then maybe you'd like to explain *exactly* what is going on here?" Gordon repeated.

This was his moment, Connor thought. His chance to prove he was right and the Wilsons were wrong. Wrong about Todd. Wrong about him. But his triumph rang hollow. He didn't need the Wilsons' approval. He wasn't sure why he'd ever thought he did. All he needed was Kelsey. Her faith. Her trust. Had his past and his secret destroyed that?

"Connor?" Kelsey's voice called to him.

Dressed in a blue-green print dress that hugged her curves, her hair free to curl around her face, she looked absolutely beautiful—strong and vulnerable at the same time, and he couldn't look away.

Whatever Gordon and Charlene saw in his expression had them quickly closing ranks around Kelsey. Surrounded by her aunt and uncle, the Wilson misfit suddenly looked at home within the golden circle, and Connor was alone on the outside.

Tearing his gaze away, he focused on Gordon and pulled the information he'd printed from his back pocket. "Your golden boy has a history of using women. His blue-blood family, who mean so much to you, has completely cut him off after he got one of their maids pregnant." He slapped the pages into Gordon Wilson's reluctantly outstretched hand.

Charlene gasped, color leaching from her face, but doubt pulled Gordon's silver eyebrows together.

"Todd, what is Connor talking about?" Emily asked, her eyes wide as she stared at her fiancé.

"He's lying," Todd scoffed. But instead of trying to console Emily, he looked to Gordon with a can-you-believe-the-nerve-of-this-guy expression. "You know you can't trust anything McClane says."

"But you can trust me, Uncle Gordon," Kelsey insisted as she stepped closer.

"What do you know about this?" her uncle asked, taking a look at the papers.

"I know Connor is a good man." She spoke the words to her uncle, but her gaze never broke from Connor's. "He's here because he's worried about Emily. That information is true."

"Don't listen to her," Todd issued sharply. When Gordon's steely gaze cut his way, filled with the same distrust he'd pinned on Connor's seconds earlier, he quickly backed down. Relaxing his features into a more conciliatory expression, he said, "I'm afraid Kelsey has fallen for McClane's lies, but it's all a smear campaign to stop the wedding."

"How exactly is Connor McClane behind the significant amount of money your family paid this Sophia Pirelli?"

Todd's confident look faded, clay showing through the once-golden facade, but he still didn't give up. "My family let her go, so she went after us for money, claiming the kid she's carrying is mine. The money was a way to keep her quiet."

"A simple paternity test would have done the same thing and been *much* cheaper," Connor pointed out. "The kind of money your family paid… That's not hush money. It's guilt money."

Connor watched with satisfaction as the truth spread across Dunworthy's face and disgust and disappointment over the Wilsons'. Realization hit Emily last, leaving her pale and shaken as she looked from Todd to her parents. Finally her gaze locked with Connor's, and she burst into tears before rushing into his arms.

Seated in Gordon Wilson's study a half hour later, Connor nodded when the older man held up the bottle of scotch. Gordon poured two glasses, handed one to Connor and took a swallow from his own glass before claiming his spot behind the large mahogany desk.

Connor took a sip of his own scotch while he waited for the older man to speak.

"We owe you our thanks," Gordon said after a minute of silence. "When I think of my little girl married to that liar—"

At the chapel Gordon had made it clear to Dunworthy that the engagement was over and the wedding off, and that he'd live to regret it if he ever went near Emily again. Gordon and Charlene had reluctantly agreed to Emily's request that Connor drive her home after Charlene immediately tried to take charge. Emily had surprised them all, demanding some time alone. Connor thought—hoped—that she was learning to stand up for herself.

"I'm glad I found the proof I needed. I only wish I had found it sooner."

"And I wish you had come to me with your suspicions sooner."

Connor couldn't choke back a disbelieving laugh as he set the glass of scotch aside. "I'm not sure how you think that conversation would have played out, but I don't see you taking my side over your handpicked future son-in-law."

"I did not *handpick* Todd. You make it sound like some kind of arranged marriage."

"Wasn't it?"

A flush rising in his face, Gordon struggled for a calming breath. "Look, I'm trying to say that I appreciate what you've done. I don't know how we can repay you."

Pay him...

Shoving to his feet, Connor ground out, "I don't want your money."

"I wasn't offering any," Gordon shot back. He rose to glare at Connor from across the expanse of his desk.

The silent stalemate lasted several tense seconds before Gordon sighed. The tension drained from his body, leaving his shoulders a bit stooped and signs of age lining his face. "Sit back down." He gestured to the leather chair Connor had abandoned. "I've had enough drama for one night."

Hesitating, Connor glanced at the study doorway.

"Expecting someone?"

"I thought Kelsey would be here by now."

In the aftermath of the argument with Dunworthy and Emily's collapse into tears, Connor hadn't had a chance to talk to Kelsey. He'd expected her to head back to the Wilsons' with the rest of her family, where he'd been counting on the chance to talk to her.

But maybe he'd misunderstood what she'd said during the phone call. He should have known Javy wouldn't keep his mouth shut just because he'd told him to, but the more time Connor had to think, the more worried he became. Did her absence mean that Javy's explanation hadn't made a difference? That she still couldn't forgive Connor for the money he'd taken?

Gordon sucked in a deep breath as if preparing for a painful blow and admitted, "I was wrong about Todd."

They were the words Connor had come to Arizona to hear. The perfect lead-in to tell Gordon he hadn't been wrong just about Todd Dunworthy; he'd been wrong about Connor, too. But as he'd already figured out, it no longer mattered. Only Kelsey…

When he stayed silent, the older man repeated, "I was wrong about Todd. I realize now you came back to help Emily, and you have. But you still have some work to do to convince me you're good enough for this family."

"Good enough—" Connor's words broke off when he caught sight of what almost looked like respect gleaming in the older man's blue eyes. Shaking his head and wondering how a single sip of scotch could so seriously impair his judgment, he said, "You don't have to worry about me being good enough. Emily and I are friends. That's all."

As if the night hadn't already been surreal, Gordon Wilson circled his desk to clap a hand on Connor's shoulder. "Who said anything about Emily?" At Connor's surprised glance, Gordon said, "At the chapel I saw the way you were looking at my niece. You never looked at Emily like that. So don't you think it's time for you to go find Kelsey?"

Sitting in her car outside her shop, Kelsey stared at the freshly painted window. Weddings Amour scrolled across the glass in a flowing, curlicued font. The script matched the business cards and letterhead she'd had made—by the thousands, since it was cheaper to buy in bulk.

Kelsey sighed. She should have gone with the rest of her family—and Connor—back to her aunt and uncle's house. But this was Connor's moment. His moment of triumph…of success. And her moment of failure.

Not that Kelsey had expected her cousin to go through with the wedding once she realized Connor was right about Todd. Still, she felt sick with disappointment. She'd worked so hard on the wedding. Her friends had worked so hard! Lisa and Sara… Like her, they had been counting on Emily's wedding, and Kelsey hated letting them down. She dreaded calling them with the news, but that, too, was part of her job. Along with canceling the reservation at the chapel and the hotel reception, phoning all the guests, arranging for gifts to be returned. The mental list went on and on, with Kelsey's hopes and dreams sinking deeper beneath the crushing weight.

But it had to be done, and sitting in her car wouldn't accomplish any of it. Grabbing her purse off the passenger seat, she climbed from the car. As she opened the door to her shop, she tried—and failed miserably—to forget her excitement and gratitude only days earlier as her friends had pitched in to help decorate. The smell of peach potpourri drifted toward her the moment she stepped inside, but it was the memory of Connor's aftershave that filled her senses, playing games with her mind and her heart.

No matter how many unpleasant tasks lay ahead of her, Kelsey would gladly face the professional failure head-on as long as she could turn a blind eye to the personal heartbreak tearing her up inside.

"You should be happy for him," Kelsey whispered as she sank behind her desk and grabbed the box of tissues. She'd placed it there with the idea that a bride might be overcome with emotion and shed some tears of joy. She hadn't anticipated that she'd be sitting alone in her shop, tempted to put her head down and cry.

Connor had done what he'd set out to do. He'd listened to his gut, proved her aunt and uncle wrong, saved the damsel in distress. If life were a Hollywood movie, now would be the time for him to once again ride off into the sunset...this time with Emily.

He said he didn't love her.

But his lack of feeling for Emily wasn't exactly an undying declaration of love for Kelsey. Especially now that Todd was out of the picture and Emily was back in Connor's arms.

She heard the front door swing open and fought back a groan. The sign in the front window still read Closed, but she hadn't remembered to lock the door behind her. She couldn't afford to turn away potential clients, but she'd never felt less like talking about weddings with a head-over-heels-in-love couple.

Pasting on a smile, she pushed away from her desk and walked to the front of the shop. "Can I help..." her voice trailed away as she caught sight of Connor standing in the doorway "...*you?*"

"I hope so." He wore his sunglasses, as he had the first time Kelsey saw him, but the reflective shades didn't offer the protection they once had. She knew now, behind the polished lenses, his eyes were a vivid, vibrant green. Just as she could read the uncertainty behind his cocky smile and the nerves his confident stance—his legs braced wide and arms loose at his sides—couldn't disguise.

Her heart was pounding so hard, Kelsey half expected the shop's glass windows to shake from the force of the vibrations, but only her entire body trembled in reaction. "What are you doing here? I thought you were—"

"With Emily?" he filled in, taking a step farther into the shop.

"She *is* the reason you came back. To stop her from getting married."

"To stop her from getting married to the *wrong* man," he clarified. He took another step forward, and it was all Kelsey could do to hold her ground.

"Are you—" Kelsey licked dry lips and forced the words out, even though they scraped like sandpaper against her throat. "Are you the right man?"

"I like to think so. But not for Emily."

No longer holding her ground, Kelsey was frozen in place as Connor drew closer. His movements slow and deliberate, he stripped off his sunglasses and set them on the wicker coffee table amid the bowl of potpourri and a dozen bridal magazines. Without the glasses, she could see not only his gorgeous green eyes, but the vulnerability and doubt she'd caused with her lack of faith.

"I like to think I'm the right man for you."

Kelsey opened her mouth to agree he was the *only* man for her, but her voice broke on his name and she surprised them both by bursting into tears. Panic crossed Connor's features for a split second before he pulled her into his arms. "It's okay, sweetheart."

Clinging to the warm cotton of his T-shirt and breathing in the sea-breeze scent of his aftershave, Kelsey swallowed against the tears scraping her throat. "I am so sorry, Connor. I should have given you the chance to explain why you took the money. I should have known you would have a good reason, an *honorable* reason."

"I took an easy way out. Don't make it into something it wasn't."

"You were looking out for the Delgados—for your family. I shouldn't have expected anything less."

"And your family was looking out for Emily. I get that now," he said, running a comforting hand up and down her spine. "Besides, I think Gordon and I have an understanding, even if it is going to take a while for your aunt to get used to the idea."

Lifting her head from the comfort of Connor's chest, Kelsey asked, "Wh-what idea?"

"The idea of me and you." His eyes steadily searching her face, he added, "The idea of me loving you."

They were the words Kelsey longed to hear, words she'd thought she would never hear, and she had trouble believing her ears. Surely her imagination had to be playing tricks. Maybe this was nothing but a dream and she'd wake up in her bed—alone—any minute.

"Kelsey?" Connor prompted.

"In my dreams, you're wearing a tuxedo."

Glancing down at his usual jeans and a T-shirt, he swore beneath his breath. "Leave it me to mess this up. Your aunt told me—"

"No, you didn't mess up at all!" Kelsey insisted.

Connor wasn't some fantasy groom who could spout

poetry and had a picture-perfect smile. He wasn't perfect at all. He was real. Loyal and determined, and she loved everything about him—including his bad-boy past. A past that had shaped him into the good man he was now.

"It's perfect and— You talked to my aunt?"

"To your aunt and uncle both. When I asked them for permission to marry you."

Heart pounding crazily in her chest, Kelsey saved wondering about *that* conversation for another time. For now, she could only focus on one thing. "You want to marry me?"

"I love you, Kelsey. I want to spend the rest of my life with you."

"But what about what you said? About love and marriage being nothing but a lie?" she babbled over the voice in her head all but screaming, *Say yes, you idiot!*

"Yeah, well." Looking a little sheepish, he admitted, "I let my parents' relationship color the way I looked at marriage. Of course, my job didn't paint a rosy picture, either. It's one of the things that makes you perfect for me. I'll have you to remind me that sometimes happily-ever-after does come true. That is, if you say yes."

The screaming voice in her head could no longer be silenced, and Kelsey burst out, "Yes, of course. Yes! I love you, Connor. I think I loved you from the minute my aunt showed me your picture and told me it was my job to keep an eye on you. You've been on my mind and in my heart ever since."

The slow smile he gave her was vintage Connor McClane, but the love and tenderness and emotion Kelsey tasted in his kiss…that was brand-new. She clung to his shoulders, never wanting to let him go, and knowing now that she wouldn't have to. He wasn't a man of the moment; he was the man she would love forever.

As Connor slowly eased away, his breath still warming

her lips, his fingers still buried in her hair, he asked, "About your shop... How much damage will Emily canceling the wedding cause?"

It took a second for Kelsey to focus on anything outside the joined circle of their arms. "Well, um, people will understand her calling off the wedding when they find out about Todd. I don't think they'll hold *that* against me. But the chance to show all the guests an amazing wedding and the word-of-mouth publicity the ceremony and reception would have generated, that's a lost opportunity. For me and my friends. I hate disappointing them," she said, a small touch of sadness dimming her joy.

"What if you don't have to?" Connor asked, a familiar gleam in his eyes. The same look he'd had before he suggested they pair up as a team. The kind of look that told Kelsey he was about to offer some crazy solution that just might work.

"What do you mean?"

"I love you, Kelsey. And while I've never thought about it before, I suspect long engagements aren't my style. I want to marry you, and I have it on good authority that the best wedding coordinator in town has the perfect wedding already planned."

"You mean—*Emily's* wedding?" A startled laugh burst from her lips. "You cannot be serious!"

"No?"

"No! I mean, sure, everything's all planned, but it was done for Emily."

"Was it?" he challenged with a knowing lift to his eyebrows. "Was it Emily who insisted on hiring all her friends? Emily who ran around with a hundred lists to make sure every last detail was exactly the way she wanted it?"

How could Kelsey argue when Connor was right? Along the way, the lines had blurred and Kelsey had planned the kind of wedding she'd dreamed about as a starry-eyed, hope-filled little girl, not the kind of wedding she'd dreamed about as a professional career woman.

"Hey, it's just a thought," Connor said. "For all I care, we can go to Vegas or a justice of the peace—"

"Stop!" Kelsey protested in mock horror, even as excitement bubbled inside her like champagne. "A Vegas wedding? If word got out, my career would be over for sure!"

"But what about switching places with the bride? Think your career can withstand that scandal?"

"Well, as long as it's just this once…"

Her words ended in a laugh as Connor spun her around the room. "Oh, I can guarantee we'll only need to do this once," he vowed, love and commitment shining in his eyes.

"You'd really be okay with a big—and I mean, *big*— wedding, with all the Wilson family and friends in attendance?"

Lifting a hand, he traced a pattern on her cheek—the five-point star he'd confessed drove him crazy. But there was only tenderness in his touch as he knowingly said, "They're your friends and family, too."

Kelsey smiled. "You're right. They are." And now that she no longer felt she had to live up to her mother's motto of Wilson women against the world, she knew they would only grow even closer. "And soon they'll be yours, too," she teased with a laugh when Connor groaned. "Are you ready for that and all the happily-ever-after, love-of-a-lifetime, till-death-do-us-part stuff?"

Kelsey could read the answer in Connor's eyes—the promise of a future filled with happily-ever-after.

"With you?" he vowed. "I can't wait."

* * * * *

THE MAVERICK'S
CHRISTMAS
HOMECOMING

TERESA SOUTHWICK

To my brothers – Jim, Mike, Dan, and
Chris Boyle. I love you guys.
Merry Christmas!

Chapter One

When he'd come to Thunder Canyon five months ago look-ing for his biological parents, Shane Roarke never expected to find out that his father was in jail for stealing from the town. So far his mother's identity was still a mystery, but maybe that was for the best. Did he really want to meet the woman who'd shown the bad judgment to hook up with a criminal? And what did that say about his own DNA?

He'd arrived a city-slicker chef with a list of questions about who he was. Now he had half the answers and a lot to lose if anyone else found out. The information and what to do about it weighed heavy on his mind.

In June he'd taken the executive chef position at The Gallatin Room, the fine-dining restaurant at Thunder Can-yon Resort. With successful restaurants in L.A., New York and Seattle it had been a career step-down, but necessary for personal reasons. Now he was the definition of a man in conflict—part of him wished he'd never come, while the other part really liked this town.

"Oh, you're still here—"

Shane looked up from the glass of wine in front of him to the redhead who'd just walked into his kitchen. Gianna Garrison was a waitress and part-time bartender on his staff. In the big cities where he'd worked his name had been linked to models, actresses and celebrities, but he'd never seen a more beautiful woman than the one in front of him now, looking like a deer caught in headlights.

"I'm still here," he agreed.

"Like the captain of a ship."

"The last to leave." He smiled.

Gianna was wearing the black slacks and long-sleeved white shirt all the waitresses wore but it looked better on her. The tucked-in blouse accentuated breasts, not too big or too small, which only left just right. Her waist was trim, her legs slim and that curly, shoulder-length red hair always got his attention even from across a crowded room. Close-up was even better.

"Sorry to bother you." She started to back out of the room. "I'll just be going."

She wasn't bothering him. In fact she'd done him a favor. Shane realized the last thing he wanted was to be alone with his dark thoughts.

"Wait. We were a waitress short tonight." Pretty lame stating the obvious, but he'd just switched mental gears and it was the best he could come up with to stop her from leaving.

"Yeah, Bonnie has a bad cold. Coughing, sneezing and breathing germs on that party of ski executives from Switzerland seemed counterproductive to the goal."

Shane nodded. "Convincing them that Thunder Canyon

has the snow, slopes and service to make it a winter vacation destination for Europeans."

"Right. And have you seen any of those movies on the flu pandemic and how disease spreads? We wouldn't want Thunder Canyon identified as ground zero by the Centers for Disease Control. The Swiss would probably hear about it."

"That wouldn't be good. Bonnie was wise to call herself off."

The humor sparkling in her eyes made them almost turquoise. He hadn't noticed that before, which wasn't surprising. Between work, looking for his birth parents and feeling guilty about it on account of his real parents who loved him unconditionally, he'd been a little preoccupied. Now she was only a couple of feet away and he noticed that her eyes were wide and beautiful, like the Caribbean Ocean. If he wasn't careful, he could drown in them.

"So one waitress less means you worked twice as hard," he said.

She lifted one shoulder in a no-big-deal gesture. "I just moved faster, smiled more and dazzled them with the Garrison wit, hoping they had no idea it was taking just a little longer to get their orders delivered. The complimentary bottle of wine you sent over to the table didn't hurt, either. By the way, they raved about the food and seemed surprised. You'd think the invention of Swiss cheese entitled them to culinary domination of the universe."

"I'm guessing you didn't say that to them."

"No." She grinned.

"The head of the delegation complimented me on the food and service before they left. He promised me maximum stars, diamonds, happy faces, thumbs-up, however they designate their rating. Without you I couldn't have pulled that off, Gianna."

Her wit wasn't the only thing about her that dazzled. When she smiled, her face lit up like the town square decorated for Christmas. "I'm flattered you noticed."

"I make it my business to notice. It crossed my mind to come out to help serve, but I couldn't get away."

"Cooking is what you do. Delivering what you cook is my job."

"There's more to it than that. Even when the food is good it's not always easy to keep the customer happy. But you make it look easy. Tonight you did a fantastic job."

"I just handled it," she said modestly.

"You always do. You're one of my best waitresses. Thanks for all your hard work. I appreciate it very much."

"No problem. It's what you pay me for but it's nice to hear you say it." Gianna backed up a little more. "I'll just be going now."

No, he thought. Her dazzle kept the dark away and he wasn't ready for it to come back yet. He wanted her to stay. Saying that straight out might make her nervous, think he was hitting on her. That wasn't his intention. The pleasure of her company was his only goal; the question was how to achieve it.

All Shane could come up with was a delaying tactic. "Did you want something?"

"Why do you ask?"

"You came in the kitchen."

"Oh, that. It's just, you know—" Her shrug did interesting things to her breasts. "Tonight's special looked and smelled amazing so…"

"You're hungry." Of course. What other reason would she have for coming here when her shift was over. After a mental forehead slap, he said, "Doing the work of two people didn't leave time for a dinner break."

"It's my own fault. I missed the staff meal before service started. I'll just grab something on the way home."

"No." He stood and walked over to her. "The least I can do is feed you. And there will be a glass of wine involved."

"Don't make a mess on my account. The dishwasher and prep crew already cleaned up."

"But I'm the boss. I have a nice Pino Grigio already uncorked and it pairs well with the spinach and crab ravioli." He led her to the stool he'd just vacated then pressed gently on her shoulders, urging her to sit. The slight touch ignited a need in his belly and the instinct to pull her against him was unexpectedly powerful.

It was his business to notice workflow in the restaurant and he had. Just because it wasn't his job to be attracted to someone working the flow didn't make the attraction any less real. But he still wasn't hitting on her. This was just a gesture. A happy staff didn't quit and contented workers kept things running smoothly. Training a new waitress was time consuming and costly.

"I was going to have something myself. Please join me."

"Okay, then. Thanks." She rested her heel on the metal rung of the stool and crossed one leg over the other.

The movement was graceful, sexy, and it was an effort to pull his gaze away. On his first day at The Gallatin Room, Gianna Garrison had caught his eye, but for professional and personal reasons he'd resisted the impulse to act on the temptation. Until tonight.

Just before Thanksgiving he'd received conclusive proof that Arthur Swinton, the most hated man in Thunder Canyon, was his biological father. The information had weighed on him over the last couple of days and he was low on willpower. That was the best explanation he could come up with for this lapse in professional judgment. It was time to do his chef thing and take his mind off other things.

While he worked assembling plates, warming food, pouring wine, Gianna chattered away. He let her, liking the sound of her voice, the warm honey with just a hint of gravel. Then something she said tapped into his dark mood again.

"The Thanksgiving dinner you prepared last week for military families was amazing. Everyone in town is talking about it. Angie Anderson and Forrest Traub told me how thrilled the families were, how special and appreciated they felt for their loved ones' sacrifices."

He'd been more preoccupied than usual since that night. People had looked at him like he walked on water and he felt like a fraud. How could he be a walk on water type when Arthur Swinton was his biological father? The man had been convicted and sent to jail for embezzling public funds. Not only that, he'd perpetrated a conspiracy to ruin the Traubs, one of the most prominent families in town. If there was someone who didn't hate Swinton, Shane hadn't met them yet.

Gianna smiled at him. "They said it really helped because of missing their loved ones overseas so much, especially around the holidays."

"I know something about missing family," Shane whispered.

"What's that?" she asked.

He slid hot food onto two plates, then looked over his shoulder. "You're missing something if you don't eat this while it's hot."

"It looks wonderful and smells even better."

He put the two steaming plates on the stainless-steel countertop, then pulled up another stool and sat at a right angle to her. "Dig in."

"Okay." After she did, her gaze met his. "This is sinfully good. I don't even want to think about the calories."

"It's a little-known fact that when you do the work of two people calories don't count."

"Thank goodness. Because this tastes even better than it smells and it smells very fattening." She licked a drop of white wine sauce from her lower lip.

For a second, Shane thought he was going to choke on his own food. The look on her face was the most unconsciously erotic thing he'd ever seen.

A sip of wine kick-started his brain again and he managed to say, "I'm glad you like it."

The words almost made him wince. He had a reputation for being charming but tonight he wouldn't win any awards for witty repartee. It was a miracle that she didn't make an excuse and run for the hills.

"How do you like Thunder Canyon?" She took another bite and chewed.

"Actually, I love it."

"Seriously?" She stared at him as if he had two heads.

"Cross my heart. If it's not at the top of my list, it's very close."

"But you've been all over the world, no?"

"Yes."

"Where did you go to culinary school?"

"CIA."

"Does that mean you could tell me but you'd have to kill me?" The corners of her full mouth turned up.

"The Culinary Institute of America. Hyde Park, New York. About two hours from Manhattan."

"Convenient."

He nodded. "I got a degree in Culinary Arts management because I always wanted to open my own restaurant. But I went to Paris to learn baking and pastry arts. I've traveled to Italy and Greece to experience various cooking techniques like liquid nitrogen chilling, and experience different cuisines. CIA also has a campus in Napa where they specialize in a different area of food preparation and wine pairing."

"So you've got a well-rounded culinary education."

"Yes. My parents are well-to-do. I didn't have to worry about student loans and could indulge every aspect of my curiosity about business trends and cutting-edge themes in the food-service industry."

Her eyes filled with a little wonder and a lot of envy. "That sounds so exciting. How can the town square in Thunder Canyon, Montana, compare to the Eiffel Tower? The Louvre? The—everything—of France?"

"Paris is something to see. No question. But it's not fair to compare places in the world. The favorites just speak to your heart."

"And Thunder Canyon speaks to yours?"

"Yes." It was true, but she probably thought he was a poetic idiot.

He didn't understand his instant connection to this small town in Montana so far off the beaten path. It crossed his mind that the answer could be in his DNA, but that didn't make sense. Not really. Arthur Swinton was a greedy opportunist who only cared about himself and that had nothing to do with the place that filled up his son's soul.

"I'd like to hear about you," he said. "Are you from here?"

"Born and raised. My mother, father, sister and her family are still here." She put the fork down on her empty plate. "After getting a business degree, I went to New York."

"And?" He poured a little more wine in her glass. "What did you do there?"

"I opened a travel agency."

"So, you took a bite out of the Big Apple." Brave girl. He was impressed. His first business venture had been close to home in L.A. She jumped right into the big time. "Apparently I'm not the only one who's been all over the world."

She lifted her shoulder, a noncommittal gesture. "I was pretty busy getting the company off the ground."

"It's a lot of work, but incredibly exciting turning a dream into reality."

"Speaking of reality," she said, clearly intending to change the subject. "You certainly turned your appearance on that reality cooking show—*If You Can't Stand the Heat*—into culinary success."

"I was lucky."

"Oh, please. If you call talent, charm, good looks and a clever way with a wooden spoon luck, then I'm the Duchess of Cambridge."

He laughed. "So you think I'm not hard on the eyes?"

"Are you kidding? You're gorgeous." She looked a little surprised that the words had come out of her mouth. "But, for the record, really? That was your takeaway from what I just said?"

It was better than wondering where his looks had come from. "Beauty is as beauty does."

"What does that even mean?"

"You got me. Do you have someone running the travel agency?" Which begged another question. "Why are you here in Thunder Canyon?"

"Personal reasons." The sparkle disappeared from her eyes and she frowned before quickly adding, "I'm only here for a little while. Not much longer."

Shane understood personal reasons and the reluctance to talk about them so he didn't ask further. "Are you anxious to get back?"

"Who wouldn't be?" She took the stem of her wineglass and turned it. "There's a rumor that your contract here at The Gallatin Room is only six months."

"Yeah." He'd thought that would give him enough time to find out what he wanted to know, but he'd only found out half of it. Now the question was whether or not to keep going and what to do with the information he already had. "So it seems both of us have a time limit here in town."

It was weird, probably part of the pathetic, poetic streak kicking in tonight, but talking to her had made him realize that since coming here he'd been a loner. And suddenly he was lonely. But the last thing he needed in his life was a long-term romantic complication. She was beautiful, funny and smart. He wanted to see her again and she wasn't staying in town. That made her the perfect woman.

"I guess you could say I have a time limit here," she agreed.

"Then we shouldn't waste any time. Have dinner with me."

She looked at his empty plate. "Didn't we just do that?"

"Sassy." He grinned and added that to her list of attributes. "I meant something away from work. Monday is the only day the restaurant is closed and every place within a twenty-mile radius is, too. How about I cook for you at my condo? It's not far, here on the resort grounds."

"I know. But—"

"It's just a home-cooked meal. How does six-thirty sound?"

"I don't know—" Her expression said she was struggling with an answer.

That's when he gave her the grin that reality show enthusiasts had called his secret ingredient. "Doing double-duty tonight deserves a double thank-you."

"When you put it that way… How can I say no?"

"Good. I look forward to it."

Gianna had been looking forward to this evening since Shane Roarke had invited her to dinner. She took the elevator to the third floor of the building on Thunder Canyon

Resort grounds where his condo was located. After five months of nursing a crush on him she could hardly believe he'd finally asked her out. Or in. It felt surreal, with a dash of guilt for good measure.

What she'd told him about herself in New York was a little sketchy. She hadn't so much taken a bite out of the Big Apple as been chewed up and spit out by it. Apartments were small and expensive. The travel agency didn't survive, a casualty of the internet, with more people looking online, eliminating the middle man. And the recession. And she'd seen no point in sharing with Shane that she kept falling into the trap of choosing men who had no intention of committing.

She hadn't lied about personal reasons bringing her back to Thunder Canyon. It was the elaborating part she'd left out. Being unemployed and penniless *were* personal and her primary motivation in coming home. A job at The Gallatin Room was getting her back on her feet. She had a small apartment above the new store Real Vintage Cowboy and the only car she could afford was a fifteen-year-old clunker that she hoped would hold together because she couldn't afford a new one. Sharing all of that with a sexy, sophisticated, successful man like Shane Roarke wasn't high on her list of things to do.

After stepping out of the elevator she walked down the thick, soft carpeted hall to the corner apartment, the one with the best views.

"Here goes nothing," she whispered, knocking on the door. Moments later Shane was there. "Hi."

"You're very punctual." He stepped back and pulled the door wider. "Come in. Let me take your things."

She slipped out of her long, black quilted coat and handed it to him along with her purse, then followed as he walked into the living room. It was stunning. The wood entryway opened to a plush beige carpet, white overstuffed sofa, glass tables and twelve-foot windows on two sides. High ceilings held recessed lighting and the expanse of warm, wheat-colored walls were covered with artwork that looked like it cost more than she made in a year.

"Wow." Gianna had been nervous before but now her nerves got a shot of adrenaline. "This is beautiful."

"I think so, too." Shane's gaze was firmly locked on her face.

Her heart stuttered and skidded. His eyes weren't the color of sapphires or tanzanite, more like blue diamonds, an unusual shade for a stone that could cut glass. Or turn icy. Right this second his gaze was all heat and intensity.

"I've never seen you in a dress before. Green is your color," he said. "It looks beautiful with your hair."

Outside snow blanketed the ground; it was December in Montana, after all. But this moment had been worth the cold blast of air up her skirt during the walk from her clunker of a car. She'd given tonight's outfit a lot of thought and decided he saw her in black pants most of the time. Tonight she wanted him to see her in something different, see her in a different way. The approval on his face as he glanced at her legs told her it was mission accomplished.

"'Tis the season for green."

She'd never seen him out of work clothes, either. The blue shirt with long sleeves rolled up suited his dark hair and brought out his eyes, she thought. Designer jeans fit his long legs and spectacular butt as if made especially for him. For all she knew they might have been.

"Would you like some chardonnay?"

"Only if it pairs well with what you're cooking," she answered.

"It does."

She followed him to the right and into the kitchen with

state-of-the-art, stainless-steel refrigerator, dishwasher and cooktop. It was most likely top-of-the-line, not that she was an expert or anything. Ambience she knew something about and his table was set for two with matching silverware, china and crystal. Flowers and candles, too. The ambience had date written all over it.

"Good to know. Because I'm sure the food police would have something to say about nonpaired wine."

"I kind of am the food police."

"That makes one of us." She took the glass of wine and sipped. Not too sweet, not too dry. It was delicious. The man knew his wine and from what she'd been able to dig up on him, he knew his women, too. She was really out of her depth. "And it's kind of a relief that you know your stuff. Because you know that thing about actors wanting to direct? I don't think it works the same in food service. Waitresses don't want to be chefs. At least I don't. Boiling water I can do. Ham sandwich, I'm your girl. Anything fancy? Call someone else. Call you. You're famous in food circles for—"

He stopped the babbling with a finger on her lips. "Call me for what now?"

"You tell me." She took a bigger sip of wine and nearly drained the glass.

"You're nervous." He was a master of understatement.

"I didn't think it showed."

"You'd be wrong." He smiled then pulled chicken, vegetables and other ingredients from the refrigerator—all obviously prepared in advance—and stuff from a cupboard beside the stove, probably seasoning or spices. Or both. He took out a well-used frying pan and placed it on the stove. "But I'm pretty sure I understand."

"What?"

"Your nerves. Thanks to reality TV, exposure about everything from bachelors to swamp people, we chefs have earned something of a reputation."

"What kind of reputation would that be?" She finished her wine, then set the glass on the granite countertop.

"Bad boy." The devil was in the blue-eyed glance he tossed over his shoulder. "And I'm no exception."

"Oh?"

"Think about it. What I do involves sharp knives and fire. Very primitive." As he lit the burner on the stove, the fire popped as the gas ignited.

"I see what you mean." And how.

"On top of that I invited you to my place for dinner. But let me assure you that I have no intention of making you the dessert course."

"That never crossed my mind." But why not? she wanted to ask. It hadn't been on her mind until just now. Well, maybe a little bit when she saw him in that shirt and those jeans because that kicked up a curiosity about what he'd look like *without* them.

He glanced over his shoulder again while tossing in the air over the hot flame everything he'd put in that frying pan. "In spite of what you may have heard, I'm not that type. I like to get to know a woman."

If he really got to know her, chances were pretty good that he'd lose interest. And speaking of types, she probably wasn't his. She wasn't a businesswoman now, more the still-trying-to-find-herself variety.

"So, what are you doing for Christmas?" Changing the subject had seemed like a great idea until those words came out of her mouth. Would he think she was hinting for an invitation? The filter between her brain and mouth was either pickled or fried. Or both.

"My holiday plans are actually still up in the air," he said. There was an edge to his voice that demanded another subject change so she did. "What are you making for dinner tonight?"

"It's something I'm experimenting with."

"So I'm the guinea pig?"

"Think of yourself as quality control." He grabbed the two plates off the table, then slid half the contents of the frying pan onto each one and set them on a part of the cooktop that looked like a warming area. Then he put liquids into the sauté pan and stirred, fully concentrating on the job. After spooning what looked to her like rice from a sauce pan, he said, "Dinner is served." He glanced at her. "More wine?"

"Please."

After filling her glass and setting plates on the table, he held the chair for her to sit down. If a guy had ever done that before, she couldn't remember. Then he sat across from her. The star lilies and baby's breath with candles in crystal holders on either side gave it all a romantic feel.

Suddenly her appetite disappeared, but she was here to eat and figured she'd better do that. She took a bite of the chicken and the flavors exploded on her tongue. "Oh, my. That is so good. It's like a party in my mouth and I thought only chocolate could do that."

"I'm glad you like it."

"What's in here?" She chewed and swallowed. "Can you tell me or would you have to kill me?" At his wicked look she shrugged. "Bad-boy rep, remember? CIA. Fire. Sharp stuff."

"I'll make an exception for you." He picked through the food on his plate. "Chicken. Asparagus. Mushrooms."

"This looks like rice, but the consistency is wrong."

"It's risotto."

"Ah." The gleam in his eyes started pressure in the vicinity of her chest and she hoped it was nothing more than pre-indigestion.

They ate in silence for several moments before he said, "So how was growing up in Thunder Canyon?"

"It was great, but keep in mind that I didn't know anything else." She put down her fork and wiped her mouth on the cloth napkin. "The pace is slower here and kids don't need to grow up so fast."

"It's slower for grown-ups, too."

Gianna nodded. "Not everyone is happy about that. Maintaining the balance between status quo and development has been and probably still is a source of conflict here in town."

That started a discussion about everything from population growth to weather to large holiday groups scheduled at The Gallatin Room the following week. It was interesting to hear about restaurant management, all that went into a successful business besides just preparing food. Time seemed to both fly and stand still.

Finally Shane looked at her. "Would you like more?"

"No, thanks." Her plate was empty and she was so full. "I guess guinea *pig* was the correct term."

"I don't think so. Clearly you enjoyed the food. In some cultures burping is high praise and a compliment to the chef."

"And in some parts of the country it's a competitive sport."

He laughed, then stood and picked up his plate. She followed his lead and carried hers into the kitchen, where he took it from her and set them in the sink.

"What can I do to help?" she asked.

"Nothing. You're a guest and I have a housekeeper. Why don't we sit in the living room?"

"Okay." But when they walked in, the tall windows were filled with the sight of lights winking in the valley below and she walked over. "That is a pretty amazing view."

"I think so. Would you like to see it from the balcony?"

"Oh, yes." She might never have another chance.

Shane opened the French door, then let her precede him outside. The cold air hit her immediately, but when they moved to the railing and he stood beside her, his nearness and the warmth from his body took the edge off.

"Oh, Shane, this is so stunning. Is it always like this?"

"Well, the mountains are permanent and don't change."

"Duh."

He grinned down at her, then pointed. "See the spotlights over there? That's the slopes and they're always illuminated for night skiing. But in the last few days since Thanksgiving, people are putting up Christmas decorations so everything is even more beautiful."

She glanced at him. "There's something in your voice, an awe, a respect, as if you're whispering in church."

"It kind of feels that way," he admitted. "There's a sense of being in the presence of God. The natural beauty here..."

"Speaks to your heart?"

"Yeah. I do love it. Especially on a night like this."

She looked up at the moon and stars. "I don't know what's more beautiful, the sky above or valley below."

"Maybe it isn't either one."

There was a raspy quality in his voice that made her look at him. Their gazes locked and his sparked with heat and intensity. His shoulders were wide, his arms strong. Suddenly she was filled with an ache to feel them around her. She *wanted* to be dessert.

As if Shane could read her thoughts, his mouth inched toward hers and again time stood still.

Until it didn't.

One second passed with him just standing there, then two before he backed away even though the expression in his eyes hadn't changed. "It's getting late. I should probably see you to your car."

Gianna blinked up at him wondering what just happened. She wasn't so out of practice that she didn't know when a man was going to kiss her, and Shane had been about to do that. Something had changed his mind, but darned if she knew what it was. But clearly she'd been dismissed for unknown reasons.

"It is getting late. I'll just get my coat."

Shane got her things, and if the atmosphere at the restaurant was as awkward as the walk down to where she'd parked her wreck of a car, work was going to be even less fun than being one waitress short while feeding the Swiss delegation.

Chapter Two

Three days later Gianna was stewing in The Gallatin Room
kitchen, which was ironically appropriate. It had been three
nights since Shane had made dinner for her at his place.
Three nights of seeing him at the restaurant where they
both worked and he hadn't said a word to her—not about
work, not even about things other than work. Even a hello,
how are you, wasn't in his repertoire. In fact he was going
out of his way to ignore her and she didn't understand why.

She also didn't have time to think about it. Waitresses
were hurrying in and out of the kitchen with orders and
busboys handled trays of dirty dishes, utensils and glass-
ware. It was busy and noisy and she was putting together a
basket of bread for the order she'd just taken. Shane stood
by the stove concentrating on sautéing seafood over a hot
flame. She stared at his back and felt like a lovelorn idiot,
but she couldn't help it. When he was in a room her gaze
automatically searched him out.

He, on the other hand, didn't even look at her when he wasn't cooking. Disappointment trickled through her and she felt incredibly stupid. Maybe she'd been hoping the third time was the charm—or third day post dinner he would finally break his silence.

No such luck.

Bonnie Reid pushed through the swinging doors separating the kitchen areas from the dining room. Her friend did break the silence.

"Wow, it's busy in there tonight, G."

"Tell me about it."

Gianna rested her hip against the stainless-steel worktable. She'd become good friends with the other waitress, a petite brunette with a pixie haircut and big brown eyes. They'd both been hired at about the same time and bonded over the good, the bad and the awe of their celebrity boss. The other night she'd thought he actually was awesome, but now? Not so much.

"I'm very glad you're over your cold and back to work." Gianna dragged her gaze away from Shane and looked at her friend.

There was sympathy in those brown eyes. "If I hadn't been too sick to crawl out of bed, I'd have been here. It must have been awful by yourself, serving that big party of Swiss businessmen."

"I managed." And now she heard Shane's voice in her head, telling her she always did. The words still made her glow, but she was doing her best to get over it.

"I hated leaving you shorthanded. You must have run your legs off."

Gianna looked down. "Nope. Still there. Cellulite, the extra two and a half pounds on each thigh and all."

"Yeah. Right." Bonnie grinned. "You're fit and fine, my friend."

"Not that anyone would notice." She glanced at Shane who still had his back to her.

"Did something happen while I was out sick?" Bonnie's tone was sharp with curiosity, but fortunately their boss was too far away to hear in the noisy kitchen. "What did I miss?"

"Nothing." That was the very sad truth, Gianna thought.

"I'm getting a vibe, G." Her friend glanced at Shane, then back. "Did Roarke the magnificent do something? Say something?"

"Said something, did absolutely nothing." Darn him. Gianna picked up the silver basket in which she'd artfully arranged a variety of herb-covered rolls and cheese cracker bread, then started to walk back to the dining room.

"Uh-uh. Not so fast." Bonnie shook her head. "You can't drop a cryptic comment like that and not elaborate. It violates every rule of friendship and is just wrong on so many levels."

"Really, nothing happened. I guess I just got the signals wrong. Wouldn't be the first time."

"You're trying to deflect me. Even if this is about all the time you wasted on too many men who have an allergy to commitment, it's not going to work. Did Roarke make a move on you?" Bonnie's eyes filled with indignant anger and she looked a little dangerous.

"Nothing like that." Gianna pulled her farther around the corner to make sure they couldn't be overheard even with the sizzle of cooking and banging of utensils. "We had a moment."

"What kind of moment?"

"When you called in sick I missed the staff dinner then did double duty and was starved at the end of my shift. I thought everyone had left and came in here to grab something to eat. Shane wasn't gone."

"You were alone with him? Did he try something?"

If only… "No. He made me food and gave me wine."

"To lower your resistance? I'll take him apart—"

"Stand down." Gianna couldn't help smiling at the thought of her tiny friend taking on tall, muscular, masculine Shane Roarke. "He asked me to dinner on Monday, at his place."

"How was it? His place, I mean. I've got more questions, but first things first."

"All I can say is rich people really are different."

"That good, huh?"

"The artwork. Furniture. Spacious floor plan and high ceilings. The lighting." She sighed at the memory. "And don't even get me started on the view."

"So he caught you in his web, or lair, or whatever, then pounced?" The fierce look was back.

"That's just it. He took me out on the balcony to show me the view of the mountains, the valley getting ready for Christmas. There was a moon and stars and lights stretching across said valley."

"Romantic with a capital *R*."

"Romantic with every letter capitalized and the whole word italicized." She sighed. "I was sure he was leaning in for a kiss and then—"

"What?"

"Nothing. He all but told me to go home, except he did it in his Roarke-like way. 'I'll see you to your car,'" she quoted.

"Bastard." Bonnie shook her head. "Gentleman bastard."

"I know." Gianna peeked at him again, busily sautéing something. "That was Monday night and he hasn't acknowledged me here at work since. I'm not sure which is worse. The let's-just-be-friends speech I'm used to or this cold shoulder."

Bonnie's frown went from fierce to puzzled. "I prefer the speech. At least you know where you stand."

Maybe that was her chronic problem, Gianna thought. If the relationship status wasn't spelled out, she went straight to hope. That meant she'd made no progress in breaking her bad habit of being a hopelessly romantic fool who wasted time on the wrong men.

"Anyway, that's the scoop." She angled her head toward the swinging doors. "I have to get back to work."

"Me, too." Bonnie gave her a sympathetic look. "I've got your back."

"Thanks."

Gianna put her shoulder to one of the kitchen's swinging doors, then opened it and walked into the quiet and elegant world where special service was the key to success. A beautiful setting during any season, The Gallatin Room was even more so, decorated for Christmas. A ten-foot tree with white lights, red, green and gold ornaments and shiny garland stood in the corner. All the tables had red poinsettias in the center on white linen tablecloths.

Now that Gianna had seen the view from Roarke's penthouse apartment, she knew this restaurant wasn't the most romantic place in Thunder Canyon, but she'd put it very high on the list. This was a weeknight but the place was nearly full, and that happened when you served the best food in town. That's what the two women at her table were after. Gianna had chatted them up while delivering menus and found out they were having a girls' long ski weekend.

She put the breadbasket on the table, then looked at the beautiful blonde and equally pretty brunette, both in their late twenties. "Have you decided or do you need another few minutes to look over the menu?"

"Too many tempting choices," the blonde said. "Do you know what you're having, Miranda?"

"I should go with salmon." She frowned, but her face didn't move. "But Shane's filet with that yummy sauce is to die for."

Gianna didn't recognize either woman and she had a good memory for faces. "So you've been here before?"

"Not here." Miranda shook her head. "But I've been to Roarke's in New York. Daisy and I do a winter ski trip every year and have been talking about trying the slopes in Thunder Canyon for a while. But we always decided on somewhere easier to get to that had restaurants with a reputation. Then we heard Shane Roarke was the chef here."

"He definitely is."

"Miranda says this menu is different from the one in New York," Daisy said.

"He's tailored his signature recipes specifically for The Gallatin Room. I can tell you that every one is fantastic."

"What's your favorite?" Daisy asked.

The chicken he'd made for her at his place. But that wasn't for public consumption yet. She smiled at the two women and hoped it was friendly because that's not the way she felt.

"It would be easier to tell you what's not my favorite. If you're in the mood for beef, the filet is excellent, practically melts in your mouth. And the sauce only enhances the flavor. I'm not a fan of lamb, but people who are rave about it here. The stuffed, grilled salmon is wonderful. And a little lighter, which would leave room for dessert."

"Tell me the chocolate, sky-high cake I had in New York is a choice."

"I don't know if it's the same, but there is one that will tempt you to lick crumbs off the plate."

"That does it." Miranda smiled in rapture. "Shane's desserts are the best. I'll have the salmon. Tell me about The Gallatin salad."

"It's greens with avocado, tomato and goat cheese in a very delicate dressing. So delicious you won't believe it's good for you."

"You talked me into it."

"Make it two," Daisy said. "And a bottle of the Napa Valley Chardonnay."

"Excellent choice." Gianna smiled at the two women. "On behalf of Thunder Canyon Resort and The Gallatin Room, I'll do everything possible to give you a perfect dining experience. If there's anything you'd like, just let me know. It's our goal to make this your ski vacation destination every year."

"Shane being the chef here made the difference in our choice this time," Miranda said.

"He's really something." Just what, Gianna wasn't sure.

"Is he by any chance here now?" Miranda asked.

"Every night."

"I'd love to say hello again." She looked at her friend. "And Daisy has never met him."

"I've certainly heard a lot about him," the blonde said. "Do you think he would come by the table?"

"I can ask." And that would give her an excuse to talk to him. "Although he's pretty busy."

"I understand. I'm not sure he'll remember me, but my name is Miranda Baldwin."

Gianna walked back to the kitchen and her heart was pounding at the thought of talking to Shane. Maybe it would break the ice. Give him a chance to say he'd just been too busy, up to his eyeballs in alligators what with Christmas parties and planning menu changes to shake things up with new dishes in January. It was a slim hope, but hope was something and a hard habit for her to break.

She went through the swinging doors into the kitchen and

saw Shane directing the sous-chef. He shifted to the cutting board on the stainless-steel table across from the stove.

"Can I talk to you?" she asked, moving beside him.

"What is it?" There was no anger or irritation in his tone. In fact there was no emotion at all, which was worse.

If only the world would open now and swallow her whole. Gianna felt her hope balloon deflate. His non-reaction made it unlikely that he would mention their dinner or anything about spending time with her. It was like nothing had ever happened. Situational amnesia. If he wasn't going to bring up the subject, neither would she.

"There's a Miranda Baldwin in the dining room who says she knows you from New York and wondered if she could say hello. I told her you might be too busy—"

"I can do that." He started toward the door and said over his shoulder, "Thanks."

"For nothing," she whispered under her breath.

In every serious relationship she'd had, the guy had strung her along and when it was time to fish or cut bait, she got cut. But Shane couldn't get away from her fast enough, which was a first. Apparently bad dating karma had followed her from New York and mutated.

Clearly he wasn't into her. Since she wasn't into wasting any more time, that should make her happy. Somehow it didn't.

Shane pushed through the double doors into the dining room and left Gianna behind in the kitchen with the hurt he'd caused evident in her eyes. She probably thought he was crazy and who could blame her? Certainly not him. He'd invited her to dinner, then stood with her looking at the night sky and wanting to kiss her more than he wanted his next breath. Every day since then he'd fought the urge to tug her into a secluded corner and see if her lips tasted as good as he imagined. There were times he wished he was as good with words as he was with food and this was one of those times.

He liked her, really liked her. The attraction was stronger than he'd felt in a very long time, maybe ever. He was still coming to terms with the truth about his father's identity so, for Gianna's sake, he wouldn't start something that he could really mess up. Cooling things was for the best and judging by the look on her face when he'd left the kitchen so abruptly, he'd done an exceptional job of it. The depth of emotion he'd seen proved that even though it would be temporary, she could get hurt and he wouldn't do that to her.

Looking over the bustling dining room a sense of satisfaction came over him. Revenue was up from this time a year ago and if that was because of him, he was glad. If the information about who his father was got out, that could keep him from drawing a local crowd, so he planned to enjoy this while it lasted.

Shane knew which tables Gianna had tonight and headed in that direction, then recognized Miranda. She was a beautiful brunette and asking her out had crossed his mind while he'd been in New York. Now she seemed ordinary compared to a certain redhead he wished he'd met while they'd both been there.

He stopped at the table. "Miranda, it's good to see you again."

"Shane." She smiled. "You remember me."

He didn't feel especially charming, but it was said that trait was what had won the reality cooking show and launched his career. He dug deep for it now.

"Of course I remember." He bent and kissed her cheek. "A woman like you is unforgettable."

"Then maybe it was my phone number you forgot. You never called me." Her eyes both teased and chastised.

"Believe me when I say that you're better off." It was easy to look sincere when telling the truth. "And there was no one else."

"Contrary to what the tabloids said."

"Because, of course, we all know that every word the rag sheets print is the honest truth." He grinned to take any sting out of that statement. "Truly, I had no personal life. It was all about opening Roarke's and keeping it open. I was practically working around the clock."

The blonde at the table cleared her throat, demanding her share of attention. "Hello, Mr. Roarke. I'm Daisy Tucker."

"It's a pleasure to meet you, Miss Tucker."

"Daisy. And the pleasure is all mine."

He didn't miss the flirty expression, the seductive tone, and there was a time when he'd have flirted back. Partly to fuel his reputation and get his name in the paper. Although he'd just mocked the tabloids, any marketing expert would tell you that even bad publicity is good, anything that gets your name out there. He was no expert, but knew the information that his biological father was a criminal would take bad publicity to a different, not good level.

"Shane," Miranda said, "after opening restaurants in so many big cities here in the States, I expected you to conquer London, Paris and Rome. It was really a surprise to find you were the executive chef here in off-the-beaten-path Montana."

"I had my reasons."

"But Thunder Canyon? What's the appeal?"

He spotted Gianna's bright hair across the room, just as she was coming out of the kitchen and a knot of need tightened in his belly. She wasn't the reason he'd taken the job but just being able to watch her was definitely appealing. The not-touching mandate was his cross to bear.

"That's difficult to put into words." He looked from one

beautiful face to the other. "I simply fell in love with Thunder Canyon."

"In that case," Miranda said, "maybe you could suggest some places to visit while we're here."

It was a hint for him to show them around and not a very subtle one. Even if he had the time, he wasn't interested. "It was actually love at first sight with Thunder Canyon. I haven't been here that long and haven't had time to explore much."

"Then maybe old friends from out of town is a good excuse to see the local highlights."

"As tempting as that would be, my schedule is really tight. I've got parties every weekend and several during the week until Christmas." It wouldn't be politically correct to tell her he wasn't interested. "You're better off checking with the concierge at your hotel."

"I'm very disappointed," she said.

"Me, too. You know what they say. This is the most wonderful time of the year."

"Ho, ho, ho." Miranda pretended to pout.

"It was wonderful to see you. Happy holidays." He kissed each woman on the cheek. "Duty calls."

He turned away and scanned the room, something he did frequently. It was a chance to make sure service was impeccable, that people were relaxed and happy. How he'd love to get a helping of happy for himself. Speaking of relaxed... He spotted a romantic booth for two and recognized the romantic couple occupying it.

Angie Anderson and Forrest Traub radiated love like a convection oven. That spontaneous thought begged the question: Where in the world had this recent poetic streak come from and when would he shake it?

He headed in their direction and when the two of them stopped gazing into each other's eyes for a moment, they spotted him. After weaving his way through the tables, he slid into the booth against the wall on the seat across from them. The other side had plenty of room for several more members of a platoon since Angie sat so close to Forrest, there was no space between them.

"Hi," he said to them.

"Merry Christmas." Angie was a college student and a volunteer at the town's teen hangout called ROOTS. In her early twenties, her shiny brown hair and dark eyes made her look like a teenager herself. "How are you, Shane?"

"Okay. What's up with you guys?"

"I'm counting the days until classes are over and it's vacation."

"Even with studying for finals she finds time to help the kids out with the holiday letters for soldiers." Forrest put his hand on hers, resting on his forearm. His hair was still military short and he had the muscular fitness and bearing of a soldier, even with the limp from a wound he'd sustained while deployed overseas.

"It makes me feel good to volunteer. What goes around comes around and I want this Christmas to be perfect for everyone," she said. "It's our first together."

"It's already perfect for me. Santa came early this year. I've already got everything I want." The depth of his feelings for this woman was right there in Forrest's eyes.

"Me, too." Angie leaned her head against his shoulder for a moment.

Shane felt like an intruder at the same time he envied them. *People Magazine*'s most eligible bachelor chef had never felt quite so alone before and he was sure that information would surprise the inquiring minds that wanted to know. It wasn't so much about this young couple as it was wanting to touch Gianna and not being able to. Denying himself the pleasure of kissing her under the stars seemed more than stupid when he looked at these two.

"Actually, Shane, I'm really glad they let you out of the kitchen tonight."

"It happens every once in a while." He grinned at them.

"We were hoping to see you," she said.

"Planning to hit me up to cater your wedding reception?" he teased.

"Maybe." Forrest laughed. "Seriously, we wanted to thank you again for all your hard work cooking such a fantastic Thanksgiving dinner for military families. Every single person said the only thing better would have been to have their son or daughter, father or mother home."

"He's right, Shane." Angie glanced at the man she loved, then back. "We can't thank you enough for what you did. You're the best."

"Not really."

He knew it was meant as a compliment but he wondered whether or not they'd feel the same if the truth came out that he was the son of Thunder Canyon's very own crook. He'd hurt Gianna tonight by brushing her off. If she knew the truth about him, she'd probably feel as if she'd dodged a bullet. Except for a strategically placed *R,* crook and cook were the same.

The burden of his father's identity still weighed heavily on him. For now it was his secret and keeping it to himself was the only way to control the flow of information. That meant not getting close to anyone.

Or kissing anyone. Immediately he thought of Gianna. Even her name sounded beautiful and exotic. The fire in her hair and freckles on her nose were a contradiction that tempted him every time he saw her.

And he saw her almost every day.

Chapter Three

At work on Friday Gianna was crabby and it was all Shane Roarke's fault. She'd seen him the previous night smiling his charming smile at the brunette and blonde, chatting them up as if they were the only two women in the world. That wouldn't bother her so much if he hadn't given her wine and food in this very kitchen and smiled his charming smile at *her*. Then he invited her to his place for a test run of a new recipe where he charmed her some more.

She loved being charmed but wished he'd kept it to himself because all of that attention had fed into her crush, the one now starved into submission because without fuel there was nowhere to go. She was doing her best to not think about him but that resolve was challenged earlier tonight when she'd seen him brooding. It was the same expression she'd noticed the night of her double duty, although what the handsome, successful, famous Shane Roarke had to brood about was beyond her.

She pushed through the double doors and he looked up from whatever he was sautéing. And that was the thing. He never looked up when he was cooking. The building could be on fire and he'd still focus on the food. A girl noticed stuff like that when she had a crush on a guy. For the last three days he'd ignored her unless special requests from a customer made a conversation necessary to get the order just right. Tonight Shane had looked at her every time she was around, no matter what he was doing.

Gianna ignored him as she put in the order for two salads with romaine lettuce and the most delicious croutons on the planet. The prep cook would toss it with Shane's special dressing, then add freshly grated Parmesan cheese. She picked up the wide, shallow bowls and set them on a tray. As she went to the double doors to go check on her tables a feeling prickled between her shoulder blades. Glancing over her shoulder she saw a hot and hungry expression in Shane's gaze. There was something up with him and she was involved.

As soon as she came back for the salads, she'd find out what was going on with him. After leaving the kitchen she walked through the maze of tables and stopped.

She knew these two, had seen them in here individually. Both were somewhere in their mid-fifties, and widowed. She saw they still had salad on the plates in front of them on the white, cloth-covered table. "Still working on those salads, Mrs. Bausch, Mr. Walters."

He was a big bear of a man with the calloused hands and leathery skin of someone who worked outdoors. "When are you going to call me Ben, little lady?"

"As soon as you stop calling me little lady. My name is Gianna."

"You got it, Gianna." There was a twinkle in his blue eyes.

"I haven't seen you two in here together before." She was curious.

"This is a blind date." Kay Bausch was characteristically direct. "Austin Anderson set us up. You probably know he's an engineer at Traub Oil Montana where I'm the secretary to the company president."

"Ethan?"

"Points to you, Gianna. That's the right Traub. And there are so many of them that sometimes it's hard to keep the names straight." She looked across the table at her blind date. "Ben has known him since he was a teenager. Austin, not Ethan."

"He's a good kid," Ben answered, his mouth curving upward to form a smile in his rugged face. "He was kind of lost after his mom died in a car accident when he was only a teenager. Turned out he just needed a steady hand."

"That's nice at any age." Kay's voice was a little wistful. "And now he's got his wife, Rose, Ethan's sister. They'll have their first anniversary on Christmas."

Gianna felt a twist in her chest that signaled a severe case of envy. She'd seen the couple in here for dinner and the glow of their love still radiated. It's what she had once hoped to find and now had all but given up on. Still, feeling sorry for herself was something she tried to do on her own time.

"Apparently Austin is quite the romantic."

"How do you mean?" Ben asked her, but the expression on his face said he knew where she was going with this.

"He fixed you two up. How's that working for you?" She looked at Kay, then Ben.

His grin was full of the devil. "So far I'm not sorry I put on this coat and tie."

"You look very handsome. And uncomfortable," Kay added. "The effort has not gone unnoticed or unappreciated."

"Good to know. Because it has to be said that there's no way to beat a comfortable pair of jeans."

"I couldn't agree more," his date said.

"Something in common already." Gianna nodded approvingly. "Can I get you anything else right now?"

"Nope. Got everything so far." Ben was looking at his companion, who smiled like a young girl.

"Okay, then. *Bon appétit.* You two enjoy."

Again weaving through the dining-room tables filled with people, she made her way back to the kitchen. Shane looked up as he was arranging shrimp in wine sauce over rice on two plates. Bonnie grabbed them, threw a nod of support, then left with the plates on a tray. She was alone with the chef and it was a sign, Gianna thought.

She marched over to where he stood in front of the stove and not all the heat she felt was from the cooking. "What's going on?"

"Excuse me?"

"Are you going to have me fired?" She folded her arms over her chest as she met his gaze. She didn't know where the question came from but her luck had been so bad it was best to get the worst case scenario out of the way first.

The surprise in his eyes was genuine. "What?"

"You keep staring at me and it's not a happy look. You're going to tell the manager to fire me, aren't you?"

"No."

She waited for an explanation, but it didn't come. "Then it's my imagination that you keep watching me?"

"No."

Again nothing further. He was the most frustrating, exasperating man she'd ever met and she had a talent for meeting exasperating men who frustrated her. "Then I don't get it. I don't understand what you want from me."

A muscle jerked in his jaw and his mouth pulled tight. He

was fighting some internal battle and it was anyone's guess which way things would go. Finally he all but growled, "Then I'll show you what I want."

He took her hand and tugged her down the short hallway and into the large, walk-in pantry where nonperishable, industrial-size supplies were kept. Canned goods, jars of olive oil, flour, sugar and spices were all stored in here on floor-to-ceiling metal shelves. Shane shut the door, closing them in.

"You know," Gianna said, her tone a little breathless, "you didn't need to bring me in here to yell at me. Public chastisement is okay. I can take it. Just tell me what—"

The words were cut off when he pulled her into his arms. "This is what I want to tell you."

And then he kissed her. His lips were soft, gentle, but there was nothing gentle about the effect on her senses. It felt as if a wave of emotions crashed over her and she was floating because her legs went weak. The scent of his spicy cologne mixed with the pleasant smell of oil, spices and fire. Blood pounded in her ears and the feel of her breasts crushed against his hard chest was simply scrumptious.

He cupped the back of her head in his palm to make the meeting of their mouths more firm, and the harsh sounds of his breathing combined with hers and filled the storeroom. She would have been happy to stay like that forever, but Shane pulled away. It could have been an hour or a nanosecond because time in this alternate sensuous universe was hard to quantify.

She blinked up at him and said, "Does that mean I'm not in trouble?"

"That's what it means." He leaned his forehead against hers. "I've been wanting to do that all week."

"Really?" Since her thoughts were smoking hot along with the rest of her, Gianna had trouble pulling herself together to call him on the fact that he'd ignored her most of the week. Somehow she managed. "You have a very odd way of showing it."

"You're right." He blew out a long breath and backed up a step, as if he needed distance to think clearly, too. "My behavior is inexcusable. Mixed signals."

"You think?"

"I don't think. It's a fact I've been running hot and cold."

"I noticed." After that kiss she definitely preferred hot, but given his recent mercurial moods it was best not to have expectations.

"Personal stuff in the workplace is a rocky road to go down. It's tricky to navigate. I was trying to take the high road, do the right thing. I'd never want to make you uncomfortable."

"You could have used your words," she pointed out, "said something. I know a thing or two about being conflicted regarding…personal stuff."

"Oh?"

"Yes." She lifted her chin a little self-consciously. In for a penny, in for a pound. Might as well use her words. Never let it be said she was a do-as-I-say-not-as-I-do person. "I understand how sometimes it's easy starting down a path, but the right time to turn off it can be tricky."

"Very Zen of you."

"Okay. Here's an example. I dated a divorce attorney for over two years before we had 'the talk' where I found out he never planned to commit. Should have turned off that path a lot sooner."

"I see."

"Then there was the accountant who saw too many joint checking accounts split, not necessarily down the middle, by messy breakups. There's a year and a half I'll never get back."

"Okay."

"The college professor who said up front that he was a loner. That one is my own fault."

"You've definitely had a conflict or two."

"Yes, I have. As with my job, I can handle it. You don't need to protect me. I'm a big girl."

"I noticed." His eyes were like twin blue flames with the heat turned up high.

"Don't hold back on my account."

"It won't happen again," he agreed.

"That was a very nice kiss."

One of his dark eyebrows lifted. "Nice?"

"Location, location, location." She looked around the storeroom and wrinkled her nose. "For the record? The balcony of your apartment has much better mojo."

"Everyone's a critic." He grinned. "Let me make it up to you."

"How?" She should be ashamed at being so easy, but darned if she could manage that.

"Meet me here after work and I'll show you."

"Okay." Way too easy. The end of her shift wouldn't come fast enough.

All it took was Shane's kiss to make her crabby mood disappear. Probably not smart, but definitely the truth.

After making sure everything in the kitchen was shut down and squared away to his satisfaction, Shane turned off the lights. Only the security ones were left on, making the interior dim. The frenzied chaos so much a part of the food-service business he loved was over for the night and eerie quiet took its place.

He waited for Gianna to get her coat and purse then meet him here. Keyed up from work, he paced while he waited. Part of him hoped she wouldn't show because he didn't need more complications in his life. Mostly he couldn't wait to see her. Fighting the temptation to kiss her had given him a lot of time to imagine what it would be like, but the actual touching of lips had been everything he'd expected and more.

What he hadn't expected was her straightforward sass and steadfast spunk. The way she'd challenged him about how peculiarly he'd been acting had surprised and charmed him in equal parts. He hadn't been surprised in a good way since the first time he'd seen Thunder Canyon.

With his parents' blessing, he'd hired a private investigator to find his biological parents and the guy had narrowed the search to this small town in nowhere, Montana. His restless need to connect the dots about himself had been stronger than his aversion to packing himself off to that small town. The surprise was his instant connection to the rugged beauty of the mountains and trees, being drawn in by the friendliness of the people.

He'd grown up in Los Angeles, for God's sake, where freeways, traffic and smog ruled. He wasn't a mountains-and-trees kind of guy. At least he'd never thought so. But the connection he'd felt had only gotten stronger in the five months he'd been here. That was already a lot to lose, and now there was Gianna.

That saying—the apple doesn't fall far from the tree—was a saying for a reason. And the sins of the father... The rest of the words eluded him but when sins were involved it couldn't be good. Something deep inside Shane rebelled at the thought of Gianna knowing who his father was.

The kitchen door opened and there she was, wearing a navy blue knit hat pulled over her red hair with curls peeking out by her collar. She had a matching scarf tied loosely around her neck and the ends dangled down the front of her coat. When she smiled, the beauty and warmth melted the place inside him that had started to freeze over.

"So," she said, "just how are you going to make it up to me?"

He wasn't quite sure, but when the moment was right, he'd know. "You'll just have to wait and see. Let's go."

"Okay."

There was a rear restaurant exit and she followed him past the pantry where he'd kissed her earlier and the big industrial-size refrigerator and freezer. He opened the outside door and let her precede him, then closed and locked it after them. The area was illuminated by floodlights at the corners of the building.

"That air feels so good," she said, drawing in a deep breath. "So clean and clear and cold."

"How do you feel about a midnight walk in the moonlight?"

Her blue eyes sparkled with merriment. "I feel like that's a promising start to making things up to me."

The restaurant employees parked here in the back and since they were the last two to leave, Shane figured the only car in the lot, an older model compact, belonged to Gianna.

He looked down at her. "You don't come out here alone after your shift, do you?"

"No. It usually works out that several of us leave together."

"Good." But tonight he would make sure she was safe. "Are you okay with leaving your car here?"

"Because someone might break in? I should be so lucky it would get stolen." She laughed and the cheerful sound magnified in the still night.

"Is it giving you trouble?"

"Trouble is too nice a word for what it gives me. Every

day I cross my fingers and say a little prayer that it will start and get me to work."

"If it ever doesn't, let me know. I can't afford to lose my best waitress."

"You might regret that offer," she warned.

They walked across the lot to the sidewalk that bordered an open grassy area. At least there used to be grass. He'd seen the green before winter rolled in and dumped a couple feet of snow. During the day the temperature was warm enough that the existing snow melted a little, wetting the walkway. The sun had gone down hours ago and it was freezing, making the sidewalk slippery. On top of that, a light snow had started to fall.

"So much for walking in the moonlight," she teased.

"I'm trying to feel bad about that. But for a boy from Southern California, the excitement of snow still hasn't worn off."

"All that sunshine and good weather must really get old."

"It's a dirty job, but someone has to live there."

She laughed. "Still, there's something to be said for Montana."

"Preaching to the choir, Gianna," he said. "And it's not just the landscape or weather. The people in this town are good, friendly, salt-of-the-earth types."

"I know what you mean." Her tone was serious and sincere. "I met people in New York. Still have a good friend there who used to be my roommate. But the city is so big and impersonal. There's an intimacy here that's unique."

"Everyone has made me feel really welcome, embraced me as one of them."

"Thunder Canyon spirit," she agreed. "But they can turn on you in a heartbeat if you let them down."

That's what worried him. But it probably wouldn't happen tonight. He made a deliberate decision to change the subject. "So, we had a pretty good crowd in the restaurant."

"We did." She glanced up at him. "Were you mad enough to spit when that man sent his steak back twice because it wasn't mooing on the plate?"

He shrugged. "People pay a lot of money for service and food. It's my job to make sure they're satisfied."

"For every persnickety person, there's a Ben Walters and Kay Bausch."

"I don't think I know them." When she slipped a little on the sidewalk, he took her hand and slid it through the bend of his elbow. It wasn't an excuse to stay connected. Not really. He was responsible for keeping her safe.

"Ben is in his mid-fifties, a rancher born and raised here. He's a widower. Kay is a transplant from Midland, Texas. She works for Ethan Traub and came with him when he opened Traub Oil Montana. She's a widow." She sighed. "I was their waitress tonight."

"Nice people?"

"Very. And the best part is they were on a blind date. Austin Anderson fixed them up."

"Angie's brother?"

"Yeah. It's really sweet. And I can't help wondering if the two of them were meant to meet and find a second chance at happiness. Romantic drivel, I know."

"Not here. To me it sounds like just another day in Thunder Canyon."

"On the surface that's sort of a cynical remark," she observed. "But digging deeper, I can see the compliment buried in the words."

They were walking by one of the resort's Christmas displays with lighted reindeer and Santa Claus in his sleigh. Animal heads moved back and forth and Rudolph's nose was bright red. The big guy with the white beard moved his hand in a wave. Old-fashioned, ornate streetlamps lined the walkways and the buildings were outlined with white lights.

"This is really a magical place, especially this time of year," he said.

"I know." There was a wistful tone to her voice as she stared at the decorations. "What is Santa bringing you this year? A Rolls Royce? 3-D TV with state-of-the-art sound system? Really expensive toys?"

Material things he had. And more money than he knew what to do with had paid for a private investigator to dig up information. But it was what money couldn't buy that made him feel so empty.

"I actually haven't written my letter to Santa yet."

"I see." She stared at the jolly fat man turning his head and waving. "Have you been naughty? Or nice?"

"Good question."

The mischief in her eyes turned his thoughts to other things and he looked at her mouth. The memory of those full lips so soft and giving convinced him that this was the right moment to make it up to her for not taking advantage of the romantic mojo on his balcony.

Shane lowered his head for a kiss, just the barest touch. He tasted strawberry lip gloss and snowflakes, the sexiest combination he could imagine. And he could imagine quite a bit. His heart rate kicked up and his breathing went right along with it. Gianna's did, too, judging by the white clouds billowing between them.

No part of their bodies were touching and she must have found that as dissatisfying as he did. She lifted her arms and put them around his neck, but when she moved, her foot slid on the sidewalk and she started to fall.

Shane shifted to catch her but couldn't get traction on the icy surface and knew both of them were going down. He managed to shift his body and take the brunt of the fall on his back in the snow while Gianna landed on top of him with a startled squeal. Then she started laughing.

He looked into her face so close to his and said, "That couldn't have gone better if I'd planned it." If he had, he'd have planned to be somewhere warm and for her not to have so many clothes on.

"So, you think it will be that easy to have your way with me?"

"A guy can hope."

Apparently the innocent expression he put on his face wasn't convincing because she chose that moment to rub a handful of snow over his cheeks.

He sucked in a breath. "God, that's cold."

"I'm so sorry." Clearly it was a lie because she did it again.

"Payback isn't pretty." He reached out to grab some snow, then lifted the collar of her coat to shove it down her back.

She shrieked again, then gave him a look. "You're so going down for that."

"I'm already down."

"Then we need to take this battle to a new level." She jumped up and staggered back a few feet, then bent down. When she straightened, she hurled a snowball with each hand, but missed him.

Shane rolled to the side and grabbed her legs, tackling her. "I learned to do that when I played football."

He looked down at her laughing face and thoughts of war and retaliation retreated. She was so beautiful he couldn't stop himself from touching his mouth to hers. Definitely going on Santa's naughty list this year.

He deepened the kiss and caught her moan of pleasure in his mouth as she slid her arms around his neck. They were already down so he didn't have to worry about losing his balance this time. That was fortunate because she felt so good in his arms, he had his doubts about maintaining emotional equilibrium.

He cupped her cold cheek in his palm and traced the outline of her lips with his tongue. She opened her mouth, inviting him inside, and he instantly complied. The touch sent liquid heat rolling through him and he groaned with the need to feel her bare skin next to his. The sensual haze lasted just until he felt her shiver.

He lifted his head and saw her shaking. "You're freezing."

"N-not yet. But c-close."

Shane levered himself up and to his feet, then reached a hand down to help her stand. In the streetlamp he could see that her coat and pants were wet. "You're soaked."

Her teeth were chattering, but she managed to say, "Th-thanks for the news flash."

"You need to get into something dry."

"I need to go h-home."

"My place is closer." The next words just popped out, but as soon as they did he knew how much he wanted it. "You could stay tonight."

"Oh, Shane—"

"Just a thought. No harm, no foul."

"I'd really like to." There was need in her eyes, but it was quickly followed by doubt. "But…"

There always was, he thought.

"I have an early day tomorrow," she said. "It's probably best if I go home. Rain check?"

"You got it." He'd never meant a promise more. "Now let's get you back to your car."

He hurried her to the parking lot and took her keys when her hand was shaking too badly to fit it in the lock. When she was in the driver's seat, she managed to get the key in the ignition and turn it. There was a clicking noise but the engine didn't turn over.

Shane met her gaze. "Did you forget to say your prayer this morning?"

"That's not the problem. This clunker is officially beyond the power of prayer. It's dead."

Chapter Four

Trouble wasn't a four-letter word but it should be when talking about her car, Gianna thought. On top of that, she was freezing. Rolling around in the snow with Shane had seemed like a good idea at the time, but not so much now.

He leaned into the open door and met her gaze. "I think the battery's dead."

"Of course it is because that's just how I roll—or in this case, don't roll. And dead is good."

"How do you figure?"

"It won't feel a thing when I beat it with a baseball bat."

"That won't help the situation."

"Says who? Hitting something would make me feel a lot better." She got out of the car, shivering when the cold air wrapped around her, then dug in her purse for her cell. "It's late. There's no way I can deal with this now. No garage will be open, so I'll call a cab to take me home."

He put a hand on her arm. "Not while I'm around."

"I don't want to inconvenience you."

If she'd taken him up on the offer to spend the night it would be very convenient, but she was pretty sure sleeping wasn't on his mind when he'd offered. It's not that she wasn't interested in sex, but this was too soon.

"I'm happy to help you out, Gianna. And I won't take no for an answer." He plucked his cell phone from the case on his belt, pushed some buttons and hit Send. A moment later he said, "Rob? Shane Roarke. Can you do me a favor? Bring my car down to the restaurant, the parking lot out back." Rob said something that made Shane grin. "Yes, a very nice Christmas bonus. Happy holidays." He put the phone back in the case. "The car will be here in a few minutes."

Gianna stared at him. "It must be amazing to be you."

"And who am I?" The words were meant to be glib and lighthearted but a slight tension in his voice made him sound a little lost.

Shane Roarke, celebrity chef and wealthy eligible bachelor? Lost? That was just nuts. She must have hit her head when they were wrestling in the snow. Or her brain was frozen. He was rich, famous, handsome. Women threw themselves at him. If this was a dream, she didn't want to wake up. And he was driving her home.

To her minuscule apartment above Real Vintage Cowboy. Yikes.

After seeing his place she was a little embarrassed to bring him inside hers. But that was just silly. After he pulled into the parking lot behind the store she'd just hop out and say thanks. There was no reason for him to know that her apartment was so small she could stand in the living room with a feather duster, turn once in a circle, and the place would be clean.

Headlights rounded the corner of the building then slowly

moved closer to them, finally stopping. A young man got out of the BMW SUV. "Here you go, Mr. Roarke."

"Thanks, Rob. Can I give you a lift back to the lobby?"

"No, thanks. The fresh air feels good, clears my head. That will help me stay awake and it's a long night ahead."

"Okay. Thanks again."

"Have a nice evening." He lifted his hand in a wave, then headed back the way he'd come.

"And just what is Rob's job title?"

"Concierge." He walked her to the passenger side of the car and opened the door. "One advantage of condo living is around-the-clock service."

"Does Rob's skill set lean toward replacing a dead car battery?" she wondered out loud.

"If you were one of my neighbors it would be his job to figure out how to do that."

"Rich people really are different."

He closed her door, walked around the front of the car and passed through the headlights, then slid in on the driver's side. "Where to?"

"Real Vintage Cowboy. It's on Main Street near the Wander-On Inn and Second Chances Thrift Store."

"I've been there. Isn't it closed this time of night?" He glanced over at her, questions and something else swirling in his eyes before he put the car in gear and drove out of the parking lot.

"My apartment is above the store. So you've been there?"

"Yes." Again his voice was tense. "I actually went shopping there. And for the record, rich people aren't different. I put my pants on one leg at a time."

"Okay. If you want to split hairs, I'll play," she said. "Have you ever been in the grocery store?"

"Here in Thunder Canyon, or ever?"

"Let's get wild. Here in town."

"No. I leave a list for the housekeeper."

"Of course you do." While he drove, she settled into the soft leather of the heated seat. Because Rob was Rob, he'd turned on the heater and the interior was warm in addition to feeling like a spaceship with all the dials and doohickeys on the dashboard. "I want a housekeeper and a Rob," she said wistfully.

"With great privilege comes great responsibility."

"Confucius says…" She glanced over at him, the rugged profile, the strong jaw and stubborn chin. There was something so appealing in his smile, a quality that tugged at her, made her want to touch him. "Would you translate that for me?"

"It means that money is a reward for hard work. A benefit of having it is being able to hire help so that when you're not working, complete relaxation is possible."

"So, getting into the milieu of my car, your batteries are recharged and you can go to work with renewed energy and make gobs more money."

There was irony in the glance he slid to her. "Something like that."

From where she was sitting, the rich were different, no matter what he said. That didn't mean their houses wouldn't burn in a wind-driven brush fire or their cars didn't break down. But when bad stuff happened there were no worries about the cost of fixing it. And you could hire someone to change a battery or flat without batting an eye.

Gianna would bet everything she had that the actresses, models and famous-for-being-famous women he dated wouldn't be fretting about how they were getting to work in order to earn the money to buy a car battery for a clunker. It was too depressing so she decided to change the subject.

"So, when you went to Real Vintage Cowboy, what were you shopping for?"

"I'm building a house."

That wasn't really an answer. "I heard a rumor to that effect. People talk about you."

"Because I'm different?"

"No. Because you're a celebrity." When the car stopped at a stoplight under a streetlamp, she saw the muscle in his jaw tighten. "So, because of the house-building rumor, I was a little surprised when you said you might not be renewing your contract at The Gallatin Room."

"All I did was confirm that it's only six months."

"Again you're splitting hairs." Now that she thought about it, he was pretty stingy with personal information. "If you're not staying, why build a house?"

"I found a great piece of land that was begging to be developed."

So, of course, he bought it and did just that, even though his time in Thunder Canyon might be limited. So much for his assertion that the rich weren't different. She thought about using what he'd just told her as evidence to support her statement, but decided against it. He would never understand.

The windshield wipers rhythmically brushed snow away as the car glided smoothly along nearly deserted Main Street. When they drove past The Hitching Post, Gianna tensed. The new and improved bar and restaurant had been thoroughly overhauled by new owner, Jason Traub. He'd managed to respect its Montana history and maintain the Western style while using reclaimed lumber and stones.

The upstairs, which used to be rooms for rent, had been converted into an intimate salon with overstuffed leather chairs, hand-carved rockers and antlers that hung on the wall. A large stone fireplace and cozy floor rugs made it a welcoming place for a quiet drink and conversation. None of that is what made her nervous.

A minute or two after going by, Shane turned the car into the lot behind Real Vintage Cowboy and pulled into a parking space closest to the building.

"Thanks a lot, Shane. I don't want to keep you." She started to open the passenger door.

"Let me turn the car off."

"Don't bother. You don't have to see me to my door. I'll just run upstairs. You've done enough already."

Her effort to make a smooth exit was wasted and she knew it when the car's dashboard lights revealed his amusement.

"If I didn't know better, I'd think you were nervous about something."

Not something, everything, she thought. "Not at all. I just don't want to take advantage of your kindness."

"Oh, please." He turned off the engine. "I'm not in the habit of barely slowing down to let a lady out of my car. Just so we're clear, I'm walking you to your door. No argument."

He'd left her no graceful way out of this and did it in such a gentlemanly way. Could be because he didn't know her very well and was on his best behavior. Could be an act meant to disarm her. If so, it was working. She was almost completely disarmed.

"Okay," she said. "But you should know. My apartment is on the third floor."

"Real men don't flinch at a second set of stairs."

"Don't say I didn't warn you."

Shane came around and opened her door, then walked beside her to the wooden stairs on the outside of the building. When they got to the landing, Gianna had her keys out. "Thanks, Shane. I had a great time tonight."

"Me, too." His gaze searched hers. "Did I redeem myself for first-kiss faux pas?"

She laughed. "Yeah."

"Good. Here's another better first."

He lowered his mouth to hers. It was soft and warm where their lips met, but the breeze swirled snow around them and made her shiver.

Instantly he pulled back. "I'm an idiot. Your clothes are still wet, aren't they?"

"Y-yes."

"You need to get inside. Good night, Gianna."

She nodded, but as he started to back away it hit her that she really didn't want him to go. A third kiss didn't mean she'd known him any longer, just convinced her that she wanted to spend more time with him. It wasn't smart, but the words came out of her mouth, anyway.

"You're cold, too. How about a cup of tea?"

"I wouldn't mind." He stared down at her, questions in his eyes. "But only if you're sure it's not too late. You've got stuff to do tomorrow."

His hand was on her arm; his gaze held hers. She was definitely sure. "It's not too late." Or maybe it was. "Just don't expect much. My apartment is nothing like your place."

Gianna unlocked the door and he followed her inside. She tried to tell herself that the actresses, models and TV personalities he dated probably had places this small but it didn't work.

The apartment was long, narrow and divided into two spaces—living room and kitchen, bedroom and bath. There was a window looking out on Main Street and the other faced the parking lot with rugged, majestic mountains in the distance. When you thought about it, she and Shane sort of shared a scenic view, but his was way better.

She'd separated her cooking and eating area with a hunter-green love seat. Braided rugs in green, coral and yellow were scattered over the wooden floor. The walls were painted a pale gold and had white baseboards and crown molding. Scattered pictures hung in groupings, a lot of them framed in cherrywood ovals. To shake things up, she'd put a two-foot section of a scaled-down ladder over the outside door and a hanging fixture over the stove held several copper pots and an orange colander. It was bright and cheerful, in her opinion.

She watched Shane, trying to gauge his reaction. "Be it ever so humble…"

"Have you ever heard the expression, 'it's not the square footage, but what you do with it'?"

She tapped her lip. "Is that like 'size doesn't matter'?"

"In a way." His grin was wicked and exciting. "You've created a space that's homey, comfortable and charming. A reflection of its occupant."

"So, let me see if I understand what you're saying. I'm homey and comfortable?"

"Don't forget charming," he said, looking around again, then coming back to meet her gaze. "Among other very attractive attributes. My place doesn't have this warmth…" He stopped. "And speaking of that, I'm an idiot. Get out of those damp clothes into something warm."

Your arms would be warm.

Gianna hoped she hadn't said that out loud and when his expression didn't change, she breathed a sigh of relief. "Okay. Let me get tea first—"

"I'll do it."

"But…"

"Do you have tea bags?" he asked.

"In the appropriately marked canister by the stove. It won't take a minute—"

"You don't trust me?" He shook his head. "I'm CIA. My culinary genius is the stuff of legend."

"Humble, too," she muttered.

"I think I can handle putting a couple of mugs with water in the microwave."

"Okay, then. Knock yourself out."

She walked through the doorway that separated the living room from her bedroom and bath. After closing the door, she stripped off her coat followed by the rest of her wet clothes. Still chilled to the bone, fashion and seduction were not her priority now. She pulled a pair of fleecy Santa Claus pants from her dresser and a green thermal shirt and put them on, then slipped into her oversize dark blue terrycloth robe, thick socks and fuzzy slippers.

In the adjoining bathroom she turned on the light and recoiled from her reflection in the mirror. "Oh, dear God."

Mascara from the lower lashes gave her "raccoon" eyes and her hair looked like she'd combed it with a tree branch. After washing her face to remove the makeup and free her freckles, she applied cream and ran a brush through her red hair. The cut that had layers falling past her shoulders was good, the color—not so much.

She was finally warm thanks to Shane getting her home as fast as possible. Inviting him in was equal parts boldness and stupidity. Conventional-dating protocol dictated three dates before sleeping with someone. Between dinner at his place and tonight's walk in the snow, they were barely at one.

She had no illusions about a future with Shane Roarke because he'd been honest about his uncertain plans. Still, she wanted him. That was the downside of giving him a first kiss do-over. The touch of his lips, the feel of his hard body pressed against hers had just made her want him even more.

And that was the stupid part of giving in to her boldness. Her heart was telling her to slow down; her head was saying take me now.

There was very little danger of him doing that, she

thought, looking at her reflection. The old robe and Christmas pants would prove to the seduction police that she hadn't dressed to lure him to her bed.

"You're comfortable and homey, the complete opposite of a temptress," she said to herself. "Charming is debatable."

With a sigh she opened the door and joined him in the kitchen. "I see you found everything."

"Yes." He'd removed his coat and settled it on the standing rack by the front door. Now he was leaning against the counter with two steaming mugs beside him. His jeans were fashionably worn and fit his lean legs perfectly. The white cotton shirt fit his upper body in the most masculine way. But what hiked up her pulse was the amusement in his eyes as his gaze scanned her from head to toe. "Love the outfit."

Looking down she said, "I'll start a new fashion trend. Montana practical."

"I think you look pretty cute." He traced a finger across her cheek. "Love the freckles."

"Yeah." She wrinkled her nose distastefully. "Me, too."

"What's wrong with them?"

"When I was in grade school, the boys wanted to play connect the dots on my face. That got really old. The curse of a redhead."

"Your hair is beautiful and unique."

"I always wanted to be a blonde or brunette."

"Boring."

The simple, straightforward word warmed her the way fleece, thermal and terrycloth never could. "Still, there's something to be said for blending in. Being different made me a target of teasing."

"It's a well-known fact that boys are stupid."

"You'll get no argument from me." She raised her gaze to find him watching her and a sizzle of awareness sprinted down her spine. When he moved closer, her heart started to pound.

"But we get smarter." He cupped her face in his hands and slid his lips over her cheek, soft nibbling kisses that made drawing air into her lungs a challenge. "How's that for connecting the dots?"

"Great technique." Her voice was a breathless whisper and she felt his lips curve into a smile. The only thing that would make this better was his mouth on hers. "Definitely smarter."

"But wait. There's more," he said a little hoarsely.

Gianna pressed her palm to his chest and felt the heavy beat of his heart then shivered at the heat in his gaze. "More sounds good to me."

Strangely enough she didn't agonize over the right or wrong of this. It just was. She wanted him, wanted to give herself to him. No questions; no regrets.

She felt his hand loosen the belt of her robe and slide inside, cup her hip. The good thing about oversize clothing was how easily you could slip it off.

When their gazes locked, she saw invitation in the smoldering depths darkening his blue eyes. "Do you want to see the bedroom?"

"Only if you want to show it to me."

Her answer was to take his hand and lead him through the doorway. The light beside the bed was on, illuminating her simple, white chenille spread. Throw pillows in light pink and rose gave it color, but she threw them onto the floor. Shane was the only man she'd ever brought in here and he seemed to fill the room, complete it somehow.

Gianna folded down the bedspread and blanket, revealing her serviceable flannel sheets. "Not sexy, just practical for a Montana winter. Otherwise I scream like a woman when I go to bed."

One of his dark eyebrows rose as his mouth curved into a wicked grin. "There's nothing wrong with screaming like a woman."

"I agree—when it's not from cold sheets."

"I promise you won't be cold." He traced his index finger along her collarbone and proved the truth of those words.

Shards of heat burned through her, warming her everywhere. Her toes curled and she stepped out of her slippers. But she hadn't let him be the first man in this room just to be a passive participant. She tugged his shirt from the waistband of his jeans and started undoing its buttons. Then she pressed her palms to his bare chest, letting the dusting of hair scrape across her hands, the nerve endings in her fingers.

The moan that built inside her refused to stay contained and Shane took it from there. He shrugged out of his shirt, then took the hem of hers and lifted it over her head.

He cupped her bare breasts and brushed his thumbs over the soft skin. "Beautiful."

She put her hands over his knuckles and gently pressed, showing him without words how perfect it felt. His breathing increased and the harsh sound of it mingled with hers. The scent of him, the heat of his skin, the feel of his hands all capsized her senses and drowned her in need. She backed toward the mattress and tugged him with her. Then she pushed off her fleece Santa pants and toed off her socks. His eyes darkened with approval and the heat of desire.

Gianna sat on the bed and even though the flannel sheets were cold on her bare skin, there was no screaming. Just acute anticipation. She watched Shane unbuckle his belt and step out of his jeans, then pull a condom from his wallet and set it on the nightstand. She wasn't sure he could see it in her eyes, but she most definitely approved. His shoulders were wide, his belly flat, his legs muscular. He was fit and fine and—for tonight—hers.

She held out her arms and he came into them, pressing her back on the mattress. He kissed her deeply and she opened, letting him stroke the inside of her mouth. While he ravaged her there, he slid a hand down her waist and belly, then her inner thigh. The touch tapped into a mother lode of desire and she could hardly breathe.

"Oh, Shane, I want—"

"I know."

He reached for the condom and covered himself, then rolled over her, between her legs, taking most of his weight on his forearms. Slowly he entered, filling her fully, sweetly. Her hips arched upward, showing him, urging him.

She could hardly draw enough air into her lungs as he stroked in and out with exquisite care. Then he reached between their bodies and brushed his thumb over the bundle of nerve endings at the juncture of her thighs.

The touch pushed her over the edge where she shattered into a thousand pieces. Shane held her and crooned words that her pleasure-saturated mind couldn't comprehend but knew were just right.

As if he knew the perfect moment, he started to move again. His breathing grew more ragged until there was one final thrust and he went still, groaning out his own release. Like he'd done for her, she wrapped her arms around him and just held on.

"Gianna—" Her name was a caress riding on a satisfied sigh.

"For the record—" She kissed his chin and the sexy scruff scraped her passion swollen lips in the nicest possible way.

"Yes," he urged.

"Boys really do get smarter."

She felt the laugh vibrate through his chest where their bare skin touched. Ordinarily that would have made her smile, but she couldn't quite manage. Boys might be smarter, but girls were notorious for making stupid choices. She had the emotional scars to prove she'd made the same ones multiple times.

She just hoped this wasn't a different kind of mistake, the kind that would make her sorry in the morning.

Chapter Five

Shane woke when Gianna mumbled in her sleep and moved restlessly against him. They were spooning, a term he used in cooking but liked a whole lot better in this context. If finding out his biological father was a criminal in jail was the worst thing since coming to Thunder Canyon, this was the best. He nuzzled her silky red hair and grinned.

Light was just beginning to creep into the room around the edges of the white blinds over the window and the number on the clock by the bed made him groan. Because his business was primarily done in the evening, he always slept in. His day usually started much later than this, but he had to admit it had never started better.

Gianna stretched sleepily then went still after her legs brushed against his. Without looking over her shoulder she asked, "Shane?"

"You were expecting someone else?"

"No." She cuddled into him. "I was sure I'd dreamed last night."

"A nightmare?"

"Oh, please. It was wonderful and you're very aware of that. I refuse to feed your ego."

"Then how about feeding me some breakfast?"

"I'll try. After I throw on some clothes. Meet you in the kitchen. Five minutes. I get the bathroom first."

Before he could ask a question or form any sort of protest, she'd thrown back the covers and raced from the bed. While waiting his turn, Shane thought about the situation. Sex was a very efficient recipe for stress relief and his body was really relaxed for the first time in longer than he could remember. That's not to say he hadn't been with women, but the vibe was different with Gianna.

Maybe it was more intense because their time together would be short. She wasn't staying and if information came out about who he really was, he wouldn't have to make a choice about his contract since it wouldn't be renewed. All he knew for sure was that as long as the two of them were in town, he wanted to see her.

Within the designated time frame, he joined her in the kitchen. She was wearing the same fleece pants, thermal top and robe from last night, which was both good and bad. She looked every bit as cute and he wanted to take the clothes off her again.

"Coffee?" She stood in front of the machine on the counter and glanced over her shoulder. When she met his gaze, a lovely blush stole over her cheeks as if she knew what he'd been thinking.

"I'd love it," he said.

"Coming right up." She added water, then put a filter and grounds in the appropriate place before pushing the start button.

"What did you mean about trying to feed me breakfast?"

"I'm not sure what I've got to cook," she explained.

"Let me have a look."

"Be my guest." She laughed. "Oh. Wait. You are my guest. And I'm the worst hostess on the planet if I let you do the cooking. There just may not be much in the refrigerator."

He slid her a wry look. "I won a reality cooking show by whipping up a gourmet meal with jelly beans, popcorn, granola, shrimp and instant mashed potatoes."

"Let me just say—eww." She folded her arms over her chest. "But far be it from me to stand in your way. Go to it, chef boy."

He lifted one eyebrow. "You do remember I'm the boss?"

"Not right now, you're not," she shot back. "At this moment you're my—guy in the kitchen."

"Good to know. Let's see what guy-in-the-kitchen has to work with."

The contents of her pantry and refrigerator were limited. It was the female equivalent of a bachelor's. Half a bottle of white wine. He grabbed the open milk container and took a sniff that told him it was still good. Individually wrapped slices of cheese. A couple of limp celery stalks and a few green onions. There was a loaf of bread touting fiber, low calories and weight control. Thank God she had half a dozen eggs.

He pulled the ingredients out and set to work with the cutting board, frying pan and a silent, solemn promise to equip her kitchen better. Starting with a decent set of knives.

He held up an old, dull one. "This is where it all starts. I recommend high carbon, stainless steel. It's the best of both worlds. Carbon is tough and has a great edge. Stainless steel keeps it from rusting and taking care of it is a lot less effort."

"Good to know. Can I do anything besides an emergency run to the kitchen gadget store?" she asked.

"Set the table and stay back."

Not that he couldn't work with her underfoot. The Gallatin Room kitchen was always swarming with people, a well-choreographed cauldron of activity, but experience had taught him how to tune everything out. He'd only ever been unsuccessful at doing that when Gianna was around.

He glanced at her in that oddly sexy oversize robe and felt his blood heat like butter in a frying pan. Now that he'd explored the curves under her quirky outfit, if she got any closer to him, resisting her would annihilate his concentration.

Fifteen minutes later they sat at her dinette just big enough for two and ate toast, cheese omelets and coffee. Gianna took a bite and made a sexy little sound of appreciation, not unlike something he'd coaxed from her in bed.

"This is so good, Shane."

"You sound surprised."

"Not at you. Just that it was possible from my survival rations." She chewed another bite. "Mmm. I can only imagine what you could whip up after a trip to the market."

Which reminded him... The reason they were here and not at his place was because she had an early day.

"So, you're up before God," he said. "What's on your agenda today?"

"I have to start my Christmas shopping."

"Really? By yourself?"

"Unlike the great and powerful Shane Roarke I don't have minions to do it for me."

"That's a shame."

"No kidding."

"Want some help?" He wasn't a fan of shopping but he was becoming a fan of Gianna's. He wanted to hang out with her even if that involved poking through stores and carrying bags. "I could be your minion."

"Singular?" Her auburn eyebrow lifted slightly. "By definition doesn't minion mean more than one?"

"How about if I chauffeur? Then it would be me and the car."

"Oh, gosh, I forgot. What with us— After we— Well, you know." She looked at him, blushing like crazy. "My car died last night."

He'd never heard sex described as us, we and you know, but definitely understood how it could push everything else from one's mind.

"Since you don't have wheels, that's even more reason to let me come along. I'll make a phone call and have the local garage bring your car back from the dead while you take care of Christmas." Sipping coffee, he watched her mull it over. "Gianna?"

"Hmm?"

"Don't think it to death. Just say yes. It's a good offer."

"It's an outstanding offer and I'd be all kinds of crazy to turn it down. Thank you, Shane." She stood and leaned over the small table to kiss his cheek. "My hero."

Right now, maybe. For as long as she didn't know the identity of his father. And there was no reason she should, even if he actually found out who his mother was. Right now all he knew was her first name. Grace.

A problem for another day. At this moment Gianna was looking at him as if he had wings and a halo. It felt really good and he didn't want that to change. Keeping his secret was the best way to do that.

Gianna was rocking a pretty awesome post-sex, post-breakfast glow while she waited for Shane to pick her up. She was scouting out Real Vintage Cowboy, the shop below her apartment, which was where they'd agreed to meet after he went home to shower and change.

There was a Christmas tree in the window decorated with ornaments made out of clothespins fashioned into reindeer, beads strung together into snowflakes, crystal dangles from old lamps and tin Santas and sleighs. Meandering the main aisle, she admired a saddle lovingly repaired and polished, a turn-of-the-century, repainted Singer sewing machine and a milk can holding a lamp as an example of how it could be used as an end table.

Everything looked beautiful to her this morning. She was happy. Being with Shane was magic and something about eating breakfast together was more intimate than sex. Her world was bright with possibilities and she believed with every fiber of her being that it really was the most wonderful time of the year.

Catherine Clifton Overton was standing by the far wall, near the cash register. She saw Gianna and smiled. "Hey, tenant."

"Merry Christmas, landlady."

The woman she paid her rent to was a willowy brunette with the warmest, darkest chocolate-colored eyes Gianna had ever seen. She was wearing a turtleneck top that came down over her hips and a coordinating gauzy skirt that skimmed the top of her signature cowboy boots. A leather belt cinched her small waist and pulled the whole outfit together perfectly.

Gianna's style leaned more to black-black jeans, gray sweater, black boots, leftovers from her days in New York. Compared to her landlady she felt as if she was on the fashion police's most wanted list.

"So how's married life?" she asked.

"Absolutely perfect." Catherine had a dreamy expression

on her face as she glanced at the wedding and engagement rings on her left hand. "Cody makes me so happy."

"You're a lucky woman. I envy you." Gianna figured if she couldn't stop the stab of jealousy, it was best to be up-front about it. "He's a great guy."

At this point in her life she'd expected to have what Catherine did—a growing business and marriage to the man of her dreams. She was a failure on both counts. As she saw it, the lesson was to not have expectations. Take it one day at a time. And today she was going to be happy.

Just then the bell over the front door rang and in walked Shane Roarke.

"Speaking of great guys..." Catherine arched an eyebrow. "I wonder what he's looking for this time."

"He told me about checking out your store." Gianna waved at him and he started toward her across the long room.

The other woman lowered her voice. "He was browsing and we ended up talking. He had a lot of questions about Arthur Swinton and the last owner of this place."

"Jasper Fowler?" Gianna had heard about the crazy old man who had conspired with Swinton to steal money and ruin the Traub family. The two were currently in jail.

Catherine whispered. "Vintage items all have a story. Shane just might be a man who appreciates that."

That implied he had a story, but Gianna was more interested in admiring the man. More caught up in the way her heart skipped and her breath caught at the sight of him. The broad shoulders and long legs wrapped in designer jeans would make it easy to mistake him for a cowboy. This was Montana after all, a little off the beaten path for a celebrity chef.

He walked up beside her and smiled at Catherine. "Nice to see you again."

"Same here. Can I help you find something?"

"I just did."

Gianna shivered at the sparkle in his eyes when she met his gaze. "My car is being uncooperative, as usual. Shane volunteered to take me Christmas shopping."

"Really?" Catherine looked impressed. And curious. What woman wouldn't be? "Most guys would rather take a sharp stick in the eye."

"I guess I'm not most guys." He grinned at them.

"My husband could take lessons from you."

"Didn't you just tell me he's perfect?" Gianna said.

"In most ways," the other woman agreed. "But, like the average man, he's a little shopping-challenged."

"I never said I'd be good at it," Shane corrected. "Just promised to do the driving."

Catherine tapped her lip as she studied him. "Do you give cooking lessons? Maybe I could persuade you to teach my husband a couple easy recipes."

"I'm happy to help out." He looked at Gianna. "Speaking of helping, I made a phone call. The garage is working on fixing your car as we speak and it will be delivered back here today. They're going to leave the keys with you, Catherine, if we're not back. Is that okay?"

"Of course. And in the spirit of good deeds—" she looked from him to Gianna "—do you know about Presents for Patriots?"

"I've already signed up to volunteer," Gianna answered, knowing what was coming. "Most of The Gallatin Room employees have."

"I haven't heard about this," Shane said.

"That's because you're not an employee," she shot back. "You're the boss."

"What is it?"

"Last year," Catherine said, "people in town got together

and wrapped donated gifts for military personnel serving overseas who couldn't get home for Christmas."

Shane nodded approvingly. "Sounds like a terrific event."

"You should come by if you're not too busy," the other woman suggested.

"I will. Where?"

"The Rib Shack. It's D. J. Traub's pet project." Maybe it was from working around things that all had a story, but Catherine warmed to telling one. "His mother, Grace, died when he was just a boy and he had difficulty connecting with his dad. They reconciled before Doug Traub died, but because of what he went through, family is very important to him."

"Okay."

It was one word, but Gianna heard something in Shane's voice and looked at him. His easygoing, relaxed manner had disappeared and there was tension in his jaw.

Catherine didn't seem to notice. "D.J. feels that we're all part of the American family and the military fights to preserve that for us. Presents for Patriots is his way of giving back to them for all they do."

"A worthy cause." Shane looked down at her. "Are you ready to go?"

"Actually, yes. There's a lot to do and a limited amount of time to do it in. Yesterday I made a date to meet my mother and sister for a late lunch. You're welcome to join us if you have time."

"Then we should get started." Shane didn't accept or decline, but put his hand on her lower back, a courtly gesture except she could feel him urging her to leave. "Have a good day, Catherine."

"You, too." She smiled. "Or just grit your teeth and get through it."

As they headed for the door Gianna didn't feel ready

for this expedition at all. It was possible she'd imagined the shift in Shane's mood, but not likely. The contrast was too stark. He'd arrived and was his usual friendly, charming self. When the subject of volunteering came up, he'd turned dark and broody. What was up with that?

Envying Catherine Overton hadn't punctured her happy balloon, but an "aha" moment did the trick. She'd slept with this man less than twelve hours before but still didn't really know very much about him.

Shane's SUV was at the curb in front of Real Vintage Cowboy and he held the door open for her. She could feel his body language change as soon as they walked outside. He was more relaxed, which made her think whatever had brought on the mood was somehow connected to Catherine or the store. Gianna slid into the car and couldn't contain a small sigh of pleasure as her body connected with the butter-soft leather.

When he was in the driver's seat, engine on and purring, Shane said, "Where to?"

Gianna returned his smile and pulled the list out of her purse. "Mountain Bluebell Bakery. It's at the corner of Nugget and Main in Old Town. Just east of the Tottering Teapot and ROOTS."

"Got it."

He put the car in gear, then glanced over his left shoulder before easing out into the stream of light traffic. Only the drifts of snow still in the shade were evidence of last night's storm. The street was clear, the sky was blue and the bad vibe was behind them.

"So, on this shopping expedition, I'm surprised the Bakery is the first stop. You've got a sweet tooth all of a sudden? Need an energy boost so you can shop till you drop? Or is there something I need to know?"

"Only that you should be warned. This will probably be

the easiest shopping of the day. I'm ordering something to send to a friend in New York."

"Male or female?" he asked.

"What?" She looked at him, the chiseled profile that made her want to touch his face.

"Your friend in New York. Man or woman?"

His tone was just a little too casual and that made her happy. "Before I answer that, I have a question."

"Okay."

"Are you jealous?"

He glanced at her and before returning his gaze to the road, his eyes burned bright and hot. "No. Just making conversation."

She was pretty sure that was a lie and a little ball of pleasure bumped against her heart. "Then, in the spirit of conversation...my friend is a woman. Hannah Cummings. We were roommates before I moved back to Thunder Canyon. I'm trying to talk her into coming for a visit."

"Will you be here that long?"

"My plans are still up in the air." That was true. She still hadn't fine-tuned her Plan B. Before he could question her more, the bakery came into view. "There it is. Looks like there's a parking place out front."

"I see it."

"That's really lucky. Lizzie Traub opened it about a year ago and this place is always busy." She chattered away. "She got some great publicity when the former owner, who was going to make Corey and Erin Traub's wedding cake, closed the place and left town with people's deposits. Lizzie made their cake and saved the wedding day."

"Is Corey related to D.J.?"

"They're cousins," she answered. "Lizzie and Ethan weren't married then. She was his administrative assistant and relocated to Thunder Canyon from Midland, Texas. Her family's bakery was a landmark there for years until her father lost money and the bank repossessed it."

"How do you know all this?" There was no teasing in his voice, just awe. "Weren't you living in New York?"

She didn't like reminders of her failed life. "My mother and sister live here. They talk to me."

"I'll keep that in mind," he said, pulling to a stop in front of the shop.

They got out of the car, walked inside and were immediately surrounded by the sweet smells of chocolate and icing. Gianna could almost feel her pores absorbing the sugar and calories and couldn't find the will to care. Her mouth was watering and she wasn't even hungry.

One glass case was filled with muffins—blueberry, pumpkin spice, banana nut, chocolate chip and more. Another display had old-fashioned donuts and buttermilk bars. Yet another showed cupcakes and specialty cakes and a book filled with pictures from various events handled by Mountain Bluebell Bakery.

A tall, beautiful woman in her twenties with gray-green eyes and dark blond hair walked out of the back room. "Hi. I'm Lizzie Traub."

"Nice to meet you. Gianna Garrison," she said and held out her hand. "And this is Shane Roarke."

"The chef at The Gallatin Room. I never missed your show—*If You Can't Stand the Heat*. You really smoked the competition. Pun intended." Lizzie smiled.

"Thanks." He grinned at her, then looked around at the bakery's interior. "I defy anyone to be gloomy in here."

"I like bright colors and since I spend a lot of time working, it seemed wise."

The shop was cheerful and bright with signs advertising Wi-Fi and tables scattered over the floor. It was the kind of place where someone could come for an espresso and muffin, set up a laptop and stay for a while. There were café lights with blown glass shades swirling with orange, yellow and blue, a sampling of the color scheme. Three walls were painted a sunny yellow and the long one behind the counter was a rich, deep burnt umber. At waist level along each wall flowed an endless chain of mountain bluebells.

"I love what you've done with the place. I hear the guy who used to own it wasn't nice, not a bluebells-on-the-walls type," Gianna commented.

"Tell me about it." Lizzie looked at the flowers. "My friend Allaire Traub hand stenciled all of that. She's so talented and great with kids. She teaches art at the high school."

"You could hate someone like that if they weren't so nice," Gianna said.

"I know, right?" Lizzie looked from one to the other. "Can I help you with something?"

"My sister highly recommended you. Jackie Blake?"

"Right." Lizzie nodded. "Three kids—Griffin, Colin and Emily. All chocolate connoisseurs, although they love the Mountain Bluebell muffins, too."

"That sounds like my niece and nephews."

"Adorable children." She smiled at Shane, then said, "But I have to say that I'm feeling some pressure. Your Gallatin Room desserts are legendary."

He smiled. "I fill a completely different business niche. And from what I see, your product is amazing."

"Thanks." She looked at each of them. "So, what can I help you with?"

"I understand that you ship orders?"

Lizzie nodded. "Anything over fifty dollars is no charge for shipping and handling. And I guarantee it will get there fresh."

"That sounds perfect."

"Did you want to sample something?"

"More than you can possibly imagine, but I already know what I want." She pointed into the display case. "Red velvet cupcakes."

"For Christmas, I assume?" At her nod, Lizzie continued. "Maybe a reindeer or Santa on the icing? Like the ones in the case."

Gianna bent to look. "Very festive. Sold."

"Wow." Shane looked impressed. "A woman who knows her mind."

It took a few minutes to fill out an order form with her choice, the quantity and the address in New York. When there was a total, Gianna handed over her credit card, then signed the receipt.

"Thanks, Lizzie. That was quick and I'm crunched for time."

"You made it easy."

Shane laughed. "She told me this would be the easiest errand of the day."

"I'm glad she was right. Come back again."

"Definitely."

They walked back outside and Gianna pulled her list out of her purse, then checked off the first item. "That's one down. Now there's my mom and dad. Jackie and her husband and my nephews and niece. A little something for Bonnie. I'm thinking maybe the mall would be good, going for a variety of stores rather than a lot of separate stops. But I'm feeling a little guilty about monopolizing your time."

"You shouldn't," he said. "I don't mind."

"Do you need to do some shopping for your family?" She looked up at his dark aviator sunglasses that hid his eyes. It occurred to her again that she knew very little about him. He'd never said much about himself. "I'm assuming you weren't raised by wolves."

"My mom and dad live in Los Angeles."

"Any siblings?" she asked, noting the dark change in tone and the way his mouth tightened.

"A sister and brother." He started to take her elbow and lead her to the car. "Next stop New Town Mall."

There was something going on with him. That was twice in less than an hour that he'd gone weird on her. If there was a problem she needed to know now. Relationships that had gone on too long had taught her not to ignore signs of trouble.

She dug in her heels. "Wait, Shane."

"What's wrong?"

"That's what I want to know." She looked up at him, took a deep breath and said, "I know you're struggling with something today. What's going on? Is it us? Are you sorry about last night?"

Chapter Six

"God, no."

Shane was sorry about a lot of things and right at the top of the list was the man who'd fathered him. But he would never in a million years regret being with Gianna. It was wonderful. She was amazing.

Standing on the sidewalk outside the Mountain Bluebell Bakery he looked into her eyes. "Last night was the best. And now who's feeding whose ego—"

She smiled as intended, but there was still concern in her beautiful turquoisey eyes. "Then what is it?"

He really thought he'd done a pretty good job of hiding his feelings. First when Catherine Overton had mentioned D. J. Traub's mother. It was the first time he'd heard her name. Grace was his birth mother's name, too. And just now when Gianna had asked him about his family, he was reminded that he was here in Thunder Canyon to dig up information about who he was. That thought was quickly followed by a whole lot of guilt.

One thing he wasn't: a poker player. He'd taken risks—on the reality show that launched his career and in business, opening restaurants. But that was different from playing a game. He didn't know if he could bluff, but this was as good a time as any to find out.

"You can talk to me, Shane." Her gaze searched his and she must have seen something. "I'm going to get coffee from the bakery and we can sit on that bench in the sun."

He saw the one she meant, a wooden bench on the side of the bakery facing Nugget Way. "There's nothing to talk about. And that will cut into your shopping time."

"The mall can wait. Somehow it will get done. This is more important."

Shane had a feeling there wouldn't be any putting her off now. "I'll get the coffee."

"No. Let me. You make sure no one takes our seats." She put a reassuring hand on his arm before disappearing inside the shop.

As soon as he sat down by himself he missed her warm presence. His darkness was no match for all that bright red hair and innate sweetness. And now he was on the spot—the classic man in conflict. He didn't want to talk about what he was dealing with because not talking was the only way to keep his secret. But obviously it was affecting him since she'd noticed his mood shifts.

He felt like a disloyal, ungrateful jerk. Gavin and Christa Roarke had done nothing but love, nurture and encourage him. He couldn't imagine a better brother or sister than Ryan and Maggie. All of them had pushed him to do what he needed to and hoped he found peace of mind. Fat chance after hearing the name Grace. It was on his birth certificate, but so what? There were probably a lot of women in and around Thunder Canyon with that name, including D. J. Traub's mother.

Gianna appeared with "to-go" cups of coffee in her hands. She sat beside him and held one out. "Cream, no sugar."

"You remembered." From breakfast just a few hours ago. Seemed like forever.

"Of course I remembered. It's my job and the boss has mentioned that I'm pretty good at it."

"He's a guy who can spot talent when he sees it."

"Also a guy who tries to hide his feelings and can't." Her expression grew sympathetic and serious. "He's got something on his mind. I'd be happy to listen and help if I can."

Shane looked up and knew why Montana was called Big Sky country. It seemed bigger, bluer and more beautiful here in Thunder Canyon. The snow-capped mountains were towering and the scenery spectacular. But that wasn't all that made this a special spot.

He'd lived all over the country in some of the biggest and most sophisticated, cosmopolitan cities. As his name recognition grew and his career soared, he'd been asked to endorse worthy causes or donate large sums of money. But he'd never been invited to cook for military families or wrap presents to brighten Christmas for a lonely soldier overseas.

That had changed here; he was a part of this community. The people had a hands-on spirit of caring that he'd never experienced before and was grateful and humbled to be part of it now. He didn't want to do anything to put him on the outside again.

And then there was Gianna. He looked at her, the sun shining on the most beautiful hair he'd ever seen. He knew she was just as beautiful inside.

"Shane?"

Damned if he did; damned if he didn't. He'd start at the beginning and wing it. "I'm adopted."

"Okay." Her expression didn't change. "The last time I checked, that wasn't a crime."

If she only knew how close that comment came to the truth.

"No, I'm aware that my story isn't one that makes a prime-time, news-magazine segment. It was too normal."

"How do you mean?" She took a sip of her coffee and angled her body toward him, listening with intense concentration.

"My parents are, quite simply, remarkable people. They're both lawyers."

"Pretty demanding careers. And yet a child was so important to them, they moved heaven and earth to have you in their lives."

"They chose me." It's what he'd always been told and a part of him had always felt special. Not anymore. "And not just me. They adopted my brother and sister—Ryan and Maggie. Also lawyers like our folks."

One of her auburn eyebrows went up. "High achievers. I realize we're not talking genes and DNA here, but how did your parents feel about your career choice?"

He smiled. "The three Roarke kids were encouraged to study what they loved and follow their passion."

"Good advice and it seems to have worked out for all of you," she commented.

"Professionally. But personally?" He shook his head.

"How do you mean? Do you have multiple wives and families stashed in cities and towns all over the country?"

"Yeah." He grinned. "Because I have so much time to pull that off. Can't you see the tabloid headline? Celebrity chef cooks up dual life."

She smiled. "So, what is it?"

"I was restless. Moved around a lot opening restaurants in Los Angeles, New York and Seattle. When I started talking about Dallas, my mother was worried."

"Why?"

"She felt I was deliberately or subconsciously avoiding settling down. And maybe I needed to look at who I was. That's when she finally gave me all the information she'd received about my birth parents from the adoption agency."

"That's incredibly courageous of her."

"No kidding." He remembered his mother's face, hesitation and concern battling it out. "She told me to use it however I wanted. Do whatever was necessary to find peace and put down roots."

"And?"

"I realized that as happy and loving as my childhood was, I'd always had questions about why I am the way I am. I wanted to connect the dots."

"What did you do?" she asked.

"Hired a private investigator."

Her eyes widened and comprehension dawned. "Is that why you took the job at The Gallatin Room here in Thunder Canyon?"

"What makes you say that?"

"You said it yourself—successful restaurants all over the country. Executive chef is a prestigious position, but this isn't Paris, New York or San Francisco. At best, it's a lateral career step. You had other reasons for taking this job."

Smart girl. He'd have to tread carefully. "Yes. The investigation and search narrowed to this town, so I contacted Grant Clifton."

"The manager of Thunder Canyon Resort."

"Right. When the previous chef's contract was up, I let Grant know I'd be interested. He jumped at the chance."

"Didn't he wonder why? A famous guy like you coming here?"

"The subject came up. I just said I'd been going at warp speed for years and wanted to throttle back for a while."

"Obviously he believed you."

"Because it was true." Shane just hadn't realized until he'd said it to Grant. And talking about it out loud now made the whole thing seem underhanded. Fruit doesn't fall far from the tree, he thought. Still, it was a good thing he'd gone about this quietly, otherwise everyone would know about his biological connection to Arthur Swinton. "But I also had personal reasons."

"To find your parents," she said. "Any luck with that since you've been here?"

He leaned forward, elbows on his knees. He didn't want her to read his expression. "Recently I found some information about my father."

"Oh, Shane—" She put her hand on his arm. "That's great. Do you know who he is?"

"Yes."

"Have you contacted him?"

"No." He laughed and heard the bitterness in the sound but hoped she didn't.

"Is he still alive?"

"Yes." And in jail. That part was best kept to himself.

"You need to talk to him."

"Not sure that's the wisest course of action."

"But it's why you started down this road in the first place." Her voice gentled when she said, "Are you worried that he'll reject you?"

That was the least of his concerns. Shane didn't want to risk *everyone else* rejecting him. The people in this town hated Arthur Swinton with the same passion that they loved being good neighbors. There was every reason to believe they would despise anyone related to their homegrown felon.

He finally met Gianna's gaze and saw the sincere desire to help shining there. She was easy to talk to, a good listener. A good friend. Maybe more than that. He didn't want to lose her by revealing what he suspected. He'd probably said too much already.

"It's complicated, Gianna."

"Of course it is. But, Shane, you're clearly not at peace the way things stand. Wouldn't it be better to get everything out in the open?"

That's what he'd thought before finding out his father was a criminal. "I'm not sure what to do with the information."

The sounds of laughter, women's and children's voices drifted to him just before he saw a large group of people round the corner. He glanced that way and the first person he recognized was D. J. Traub. They both worked at Thunder Canyon Resort restaurants so their paths crossed occasionally. They'd talked a few times.

And they both had mothers named Grace.

Gianna saw the exact moment when Shane's expression changed and he got that weird look on his face again. Before she had time to wonder what put it there, the two of them were surrounded by a big group of Traubs, Dax, D.J., their wives and three kids between them. Everyone was saying hello at once. Everyone, that is, but Shane, who stood a little apart. It was impossible to grow up in this town and not know these guys. Since she wasn't sure who Shane had met, she decided to make introductions.

"Shane Roarke, this is Dax Traub and his wife, Shandie."

"Nice to see you." Dax extended his hand.

He was a year older than his brother with dark hair and eyes, a brooding, James Dean type who oozed sex appeal.

His wife was tall, with shoulder-length blond hair cut into perfect layers.

"Dax owns a motorcycle shop here in town and Shandie works at the Clip 'n Curl," she explained.

"Nice to meet you," Shane said, cool and polite. He looked down when a little bundle of energy tripped over his shoe and nearly took a header. "Hey, buddy. You okay?"

Shandie steadied the little boy. "This is Max. Say hello to Mr. Roarke."

"Hi." The little guy had his father's dark hair and eyes. As soon as he dutifully said what was expected, he took off running down the sidewalk again.

Shandie called after him, "Slow down, Max."

Dax tugged on a young blond girl's pony tail. "This is our daughter, Kayla."

"Nice to meet you," the child said.

"The pleasure is mine, Kayla." Shane leveled all the considerable Roarke charm on her and a becoming pink stole into her cheeks.

"Sorry to be rude," a concerned Shandie said. "But I have to catch up with my son, the budding Olympic sprinter, and keep him out of trouble."

"I'll give you a hand, honey." Dax looked at Shane. "I'm sure we'll run into you again soon."

"We'll catch up with you, bro," D.J. said.

He was an inch or two shorter than his brother and not as dark. His brown hair had strands of sunlight running through it and his eyes were more chocolate than coal colored. "Shane and I have met, but I don't think you know my wife, Allaire."

The pretty, petite, blue-eyed blonde smiled. She had her hand on the shoulder of their little guy, who was quivering with the need to follow the other family and be with the kids.

"And this is our son, Alex." The proud mother smiled as she ruffled hair the same color as his father's.

"I'm four," the boy said. "Just like Max. People say I look big for four."

"I thought you were at least five and a half," Shane said seriously.

"There are days he makes me feel twice my age." D.J. shook his head.

"Mommy? Daddy? Can I go with Uncle Dax and Aunt Shandie?"

Allaire glanced up the street to the group gathered in front of a gift-shop window. "If you hurry."

"I'll run fast, like I'm already five." And he did.

"Dax?" D.J. called out and when his brother glanced over, he pointed to the boy running toward them. There was a nod of understanding and he settled a big hand on the small shoulder when Alex caught up and joined the merry little band.

Gianna glanced between them. "Is that a brother thing? Silent communication? Because my sister and I don't have that."

"Maybe because you're in different places in your lives," Allaire suggested. "Dax and D.J. both have four-year-olds and a protective streak as big as Montana."

Gianna knew it was a nice way of saying her sister Jackie was married with three kids. And she, Gianna, was a spinster with no prospects. Time to change the subject.

"So, Allaire, Lizzie was just singing your artistic praises. She said you hand-stenciled the flowers on the walls of her bakery."

"I did." The other woman smiled with pleasure.

"Beautiful job," Shane said. "I understand you're a high school art teacher."

"Yes. I wasn't cut out to be a starving artist." She looked

up at her husband. "And I'm not. Thanks to D.J.'s Rib Shack and my teaching job."

"What else do you like to work on?" Shane asked.

Gianna thought it was interesting that he was chatting up Allaire and hadn't said much to her husband. Probably the art connection. He had an interest in it judging by the collection she'd seen in his condo. The four of them moved closer to the building to let a mother with a baby in a stroller get by them on the sidewalk. The movement put Shane beside the other man.

"I really like portraits," Allaire answered. "But just for fun. I'm not very good at it. But it lets me indulge my people-watching tendency."

"She's way too modest about her amazing talent." D.J. slid an arm across her shoulders and looked at Shane. "So, how do you like Thunder Canyon?"

"Fine."

Along with the other couple, Gianna waited for him to elaborate. When he didn't, she put a teasing tone in her voice when she asked, "What happened to the poetic guy who said the scenery around here speaks to your soul?"

"If I was Shane," D.J. said with a knowing expression, "I'd never admit to that, either."

Gianna looked at Allaire and together they said, "Guy thing."

"Speaking of guys…" D.J. met her gaze, then glanced at her companion. "How's everything?"

Gianna knew he meant her love life. She'd gotten to know him since coming back to town. She'd applied for a job at the Rib Shack and he wasn't hiring, but steered her to The Gallatin Room. Then he'd taken her under his wing and become the big brother she'd always wanted.

"D.J." Allaire's voice had a scolding note to it. "Don't put her on the spot right now."

"Why?" His expression was clueless. "We talk."

"We do," she confirmed. "And I can tell you that everything is…" She'd ended up confessing to him her pathetic love life and all the time and energy she'd wasted in New York. D.J. wanted to know what was up with Shane and she wasn't going to talk about that in front of him. So she resorted to a girl's succinct fallback response. "Fine."

"You know…" Allaire glanced back and forth between the two men.

"What?" Gianna wasn't sure what was on her mind, but encouraged a change of subject.

"Speaking of people watching to indulge my artistic streak," the other woman said, "I've just noticed something."

"That I'm better looking than Ryan Reynolds?" D.J. said.

"No." She playfully punched him in the arm. "There's a very strong resemblance between you and Shane."

"Really?" Gianna studied them.

"Not the eyes." The other woman thoughtfully tapped her lip. "D.J.'s are brown and Shane's are strikingly blue. But the shape of the face is identical. And you both have a strong chin. So does Dax."

Gianna looked carefully at the two men standing side by side and saw what Allaire meant. She wondered why she'd never noticed before. Probably because she'd never seen them in the same room together, let alone side by side.

"You're right. I see it, too."

"They say everyone has a twin." D.J. pointed playfully at Shane. "Just don't pretend to be me and go changing the Rib Shack menu to snails and frog's legs."

Gianna snapped her fingers. "And you both make a living in the restaurant business. What a coincidence."

That's when she noticed Shane's weird look was back and even more intense. Not only that, he hadn't said a word since Allaire mentioned the strong resemblance. The face might resemble D.J.'s but it was not the face of the charming, playful man who'd said her fleecy pants and ratty robe were cute. Was that only last night? Seemed so much longer.

Even this morning at breakfast he'd been carefree and gallant, offering to drive her wherever she wanted to go. His mood had changed when Catherine had mentioned Presents for Patriots. Then again when Gianna had asked him about shopping for his family. That led to the revelation about him being adopted and searching for his birth parents.

He took her arm. "We should probably get to the mall."

"That's where we're going," Allaire said.

D.J. looked down at his wife. "We should meet them for lunch. You can compare the shape of Dax's face to mine and Shane's."

"I wish I could. I already have lunch plans with my mother and sister. But maybe Shane—" She'd invited him to join her but he hadn't responded one way or the other. Now Gianna felt his hand tense. Even if she were free, it was clear he'd rather eat bugs than join them.

"I can't," he said. "I have a meeting with a vendor this afternoon."

"Too bad." The other woman slid her hand into her husband's.

"How about a rain check?" D.J. suggested.

"That would be great." Gianna figured like a typical man he hadn't noticed that Shane was quiet. But she'd bet everything she had that observant Allaire had sensed something. "See you guys soon."

"You're coming to Presents for Patriots?" D.J. asked.

"Wouldn't miss it. I'm all signed up," she said, but Shane remained quiet.

"Okay, then. Bye, you two," Allaire said before they strolled down the street in the same direction the rest of the family had gone.

Shane walked her to his SUV parked in front of the bakery and handed her inside. Then he came around to the driver's side and got in. "Do you still want to go to the mall?"

His tone said he hoped to get a rain check on that, too, and suddenly she lost the Christmas spirit.

"Shane, talk to me. What's bothering you so much?"

"I already told you. Just some family stuff."

"Come on. I'm not artistic like Allaire, but I observe people, too. I'd make a lousy waitress if I didn't notice things. You barely said a word to D.J. That's not like you. You're probably one of the friendliest, most charming men I've ever met. So, I ask again. What's wrong? And don't tell me nothing."

His hand tensed on the steering wheel and a muscle in the jaw so much like D.J.'s jumped. "It's complicated."

So, back to square one. He'd shut her down again. It didn't take Cupid to clue her in that she was beating her head against the wall. By definition, romance required two people to participate in order to achieve the desired result. Clearly she was the only one here doing the work.

At least it hadn't taken her very long to figure out that he had no intention of committing. And really, it was almost funny given her history of hanging on until all hope was gone.

She'd just set a personal record in the least amount of time it took her to lose a guy.

Chapter Seven

After asking Shane to take her home, Gianna hadn't had much to say. That technically wasn't true. She'd actually had a lot to say but kept it to herself since it was impossible to have a meaningful conversation with an obviously pre-occupied man who would only tell her "it's complicated." Still, when the man said he would do something, he did it.

At Real Vintage Cowboy, Catherine Overton had her car keys. Per Shane's instructions, the car had a new battery and they'd dropped it off for her. Note to self: find out the cost and pay him back. She didn't want to owe him. On the other hand, at least she now had wheels, such as they were.

She never made it to the mall, but managed to get in a little Christmas shopping before it was time to meet her mother and sister at The Tottering Teapot. The customer base was primarily female and the restaurant was located in Old Town on Main Street near Pine, between the teenage hangout ROOTS and Mountain Bluebell Bakery. Not far from this morning's disaster with Shane.

She drove around for a while looking for a parking space because, of course, she was running late. The place did a brisk business but seemed more crowded than usual today. A lot of people were probably out Christmas shopping and stopped for lunch.

Gianna finally found a spot to park that felt like a mile up the block, then nearly jogged all the way to the entrance where the double, half-glass doors were covered with lace. She pushed her way inside and immediately the sweet scent of lighted candles surrounded her. She knew the fragrance was called Mistletoe and that made her think of kissing Shane. Thinking of him was like a sudden pinch to her heart so she tried not to.

A podium just inside the door had a sign that said "Please wait to be seated" but the hostess must have been leading another party because no one was there. Peeking into the dining room, she spotted her mother and sister already at a table.

"Because, of course, they have well-ordered lives with men who probably confide in them," she muttered to herself.

Without waiting for the hostess, she walked halfway through the restaurant. In addition to the menu of organic food, free-range chicken and grass-fed beef, everything about the place was female friendly. The tables were covered with lace tablecloths, no two the same. Food was served on thrift-store-bought, mismatched china. In deference to its name, there was an endless variety of teas, both herbal and otherwise. Normally this was Gianna's favorite restaurant, and catching up with her mother and sister was something she looked forward to. But not today.

Because getting grilled like a free-range chicken was really unappealing, Gianna pasted an everything's-just-peachy smile on her face just before sliding into the third of four chairs. The other held purses.

"Hi. Sorry I'm late. Took a while to find a place to park."

"Oh, sweetheart, don't worry about it. We haven't been here very long," her mother said.

Susan Garrison was in her early fifties and was walking, talking proof that fifty was truly the new forty. She was blond, with some chemical help at the Clip 'n Curl to cover just a sprinkling of gray. Her beautiful blue eyes had been passed on to both of her daughters.

Her sister, Jackie Blake, was about Gianna's height and had a trim figure even after three kids, but she'd inherited their mom's blond hair. There was no obvious link from either parent to Gianna's red shade and the family joke was that her father was the mailman. No one believed that since her parents only had eyes for each other.

"It seems like forever since we've done this," her sister said.

"Everyone is busy," Susan commented.

"No kidding." Gianna looked at her sister. "What's up with the kids?"

"Griffin wants to play basketball, but isn't he too short? Colin is in preschool, as you know, but he thinks he's such a big boy. Can you believe Em is two already? She's home with Frank. He doesn't have a firefighter shift for a couple of days and said I could use the break."

The brunette, twentysomething waitress brought a tray containing a china teapot filled with hot water and three cups, each with a mismatched saucer. Her name tag said "Flo." "Peppermint tea for three."

"I hope that's okay, Gianna. It's what you usually have," her mother explained.

"It's fine, Mom."

With the plastic tray under her arm, Flo pulled out her pad. "Are you ready to order?"

"I think so. I'll have the portobello mushroom sandwich and salad," Jackie said.

"Me, too." Susan folded her menu closed.

Gianna hadn't had a chance to look, but knew the choices pretty well. She usually ordered exactly like the other two but after the morning she'd had, her rebellious streak kicked in for unknown reasons.

She looked at the waitress. "Grass-fed beef burger and sweet potato fries."

"The fries are a new addition to the menu. Really yummy," Flo added. "I'll get it right out for you."

When they were alone, Susan poured hot water from the teapot into their cups. "So, how's work? What's new?"

Gianna knew the question was for her. Jackie was a stay-at-home mom and couldn't be more different from herself. She'd never had career ambitions or wanted to leave home and see the world. She married her high-school sweetheart shortly after graduation and their first child was born nine months later. Frank Blake was a county firefighter and they'd been married seven years and had two more children.

Gianna had a failed business, no romantic prospects and a junker car. She didn't really want to talk about any of it. "Work is fine."

"That's it?" Jackie asked.

"Pretty much."

"I want to hear about celebrity chef Shane Roarke." Her mother's blue eyes twinkled. "I watched *If You Can't Stand the Heat*. He's a hottie and that has nothing to do with cooking over a steaming stove."

"Mom," Gianna scolded. "What would Dad say?"

It was a deflection because she really didn't think her

carefree act would hold up to scrutiny if she was forced to talk about her boss.

"Your father would say there's nothing wrong with looking as long as I come home to him."

"Frank would agree with that." Her sister looked thoughtful. "This isn't the first time I've noticed that he and Dad are a lot alike."

Susan took a cautious sip of the hot tea, then set the cup on the saucer. "They're both good men. Solid. Stable. Dependable. It's what eased my worries a little bit when you insisted on getting married so young."

"It all worked out for the best," Jackie said.

And then some. It was everything Gianna wanted. Up until this morning she'd been sure Shane was cut from the same cloth as the other two men, but now she didn't know what to think. His behavior had changed so suddenly. Where he was concerned, her emotions were all over the map. One minute she was angry, the next worried about whatever was so "complicated."

"Are you okay, honey?"

"Hmm?" Gianna had zoned out and it took a couple of seconds to realize her mother was speaking to her. "Sorry, Mom. I'm fine. Just tired."

"Any particular reason?"

"No. Just that time of the year when we're all busy."

It wouldn't do any good to tell them that she'd lost sleep because of playing in the snow last night with Shane, then he drove her home and made love to her. Her head was still spinning at the speed at which everything had changed.

She looked at her sister. "What's going on with you?"

"Things are good. The kids aren't sick and I hope we make it through the holidays with everyone healthy." She crossed her fingers for luck. "Griffin is in the Christmas pageant at his school. Colin's preschool is going to the hospital to sing carols for the patients. I'm the room mother in both of their classes and responsible for the holiday parties. I love doing it, but when Emily is old enough for school, I'm not sure how I can spread myself that thin."

"You need minions." Gianna remembered talking about that with Shane and wondered how long casual conversation would set off reminders of him.

"She has minions," Susan said. "It's called family."

Jackie snapped her fingers. "That reminds me."

"What?" Gianna and her mother said at the same time.

Her sister grabbed her purse from the chair and pulled something from the side pocket. It was an oblong-shaped piece of cardstock and she handed one to each of them. "This is the Blake family Christmas card."

Gianna's heart pinched again in a different way as she looked at her sister's beautiful family. Handsome dark-haired Frank with four-year-old Colin on his lap. Beautiful Jackie holding Emily. She was wearing a sweet little red-velvet dress, white leggings and black-patent shoes. Griffin, seven and a half, stood just behind his parents, little arms trying to reach around their shoulders.

"Oh, sis—" Gianna's voice caught. "This is a fantastic picture."

"It really is, honey." Susan smiled fondly.

"Thanks." Her sister beamed. "It's a Christmas miracle. You have no idea the level of difficulty there is in getting a decent photo of three kids and two adults. No one is crying and by that I mean Frank and I. There are no spots on the clothes—at least none that show up."

Gianna laughed in spite of the fact that she was simultaneously rocking a case of jealousy and feelings of failure. She loved her sister very much and was so happy for her. But the picture she held in her hands was everything she'd ever wanted and thought by now she would have. She was thirty years old and had nothing to show for it except a string of broken dreams and long, unsuccessful relationships.

She wasn't sure Shane could be considered a relationship, but he was definitely the shortest. So it didn't make sense that what happened with him hurt so much more than all the others.

And it was going to get worse. She had to see him at work in a couple of hours.

Shane paced back and forth in the living room of his condo but today the fantastic mountain view and heavenly blue sky did nothing to fill up his soul. On the other hand, his mind was overflowing, mostly about how rude he'd been to Gianna that morning.

"I'm an idiot." An idiot who was talking to himself. "At the very least she just thinks I'm nuts. It's complicated? How does that explain anything?"

His cell phone rang and he plucked it from the case on his belt then checked the caller ID because he didn't want to talk to anyone unless absolutely necessary. This person was most definitely necessary.

He smiled and hit the talk button. "Hi, Mom."

"Shane. Is it really you? Not your voice mail?"

"Okay. I officially feel guilty."

She laughed. "Is this a bad time? Are you working? I don't want to interrupt—"

"You're not interrupting anything." Except him beating himself up. He had a little time before work. And facing Gianna. "I'm at home."

"Great." Christa Roarke's voice suited her. She was strong, sweet, tough and tender. A green-eyed brunette whose face showed the traumas and triumphs of life but remained beautiful. She practiced family law and after struggling to have a family of her own, it seemed appropriate.

"Is Dad okay?" Gavin Roarke was the strongest man he knew, but Shane always needed to check.

"Fine. Why?"

"Ryan and Maggie?" His siblings, lawyers like their parents. He'd wondered more than once if that's part of what made him question who he was. Though they were all adopted, he was the only one who didn't follow in their parents' footsteps, but took a completely different career path. He couldn't remember when he'd seriously begun to wonder why.

"Your brother and sister are fine." There was humor in her voice. "But the focus of your questions leads me to believe you think I called because of a family crisis."

"Did you?"

"Everyone here in L.A. is fine."

"Good." That left him the only family member in a mess. "What can I do for you, Mom?"

"I just haven't talked to you for a while." There was a slight hesitation before she added, "That comment was in no way meant to make you feel guilty."

He laughed. "If you say so."

"Maybe because it's the holidays and you're so far away, I've just been thinking a lot about you. Wondering how you are."

He stood beside the floor-to-ceiling windows and leaned a shoulder against the wall as he looked out. His mother was as transparent as the glass. She knew why he'd come to Thunder Canyon and was fishing for information. "I'm okay."

There was silence on the other end of the line for a few moments before she asked, "That's it? Just okay?"

"Yeah."

"This is why you're not an attorney like the rest of the

Roarkes. Practicing law frequently requires the use of words and apparently that's not your strength."

He grinned. "I communicate through food."

"That's all well and good. The culinary world loves you. The camera loves you. And I love you. But it's a mother's job to encourage her child to use words."

"It's a dirty job, I guess, but someone has to do it."

"And you know what an overachiever I can be," she said.

"What is it you're asking, Mom?"

"You just love to torture me, don't you?" She sighed. "Okay. You asked for it. Here comes the maternal cross-examination."

"I can hardly wait." A rustling sound on the line made him picture her sitting up straight in the chair, probably behind the desk in her office.

"Mr. Roarke, you've lived in Thunder Canyon, Montana, for nearly six months now. How is it going?"

He thought about the question and knew she was asking how the search for his birth parents was progressing. When he'd first stepped foot in the town something clicked into place inside him and it seemed crazy at the time. But the more he learned, the longer he stayed, the less crazy that feeling felt. Still, he wasn't ready to tell his family what was going on. So much of it was conjecture. Getting into her milieu, he only had half the facts to build a case.

So, Shane decided to use his words to go in a different direction. "When I made the decision to come here, I braced myself for a wilderness adventure."

"Survivor Montana?" she teased.

"Something like that." He studied the jagged snow-capped peaks with evergreen trees standing out in stark relief against the whiteness. "You can research anything on the internet, but there's no way to experience a place until you do it in person."

"There's a reverence in your voice, as if you're in church."

"Someone else said the same thing to me," he answered, thinking of Gianna. "And it feels like being in the presence of God sometimes. You can't know unless you see."

"And what do you know now, Shane?"

"I like this place. More than I thought." He pretended she wasn't asking about his search. "Thunder Canyon is small. Really small compared to anywhere I've ever lived."

"That could be a double-edged sword."

"People talk." He knew that and what he'd uncovered could give them a lot to talk about. "Around here everyone knows your business even if you haven't shared it with them. But that can also be a good thing. When there's a problem, they don't look the other way. They don't avoid getting involved or feel inconvenienced. Folks help each other out."

"And you like that?"

"Let me put it this way," he said. "I've donated money to charity and felt good about it, but was never personally touched by the cause. But it's different here. There's no comparison, no way to describe how good it feels to use your talent to make a difference. To be included in a cause bigger than yourself."

"Such as?"

"Just before Thanksgiving I prepared a dinner for the families of military members serving overseas. You could see the gratitude in their eyes, Mom. It was a fantastic feeling."

"Sounds wonderful."

"Of course I didn't do it alone. The staff at The Gallatin Room pitched in. Gianna was pretty amazing."

"Gianna?"

"Gianna Garrison. She's one of the waitresses who volunteered her time to serve that dinner." He pictured the sassy redhead with the beautiful smile that warmed him in dark places he hadn't even been aware of. "She worked her tail off and I never once saw her anything but considerate. Always laughing."

"Is she pretty?"

"What does that have to do with anything?"

"Humor me." There was a tone that said resistance was futile.

"She's very attractive." Such plain words to describe someone so bright, so special. And before his mother asked, he added, "A blue-eyed redhead."

"Hmm."

He wished he could see her expression. "What does that mean?"

"Nothing. Go on."

"That's it. I was finished."

"Hardly." Along with sweet and strong, his mother's voice could also be sarcastic. "There's a lot more you're not saying."

Mental note, he thought. Never play poker with this woman. But he added something that was completely true and also too simple to explain what he felt. "I like her."

"That does it. I really want to meet the new woman in your life."

"That's not how it is." At least not after the way he'd acted this morning. He probably blew it big time.

He just hadn't been able to pull off a casual act after Catherine Overton mentioned D.J.'s mother's name was Grace. If their mothers sharing a first name was the only coincidence, he could have laughed it off. But then Allaire Traub commented on his resemblance to Dax and D.J. She'd stopped short of calling it a family resemblance, but...

He and D.J. both had the food-service industry in common and every time he'd seen the other man there'd been a feeling. A shared sense of humor. A connection that Shane couldn't explain. Because they were brothers?

It *was* complicated. If he'd told Gianna all of his suspicions, she'd think he was crazy and call the shrink squad. Shane had heard the rumors of Swinton's unrequited love for Grace Traub, but everyone laughed it off as the raving of a lunatic. What if that was true? What if Arthur Swinton had slept with Dax and D.J.'s mother and he, Shane, was the result?

"Shane?"

His mother's voice yanked him out of the dark turn his thoughts had taken. "Sorry. What did you say?"

"I asked how it is with you and Gianna?"

It was nowhere because he'd pushed her away. Even a bad shrink would say it was because he didn't want to see the look of disgust in her eyes when she learned who his father was. Why would she not believe that an evil man's son didn't have evil in his DNA?

"I consider her a friend," he finally said.

"Hostile witness."

"Really, Mom?" He had to smile. "Now you're going all lawyer on me?"

"That's what you do when a witness holds back." She sighed. "But, it's all right. You're entitled to your secrets."

That word grated on him. He was learning the hard way that secrets could corrode the soul. Should he come clean with Gianna, give her the explanation? Maybe stop the blackness inside him from spreading? The risk was that everyone in town would find out. But maybe if he asked her to keep it to herself, it might be possible to control the flow of information even in a small town.

When he didn't comment, his mother continued, "Another reason I called is…what are your plans for Christmas?"

"I hadn't really thought that far ahead." What with everything else on his mind.

"It's a couple of weeks, so not really that far ahead. Will we see you for the holidays?" Her voice was carefully casual, an indication that seeing him meant a lot.

The truth was he missed his family. He'd never not been there for Christmas. No matter where he worked his heart was with the Roarkes—his parents and his siblings. Nothing he found out would ever change that.

"Of course I'll be there."

"Wonderful." There was a subtle sound of relief in her voice. "We'll look forward to seeing you, sweetheart."

"Same here, Mom."

"Hold on." There were muffled voices in the background, then she came back on the line. "I'm sorry, Shane. My next appointment is here."

"No problem, Mom. I have to get to work."

"Love you, son."

"Love you, too."

He clicked off and thought about the conversation. It didn't escape his notice that he no longer thought of Los Angeles as home. Something twisted in his chest when he opened the French door and walked out on the balcony to look at the big sky and mountains. The cold snapped through him and sliced inside.

He wasn't at all sure he would survive Montana unscathed. This place had become home and Gianna had become more important than he'd intended. It was entirely possible that he could be more lost now than when he'd first arrived in Thunder Canyon.

Chapter Eight

At work Gianna looked over the empty dining room, searching for anything out of place. Silverware was wrapped in cloth napkins and ready in a corner, out of the view of customers. Fresh linens and flower vases were on the tables along with lighted candles. She'd done everything ahead of time that could possibly be done and not compromise the quality and freshness of food.

The service business was always a delicate balance, not unlike navigating a relationship. Never give anyone a reason not to come back, but if a mistake was made, do whatever was necessary to make things right.

With all the prep work done, this would be a good time to grab a quick bite to eat. At lunch with her mother and sister she'd lost her appetite, but was starving now. The rest of the staff had already finished their pre-service meal and were gearing up for a busy night. A local company was having their Christmas party in the banquet room.

In the kitchen there was food left from the staff meal. She was just taking a bite when Shane walked in. This was the first time she'd seen him alone since he'd dropped her off at her apartment this morning. Not that she'd done anything wrong, or that she wanted to give him a reason to come back, but speaking of making things right... They did have to work together, at least for the time being.

There was a nanosecond of awkwardness between them before she finally said, "Hi. How are you?"

"Keeping my head above water." He shrugged. "How's the car?"

"Not getting any younger and still holding together with bubble gum and prayer." That produced a smile, which was good to see. "But running now, thanks to you. I left a check for the battery on the desk in your office."

"You didn't have to. I was happy to take care of it. And I'll be tearing up that check." She opened her mouth to protest, but he held up his hand. "No argument. Just say thank you."

"All right. Thank you. I appreciate it very much."

"You're welcome." He hesitated a moment. "So you saw your mother and sister?"

"Yes."

He moved closer, leaned a hip against the counter beside her and crossed his arms over his chest. The spicy scent of his cologne burrowed inside her and pushed every nerve into a spasm of need. If she hadn't been with him skin to skin maybe she could fight off this overwhelming feeling, but that wasn't the case. She had slept with him and there was no way to unremember the practically perfect way his body had felt against hers.

"How was lunch?" His gaze settled on hers.

Why was he suddenly so chatty? She'd take it as a good thing if the shadows weren't still in his eyes, just the way he'd looked outside of Mountain Bluebell Bakery. But her questions, even though asked with the intention of helping, hadn't helped either one of them.

She ran a finger around the edge of her plate. "It's always good to catch up with Jackie and my mom. They're busy getting ready for Christmas. Making plans."

"Apparently this is the day for it." He rubbed a hand across the back of his neck.

"Oh?" She took a bite of her food, although her appetite was missing in action again.

"My mother called."

"How was it?" He'd already opened that door by asking her the same question.

"Before or after she let me know I don't phone home often enough?"

"I can see how that would lead directly into holiday plans," she agreed.

"It did. And I'm going to Los Angeles."

"You're leaving?"

"For Christmas," he confirmed.

Even she had heard the shock and hurt in her voice. If only she were a computer and could backspace and delete those two words. She had no claim on him. Yes, he'd taken her to bed and she'd gone enthusiastically. But there was no reason to think it was more than fun. They'd gone into it with the understanding that one or both of them would be leaving town. Nothing serious.

Except somewhere in her subconscious she must have been thinking about spending the holiday with him. Otherwise she wouldn't feel like the rug had been yanked out from under her because he wouldn't be here for Christmas. The depth of her disappointment was a surprise, a very unwelcome one.

"Gianna—" He cupped her cheek in his palm. "Please don't look like that."

Obviously she wasn't very successfully hiding her disappointment. "I'm not looking any way. Not on purpose. You just surprised me. It's your first Christmas in Thunder Canyon and the way you talked—" She'd assumed when a place filled up your soul, it's where you'd want to be at the most wonderful time of the year. Apparently his soul was taken and this was proof that she had no claim on his heart. "I understand. They're your family."

"They are. And I love them." His gaze searched hers and he let out a long breath. "Look, I feel like a jerk—"

"No. Please don't. Of course you should be with your family. I didn't mean anything. I'm fine."

"You are fine." For just an instant as he caressed her cheek with his thumb, heat burned in his eyes. Then it was gone and the shadows returned. "And I acted like an idiot earlier. You deserve an explanation."

"That's not necessary—"

"I know it's not, but I want to tell you. I need to talk about this with someone. It's eating me up inside." There was a dark and dangerous expression on his face. He took her hand and led her away from the noise and bustle of the kitchen, into the pantry where he'd kissed her. He didn't look like he planned to kiss her now.

So she was right to be concerned about him. "What is it, Shane? Of course you can talk to me. I'm happy to listen."

"You might change your mind when I tell you what's going on."

"Be a Band-Aid."

"What?"

"Do it quick. Just spit it out."

He hesitated for a moment, then said, "Arthur Swinton is my biological father."

Gianna couldn't believe she'd heard him correctly. "What?"

"The man who embezzled from the city, disappeared with the money and was behind all the bad stuff that happened to the Traub family is my father."

"You're joking."

"If I was going to joke, it wouldn't be about that." He dragged his fingers through his hair. "The way everyone in town feels about that weasel makes him the last man on the planet I'd claim for a father unless it was true."

She stared at him. "Are you sure about this?"

"I have a DNA test confirming it to a ninety-nine percent certainty."

Her brain was spinning. "But don't you need a sample from him? I thought he was in jail."

"He is." Shane's gaze slid away for a moment. "I told you my mother gave me all the information she had on my birth parents? She also told me the adoption records were sealed and she didn't know what good it would do."

"Right."

"The private investigator said with everything on computers, now no records can be completely sealed. Nothing is hack-proof. My biological mother's first name and the first initial of her last name are on the birth certificate. It only has my father's initials. The guy I hired found the hospital and narrowed the search to Thunder Canyon. After tightening the parameters of age, names with those initials, then cross-referencing employment and personal interests, which included political ambitions, one name stood out."

"Arthur Swinton was on the town council for years," she remembered.

"He ran for mayor against Bo Clifton on a family-values platform." Bitterness hardened his eyes. "How hypocritical is that? Add being a fraud of a human being to his long list of sins."

Gianna was in shock. "I was in New York when that happened, but my mom told me what was going on. How did you get the DNA?"

"The P.I. visited him in jail. He made up something about being a journalist and doing a story on Thunder Canyon politicians. Swinton was only too happy to talk about how he was a victim of the Traubs. That they always hated him."

"And the investigator was able to get something to compare DNA?"

Shane nodded. "A soda can. He said it was easy and the guy never suspected anything."

"And the test is back?"

"I got a report just before Thanksgiving." His mouth twisted as if he'd eaten something bad. "*There's* something to be thankful for. Being the son of Thunder Canyon's most despised person."

"Oh, Shane—" Gianna suddenly got it. He was concerned that if anyone found out about this the whole town would turn against him, making him an outcast in the place he'd come to love. And the worst part was that he could be right. Some great person she was to talk to. She couldn't think of anything helpful to say.

"It will be okay." That was lame. So she put her hand on his arm.

"Careful." He pulled away from her touch. "You probably don't want to get too close to me."

"Don't be ridiculous. This doesn't change the good man you are." She met his gaze even as the struggle to wrap her mind around this raged inside her. "Did the investigator find out about your mother?"

"No." He slid his fingers into the pockets of his jeans. "But you've heard the rumors of Grace Traub and Arthur

Swinton. How he ranted and raved about them being a couple. Everyone in town thought he was just a wacko, but the name on my birth certificate is Grace S. Dax and D.J.'s mother's name was Grace."

"That doesn't prove anything."

"Not by itself. But you heard Allaire Traub. The resemblance—"

"Shane—" The ramifications of that rippled through her. "Do you think you're related to the Traubs?"

"I don't know. But that family has every reason to hate the man. He tried to destroy them, personally and professionally. How do you think they'd feel to find out he's my father and we could be half brothers? What does that information do to their mother's memory?"

He was so right. This *was* complicated and that word didn't even do it justice.

"Gianna?"

She looked up as the blond, thirtyish restaurant hostess poked her head in the door. "Hi, Ashley. What's up?"

"I just seated a party of four in your station."

"Thanks. I'll be right there." She looked at Shane. "I don't want to leave you like this—"

"It's okay." But there was nothing okay in the look on his face, or the tension coiled in his body. "We have a job to do."

She nodded, then slid off the stool and tossed her food in the trash. If only her thoughts could go with it. The fact was she needed time alone to let all this sink in. She wasn't sure how she felt, which was why Shane was justified in his concern. If this information got out, his reputation and standing in Thunder Canyon could be destroyed.

Shane wasn't sure if this was the smartest move, but he'd felt compelled to drop by D.J.'s Rib Shack. Both of their restaurants were on resort grounds and when business slowed at The Gallatin Room, he'd left the sous-chef in charge, with orders to call if there was an emergency.

It was possible he was jumping to conclusions about Grace Traub and Arthur Swinton. Somehow he couldn't think of the man as his dad. And he couldn't very well ask D.J. about what happened, so he wasn't sure what this visit would accomplish. Curiosity, maybe.

Now he stood in the doorway of the Rib Shack looking around. Really looking. He'd been in here before, but it all felt different now, given the things he'd learned. There were a few customers scattered around the large, open dining room in this primarily family restaurant. Booths lined the exterior with picnic-style tables and benches filling the center. The walls were covered with sepia-toned pictures of cowboys, ranches and a hand-painted mural depicting the town's history. He was surprised it didn't include a section with Arthur Swinton being led away in handcuffs.

That kind of thinking proved that this was a stupid idea. He started to leave then spotted D. J. Traub himself walking toward him. So much for a clean getaway.

"Shane. Hi." The other man held out his hand and gave him a firm handshake. "To what do I owe the pleasure of a visit from Thunder Canyon's celebrity chef?"

"Celebrity?" He shrugged. "I had an opportunity. I'm just a guy who's fearless with food."

"You just happened to be fearless on reality TV in front of millions of women. Thunder Canyon ladies are lucky to have you."

Shane couldn't suppress a grin at the good-natured teasing. "It's a dirty job, but someone has to do it and do it well."

"Modest, too. I can respect that." D.J.'s dark eyes glittered with amusement. "Do you have time for a beer?"

"Why not?" Actually he could think of a lot of reasons, but his curiosity was telling him to follow through on this.

"Follow me."

The other man led him to a quiet corner in the back of the restaurant where there was a table and two wooden barrel-backed chairs. He said something to one of the waitresses and she returned with a couple of frosty mugs of beer.

"Thanks, Jan," D.J. said to her. He looked across the small table at Shane. "So, how are things at The Gallatin Room?"

"Busy. Business is up compared to last year."

"That could have something to do with the famous and fearless chef running the place."

"Whatever." Shane took a sip of his beer. "It's all good."

He couldn't say the same for his personal life. Probably he didn't deserve it, but at least Gianna was speaking to him. If only he could forget the look in her eyes when he'd confessed about who his father was. He wouldn't have blamed her if she'd run screaming from the room.

"What about you?" he asked, glancing around. "How are things here?"

"The books look better than they have in a while. Grant Clifton says resort traffic is better than it's been in a while, so there's a direct connection. Part of the increase could be because Traub Oil Montana is gearing up, bringing jobs into the area."

"That means more families," Shane commented.

"Right. Since that's the Rib Shack demographic, we've been more in demand. I've been able to hire some people. Business is improving."

"Do you like it? Food service?"

D.J. nodded. "Yeah. I enjoy the chaos, seeing the customers having fun. How about you?"

"Can't imagine doing anything else. The complexity, creativity and everything you just said, too."

Their careers were in the same field and it felt good to

talk to someone who understood. They each filled a different niche under the Thunder Canyon Resort umbrella. Not for the first time he wondered if it was a coincidence or something in the genes.

Their thoughts must have been traveling a parallel path because D.J. said, "I'm glad our customer base is different."

"You mean because I get to serve romantic dinners to local lovers Forrest Traub and Angie Anderson? And budding couples like Ben Walters and Kay Bausch?"

"Ben and Kay?" One of D.J.'s dark eyebrows lifted in surprise.

"I understand it was a blind date." And now he was talking about people as if he was just like everyone else here in Thunder Canyon.

Gianna had told him about the older couple. She thought it was cute and he agreed. He also thought Gianna was pretty cute and so much more. He wasn't sure how he'd have come this far without her. She'd listened to him and he felt better after confiding in her. Although not if his revelation had cost him that connection with her. But that was something for later.

"Apparently Austin Anderson set up the two of them."

D.J. looked amused. "So you're saying your place is all about romance?"

"And you get what comes after. Families." Shane had meant it in a teasing way, but had an uncomfortable hollow feeling inside, a sense of loneliness he'd never felt before. That something was missing from his own life. "You're a lucky man, D.J. To have Allaire and your son."

"I've loved her for a long time." The other man toyed with his mug. "You know she was married to my brother Dax for a while."

"No, I didn't." Shane was surprised. The two brothers had looked like they were extraordinarily close and he'd envied the shared bond of growing up together. How could they maintain that when they had both loved the same woman?

"The look on your face says you've got a lot of questions about how we can still hang out." D.J. smiled. "It was a long time ago. They both knew it wasn't right and stayed friends. Things have a way of working out the way they're supposed to."

Shane wasn't so sure about that but hoped it proved true. He felt comfortable with this guy. Liked him. D.J. was honest, funny and could maintain a relationship with his brother, even though they'd been married to the same woman. That was extraordinarily open-minded. Maybe a friendship was possible, even if the truth of Shane's real father came out.

But it wasn't coming out now. He traced a finger through the condensation on the outside of his mug.

"So, do you think the Packers will make it to the Super Bowl?" D.J. must have sensed the need for a subject change.

"Not if the Forty-Niners have anything to say about it."

"Ah, a California guy loyal to the state's teams."

Shane shrugged. "I've moved around a lot. Seattle for a while. New York. Los Angeles is just where I grew up."

"But you could be persuaded to root for the Packers?"

"Maybe." He looked around the big room. "Is this where you hold the Presents for Patriots event?"

The other man nodded. "We've been collecting donations for a while now. Storing them in a back room here. Small electronics, toiletries, socks, candy. Baked goods are brought in the day when all the volunteers wrap and box it all up for shipping out."

"It's quite an undertaking."

"I'm privileged to do it. Family is precious," D.J. said,

suddenly serious and sincere. "No one knows that better than I do."

"Me, too." Catherine had mentioned that his mother died when he was young and there was a time that connecting with his dad was difficult. Shane loved his parents and would do anything for them, but he had different family issues.

"Our military men and women sacrifice so much every day," D.J. continued. "But even more this time of year. They give up holidays with their loved ones so that we can be safe and secure and enjoy ours. In some small way what we do says thanks for that."

Shane could see for himself that the other man felt deeply about family and roots. Would he understand why Shane needed to find out about his birth parents? Would D.J. have done the same thing if he'd been given up for adoption?

D.J. took a swallow of beer. "Wow, I can't believe it's been a year already."

"Since the last Presents for Patriots?"

"That. The holidays. Rose and Austin were married last year on Christmas Day." D.J. looked thoughtful. "It was a year ago that she was kidnapped."

"What?" Shane couldn't believe he'd heard right. Things like that didn't happen in Thunder Canyon.

"That's right. You weren't here then."

"She was kidnapped? By who?"

"Jasper Fowler."

The man who was linked to Arthur Swinton. It seemed as if everything bad that happened in this town could be traced back to his father. "What happened?"

"Rose works in public relations for the mayor and was helping clean out paperwork from the previous administration. She found evidence of Swinton's embezzling money from the city council and a link to Fowler as an accomplice."

Shane's stomach knotted. "I heard about that."

"Common knowledge," D.J. agreed. "But everyone thought Swinton had died in jail. Turned out he faked a heart attack and with inside help he escaped. He and Fowler conspired to ruin my business and launder the stolen money through The Tattered Saddle."

"Which is now Real Vintage Cowboy." Shane was concentrating on not reacting as if any of this concerned him personally.

"Right. Rose decided to pay Fowler a visit and ask him about what she found. It never occurred to her that the man could be dangerous. But she was wrong. He was desperate and crazy and took her at gunpoint."

"But she got away." That was stating the obvious but he couldn't manage much more than that.

"Smart girl." There was a dark satisfaction in D.J.'s eyes. "She managed to call Austin and leave the cell line open while she talked to the old man about where he was taking her. They were intercepted by her brother Jackson and Austin. I think a couple more of her brothers showed up, too, and then the cops. Fowler gave up Swinton and he was re-arrested. He won't be getting out of jail anytime soon."

"That's quite a story."

D.J. shook his head. "It really ticks me off that the rumor linking my mother to Swinton refuses to go away."

"I can understand that." If Shane could make his own connection to the man go away he'd do it in a nanosecond.

"Swinton is corrupt. A convicted criminal."

Anger and resentment twisted together in D.J.'s expression along with distaste and revulsion. Shane hoped it wasn't a preview of what he could expect. If he had it to do over again, he'd refuse to take the information his mother gave him. It came under the heading of be careful what you wish for. Or let sleeping dogs lie. When you went out of your way to connect the dots, you might not like the picture that emerged.

"I can't believe people would think my mother could be involved with someone like that," D.J. continued. "No way Grace Traub would associate with him. Actually it would have been before she married my dad. She'd have been Grace Smith then. She'd never have gone out with Swinton."

Shane went cold inside as the dots connected. If she'd only gone out with him, Shane thought, he and D.J. wouldn't be sitting here talking. Under the table his hands curled into fists. All the puzzle pieces fell into place and explained his resemblance to the other man. Only a DNA test would prove it to a ninety-nine percent certainty, but Grace S. was his mother's name. Smith was such a common last name that the P.I. wouldn't be able to pin down his mother's identity for certain. Evidence from his own search was piling up, though.

Shane was convinced that Dax and D. J. Traub were his half brothers.

Chapter Nine

Gianna stood in the shadows off to the side in The Gallatin Room. The customers at her tables were enjoying various courses of their meals. At the moment there was nothing for her to do and it was nice to take a breather. Interrupting every five seconds to ask if they needed anything was as bad as ignoring them.

Especially when there was romance in this room. Candles still flickered on pristine white tablecloths and there was a quiet hum of conversation and laughter. *She* didn't feel much like laughing as she watched Shane performing the public relations part of his job.

The information about who his father was had overshadowed her disappointment that he wouldn't be here for Christmas. What he'd talked to her about a little while ago was shocking enough, and then he'd disappeared. He was back now looking even more troubled.

He frequently schmoozed with the customers, moving

from table to table, meeting and greeting, using his natural charm and enjoying the connection. He was doing that now, but something was off. There was tension on his face in spite of the smile, and something like shock in his eyes. Each encounter was brief and smacked of duty, not the usual friendly and relaxed way he interacted. The lines of his body looked tight, as if he might snap.

Bonnie moved beside her and let out a long breath. "It's been so busy. I haven't had a chance to talk."

"Tell me about it." She smiled at her friend, then glanced at Shane. "How's everything with you?"

"Jim and I broke up."

"Bon—" Gianna gave her a quick hug. "I'm sorry. What happened?"

"He wasn't that into me." She tried to look spunky, but the disappointment leaked through. "I'm swearing off men. It's time to go back to college. No distractions."

"College is good. But don't back yourself into a corner with grand declarations about no relationships." If anyone could sympathize it was Gianna. "You really thought he was the one."

"Isn't it a rule or a law of physics or something that you can't be in love by yourself?"

"It's definitely more fun with two."

Her friend's gaze wandered to their boss, who was on his way back to the kitchen. "What's with Shane tonight?"

Gianna had to decide how to answer that question. She'd seen romances here at work burn bright and hot then fizzle and get awkward. The ones involved always thought they were discreet and keeping things under the radar. But when people worked as closely together as they did in food service, secrets were hard to keep. Although she'd managed. She hadn't said anything about sleeping with the boss, and wondered if her friend had noticed a change in anything.

"You think he's different tonight?"

"Not at the start of my shift," Bonnie said carefully.

"Then when?"

"The last hour or so. I've put in requests from customers, nothing out of the ordinary because he insists on one hundred percent satisfaction. But he's had to redo several meals, like his mind is on something else. One guy asked for no mango, not even a garnish on the plate. Shane put on the mango. Fortunately I noticed and fixed it."

"That's so unlike him," Gianna said.

"Tell me about it. His mind is somewhere else and the rest of him is on autopilot. I had to tell him about the mistake. He's always encouraged us to do that. It's one of the things I like best, that he's not a prima donna. But this time he practically bit my head off. He was gone for a while and came back different."

Gianna had noticed that, too. "Do you know where he went?"

"No. He's not in the habit of confiding in me."

Gianna couldn't say the same, except about where he'd gone, but when he walked back in the kitchen, he looked like a shell-shocked soldier on the battlefield.

"Don't be too hard on him." She looked at her petite, brown-eyed friend. "He's going through some stuff."

"So am I. Isn't everyone?" Bonnie dragged her fingers through her pixie haircut. "But it's not okay to bring it to work."

"We need to cut him some slack. He's dealing with more than a broken relationship."

Her friend's eyes widened into an "aha" expression. "Is there something you'd like to tell me?"

"Such as?"

"For starters how do you know so much about him? Like

what could he be dealing with other than cooking a filet to the customer's exact specifications?"

"Oh, you know—"

How could she? Who could possibly guess that he was Arthur Swinton's son?

And Gianna was torn. Part of her really wanted to talk to someone about her conflicted feelings and Bonnie was her best friend. But this information had the potential to ruin Shane's life.

"No, I don't know." Bonnie stared at her, waiting. "What's going on with you and Shane?"

"That's a good question." Maybe she could share just a little. "Remember when you called in sick?"

"Right, the Swiss travel delegation was here."

"I told you he invited me to his place and cooked dinner to thank me for efficiently filling in."

"More like working your butt off." Interest sparkled in her friend's eyes. "Yeah, I remember you thought it got awkward at the end."

"It did until…"

Did she say that out loud?

Bonnie's raised eyebrow told her she had. "Until he saved his moves for the pantry?"

Gianna's cheeks burned and she was grateful for the romantic lighting that hid her reaction. "You saw?"

"You didn't just ask me that. Of course I saw. Not much goes on in a restaurant kitchen that doesn't get seen by someone." There was nothing but teasing and the concern of a friend in her tone. "So give. I want details."

Gianna sighed. "It was maybe the best kiss of my entire life."

"In the pantry? He couldn't have picked somewhere—I don't know—with ambience?"

"That's what I said. He promised to make it up to me

because the first kiss didn't happen on the balcony of his condo."

"He passed up moonlight and a view of the mountains for a closet at work?" Bonnie sounded shocked and appalled. "That's just wrong in so many ways."

"He made up for it."

"Did he now?"

"It's not what you think," Gianna protested.

"I think you slept with him."

"Okay. It is what you think, but— But we're just having fun. No expectations."

"No one expects to fall in love. It just happens." Sadness slid back into her friend's eyes.

"It's not going to happen to me. Been there, done that. Not again." But caring about him was different, wasn't it? She hoped so because she couldn't help caring.

"Look, I know you, G. You don't have to pretend with me. You're not the type to take advantage of a situation. You pull your own weight and work harder than anyone because it's who you are." Her smile was sincere. "But if he hurts you, I'll make him sorry even if it costs me my job."

"Thanks, Bon." Gianna meant that from the bottom of her heart.

Her friend glanced at her tables. "I have to clear salads. Then hope the real Shane is back in control."

"Thanks for listening."

"Anytime."

"And Bonnie?"

"Right." She grinned. "I'll keep it to myself."

Gianna wasn't sure whether or not she felt better. And right now it didn't matter. She was here to work. Her shift was nearly over; the hostess wasn't seating any more customers. It was time to take care of her last few tables for the evening.

Gianna checked in with the diners and brought whatever was needed. With a little time on her hands, she walked back in the kitchen. Shane was the only one there, standing with his back against the stainless-steel counter, his dark eyebrows drawn together. This was not a man thinking happy thoughts.

"Shane?"

He looked up. "Hmm?"

"What's wrong?" She held up a hand when he opened his mouth, body language signaling a denial. "Don't waste your breath. It's obvious something is bothering you. I'm not the only one who noticed."

"I don't want to talk about it."

"Where did you go before?" she asked, trying to draw him out.

"What part of 'I don't want to talk about it' did you not understand?"

She blinked up at him. "Okay. It's just that you look upset. I wanted to help."

He drew in a deep breath. "Sorry. I didn't mean to snap. It's just—I can't do this now."

He stared at her long and hard before he simply turned and walked out the back door of the restaurant. Gianna started to go after him then stopped. She had to finish up her shift, but she hated the delay. Her heart ached for him because he had the look of a man who desperately needed to get something off his chest.

What more could there be? He'd already confessed who his father was. The disclosure had really rocked her and at the time, she wasn't sure how she felt. But she did now. Her feelings about him hadn't changed. He was a good man, the same man she couldn't wait to see every day at work.

The one she'd hoped for so long would notice her. Now

that he had, she couldn't walk away. No matter what else had happened between them, she considered him a friend.

Letting him brood alone wasn't an option.

After leaving work, Gianna drove the short distance to Shane's condo. She rode the elevator to his floor and stepped out when the doors opened. For so many reasons it was tempting to step right back in. She was more tired than she ever remembered being in her life. It had been a very long day. She could hardly believe that only twenty-four hours ago they'd walked in the snow and he'd kissed her. The battery in her car rolled over, died and Shane drove her home.

Then he'd made love to her—thorough, sweet love.

It had been only this morning they'd had breakfast in her apartment and were intimate, carefree. He'd been relaxed, funny and sweet. Rumpled in the best possible, sexiest way. The thought made her stomach shimmy like it had when the elevator whisked her up to his floor.

The expression on his face when he'd left work a little while ago was so different from this morning. It was a lot like his expression outside the bakery when Allaire commented on his resemblance to Dax and D.J. It was similar, but worse somehow.

And she had to know he was all right.

"Here goes nothing." She squared her shoulders, marched down the hall and rang his bell.

It wasn't answered right away and she was about to push the button again. She was prepared to pitch a tent in the hall if necessary because she had to see him face-to-face. Fortunately he finally opened the door.

"Hi." She lifted her hand in a small wave.

The only way to describe him was ragged. That seemed contradictory since his designer jeans were impeccable so it was more about attitude. His eyes were shadowed and his white cotton shirt untucked. His mouth was tight and the muscle in his jaw jerked. He had a tumbler in his hand with about two fingers of what looked like Scotch in it.

"I'm not very good company, Gianna."

"I'm not here to be entertained."

"Why did you come?"

"You look like a man in desperate need of a hug."

Nothing about him was welcoming, but she stood her ground. For some reason he'd confided things to her. His family might know, too, but they weren't here and she was. Whether he knew it or not, he needed someone and she was it.

"Can I come in?"

He rested his forearm on the doorjamb. "If you were smart, you'd turn around right now. I'm trouble. When it all blows up, you don't want to be close to me."

The devil of it was she *did* want to be close to him. That wasn't something she seemed to be able to change, even though there was every indication this wouldn't end well.

"I'll risk it. Tell me what happened, Shane. Where did you go tonight?"

Blue eyes, dark and assessing, stared into hers for several moments. "You're not going to leave, are you?"

"No."

Reluctantly, he stepped aside to let her in. "Do you want a drink?"

"What are you having?"

"Scotch."

Did she know her liquor or what? Tending bar part-time did that to a girl. "I'll pass."

She followed him into the living room. Unlike the last time here, she wasn't preoccupied with the expensive artwork and spectacular view. Her only concern was Shane.

She watched his shoulders shift restlessly as he stood by the big windows and stared out at the lights on the ski slope.

She moved behind him and put her hand on his arm and felt the muscles tense. "Let's sit."

He nodded and they walked to the couch, then sat side by side, close enough that their thighs brushed. She felt heat and awareness burn through her, but pushed it away. This wasn't about that.

"So, tell me," she said simply.

"I went to see D.J. at the Rib Shack."

"And?"

"We talked."

"Really? You didn't just stare at each other and grunt?" She tried to lighten the mood.

"We joked around." He rested his elbows on his knees, the tumbler of Scotch held loosely in his fingers. "He told me Dax and Allaire used to be married."

"I'd heard that."

"And yet they've managed to work through the past and still be close. Maybe because of the blood connection."

"Possible. Although a lot of siblings don't speak to each other over a lot less than that."

He lifted a shoulder. "Then he told me about what happened a year ago. How Jasper Fowler kidnapped Rose Traub. How everyone thought Swinton was dead."

"Yeah. You can take the girl out of Thunder Canyon, but you can't take Thunder Canyon out of the girl. My mom clued me in. It was pretty sensational."

He met her gaze. "Then he said something that makes me pretty sure his mother is also mine."

Shocked, she stared at him, the misery on his face. "What?"

"Her maiden name was Smith. Grace S. is the name on my birth certificate." His eyes were bleak. "D.J. said there's no way, but I'm almost certain she had an affair with Arthur Swinton and I'm the result."

"Think about this, Shane." She struggled to pull her whirling thoughts together and form a rational statement in order to help him. "Grace Smith is a common name. Is it possible you're jumping to conclusions?"

"Of course. Anything is possible. But the private investigator narrowed down the search criteria and the population of Thunder Canyon isn't that big. It was even smaller all those years ago. When you factor in the strong resemblance between me and the Traubs, that narrows the odds."

Gianna stared at him, trying to make sense of all this. "An affair?"

He nodded. "The whole Traub family believes Arthur Swinton fantasized about their mom, that not having her drove him crazy. To the point where all he could think about was getting even with them."

The implications of that sank in. "If she had his baby, that would challenge every belief they've ever had about their family. And they have the highest possible regard for their mother and her memory."

"I know." His tone was hard, tortured. "It would be so much easier if they were jerks. But I like them, Gianna, all of them. It feels as if we could be good friends, under other circumstances. If I'm right about this, I've got brothers. Another family. You can't have too much, right?" He tried to smile, but it just didn't work.

"Some people would argue that, but I'm not one of them." She blew out a long breath. "What are you going to do about this?"

"There's the question." He dragged his fingers through his hair. "Information like this could tear them apart after they worked hard to be close. I could tell them about my suspicions and they'll hate my guts, destroy any possible connection I might have had with them."

"Or?"

"Keep it to myself."

"And let it tear you apart instead?" Her heart cried out against that. It was an impossible choice.

He looked down, then met her gaze. "How can I trash their mother's memory? Especially at Christmastime?"

"No matter when they hear, news like this will rock their world," she pointed out. "They have a right to know that you might be a brother."

"I don't know if I can do that to them."

"Then you'd have to continue living a lie." Gianna put her hand on his forearm, feeling the warmth of his skin beneath the material of his shirt. It wasn't clear why, but she needed the connection to say what she had to say. "Hiding the truth is just wrong. Take it from me. I lied to you."

There was a spark of heat in his eyes for just a second, then it disappeared. "How big a lie can it be?"

"Not in the same league as keeping information about who you are from Dax and D.J. But I haven't been completely honest, either."

"About what?"

She looked down, not quite able to meet his eyes. "I did have a travel business in New York, but I lost it. Between people booking trips online and the recession costing them jobs and not traveling at all, I couldn't make a go of it. I lost everything."

"I'm sorry, Gianna."

"I'm thirty years old and have to start over, figure out what I want to be when I grow up. Do you have any idea how humiliating it is to have to move home with your parents?"

"You could have told me the truth."

"Saying I was only in town for a short time was just a

way to save face." He hadn't been sure about his long-term plans and it never occurred to her that things between them could get serious. So, here they were. "It was still a lie and I can tell you that I didn't particularly like living with it."

He looked at her for several moments, then his mouth twitched and he started to laugh.

That was unexpected and hit a nerve. "I bared my soul just now. I'm glad you think it's so funny."

"Sweet Gianna." He kissed her softly. Just a brush of his lips that was more promise than passion. "If anyone had told me that I could laugh at anything tonight I'd have said they were crazy."

"Happy to help."

"You have. More than you know." His mouth curved up again. "And you're right. Your lie of omission is nowhere near as bad as my mess." He took her hand in his. "But no one else could have coaxed a smile out of me. I'm glad you're here."

"I hope you still feel that way because I have to say what I think."

"And that is?" His fingers tensed around hers.

"You have to tell Dax and D.J. If you were in their situation, wouldn't you want to know you have a brother?"

"Yes, but—"

"Okay. Whatever their reaction, they have a right to know about this. Otherwise you're forcing them to live a lie, too."

"You have a point." For several moments he looked thoughtful. "Assuming I tell D.J., I wouldn't want to drop that on him until after Presents for Patriots. It's a big event and he's got to be under a lot of stress. That's more important. This secret has waited all these years—it can wait a little longer."

She put her head on his shoulder. "You're a good man, Shane Roarke."

"I'm glad you think so."

She was glad he couldn't see her face, guess how she felt inside. Her stomach was bouncing like a skier who took a tumble down the slope. Just because she believed what she said didn't mean she wasn't scared for him.

This could all go so badly and she would be to blame for convincing him to do it.

Chapter Ten

On Monday night the restaurant was closed so Gianna accepted her mother's invitation to dinner with the whole family. She parked at the curb and saw her sister's minivan already in the driveway.

This was her first holiday at home in a couple of years because she hadn't been able to afford the trip. Her parents knew now about her business failing and money problems, but at the time she'd been too proud to let on. She sat in the car, looking at the Christmas lights lining the roof of the house where she'd grown up. They didn't flash off and on, or do anything high-tech like change color. It was just happy and solid and stable.

Traditional.

The tree stood in the living-room window with white lights and ornaments, some of them made by Gianna and Jackie in school. Lights in the shape of candy canes lined the yard. Santa with sleigh and reindeer stood on the snow in the center.

Tears filled her eyes. She'd missed everyone so much and was looking forward to Christmas with her family. If only Shane was going to be here it would be perfect.

She brushed the moisture from her cheeks, got out of the car, and walked to the front door with the holiday wreath made of ribbons and pine cones.

After knocking, she let herself in. "Hello?"

Her mother walked down the long wooden floor of the entryway and hugged her. "I'm so glad you could make it, sweetheart."

"Me, too, Mom." Breathing in the scent of pine, she looked at the living room on the right and formal dining on the left. The table was covered with a red tablecloth and set for seven and a high chair. There was a poinsettia in the center with Santa Claus candles in brass holders on either side of it. "The house looks great. So festive. And I think I smell a roast?"

"Your nose is right on. Just put your things on the sofa," Susan said, pointing to the hunter-green, floral love seat by the Christmas tree. "Everyone's in the family room. The men are watching Monday Night Football."

"Okay."

Gianna did as directed, then joined the group in the room that always felt like the heart of the home. The kitchen with granite countertops and island opened to the family room with its overstuffed corner group and flat-screen TV.

Ed Garrison was lifting the roast out of the oven. He was tall and trim, with light hair that hid some of the silver streaking it. He had a distinguished look that could have him reading the nightly news on TV if he wasn't the most popular math teacher at Thunder Canyon High. Her mother worked part-time in a gift shop in Old Town and loved it.

The two of them were partners in life and tonight in the kitchen. They were working together to get the roast out of the oven, make mashed potatoes and gravy. She saw her dad's randy touch on her mom's rear. The playful way she pushed his hand away followed by a kiss on his cheek and a look filled with promise for later.

Jackie was following toddler Emily to make sure she only looked and didn't break any of the Christmas decorations. Her husband, Frank, was on the floor with the two boys, wrestling and tickling. The loud and loving scene made Gianna smile.

It also made her ache with missing Shane.

Jackie turned and spotted her in the doorway. "Look who's here."

The children stopped laughing and shrieking to look at her, then they jumped up and started shouting. "Auntie G!"

"Hi, guys." She went down on one knee and braced for impact as the two boys threw themselves into her arms.

Emily followed moments later, doing her best imitation of her older brothers. "Annie G!"

"Hey, baby girl."

She kissed each of them in order of age. Griffin, the dark-haired firstborn. Then Colin, with his lighter hair and sensitive soul. Finally, little Em, her legs and cheeks not as chubby as six months ago when Gianna had come back home.

She met her brother-in-law's gaze over the heads of his children. "Hi, Frank."

"Hey, G." He grinned. "I can't tell you how grateful I am that reinforcements have arrived."

"Are they wearing you out?"

He was a big guy, over six feet, with dark hair and eyes. Hunky and husky. All that firefighter training equipped him for all kinds of emergencies. If anyone could handle this group, it was Frank Blake.

He stood and grinned. "If I could bottle all their energy and sell it, I'd be a billionaire."

"No kidding." She looked at the three still hanging on her. "How are you guys?"

"Hungry," Griff said.

"Me, too," Colin chimed in.

"How's school?" she asked.

"I like recess best."

"Me, too," the little brother added.

The older boy scoffed. "You go to baby school. It's recess all the time."

"Nuh uh." The middle child shot a glare at his older brother. "You're a baby."

Emily held out her arms. "Up."

While their mother tried to referee, Gianna happily obliged her niece and held the little girl close. She breathed in the mingled scents of shampoo and cookies. "I could just eat you up, Em."

Jackie separated her boys. "Go watch the game with your dad."

"But, Mo-om—" Griff stopped when he got the look.

Gianna recognized it and knew her sister had learned from their mother. She wondered whether or not she'd do it, too, if she had kids. Her thoughts went to Shane and her heart ached for him again. So much had happened since he'd cooked for her at his place. He was trying to come to terms with everything he'd learned about himself and the consequences for others if it was revealed.

Now she understood the brooding expression she'd noticed in his eyes, the conflict about family and where he fit in. She'd never experienced that and hoped for the bazillionth time that her advice was sound.

"Dinner's ready," her mother called out.

Those words sent Jackie into field-commander mode. She and Frank rounded up the kids for hand washing then asked Gianna to put Em in the high chair already in the dining room. Like an intricately choreographed ballet, the adults worked together getting children and food to the table at the same time.

Griffin started to take some mashed potatoes and got another look when Jackie said, "Prayer first. Why don't you say it, sweetie?"

He nodded, then bowed his head and linked his fingers. "Thanks, God, for all the food. And for Mommy and Daddy, Grammy and Granddad and Auntie G." He looked at his parents then added reluctantly, "And for Colin and Em. Is that okay?"

"Good job, son."

"That's exactly what I would have said, Griffie." Gianna was surprised the words got past the unexpected logjam of emotion in her throat.

The next few minutes were a flurry of passing dishes, filling plates and making sure everyone had what they needed.

Her mother looked around the table and said, "Okay, everyone, enjoy."

"And if you don't," her father added, "keep it to yourself."

"So, Auntie G.," Jackie took a bite of mashed potatoes and gravy. "I saw Lizzie Traub at the bakery today. She said you and Shane Roarke were in a couple of days ago. Together."

That brought her up short. She'd forgotten how something like that could spread in a small town. Since coming home she hadn't done a thing that was gossip worthy. Until now. "That's right. I wanted to send something to my roommate in New York."

"At lunch you didn't tell us you were seeing him," her sister added.

At lunch Gianna wasn't sure about that herself. She still wasn't sure what they were, but had to tell them something. "I've gotten to know him recently. We're friends."

"Do you like him?" her mother asked.

"Of course. He's great to work for. Funny and charming."

"Mom and I and every female under seventy-five here in Thunder Canyon think he's drop-dead gorgeous," Jackie added. "What's not to like?"

Frank gave her a teasing look, clearly not threatened. "Should I be jealous?"

"If you'd like," his wife said, sass in her voice. "And I'm glad you even thought to be after all these years and three kids."

"Tell me, Gia—" Her father set his fork on his plate as he looked at her. "Do I need to ask him what his intentions are?"

As much as she wanted to know the answer to that question, she shuddered at the thought. "Please, Dad, I'm begging you not to do that."

"There's the reaction I was going for. My work here is done."

"Ed Garrison, you're going straight to hell," her mother scolded.

"Grammy said a bad word." Griffin's expression was angelic and superior because he wasn't the one in trouble.

Gianna was grateful for the diversion, and conversation for the rest of the meal was about other things. She could just listen, laugh, be with loved ones and distracted from worrying about Shane.

Later, after her sister's family had hustled home because of school the next day, Gianna was alone with her mother.

Her father was dozing on the couch in front of the TV. She wanted to hear again about her parents' first meeting.

"Mom? When did you know that Dad was 'the one'?" She was standing by the sink, a dish towel in one hand, wineglass in the other and braced for the personal questions that would follow about Shane. It was worth the risk given how confused she was.

Susan glanced at her husband and smiled lovingly. "I knew almost from the moment we met."

"Really?"

"Yes. There was attraction, of course." Her face went soft and sort of dreamy. "I still remember exactly how it felt. We were in a room full of people at a friend's wedding reception, but he was the only one I saw. And I stopped looking right then."

"It was that way for Jackie and Frank, too? In high school?"

Her mother nodded. "I worried some about them getting married right after graduation because they were so young. But I didn't try to stop her."

"Because of you and Dad?"

"Yes." Concern put creases in her mother's forehead. "Is there something with you and Shane?"

"No. Yes—" The first time she'd met him there'd been a room full of busboys, waitstaff and restaurant employees when Grant Clifton introduced them to the new chef. She'd felt the "wow" thing her mother just described. "Maybe."

Susan took the glass from her and put it in the cupboard. "Sweetheart, I know you've had disappointments. But you'll know when it's right."

"I guess."

Disappointment was a word designed to sugarcoat her catastrophe of a love life. She realized now that time invested didn't make a man less selfish or more right for her. She envied her sister and mother, getting it right the first time.

She wanted a solid relationship like her parents had. She wanted a guy like her brother-in-law. Six months ago she'd met Shane and had a crush on him from afar. Now she knew him, a man who thought of others first. The kind of man who would let the explosive information about who he really was eat him up inside rather than make trouble for the family he believed was his, one that had already been through a lot.

She'd felt that certain something the first time she saw him but...how could she trust her judgment after so much failure?

And more important, could Shane put the missing parts of himself together and find the peace he needed to settle down? That question might be answered after Presents for Patriots tomorrow night. He'd decided to talk to D.J. about his suspicions when the event was over.

Gianna looked around the Rib Shack's main dining room and hardly recognized it. The same historical town mural and sepia-toned pictures were on the walls, but all the tables usually scattered around in the center of the room had been pushed together for work space. People crowded around them and had an assembly line going. At several workstations, volunteers wrapped small electronics and toiletries in red, green, silver and gold Christmas paper, then passed it down for whoever was doing the ribbon.

Piles of presents waited for a volunteer to pick them up for delivery to where brown shipping boxes waited to be filled, addressed and stacked for transport.

Everyone who'd signed up for the event performed a function that utilized their talents as much as possible and her job was to circulate with hors d'oeuvres. She moved back and forth from where the volunteers were working and D.J.'s kitchen, where Shane was deftly balancing an assembly of ingredients, cooking and keeping things warm.

She pushed through the kitchen's double doors where he was working. "How's it going?"

"Good."

Stainless-steel bowls were in front of him, one with a tomato mixture, the other looked like cheese. Trays of sliced, toasted French bread marched up the long counter.

"Are you holding up okay?"

His expression was hooded but tension in his body said he knew she wasn't talking about food preparation, but what was coming after. "I'm made of stern stuff."

"Yes, you are." The only problem was some of that same stuff made up D.J. and Dax Traub. They didn't know yet that their world was going to turn upside down. She hated this and could only imagine how Shane felt. Stiff upper lip. "Everyone is raving about those little pastry things."

One corner of his mouth turned up. "It's a new recipe."

"Talk about a spectacular debut." Chalk up one good thing. "I'll just refill my tray. Hang in there."

She saw him nod and the way the muscle in his cheek moved. He was strung pretty tight and there was nothing to do but wait until this event was over.

After refilling her tray with napkins and food, she moved back out into the big room. The high ceiling held in the hum of voices and laughter. In one corner, the Thunder Canyon radio station was broadcasting Christmas music and live updates from the affair. On the opposite side of the room a TV reporter from a local affiliate was interviewing D. J. Traub, who looked happy, excited and intense. That was probably a family trait because she saw a lot of it in Shane.

She stopped at a table where Angie Anderson and Forrest Traub were working together. Holding out the tray, she said, "Care for a snack?"

"Wow, those look good. What is it?" Angie looked up from the MP3 player and paper she was lining up.

"Crab puffs."

Forrest put a piece of tape on the seam to hold the paper together. He shifted his weight to take the strain off his leg, still healing from the wound he'd sustained in Afghanistan. Better than anyone in the room, this former soldier understood what presents would mean to service personnel stationed in a foreign land at Christmas. He met her gaze and there was a twinkle in his light brown eyes. "You could just leave that whole tray right here if you want."

Angie laughed. "That's the spirit. Pig out for Patriots."

"I have to keep up my strength in order to help out my brothers in arms," he defended.

"Uh-huh. You're a giver, Forrest Traub." Angie put several of the puffs on a napkin. "Thanks, Gianna."

"You're welcome. And, Forrest?" She grinned at the former soldier. "If there are any of these babies left over, they're yours. I'll do my best."

He saluted. "If I wasn't already head over heels in love with Angie…"

"But you are," she reminded him, her voice teasing.

"I definitely am." He met her gaze and there was absolute sincerity in his own.

Gianna sighed as she moved to the next table. Antonia and Clay Traub were doing ribbon duty. She was surprised to see them. "Hey, what are you two doing here?"

Antonia pushed a long, wavy strand of brown hair behind her ear. Green eyes glowed with good humor, but looked a little tired around the edges. "What you really want to know is what have we done with the kids."

"No," Gianna said. "What I really want to know is how

you can possibly look so beautiful and *slim* after giving birth less than two months ago."

Clay gazed at his wife and the love there was clear for everyone to see. A boyishly handsome man with brown eyes, he'd been raising his own six-month-old son when he rented a room at Wright's Way, Antonia's boarding house, when she was in the third trimester of pregnancy. Her plan was to be a single mom, but they fell for each other and got married. Now they were mom *and* dad to two babies.

"She's an amazing mother," Clay said, then kissed his wife's cheek, "and an even more amazing woman."

"And that's my secret," she said, sending the love right back to her husband. "A man who thinks everything I do is perfect."

Gianna held back a sigh. "Okay. Now I want to know what you've done with the kids."

"It's a wonderful invention called grandparents." Clay laughed. "My folks are here from Rust Creek and will stay on through the holidays."

"Ellie and Bob are really good with the babies," Antonia gushed.

"They should be," Clay told her, "after having so many kids of their own."

"Maybe they should hire out," Gianna said, giving them some crab puffs.

If she had babies, her folks would be there for her. They were fantastic grandparents to Jackie's kids but it was looking like that would be it for Susan and Ed Garrison, thanks to the failure of their older daughter to provide any. Envy seemed to be Gianna's new best friend these days. She was jealous of everyone. Everywhere she turned people were deliriously happy and sappy with romance. Was she the only person in the room who had the love carrot dangling in front of her just out of reach?

She moved past more tables where she saw her landlady and husband, Cody Overton. After that came Joss and Jason Traub, who had renovated and updated The Hitching Post. They'd pretended to be a couple and ended up falling in love. Gianna was pretending to be full of holiday spirit but was falling into a funk.

Envy was nothing given the fact that she just wanted to be with Shane. But when she looked at the road ahead for her, all she could see were speed bumps. His biological parents were like a cloud hanging over him and he might not stay in Thunder Canyon.

She had a few hors d'oeuvres left on the tray when she stopped at the place where Dax and D. J. Traub were filling the brown packing boxes with gifts and sealing them with heavy duty tape. Apparently D.J. had finished his interview. Both men straightened and towered over her.

"Hungry?" she asked.

Dax took a napkin and popped one of the seafood-filled pastries into his mouth. "Mmm. What is this?"

"Crab puff," she said without much enthusiasm.

"Good," Dax said after chewing and swallowing. He took another. "Have you been scarfing these down?"

"No. Why?"

"Because you are what you eat and you look crabby."

"He meant thoughtful," D.J. said, glaring at his brother. "Maybe preoccupied. Or pensive."

"No." Dax folded his arms over his chest. "I meant crabby. Where's your Christmas spirit? What's up, G?"

The words yanked Gianna out of her funk with an almost audible snap. She was selfish, shallow and self-centered. These two brothers had no idea that their world was about to tilt. That when the evening ended everything they believed about their mother would be changed forever and not in a good way.

She didn't want to talk about what was bugging her. "Speaking of Christmas, it's only about two weeks away. Will these boxes get to Afghanistan in time?"

"The Air Force National Guard is on Operation Santa Claus," D.J. explained. "They've got transport aircraft standing by to take everything, and staff in place to get it distributed by Christmas."

"Thank goodness," she said.

D.J.'s expression was curious. "Nice try, G. But you didn't answer the question. How come your Christmas spirit is missing in action?"

She forced herself to look them in the eyes. "We're here to do our part to make Christmas merrier for the men and women halfway around the world who are protecting our freedom. Please don't make me feel as shallow as a cookie sheet and admit out loud, here of all places, that I'm feeling sorry for myself."

"Is there a guy involved?" D.J. took the last of the hors d'oeuvres on her tray.

Of course he'd go there. Since she'd been working at the resort restaurant, she'd stopped in the Rib Shack from time to time and D.J. took her under his wing. She'd confessed her pathetic and unfortunate relationship history and his advice was to pick better guys. Talking to him had helped, but now she wished she hadn't. She wasn't sure he wouldn't see through whatever lie she pitched him.

"Oh, you know—"

"The classic non-answer," he said nodding. "That's okay. It's not necessary for me to know details. But you don't have a big brother so I'll do the honors and beat him up for you if necessary."

Oh, God, don't say that, she prayed. She didn't want Shane hit. Not for her and especially not by the man who was his half brother.

"I appreciate the offer, D.J., but I can take care of myself." At that moment she saw Shane nearby with a tray of bruscetta. Her heart boomeranged in her chest as he took out his reality TV smile and worked everyone over with it. She wasn't immune.

Dax's voice penetrated her haze with a comment that sounded as if he'd just remembered. "You and Shane were out shopping together."

"That's right." D.J. followed her gaze. "You and Shane? What's up, G?"

Good question. One she didn't want to answer. So she asked the first thing that popped into her mind. "What do you think of him?"

The brothers stared at each other for several moments, then Dax said, "His crab puffs are really good."

"Better than the ribs here at the shack?" D.J. challenged.

"Tomato, tomahto." Dax shrugged. "Just saying…"

"Seriously?" Gianna was aware that she was pushing, but this was important. The answer could make a big difference in how they received the news he planned to give them. "You do know I wasn't talking about his cooking skill, right?"

"Well," Dax mused, "he's stepped up every time someone asked him to pitch in. Thunder Canyon is lucky to have a celebrity who's also not a jerk."

"That's true," she said. "He spent his day off making all the hors d'oeuvres. And tonight The Gallatin Room only took a few reservations from people staying here at the resort so that the staff would be free to volunteer for your event. Shane figured most everyone from town would be here and not going out to dinner, anyway."

Dax nodded his approval. "Above and beyond the call of duty."

"I hate to admit my brother is right about anything." D.J.

grinned. "But Shane's willingness to be a part of this town goes a long way toward earning my loyalty. He and I have talked some and he seems like a great guy."

"He is. Really, really is."

Gianna knew her tone was more enthusiastic than necessary when the brothers exchanged a questioning look. This felt a lot like watching an air-disaster movie where she wanted to shout, "Don't get on the plane!"

There was nothing she could do and that was frustrating when she wanted so badly to help everyone involved because she liked, respected and cared about all of them. Shane was going to drop a very big bomb on this family tonight and she didn't want Dax and D. J. Traub to hate him for it.

Chapter Eleven

Gianna had left the Rib Shack a while ago after giving Shane a kiss and hug that went on so long he'd hated to let her go. She'd offered to stay, but this was something he had to do alone. He'd given her the key to his condo when she said sleeping wasn't likely until she knew what happened, and he was grateful to her yet again. If he was being honest, he wasn't sure how he'd have gotten this far without her.

Shane took his place in a line of volunteers who passed the brown cardboard boxes filled with presents into trucks for the next part of the journey to soldiers overseas. After that he pitched in with D.J. and a half dozen other men to move tables and chairs, put the Rib Shack's main dining room back the way it was before being taken over by patriotic holiday elves. At least he was doing something good while killing time waiting to do something not so good.

D.J. inspected the room after he and Shane moved the last table and settled the two chairs on either side. He nodded with satisfaction and announced, "Okay, everyone, I think that does it. Thanks for all your help. I literally could not have done this without you."

Shane watched D.J. shake hands with the men who left through the restaurant doors that led to the public parking lot just outside, which was nearly empty now. He locked up and wearily rubbed the back of his neck.

D.J. turned and seemed to realize he wasn't alone. He looked tired. "Shane— Sorry—I'll unlock the doors if you're going this way."

He was going to hell, but not through those doors. The Rib Shack had a rear entrance just like The Gallatin Room. "No. I'll head out through your kitchen, if that's okay."

"No problem. Would you like a beer? I could sure use one. And a little company would be welcome if you're not too tired."

"I'm used to these hours. Kind of goes with a food-service career," he said. "A beer sounds good."

"Follow me." The other man turned and led the way.

As they walked toward the kitchen, D.J. detoured into the bar and came out with two longnecks. He handed one to Shane, then continued to the back of the restaurant, turning off lights as he went.

He pushed through the double doors and glanced around. Shane knew that look, the one a chef used to make sure there's nothing out of place. To make sure heat sources are shut down, food put away, everything clean. Shane had been the last one in here and followed the other man's gaze.

The long, stainless-steel counter was spotless. Mixing bowls were nested and stacked on shelves. Recently washed pots and pans hung on overhead racks and different size knives back where he'd found them. After doing his volunteer part with the food, Shane had made sure this room was locked down.

"Looks good in here, too. Thanks." D.J. twisted the cap off his beer, then held it out for a toast. "Another successful Presents for Patriots. Here's to pulling it off."

"A job well done, thanks to you." Shane tapped the other man's bottle with his own.

"By the way," D.J. said, "my brother liked the crab puffs."

He's my brother, too, Shane thought. *And so are you.*

He hated this. They were good guys and he was tempted to walk away now, keeping the scandal to himself. But he couldn't fault Gianna's point. If the situation were reversed, he'd want to know. It was the right thing to do.

The timing couldn't be worse, just before Christmas, but there would never be a good time. This wasn't something he wanted overheard and indiscriminately spread around town.

Shane leaned back against the stainless-steel counter and took a long drink of beer. After drawing in a deep breath, he said, "D.J., there's something I need to talk to you about."

"Gianna." The other man nodded knowingly.

"What?"

"I saw the way you two looked at each other tonight."

"Excuse me?"

"My wife is a teacher, as you know. She's educating me in the touchy-feely stuff." He took a drink from his bottle, then leaned back against the cold cook top across from Shane. "Don't tell her I said this, but she's right."

"About?"

"If you watch body language, two people are having a conversation without words. Couple's shorthand, Allaire calls it."

"But Gianna and I aren't a couple."

"That's what all the guys say before they are."

"In my case it's true," Shane protested.

He thought about the sexy redhead constantly and she starred in his dreams. When he wasn't with her, he felt hollow inside and that had never happened to him before. The night he'd spent in her bed was seared in his memory, but he was the son of the town villain. He was pretty sure that was a deal breaker.

D.J. studied him. "Just so you know, I'm Gianna's honorary big brother and I offered to beat you up."

The words were teasing, the sort of banter Shane and his own brother did. Under the circumstances, he hadn't expected to smile, but he did. That only made him angrier about what he had to do.

"Did she take you up on it?" he asked, putting it off just a little longer.

"No. She said she could take care of herself."

"And there's nothing to take care of because we're not a couple."

Since coming to Thunder Canyon, Shane had been careful to not get involved, what with all the baggage he had. Gianna, with her sweetness and light, had made him forget just long enough to slip up. He'd only suggested dinner because it couldn't go anywhere. They were both leaving. But she hadn't been completely honest about going back to New York and he couldn't be sorry. If she'd told him the complete truth, he might have passed up the chance to know her and what a loss that would have been.

"Just don't hurt her," D.J. warned. "I'd really rather not have to hit you."

That was going to change. If only Shane could change who he was. He was doing his level best to keep his feelings in check so he wouldn't have hurting Gianna on his conscience along with deceiving everyone in town who'd welcomed him.

And it was time to quit stalling and say what he had to.

"D.J., there's something I need to tell you—"

The other man's eyes narrowed. "You're looking pretty serious. Did someone die?"

Not yet, but what he was going to say would be the death of something. "I came to Thunder Canyon for a reason—"

"Old news. There was a job opening."

Shane figured the best way to break this was to connect the dots from the beginning. "You said to me last week that Thunder Canyon was lucky to have me, but it's not about luck. I'd been researching this town. When I heard the executive chef position would be available, I contacted Grant Clifton to let him know I was interested. He jumped at the chance after a visit to my Seattle restaurant. Career-wise, coming here wasn't the best move. For me it was about getting answers."

"What are the questions?" D.J. tensed.

"As an infant I was given up for adoption. My adoptive family lives in Los Angeles. Mom and Dad are attorneys. Maggie and Ryan, my sister and brother are also adopted, and also lawyers." He set his half-empty beer bottle on the counter beside him. "I always knew I was loved, but still felt different from them."

"So you're looking for your birth parents." D.J. skipped steps and cut to the chase. "But why Thunder Canyon? This is a small town and pretty far off the beaten path."

"About a year ago my mother gave me all the information she'd received from the social worker at the adoption agency in Montana. I hired a private investigator who narrowed the search parameters to this town."

"Montana is a long way to go for a baby."

"I guess they wanted me to be far removed from the past." Shane shrugged. "My mother loves me enough to let me do what I need to do."

"And you needed to come here."

"I wanted to get some information on my own and the

kind of questions I had wouldn't get answers on a long weekend."

"So you took the job and positioned yourself to gain trust." D.J. finished his beer and still looked anything but relaxed. "Did you find what you were looking for?"

"I know who my father is, but it's not what I was looking for."

"You wouldn't have started this conversation if you didn't want me to know, too."

"I'd rather no one knew but it's not that simple." Shane dragged his fingers through his hair. Again he remembered what Gianna had said. Be a Band-Aid. Do it quick. "The P.I. managed to get a DNA sample and tests were run proving that Arthur Swinton is my biological father."

D.J.'s mouth dropped open, but no words came out. It took several moments for the information to sink in before he finally said, "He's in jail where he belongs."

"I understand why you feel that way." Shane didn't know what else to say except, "I'm sorry for what he did to you."

D.J. shook his head. "Not your apology to make. This is unexpected, I'll admit. But you're not responsible for his actions."

He figured D.J. continued to be in shock. That was the only reason he was still standing there and hadn't abruptly walked out. What Shane had to say next would probably do the trick.

"I found my mother, too. The name on my birth certificate says Grace S. I'm convinced the 'S' is for Smith."

"That's my mother's name, too." D.J.'s dark eyes narrowed angrily. The information sank in too fast for his mind not to have been moving in that direction. "But what you're implying can't be true."

"It is."

"No way. That would mean my mother slept with Arthur

Swinton and that's impossible. She would never have been with a man like that."

"I'm not making this up. Remember what Allaire said about the resemblance between us?"

"It's bull." D.J. slammed his empty beer bottle on the counter and glared. "What's this really about? Money? Is this a shakedown? You want me to pay so you don't spread dirty lies about my mother?"

"I don't need your money." Shane understood the surprise, shock and resulting anger, that his nerves were strung too tight. But he was treading on thin ice, suggesting Shane was like Arthur Swinton. "My family is wealthy and I've made a fortune on my own. That's not what this is about. We're brothers—"

"Get out." D.J. took a step closer. "I don't want to hear another word."

Shane started to argue, wanted to settle this, but he could see by the other man's expression that he'd shut down. He wouldn't listen to reason. Or anything else, for that matter.

"You can throw me out, but it won't change anything." Shane met his gaze, then headed for the back exit.

D.J. followed. "Don't even think about repeating this crap. I won't have my mother's memory and reputation ruined by a pack of lies."

"I don't lie," Shane said quietly. "And if I wanted everyone to know, I would have said something a couple of hours ago in the dining room when the whole town was there."

"I have no idea what sick game you're playing, but I want no part of it." D.J. opened the back door. "Now get out."

Shane nodded and stepped outside. The door shut instantly and he heard the dead bolt slam home. Cold and dark surrounded him.

When this journey of self-discovery started, he'd be-

lieved the truth would enlighten him. The real truth was
that he'd never felt colder or more in the dark.

As the saying went, one picture was worth a thousand
words and the instant Gianna saw Shane's face, she knew
that was true. Things with D.J. hadn't gone well.

She'd been pacing in front of the spectacular windows
looking out on the ski slope, snow-covered hills and lights
but all she could think about was Shane, all alone while
doing the hardest thing he'd ever done. As soon as she heard
the condo door open, she rushed to meet him in the entryway. He looked tired, defeated. His mouth pulled tight and
there was tension in his jaw.

Gianna asked anyway, "How'd it go?"

"Could have been better."

"He didn't take it well."

"How would you interpret getting thrown out of the Rib
Shack?"

"Oh, Shane—"

She moved close and put her arms around him. He resisted for half a second, as if he didn't deserve her comfort,
then pulled her tighter against him. He buried his face in
her neck, breathed in the scent of her hair and held on as if
he never wanted to let her go.

"I don't know, Gia—"

He'd never called her that before. He'd always used her
full name. Something about the nickname got to her, intimate in a way sharing the pleasure of their bodies hadn't
been. Her heart squeezed painfully in a way *it* never had before, and felt as if she'd stepped over the edge into feelings
deeper and more profound than she'd ever known.

But she couldn't think about that now. She was simply grateful that he didn't seem angry at her for convinc-

ing him to tell D.J. they were half brothers. She hoped that didn't change.

Gianna slipped her arm through his. "Let's go sit in the living room."

He nodded and let her lead him over to the couch. On the coffee table there was a tumbler with two shots of Scotch in it waiting for him.

He kissed her softly and said, "Thank you."

"Anytime." And she sincerely meant that.

With a weary sigh he took the glass and tossed back half the liquor, closing his eyes as it burned all the way to his belly. "I needed that."

Gianna sat on the couch and looked up at him. "What did he say?"

"That it was a lie and I must be trying to shake the family down for money."

She shook her head. "He was just lashing out. This really came out of the blue for him. When it sinks in he'll realize that you don't need the money."

"That's what I told him. More or less." He drank the rest of the Scotch, then sat beside her, close enough that their arms touched and thighs brushed.

"I wouldn't hold it against him, Shane. Anyone would have reacted that way."

"Agreed. That wasn't a surprise. I expected it."

"But you're still upset." It wasn't a question. One look at his face had confirmed his inner turmoil.

"Yeah, I'm upset." He dragged his fingers through his hair. "The thing is… I like him, Gia. And Dax. The whole extended family. We could have been good friends. But now—" The look on his face was tormented. "I have a better chance of opening a restaurant on Mars."

He hadn't expected to be this troubled, she realized. The Traubs hadn't been in his life until a few months ago. But like the town of Thunder Canyon, he'd connected with the family in a way friendship didn't completely explain.

She cared deeply for this man and wished there was a simple, easy way to make his pain disappear. But the only weapon she had was words. Maybe talking it through would help. And she had to know…

"Are you upset with me for pushing you to say something to D.J.?"

"You didn't push me. No one could if I wasn't leaning in that direction in the first place. I'm stubborn that way." He linked his fingers with hers. "And I don't think I could ever be upset with you. I didn't say it before, but I'm glad you're here."

"There's nowhere else I'd be." She leaned her head on his shoulder.

"But," he said, "I can't help thinking that it would be better if I'd just left things alone. Not disturbed the ghosts of the past."

"For what it's worth, I don't think the Traubs are the type to run away from a problem. Seems to me they face things head-on, in a proactive way. Like you did tonight." She looked up at him, the strong profile, determined set of the jaw. "It occurs to me that besides the strong resemblance, that head-on thing is a trait you have in common with them."

"Did you just pay me a compliment?"

"That was my intent, yes." She rubbed her thumb over his. "The point is, and I do have one, regardless of the fall-out from all of this, the truth is always best."

"I'm not so sure about that." His voice was soft, sad, with a touch of self-loathing.

She thought carefully about what to say next. "How about looking at this another way."

"I'll take anything I can get."

"Okay, here goes. You already know Arthur is your father."

"Unfortunately, yes."

"This is where I argue that you need an attitude adjustment."

"Oh?"

Gianna knew if she looked at him, one dark eyebrow would be lifted. "Think about it. Whatever combination of DNA made you the way you are is something I'm grateful for. You're a good man. If not, the people of Thunder Canyon would not have embraced you so completely. They're funny that way. And you're awfully pretty to look at."

He laughed, the desired reaction, and hopefully that eased some of his tension. After several moments he sighed. "But the things my father did. He messed with people's lives, stole money. Conspired to commit God knows what kind of felonies."

"All part of the public record. But—" She met his gaze. "You're wondering about bad traits you might have inherited. If you had criminal tendencies, they'd probably have surfaced by now. Have you ever had a run-in with the law?"

"Just a couple of speeding tickets."

"That's so small-time," she scoffed. "And proves my point. The tests confirmed that he's your father. But the evidence is circumstantial that Grace Traub was your mother. Is it possible she's not? That she and Arthur never had a relationship and he is crazy just like everyone thinks?"

"Anything's possible," Shane admitted. "My parents told me everything they know and my mother turned over all the information she has. Grace died years ago. The only way to prove something like that would be a DNA test for Dax, D.J. and me. They'd never agree."

Gianna knew he was right. Grace was gone and couldn't confirm or deny. Dax and D.J.'s father had died, too, so there was no way to even find out if he knew anything. Obviously their children were all in the dark about the past. There must be another way to get the truth besides DNA testing. She just couldn't stand the idea of Shane not being able to know for sure and put this to rest.

If he was the type to let it drop, he never would have undertaken this journey in the first place. If it wasn't so important for him to find the peace to settle down, his mother wouldn't have given him her blessing for the journey that led him to where he was now. Gianna was afraid that not knowing for sure about his biological mother would cost him the piece of himself that he would need to have a life. And that gave her an idea.

"There's someone you haven't talked to yet about this. He might have the answers you're looking for."

Shane's body tensed, the muscle in his arm flexed. "I've talked to everyone I can think of. Who could possibly be left?"

"Your biological father."

"You're joking."

"No. I'm completely serious. Think about it. He's the only key player still alive. The only one who can tell you what really happened."

"But everyone says he's crazy. Delusional. A nut case. And even if he wasn't, there's the whole issue of not being truthful and less than an upstanding citizen."

"He did some bad things," she admitted. "But the Traubs are the most vocal about him being crazy. I think that's about them not wanting to believe their mother could ever have hooked up with a man like Swinton. What if they're wrong? You owe it to yourself to find out the truth."

"Even if I decided to go see him, what makes you think he'd tell me the truth? How could I know for sure whether or not to believe anything that comes out of his mouth?"

"Face-to-face you'd probably get a sense of whether or not he's delusional. The rest..." She shrugged. "I can't see that you've got a choice, Shane. It's the only thing left."

He thought about it for a long time. Finally he looked at her and said, "You're right about me being the type to face problems head-on. Whether or not I find out anything, no one can say I didn't at least try."

Gianna knew he meant himself. He didn't want to look back and hate himself for leaving even one stone unturned.

"I guess we're going to the jail," she said.

He lifted one eyebrow. "What's this 'we' stuff?"

"You don't think I'm letting you go alone, do you?"

There was a fiercely rebellious expression on his face. "This is my problem. More important, I don't want you in a place like that. Yes, I'm going alone."

"Wrong. I'll be there with you."

"I won't allow it," he said.

"At the risk of sounding childish..." She lifted her chin. "You're not the boss of me."

"Actually, I am," he reminded her.

"Only at work. This is different." It was personal.

Her track record proved that when things got personal she was the queen of perseverance.

Chapter Twelve

Shane wasn't sure what he'd expected of the county correctional facility half a day's drive from Thunder Canyon. Even at the holidays, or maybe because it was closing in on Christmas, this place was grim. No decorative lights on the outside. Not a Santa, sleigh, or reindeer in sight. Just a series of buildings enclosed by high concrete walls and law-enforcement personnel dressed in navy pants with contrasting light blue shirts.

With Gianna beside him they walked from the parking lot, then stopped at a guard station to show identification and declare their purpose for being there. Visiting was all Shane said and the guard directed them to the visitor center where they followed signs to a room with scratched tables and battered chairs. There was a surveillance camera mounted on the wall and a big window allowed guards to monitor everything that went on.

A few people were there talking to inmates wearing orange jumpsuits. A sad-looking artificial Christmas tree with a handful of red and green ornaments and tacky gold garland stood in the corner. This was where they'd been instructed to wait while someone went to get Arthur Swinton.

Shane walked to an empty table with three chairs in the farthest corner of the room. Gianna sat beside him and glanced around, blue eyes wide, looking curious and a little apprehensive.

"Scared?" he asked.

"No. You're here."

In spite of this surreal situation, he felt himself smile. "As good as I am with a knife in the kitchen, I'm not sure my skill set would be of much help in a jail riot."

"You've been watching too many prison shows on TV. I don't think this is that kind of place. It's not maximum security." She looked around at the dingy, institutional-green walls. "But we're not in Thunder Canyon anymore."

"I tried to talk you out of this. Are you sorry you came?"

She shook her head and slid her hand into his beneath the table. "Not even a little."

"That makes one of us." He listened to the low murmur of voices and glanced at the two prisoners with multiple tattoos, each talking to a wife or girlfriend. There was a hardness in the eyes, a toughness in the posture and he didn't doubt for a second that either or both could *lead* a prison uprising. These felons were his father's peer group and social contacts.

"I'd rather be anywhere else," he said. "If only I were cooking a five-course meal for a thousand pompous and pretentious food critics who don't know marjoram from parsley. That sounds like a warm and happy good time compared to this."

"Which is why I couldn't let you come here alone."

As much as he'd wanted to protect her from this toxic

environment, Shane was grateful for the stubborn streak that made her dig in and defy him. "Thank you. I appreciate it very much…"

Then the door opened and a uniformed guard walked in with an inmate wearing the same orange jumpsuit that would make it difficult to blend into a nonprison population should Arthur Swinton escape again. Shane's stomach knotted as he studied the prisoner.

His father.

The man was shorter and less significant than he'd expected, slightly built with gray hair. He was probably around sixty, but looked much older.

Since he and Gianna were the only other visitors without an inmate, the man walked over to them and sat down on the other side of the table. His blue eyes were sharp with suspicion.

"Are you Arthur Swinton?" Shane asked.

"Yeah. Do I know you?"

"We've never met. I'm Shane Roarke."

Gianna held out her hand. "Gianna Garrison."

He ignored it. "What do you want?"

"I'm here to ask you some questions."

He sniffed dismissively. "Another reporter. I don't—"

"It's not like that." Shane knew Swinton was referring to the private investigator's cover story when he'd posed as a journalist to get a DNA sample. "Actually I'm a chef in The Gallatin Room at the Thunder Canyon Resort. Gianna is a server there."

He was aware that she hadn't said anything since introducing herself, but knew she was studying both of them, comparing. Searching for a family resemblance. As far as Shane was concerned they looked nothing alike.

"What do you want?" Swinton asked again. The introductions hadn't done anything but deepen his distrust.

"I'd like to know about you and Grace Smith—you might know her as Grace Traub."

"She'll always be Grace Smith to me." Something that sounded a lot like sorrow took the sharp edge out of his voice. "What about her?"

"Obviously you knew her?"

"Yeah."

"Did you date her?"

"Yeah."

This was like pulling teeth, Shane thought, feeling frustration expand in his gut. Just then Gianna squeezed his hand, as if she knew what was going on inside him. It kept him focused. Allowed him to see that self-preservation was instinctive in a place like this. In navigating the criminal-justice system, offenders learned not to trust or give up anything that might incriminate them.

"There's no reason you should believe me," Shane assured him, "but I'm not here to do you any harm. I just want information about the past."

"Me and Grace."

"That's right." He stared hard into blue eyes that seemed familiar. "Were the two of you close?"

"You're asking if I slept with her. Not that it's any of your business or anyone else's. No one believed it then, why should you now?" The man was nothing if not direct. There was a vacant look on his face, as if he were remembering something from a long time ago. And apparently he wanted to tell his story because he added, "I slept with her, but it wasn't just sex. Grace is the only woman I've ever loved."

The guy had no idea who he was. As far as Shane could see, he had no reason to lie about that, but the admission profoundly shocked him. Probably because every time Swinton's name came up in Thunder Canyon it was in a negative context painting him as a heartless, unprincipled nut case who was incapable of deep feeling.

"Why did you break if off?" Shane asked.

"Of course I'm the bad guy." That was an ironic comment since he was the one in prison, but Swinton's gray eyebrows pulled together. "Who told you I did?"

"No one. I just—" Shane figured he was a heartless nut job.

"Gracie broke up with me. I tried to get her to reconsider, but she swore it was over." He took a deep, shuddering breath. "Her folks didn't like me much and Doug Traub was interested in her. They thought he walked on water."

So far the man hadn't said anything that convinced him Grace was his mother.

"She started going out with Doug?" Shane prodded.

"Not right away. At least not that I knew. I tried to see her, but her folks wouldn't tell me where she was."

When Gianna's hand tightened on his, Shane looked at her and knew they were thinking the same thing. Had she been sent away to hide a pregnancy? "She left town?"

"Yeah."

"But she came back."

"About six months later," he confirmed.

"Did she tell you why she went away?" His heart was pounding.

"Hell, no. She wouldn't even look at me, let alone be caught in a conversation."

Out of guilt? Shane wondered. Did her parents pressure her to keep quiet? Because it was sure looking like she was pregnant with Swinton's baby and didn't tell him.

"What did you do?"

"I kept trying to call her, see her, tell her I loved her. Then it was all over Thunder Canyon that she was dating Doug Traub. Next thing I knew she was engaged to him."

His hands clenched into fists on the table, right beside the word "hell" carved on the top. "She was making a mistake and I couldn't get past her father or Traub to make her see what she was doing."

Shane could feel the man's pain and didn't know what to say. This part of the story was history. "She married him."

"Yes." Swinton snapped out the single word. It was rife with bitterness, and sadness etched lines in his craggy face. "Then she died. So damn young. I hated that I didn't get time with her. The Traubs had her all to themselves. I never got to tell her I'll always love her. Never got to say goodbye."

"Mr. Swinton—" When Gianna finally spoke up, her voice was gentle. "Is that why you were trying to ruin the Traubs? To get even because you were shut out?"

"They had everything. I had nothing. It kept eating at me."

"But they're Grace's children."

He looked down, miserable and unhappy. "She'd hate me for it and I'm sorry for that." He looked sorry. "Grief does crazy things to a man. I was desperate for a way to get out from under it."

Shane studied the man. He looked alternately sad, angry and lonely, but not crazy. Loving a woman who didn't return his feelings had started him down a path of bitterness that led to a series of crimes that were all about revenge against the family he blamed for a lifetime of unhappiness. But he wasn't the only one with a black mark.

Grace Smith never told this man that she was pregnant with his child. Shane couldn't help wondering if knowing would have made a difference.

Swinton shook his head sadly. "I thought being left out in the cold was bad, but it's nothing compared to not having Gracie on this earth at all. Now I've got no one."

When Gianna squeezed his hand, Shane looked at her

and saw a slight nod. He knew what she was saying and agreed. "It's not entirely true that you have no family."

The suspicion ever present in the man's expression now turned to bitterness. "What are you talking about?"

"I'm your son. Yours and Grace's."

Blue eyes narrowed and turned angry. "If this is some scheme to get money out of me, you can just shove it—"

"No." Shane held up his hands in a take-it-down-a-notch gesture. Why was it that everyone accused him of a scam when his only goal was to get at the truth? "I had a DNA test."

"You didn't get a sample from me."

"Yeah, I did. Remember that reporter who came to see you?" There was a slight nod along with an expression that said he was wondering how Shane could know that. "He's a private investigator. I hired him to get a sample from you. The test results show to a ninety-nine percent certainty that you're my biological father."

"Is this some kind of sick joke, because I don't think it's funny."

"Tell me about it. You're in jail. I have restaurants in big cities across the country. This is not the kind of thing that would help my business. What possible good would making up this connection do me? My reputation could be ruined. The fact is that you *are* my father."

After several moments the old man's expression softened as the truth of the words sank in. "You're my son? Mine and Gracie's?"

"That's what I believe, yes."

"I have a son?" He stared across the table and didn't look quite so old and broken. "I can't believe it. I have a son."

Gianna looked at Shane, then his father. "You're not physically alike, but the eyes are the same, in shape, color and intensity."

"I didn't know she was pregnant. So that's why she went away. This is amazing. I don't know what to say. You're a part of me and Grace." He started to reach for Shane's hand, then stopped. "I don't know what to do. What's right. Sorry. I can hardly wrap my head around all of this."

Shane understood exactly what he was saying because he'd just confirmed the worst. He was the son of the man who was serving time in jail for crimes against Thunder Canyon and the Traub family.

His family, although they would reject that.

What the hell was he going to do?

"Shane, say *something*. You're starting to scare me."

Truthfully, the dark expression on his face had scared Gianna twenty miles ago, when they'd driven away from the jail. Now his chronic silence had her approaching frantic. She glanced at him, then turned the radio volume down.

He kept his eyes on the long, straight road. Most of the snow had melted, but there were still pockets of white where tree trunks and bushes shaded and protected it from direct sunlight. His hands gripped the wheel so tightly, she expected it to snap any second.

"I don't have anything to say."

"That's impossible. You just met your birth father for the first time." She didn't add that it was in jail, but knew he was thinking it, too. "I'm not buying the fact that you've got nothing."

"What do you want to hear?"

Stubborn, exasperating man. If she were bigger and he wasn't so tall, broad and muscular, she'd shake him.

"I don't have a script for you." She studied his profile, the lean cheek and stubborn jaw. There must be feelings, impressions—*something*—rolling around in his head. From the look of his expression, the thoughts were pretty dark. "Tell me what you're thinking."

"It's a nice day for a drive."

She sighed and shook her head. "Don't make me hurt you."

"So, you do have a script. Or a list of acceptable subjects."

"Not so much that as a specific topic," she said. Maybe questions would draw him out. "What did you think of him?"

"Arthur?"

Okay. He wasn't going to call the man dad. "Yes. Arthur."

"He's pretty intense."

So are you, she wanted to say, but decided he wasn't in the mood for a DNA characteristics comparison spreadsheet. It might get him to open up if she shared her impressions.

"I sort of expected him to look, I don't know, edgier somehow. More convict tough. Kind of like a hardened criminal."

"He's an old man." That sounded like he agreed with her and there was the tiniest bit of pity in his tone.

"Did it seem to you like he was telling the truth?"

"You mean do I think he's crazy?" Shane glanced at her. "No. He's a lot of things, but crazy isn't one of them."

"So you believe he and Grace were involved? That she left Thunder Canyon to give birth?"

He nodded without meeting her gaze. "Yeah, I do. I'm all but certain that Grace Smith Traub was my mother."

She was glad he knew the truth, but it also made her sad. After all his efforts to find his birth parents now he'd discovered his father in jail and his mother had died. It all seemed like a cruel twist of fate.

"So you'll never have a chance to know her."

"Not face-to-face."

She knew what he was saying. Grace had died when they were pretty young, but her sons, his half brothers, could share memories of their mother. "You could talk to Dax and D.J. about her."

"Not likely." He pulled off the road when a service station, convenience store and diner came into view. "I'm going to get gas. Are you hungry?"

Not really, but it was way past lunch and both of them needed food. "I could eat."

He nodded and parked by one of the pumps, then fueled up. Gianna watched his face as he worked and knew by the shadows swirling in his eyes that the surface of his feelings hadn't even been scratched yet. When he opened the driver's-side door and got in, cold air came with him and she shivered, but that was more about the emotional morning than winter in Montana.

He started the car and drove around the building and parked in front of the Pit Stop Diner. The windows were painted with snowflakes, a Christmas tree and other traditional signs of the season, with a big "Happy Holidays" in the middle. There weren't any cars in the parking lot, so it was no surprise when they walked in to find the place empty.

A thirtyish waitress wearing jeans, a Santa Claus sweatshirt and jingle bell earrings greeted them. Her name tag read Jamee. "Merry Christmas, folks. Sit anywhere."

"Thanks." Gianna picked a booth by the window and sat on the red plastic bench seat. The menus were tucked behind the salt and pepper shakers and the napkin holder. "May I have a cup of tea, please?"

"Sure thing." Jamee stared at Shane as if she were trying to place him, then there was a glimmer of recognition. "Wow. You're Shane Roarke."

"Guilty as charged."

"Wait till I tell Carl." She cocked a thumb toward the counter with swivel stools and the kitchen beyond. "He's the cook here. No pressure, huh?"

Shane smiled and only someone who knew him could tell his effortless charm was missing in action and his heart wasn't in it. "I'm sure the food is great."

She took a pencil from behind her ear and held a pad. "What are you doing all the way out here in the middle of nowhere?"

There wasn't much around except the jail compound they'd been to and Gianna was pretty sure he wouldn't want to share that he'd just visited his father there. She was at a loss with an answer, but Shane handled it with ease.

"I'm working at Thunder Canyon Resort, The Gallatin Room. I wanted to take a drive, clear my head." He looked across the table. "Gianna works with me and kept me company for some sightseeing."

"Not a lot to look at, but I'm glad you stopped in. I'm a big fan. Never missed an episode of *If You Can't Stand the Heat.*" Jamee was gushing now and who could blame her? Of all the diners in all the world, a celebrity had just walked into hers. "I voted for you every week."

"I appreciate that."

"You're a lot better looking in person."

"Thanks." The brooding expression was back and pretty easy to read. He was thinking that probably his looks came from his mother because of the strong resemblance to Dax and D. J. Traub. "I think I'll just have a burger. Medium."

"That comes with fries."

"Fine," he said.

"Me, too, and a cup of tea." Gianna grabbed a couple of napkins from the container and put one in her lap.

"Coming right up."

She watched the waitress disappear through a swinging door, then met Shane's gaze. There was doubt, questions and confusion in his eyes and her heart ached for him. She wished she could wave a magic wand and take it all away.

"What are you thinking?" she asked.

His mouth tightened and anger took over his features. "How could she not tell him she was pregnant with his child?"

"I don't know." Gianna knew the "she" in question was Grace. "She was probably scared. It sounds like her parents were strict and controlling."

"It was wrong."

"I can't argue with you there. Arthur had a right to know. Just like Dax and D.J. have a right to know they have a half brother."

"To share memories of their mother with?" His tone was mocking. "That's not going to happen. D.J. made himself pretty clear. They don't want anything to do with me. My very existence puts a big bad ding in her perfect reputation and their memories."

She wasn't so sure he was wrong about that. "Who knew Arthur Swinton would turn out to be the injured party in all this?"

"Injured?" The single word was spoken in a soft, scornful voice. "That implies something he could recuperate from. She ripped his heart out and he never recovered. He fell in love and it ruined his life."

Just then the waitress brought their burgers and fries and set the plates down. "I'll get your hot tea right out. Anything to drink for you?" she asked Shane.

"Not unless you've got something stronger than coffee."

"Sorry." Jamee looked it. "Anything else?"

A miracle, Gianna thought. All she said was, "This is fine."

Her stomach was in knots and there was no way she'd get this or anything else down. Shane was slipping away. She could feel it and there was nothing she could do to stop it.

Leaving her food untouched, she stared across the table. "Shane, look at it from Dax and D.J.'s point of view. This has rocked your world and you always knew you were adopted. The Traubs are just finding out their mother had secrets. Give them time to process what's going on. You, too. Now you know what happened. You'll come to terms with the past."

"There's nothing to come to terms with." He shrugged. "I found out what I wanted to know. It's over."

That sounded so final. As if he was finished with a part of his life, the part that included her.

"What are you going to do?" she asked.

"It's the holidays. I need to see my family. The one that actually *does* want me around," he clarified. "I'm going to Los Angeles."

She had a bad feeling about this. Just the way he said it made her want to put a finer point on his plans. December 25th was a little over a week away and he was making a trip sound imminent. "For Christmas?"

He shook his head. "As soon as I can get a flight out."

"But that's earlier than you planned." Duh, stating the obvious.

He shook his head. "I never should have started any of this in the first place. If I just go away quietly, the Traubs can get on with their lives and Grace's memory will be preserved."

"But it's not the truth. She was human. She had flaws and made mistakes. That doesn't mean she was a bad person and they shouldn't love her. Or you."

He went on as if he hadn't heard her. "D.J. is the only one who knows. He probably didn't say anything to the rest of them because he didn't believe me, anyway. It's time for me to move on. Like you said, I found out what I came here for."

But was that all he'd found? What about her? What about the two of them? Neither of those were questions she could ask. Instead she said, "What about the restaurant?"

"The sous-chef can take over for me. I've trained her. No one is irreplaceable."

He was wrong about that. He couldn't be replaced in her heart. And that's when she knew she'd fallen in love with him. It was implied when she'd told him there was nowhere else she'd rather be than with him, even meeting his father for the first time in jail. And no matter that he denied it, she was pretty sure he blamed her for convincing him to tell D.J. the truth. The look on his face said he wouldn't forgive her, either.

She'd wasted years on relationships that were wrong and not long at all on one that she'd thought was right, only to find out it was one-sided. He'd connected the dots of who he was and his contract at The Gallatin Room was almost up. So, he had no reason to stay and every reason to go back to Los Angeles.

Somehow it was no comfort that she hadn't put in a lot of time falling for him. Fate had a way of evening the score and she was going to spend the rest of her life missing him.

Chapter Thirteen

In her apartment after work, Gianna took her cup of tea and walked over to the tiny Christmas tree on a table in front of her window. She'd changed out of her work clothes and put on fleece pajama bottoms and a red Henley top for warmth. It was a schleppy outfit, but what did it matter? No one was coming, and by no one she meant Shane. He was either in Los Angeles or on his way.

Between her regular time off and The Gallatin Room's Monday closure she hadn't seen him for a couple of days. Tonight when she'd gone to work Bonnie had broken the news that Shane told the staff he was leaving for the holidays. It felt as if he'd whipped her heart with a wire whisk. The rest of the staff thought he'd be back to work after New Year's, but Gianna knew better.

He was gone for good.

The last couple of days had given her a sad and painful preview of how life without Shane would feel. It was as if someone turned off a light inside her and not even holiday decorations could power it back up.

"The most wonderful time of the year, my backside," she mumbled to herself.

She set her steaming mug on the table where the tree stood and looked at the assembled presents. The packages for her family were arranged on the floor, too big to fit underneath in the traditional spot. Only one was small enough and the tag had Shane's name on it.

She picked up the square box wrapped in gold foil paper with red holly berries. She'd spent a long time getting the three-dimensional red bow just right. That investment of energy was nothing compared to how she'd agonized over what to buy for the man who had everything. Aftershave was a cliché. He didn't wear neckties—also a cliché. Nothing too personal—even though they'd made love and things didn't get much more personal than that. Her body ached with the memories of that magic night, doomed to be a single, life-changing event.

Of course she hadn't known that when picking out his present. It couldn't be too expensive, mostly because her budget would only stretch so far. But still the gift had to mean something.

She looked at the box holding the blue wool neck scarf that matched his eyes. "It means I'm an idiot."

He was gone and she should give this to charity so someone could use it.

Then she realized she *was* the charity case who could use it. "For a horrible warning to never fall in love again."

A knock on the door startled her because it was late and she wasn't expecting anyone. Her family would have called. No one would just drop in unless it was someone who knew her schedule. Someone like Shane.

Her heart started to pound and she walked to the door,

then peeked out the window beside it. He was there on the landing and the light that had gone dark inside her blazed brightly again. He was here; he hadn't left town. He was...

What? Her hands shook as she looked at the box she was still holding. How quickly the horrible warning was forgotten. But, she realized, the warning was too late, anyway, since she was already in love with him.

She opened the door and the outside cold made her shiver. His coat was open and his hands were in the pockets. He could really use a scarf to keep him warm.

"Shane. What are you doing here?"

His gaze dropped to her fleece pants and long-sleeved shirt. Maybe it was wishful thinking, but his eyes seemed to go intense for just a moment while lingering on her chest. "I saw your light was still on."

"I thought you'd left town. That's what they told me at the restaurant." Could he tell how hurt she was?

"I had a flight out tonight," he admitted. "I actually made it all the way to the airport, but it felt wrong."

"Define 'it.'"

"Can I come in? Would that be all right?"

No, it wasn't all right. This was like grinding his heel into her already broken heart, but closing the door in his face wasn't an option. And it was too cold to stand here.

She pulled the door wide. "Come in."

"Thanks. I won't stay long."

As he moved past her the air stirred with the spicy masculine scent of his skin and she knew forever wouldn't be long enough for him to stay. But she had no illusions about that wish coming true.

She closed the door and said, "I'm just having some tea. Would you like a cup?"

"No."

She picked up her mug and sat on the sofa, leaving room for him beside her. "So, why are you here?"

"I just wanted to talk to—" He stopped, then slid into the space next to her without taking off his coat. "We're friends, Gianna."

"I thought so." Even she could hear the hurt in her voice.

"I've been an ass and having a lot on my mind is no excuse. I thought going to L.A. would help me sort things out. Then I got to the airport and couldn't go. I've sort of gotten used to talking to you and it was unprofessional to leave the restaurant on short notice."

"What about D.J.?"

"So far I haven't heard anything from him. If there's any fallout from what I said, I'll be here to face it. I'm not hiding."

She nodded approval. "There are no more secrets and that's the way it should be. It's a good plan, Shane."

"It feels good." He met her gaze. "And I don't think I ever told you just how much I appreciate your support through everything. You didn't just listen. You were there for me."

She saw the light dim in his eyes and knew he was talking about that day at the jail. The day his father found out he had a son and the woman he'd loved all his life had kept that from him.

Friendship wasn't nearly enough for her, she thought, but it looked like that was all he was offering and she'd take what she could get. She stared at him to memorize the shape of his nose, the stubborn line of his jaw, the exact shade of blue in his eyes.

"I couldn't let you go to the jail alone," she said. "It's not what friends do."

He looked like he wanted to say something to that, but shook his head and let it go. "Anyway, I had another reason for stopping by."

She felt something quiver inside her and knew it was hope stirring. If she could slap it around and discourage the emotion she would, but that was hard when hope had a life of its own.

"Oh?"

"Yeah. I know you want to travel."

"It was a dream." She was surprised he remembered. "I was always told to study what you love in school. Do what you love in your job. I was good at business and marketing and wanted to see the world. A travel agency seemed like a perfect fit." She shrugged. "It was just a cruel twist of fate that I never got to go anywhere."

"Well, it's not the world, but I'd like to take you to L.A. for Christmas. You've been supportive of me through this weird, crazy, biological-parent journey and I'd very much like you to meet my real family."

"I'm sure they're wonderful people. How could they not be? They raised you and you're a very good man. I wish I could…"

He frowned. "I hear a but."

She squeezed the mug in her hands tightly. "This is my first Christmas with my family in a couple of years. I couldn't afford the trip from New York. I was trying to keep my business afloat and after I lost it, jobs were hard to find. Keeping a roof over my head was important and the city is a pricey place to live. I didn't have the money."

"You couldn't foresee what a toll the recession would take. A lot of businesses didn't make it. Not your fault."

She met his gaze and realized talking to him about her career disaster didn't embarrass her. Even though he was so phenomenally successful, he'd never made her feel less because she didn't hit it big. She appreciated that. "Anyway, this Christmas is all about reconnecting with my folks, my sister, my nephews and niece."

"I understand the importance of family in a very profound way." He was quiet for several moments, thinking. "I'm also not a man who gracefully takes no for an answer."

"Oh?"

"If so, I wouldn't have annihilated my reality show cooking competition by making an edible dish out of beef jerky, kidney beans and wine."

"Eww." She stared at him. "You're joking."

"Only about the jerky." He grinned. "Not about giving up easily. How about a compromise? You have Christmas Eve with your family. I'll take you to L.A. on Christmas day to meet mine."

She didn't like the idea of him being alone for any part of the holiday. "Do you have anywhere to go on the 24th?"

"No, but that's okay." He shrugged. "I'll manage."

"That's just wrong." She couldn't hold back the words. "I'm sure there's room for one more at the Garrisons."

"I wouldn't want to impose," he said.

"My family would love to meet you."

"I'd like to meet them. On one condition," he said. "Come with me to the west coast on Christmas. You've been an incredible friend, more than I deserve. Let me thank you for all you've done. I only want to hear a yes."

And she wanted to hear him say he loved her, but that wasn't going to happen. He was only interested in friendship and she understood why, because she'd been there when he met Arthur Swinton. Love ruined the man's life and Shane wasn't going to let that happen to him.

Where was a horrible warning when you really needed it? If she was smart, she'd tell him no. But she wasn't smart because she couldn't say it. She didn't want the light inside to go out sooner than necessary. Whatever time she had with him she would take, if only to store up memories for when she was alone.

"You win, but then you always do. I'd love to go to Los Angeles with you."

After following Gianna's directions, Shane pulled the car to a stop at the curb in front of her parents' house at the appointed time on Christmas Eve. Her gifts were in the backseat next to a pile that he'd brought. He'd quizzed her about the kids' ages, likes and dislikes, then shopped so he didn't come empty-handed.

He was in a great mood. To her knowledge, in the days since he'd postponed his trip to Los Angeles, he hadn't heard anything from D. J. Traub. Shane hadn't told her how he felt about it and she wasn't going to ask tonight. He wasn't brooding anymore and that was good enough for her.

Gianna removed her seat belt. "Do your brother or sister have any kids?"

"No."

"Can I assume that your career hasn't afforded you the opportunity to spend time with children?"

"That's an accurate assumption." There was a big dose of amusement in his tone.

"Then I have to ask, are you sure you really want to go in there? I love them with every fiber of my being, but they're loud. Probably sugar and any number of chemical food dyes have amped up their normally high energy level. The night before Santa Claus comes there's only peace on earth when they fall into an involuntary, exhausted sleep."

"Are you trying to scare me?" He opened his car door, and the overhead light illuminated his wry expression.

"Just keeping it real in case you want to beat a hasty retreat." She pointed to the driveway. "See that minivan? It means they're already here and waiting to pounce."

"Then let's go join the party."

"Don't say I didn't warn you." She got out of the car then retrieved her presents from the back.

Arms loaded with gifts, they walked to the front door and Shane managed to ring the bell with his elbow. Moments later it was opened and Griffin stood there.

"Auntie G is here," he announced in an exceptionally loud voice.

"Hi, Griff. You know," she teased, "I think there are some people a few streets over who didn't hear you."

"You're funny." He gave Shane a long, assessing look. "Is he your friend?"

She winced at the word, but probably her mother had told him that. "Yes. This is Shane Roarke. My boss. Shane, this is Griffin, my nephew."

"Nice to meet you, Griffin."

"You're the cook?"

"Chef," she corrected.

"What's the difference? Does he cook food?"

"Yes," Shane answered.

"My dad is a good cook. So is Grammy."

"We're coming in now, Griffie." She kissed the top of his head on the way to pile gifts under the living-room tree. "It smells good in here. Turkey, yum."

Griffin stared at the exquisitely wrapped boxes Shane put beside hers. "Did you bring me something?"

"Griffin, it's rude to ask that," she scolded.

"But I wanna know. How am I gonna know if I don't ask? Mommy says it's good to ask questions."

"Your mom is right," Shane said. "And the answer is yes, I did bring you something."

The boy grinned. "Can I open it now?"

"Let's go talk to Grammy and find out what the plan is."

"Okay." He grabbed Shane's hand. "I'll show you where she is."

"Lead the way." Shane whispered in her ear. "Retail bribery works every time."

When they walked into the combination kitchen/family room, the boy stopped. "Auntie G is here and Shane brought us presents. Can we open 'em, Grammy?"

Colin left his fire truck and toy firefighter figures on the rug in front of the TV and ran over to give her a hug. "Hi, Auntie G."

Right behind him was Emily, trying to keep up on her short, pudgy legs, saying, "Annie G!"

Gianna grabbed her up and spread kisses over her cheek until the little girl giggled. "Hey, baby girl. You smell like sugar cookies."

"Cookie." She held up her sticky, crumb-covered hands for inspection. Then she spotted Shane, who grinned at her. Apparently his charm translated to women of all ages because the normally shy-of-strangers child held out her arms to him. "Pick me up."

Jackie rushed over. "You don't have to take her. With those dirty hands she'll ruin your sweater."

It looked like cashmere, a cream color that wouldn't hold up well to grubby hands, Gianna thought. "This is my sister and her husband, Frank."

The two men shook hands, then she introduced her parents. "Shane Roarke, Susan and Ed Garrison."

Her father shook his hand and her mother smiled. "We're so glad you could join us for dinner, Shane."

"Thank you for including me."

"Any friend of my daughter's…" Her father had no idea how that touched a nerve.

Gianna decided for tonight she was not going to let that word get to her. "I smell mulled wine."

"On the stove." Her dad raised his voice to be heard over Emily's wailing.

"Pick me up!" Apparently oblivious to the fact that she was up, the little girl kept holding her arms out to Shane.

"Dirty hands don't scare me. Obviously it's early childhood training for a career in the food-service industry." He took the child who pointed into the family room. "I guess we're going that way."

While Em chattered to him in a language only a two-year-old could understand, he carried her to the pile of toys on the family-room floor. When he set her down, she grabbed a ragged plastic doll with all the clothes removed and pointed to the face.

"Eye," he said.

"Eye," Em repeated.

Gianna watched as he patiently played the naming-the-limbs game until the boys moved in to get his attention. Frank tried to run interference, but apparently two grown men were no match for three small children. The toys were forgotten in favor of wrestling, tickling and roughhousing. Shane easily went from instigator to casualty, alternately taking one of the boys on his back to letting them tackle him. Jackie and her dad tried to play referee, but no one was listening to them.

Her mother handed Gianna a glass of wine. "He's even better-looking than on TV."

"Am I the only one on the planet who never saw that show?" She was remembering the woman in the middle-of-nowhere diner who'd recognized him. The man playing with her nephews and niece was much different from the shell-shocked one who had just found his birth father.

"Apparently you are," Susan said. "He's a wizard with food and if I weren't so secure in my cooking skills, having a world-famous chef to dinner could be just a little bit intimidating."

"Your turkey is the best, Mom."

"You have to say that, sweetheart, but I appreciate the sentiment."

"It's the absolute truth."

"You were looking pensive just now." Her mother studied her face. "What are you thinking?"

"Just that Shane looks really happy and relaxed."

Susan glanced at the rowdy group with Shane in the center of it. "If that's noteworthy, it would seem he's lately been just the opposite."

This wasn't her story to tell so Gianna gave the heavily edited version. "He's had a lot on his mind lately, but I think the weight has finally lifted from his shoulders." When one of the boys climbed on his back, she laughed. "He's got Colin there now."

"Yes, he does. Also noteworthy is that the kids took to him right away." Susan was using her mother's-seal-of-approval voice. "They have a finely tuned BS—bad stuff—meter and can see through phoniness instantly."

Gianna could read through the lines and the same thought had already crossed her mind. He would make a wonderful father. Tears burned her eyes because no matter how determined she was to put the "friend thing" out of her mind, it would take a Christmas miracle to pull that off.

She ached to be more than that because he was everything she'd ever wanted.

"I like your family." Shane braked at a stoplight a few minutes after leaving the crazy, wonderful Christmas chaos at the Garrison house.

"I do, too," she said. "My mother thinks you're better-looking in person than on TV."

"Good to know." He was feeling a little reflective. "They make me miss my family."

"You'll be seeing them tomorrow."

"As will you."

He glanced at her in the passenger seat, streetlights making her red hair glow. God, he wanted her. In every way. How could he ever have considered leaving her at Christmas?

"Speaking of that," she said, "what time are you picking me up to go to the airport tomorrow?"

"Are you packed?"

"Are you kidding? This is me. I've been packed for a couple days. All ready except for the last-minute things."

That's all he needed to hear. "Then I'm not picking you up."

"Okay." She slid a puzzled glance across the leather console between them. "Do you want me to come by your place?"

"That won't be necessary."

She frowned. "If you changed your mind about me going with you—"

"Just the opposite." He accelerated when the light turned green and passed the street for her place. "Technically I won't need to pick you up because I'm taking you home with me tonight. We can get your things tomorrow on the way to the airport."

It was quiet on the passenger side for so long that he looked over. Gianna was staring at him.

Maybe he'd blown his chance with her after all, but every part of him fought against that. It couldn't be too late. "Do you want me to take you home now?"

"No," she said emphatically. "It's just that I'm confused. You pulled back— I thought— You said we're friends."

"About that—" It felt like he'd been in a fog for months,

a haze that just now cleared. "After seeing Arthur, I guess I went a little crazy. Like father, like son."

"It's called processing the information," she defended.

Loyalty and support were two of his favorite things about her. "In my case it was more about going to the bad place and moving in for a while." He looked over and saw her watching him intently. "I started ticking off the things about me that are like him, none of them good."

"Shane, he has positive qualities. And you didn't get all your DNA from him. You didn't know Grace, but look at her children. They're all good men. Salt of the earth."

"I know. I've thought a lot about everything and had to work it through. Just because he buckled under the weight of disappointment doesn't mean I will."

"That's right," she agreed. "He's not a bad man, I don't think. Just one who lost his way."

"So did I. For a while." Almost to his place, he took her hand while keeping his other on the steering wheel. "Now I've got my head on straight."

She squeezed his fingers. "I'm glad."

He pulled the car into the parking garage and guided it into his space. After getting out, he went to the passenger side and opened Gianna's door, then held out his hand. "Do you mind if we unload the gifts in the morning?"

He'd missed her more than he thought possible and was in kind of a hurry to get her inside. Besides, he had a lot to make up for.

"I don't mind at all." Her expressive eyes hid nothing and promised everything.

She took his breath away.

They went into the elevator and pushed the button for his floor, then walked down the hall to his place where he unlocked the door and led her inside.

"Alone at last," he said, taking her face in his hands. "You're cold."

"Not for long. And my mom gave me something." She reached into her pocket and pulled out a red-ribbon-trimmed sprig. "Mistletoe. Sometimes a girl has to take matters into her own hands."

She held it up as high as she could to get it over their heads. He took it from her and did the job as she slid her arms around his neck.

Need exploded through him as she touched her mouth to his, then pushed at his jacket, trying to get it off. In a frenzy of kissing and wanting he dropped the mistletoe because he needed both hands. They tugged at buttons and closures until coats and keys were on the floor and the raspy sound of their breathing filled the entryway. He could hardly wait to have her, but not here, not up against the wall.

Shane swept her into his arms and laughed at her shriek of surprise. "You know it's Christmas Eve and Santa won't bring presents until you're in bed."

She grinned. "Then what are you waiting for?"

"Not a damn thing."

He carried her to his room where they undressed each other then fell on the mattress in a tangle of arms, legs and laughter. He hadn't realized how lonely the past six months had been until Gianna. Or how much he didn't want to be just friends with her.

He concentrated on her pleasure, touching her breasts, finding the place on her thigh that made her breath come faster, kissing a certain spot near her ear that made her moan. And he couldn't hold back any longer. He entered her and brought her to the peak where she cried out with satisfaction. A heartbeat or two behind her, his release came sooner than he would have liked.

But they had all night.

He pulled her against him and felt her hand on his chest. "You're the reason I didn't go to Los Angeles sooner."

"Me?" Her voice was a little breathless, a little sleepy.

"I couldn't leave you on Christmas." Or any other time, he added to himself.

"Merry Christmas, Shane." She snuggled into him and relaxed, quickly falling asleep in his arms.

"And to all a good night," he whispered, kissing her forehead.

The journey he'd started in June had brought him to an unexpected place and the future was still unsettled. He wasn't sure where he and Gianna went from here because Thunder Canyon wasn't big enough for him and the half brothers who wanted nothing to do with him.

Chapter Fourteen

Gianna stretched sleepily and touched something that felt a lot like a man's broad back. That didn't happen often in her world so she opened one eye and grinned from ear to ear. *Merry Christmas to me,* she thought. Memories of loving Shane the night before warmed her everywhere. He hadn't said he loved her, but he hadn't turned his back. Metaphorically speaking, since she was loving the view of his very real, very wide shoulders.

"I can feel you looking at me." Shane's voice was raspy with sleep and tinged with amusement.

"How did you know?"

"Like I said—I can feel it." He rolled over and pulled her against him, resting his chin on her hair. "Merry Christmas."

"Merry Christmas, Shane." She snuggled her cheek on his chest and caught a glimpse of his digital clock on the nightstand. "Holy cow. We have to get moving. There's a plane to catch and I bet you're not packed. All my stuff is at my apartment and I have to do an overhaul—hair, makeup, just the right outfit—before flying to Los Angeles."

"Why? You're beautiful."

"Thank you." The compliment made her glow from head to toe, but a look for meeting his folks didn't happen without some effort. "But your family will be there."

"Yeah." He laughed. "What with Christmas dinner being at their house and all."

"Right. And I can't meet them for the first time looking like I just rolled out of your bed."

"Why not?" He tipped her chin up and their gazes locked. "I like you right where you are."

"Shane—"

"Okay." He kissed the tip of her nose. "But let's have coffee. We've got time. Weather's good. I've been watching the forecast all week. Flights will be on time. We'll be having Christmas dinner in L.A."

"And I have to look fabulous."

He rolled out of bed and picked up his jeans, then slid them on. "You need to stop worrying so much."

"And you need to start worrying just a little more."

Gianna got up and grabbed his long-sleeved white shirt. She was feeling a little shy, even though last night he'd seen every inch of her naked. The soft cotton was like wrapping herself in the scent of him and came down to midthigh. She buttoned it as she followed him to the kitchen.

Resting her elbows on the granite countertop, she watched him put warm water in a state-of-the-art coffeemaker that had more bells and whistles than her car. He ground up beans then added them to the disposable filter before pushing some of those bells and whistles. Several moments later the thing started to sizzle and spit.

He turned toward her. "It won't be long now."

"Okay."

She'd have said okay to anything. The sight of his bare chest and the dusting of hair that narrowed down his belly to the vee where his jeans were unbuttoned absolutely mesmerized her. Tingles danced up and down her spine and for a second she thought there was a tune involved. Then she realized it was the doorbell.

"Are you expecting someone?"

"No. It's probably whoever is manning the front desk."

"On Christmas?"

"It's part of the job, like bringing my car to the restaurant." He shrugged. "Someone might have dropped off a package and the front desk is delivering. I'll be right back."

Gianna listened to the front door open then heard a very loud, "Surprise! Merry Christmas!"

Shane's voice drifted to her as he said, "Mom. Dad. Wow. Ryan and Maggie, too."

His family was here? *Now?* Gianna's heart started pounding as she frantically looked around for an escape route. There wasn't a cupboard big enough in the kitchen to hide her and no way to make it to the bedroom without being seen. She was pretty sure Shane didn't have an apron as he wasn't an apron-wearing sort of guy. It was just a case of being royally up doo-doo creek. This was like the bad dream where you somehow ended up in the mall ladies' room naked to the waist with no choice except to suck it up and walk out, knowing humiliation would happen no matter how much you pretended otherwise.

It would just be worse the longer she stayed put so, head held high, she moved just into the kitchen doorway, visible from the living room where the Roarke family stood. It was clear they all saw her because suddenly everyone went silent.

"Merry Christmas," she said, forcing cheerfulness into her voice.

"You must be Gianna Garrison." An attractive older woman with a stylish brunette bob separated from the group. "Shane said you were a blue-eyed redhead."

She touched a tousled curl by her cheek. "Guilty."

The woman, who had to be his mother, laughed. "He said you were friends."

Shane moved beside her, his expression sheepish and apologetic. "It was an ambush phone call, I was under oath and she was cross-examining me."

"He gets that a lot." The older man, obviously his father, had silver hair, very distinguished-looking. "I'm Gavin Roarke."

"My dad," Shane confirmed. "This is my mom, Christa. That's my little brother, Ryan and baby sister, Maggie."

"Hi." Gianna smiled as confidently as possible at the tall, good-looking guy with brown hair and eyes. His sister was wearing a navy knit hat pulled over long blond hair that spilled down her back.

"Are you surprised?" Maggie asked.

"Yes. Now, what are you guys doing here?"

"Your mother wanted to be with you for Christmas," Gavin explained.

"What part of me flying out for dinner did you not understand?"

"It's a mom thing." Christa's shrug was apologetic. "I miss the days when you guys were kids and ripped into presents first thing. You're all grown up so the best we could do is surprise you and be here in the morning."

"So you took a red eye?" Shane asked, shock and pleasure mixing in his voice.

"Yes," Gavin said. "Your brother and sister haven't stopped whining about it yet."

"But I'd do it all again just to see the look on your face. And everything," Ryan said, sliding a glance at Gianna's bare legs and feet, then grinning at his older brother's obvious discomfort. There was no way his family didn't know they'd slept together.

"I can't believe we actually pulled off this surprise," Maggie said. "It's nice to meet you, Gianna."

"Likewise." She was trying to hide behind Shane. "I usually look so much better than this."

"You look fine," Christa said and sounded like she meant it sincerely. "Attractive doesn't do her justice, Shane."

"Attractive was the best you could do?" Gianna didn't know whether to be flattered or not.

Looking down, Shane met her gaze. "Again, under oath."

"Don't pay any attention to him," his mother scoffed. "You're stunning. And all my children will tell you that I don't say anything I don't mean."

"It's true. She doesn't suck up," Ryan agreed. "So, about last night—"

"There's coffee in the kitchen." Shane cocked his thumb toward the room behind them. "I'm going to put on a shirt."

"Preferably not this one." As they laughed, Gianna sidled in the direction of the master bedroom and after going into the hallway, she turned and ran.

She grabbed her things from the floor where Shane had tossed her sweater and jeans last night. It seemed the arms and legs were pulled inside out. That happened when someone was in a big hurry to get your clothes off. Quickly she put them back on while Shane dressed.

"I can't believe this is happening. I just said I didn't want to meet your family looking like I rolled out of your bed. It's official. I'm being punished because I did just roll out of your bed." She turned a pleading look on him. "Tell me there's a back way out."

"Sorry." He moved in front of her and cupped her face in his palms. "They love you."

"We barely met. And I do mean barely what with wearing nothing but your shirt. There's no way they like me."

"They do. I know them and there was nothing but approval. Now let's have coffee."

When they returned, only his parents were there. Shane glanced at them, surprised. "So much for being together this morning. Ryan couldn't wait ten minutes to start checking out Thunder Canyon women."

"He does have a talent for that," his mother said, fondness and exasperation swirling in her eyes. "Although I do wish he'd find the right one and settle down. But, no. He and Maggie are using your guest rooms for a cat nap. They've been up all night."

"So have you guys," Shane pointed out.

"And worth it. But those two…" Christa shook her head sympathetically. "Rookies. It doesn't matter that you're all grown up, your father and I remember being up all night with babies. We've still got it, don't we, Gavin?"

He put his arm around her shoulders. "We do, indeed."

His mother's eyes were suspiciously bright. "'Tis the season to be with the ones you love."

"Yes, it is." Shane walked over and kissed her cheek. "Can I buy you a cup of coffee?"

"Sounds heavenly."

When they were settled around the table in the kitchen, his mother said, "So, you seem much more relaxed than you did last time we talked."

"Yeah." Shane picked up his steaming mug. "I found my biological mother and father."

Gavin exchanged a glance with his wife before asking, "Do you want to talk about it?"

"Of course. You're my parents." He took a deep breath

and said, "Grace Smith died a long time ago, when her sons were pretty young."

"You have brothers." It wasn't a question and Christa's tone was carefully neutral.

"Yes. But they're not happy about it. My birth father's name is Arthur Swinton and he did some bad things, to them and the town. He's in prison."

"Oh, my—" Christa shook her head. "You tease me about having a gift for words, but at this moment I'm at a complete loss."

"It's really complicated," Gianna said. "Grace was pregnant with Shane and didn't tell Arthur. He was so in love with her and couldn't accept that she loved another man. It made him a little crazy."

The other woman studied her son. "How do you feel about all that?"

"I had a rough time in the beginning," he admitted. "I've come to love this town and finding out you're the son of public enemy number one was hard." He set his coffee down and took Gianna's hand. "But I got lucky. My *friend* talked me through it."

"I'm glad Shane has you," his mother said.

"Me, too. No one should have to go through something like that alone."

Shane squeezed her fingers. "I've been thinking, Mom. Since there are four lawyers in the family, maybe something can be done for Arthur."

That surprised Gianna. He hadn't said anything to her, but she approved. The man wasn't a danger to society. His was a crime of revenge and it was over now.

"We can look into his case," Gavin said. "There might be mitigating circumstances to bring before a judge when he's up for parole. If he can return the money he took while on the city council there could be a reduced sentence. Time off for good behavior."

"Thanks. You guys are—" Shane's voice caught. "I got really lucky when you picked me."

"We're the lucky ones," his mother said. "We loved you the moment we laid eyes on you, so tiny and sweet. Instantly I felt as if you were meant for us. All I ever wanted was for you to be happy. I hope that everything you found out will help you to find serenity and stop searching. Stop running."

"I have." He met Gianna's gaze, but his own was impossible to read.

She had no idea what he meant, but if she'd helped him find peace, that would have to be good enough.

"That was the best Christmas dinner ever." Maggie Roarke leaned back in her chair and groaned dramatically. "I've never been so full in my life."

Gianna glanced around Shane's dining-room table, set for six. He sat at one end, she at the other, sort of host and hostess. His parents, Maggie and Ryan were on either side, facing each other. The big windows made the majestic, snow-covered mountains an extension of the room and gave them a spectacular view.

"I'm glad you liked the food, little sister." Shane sipped his chardonnay. "When you drop in on a guy, you take potluck."

"Then we should drop in every weekend," his mother said. "That beef Wellington is, without a doubt, the best thing I've ever had."

He'd never looked so pleased and personally satisfied at work. "If I hadn't been able to pillage stuff from the restaurant it would have been grilled cheese."

"Right," his brother scoffed. "So speaks the cooking genius who won *If You Can't Stand the Heat* by putting together a little something with lima beans, honey and tofu."

"You're exaggerating."

"Maybe just a little," Ryan admitted. "I don't think even you could make something edible out of that."

"Never underestimate the palate appeal of tofu," Shane said.

Gianna loved watching him banter with his family and was very happy to be included in the group. She'd been looking forward to the trip to L.A., but didn't mind that the plans were altered. This was one of the best holidays ever. Her financial position hadn't changed, but she was rich in so many other ways.

Definitely there'd been recent ups and downs, but today had been perfect, if you didn't count meeting the Roarkes wearing nothing but Shane's shirt. While his family napped, he'd driven her home to clean up, then they'd stopped by The Gallatin Room to get what he needed for dinner. Judging by the satisfied groans all around, he was a smashing success.

His mother looked out the window and sighed. "I can see why your voice was full of reverence when you told me about Thunder Canyon. It certainly is beautiful. God's country."

"Amen," her husband said.

Gianna couldn't agree more. She'd come home with her tail between her legs, feeling like a failure, but somehow this place had healed her soul. Her heart was in jeopardy, but maybe life was always a trade-off.

"It makes you hardly notice that your place has no Christmas decorations," Maggie said. "Next year."

"Maybe." Shane's tone was noncommittal.

"I'm going to earn my keep and clear the table." Gianna stood and started stacking plates.

"I'll help you."

When his mother started to stand, Shane stopped her. "No, you don't."

"I'm not a guest," she protested.

"Tomorrow you can help. But you were up all night getting here. That buys you a pass on doing dishes. All of you," he said, looking at each of them in turn.

"He just wants to be alone with Gianna," Ryan teased. "If you can't stand the heat…"

Shane lifted one eyebrow at his brother. "Can you blame me?"

"No."

Gianna blushed. Ryan grinned. Shane glared.

While Shane stacked plates at the other end of the table, she carried hers to the kitchen. Behind her she heard his mother say, "You two make a good team."

Gianna thought so, but what did she know. Her judgment was questionable. She was the one who'd wasted so much time on the wrong guys. After setting dishes in the sink, she turned to go back for the rest, but Shane was right behind her.

"I'll get the food," he said, turning back the way he'd come.

That was her prompt to rinse and arrange the plates and silverware in the dishwasher. By the time she'd finished, he was putting leftovers in the refrigerator, beside the pumpkin chiffon pie he'd "borrowed" from the restaurant freezer, from the stock he'd made for the restaurant's holiday menu.

"Do you want to wait to serve dessert?" she asked.

"Good idea."

They assembled small plates and forks. He got coffee ready but didn't push the "on" button. Then they looked at each other.

"Christmas is almost over," he said.

"I know. At the same time I'm relieved, it kind of makes me sad."

"Did you get everything you wanted?"

"I love the perfume," she said, not really answering.

His question made her think and not about the gift he'd given her. There was only one thing that could possibly make this day perfect and it couldn't be bought in a store. She just wanted to hear that he cared.

"How about you?" she countered. "Did you get everything?"

"Almost." He rubbed the back of his neck. "It's silly, I guess. And unrealistic given the circumstances. But I'd hoped to talk to D.J. and Dax. It's not that I'm looking to be embraced as a brother. I'm not asking for a kidney or bone marrow transplant."

"But?"

"I like them." He shrugged. "It was natural. I'm going to miss the friendship."

"That could still happen. Your paths are bound to cross if you stay in Thunder Canyon." She still didn't know what his long-term plans were.

"What about you?" The question turned the conversation away from him, his goals. "Is traveling still what you want?"

What she wanted had certainly changed since she'd returned to her hometown. She'd thought she was confused and lost then, but the feeling had multiplied a hundred fold. There was only one point she was clear on.

Gianna looked up at him. "In the last six months I've found out that Thunder Canyon is in my blood. I was so anxious to get away, but now I can't imagine being gone forever. I saw this place through your eyes and fell in love with it all over again." She left out the part about falling in love with him at the same time.

"I know what you mean."

"So, I'm going to put my business degree to work as soon as I figure out what business *will* work."

He nodded and a dark expression settled on his face. "There's something I have to say."

Gianna didn't like the sound of that. It was the male version of "we have to talk" and it was never about anything good. But she'd wasted a lot of time on relationships that didn't work. If this "thing" with them was heading over a cliff, it would be best to find out now. Knowing wouldn't stop the hurt, but... She couldn't really think of an upside to knowing. Best get it over with.

"Okay. What's on your mind?"

"You and I," he started. "And the Traubs. There are a lot of them here in town. Based on D.J.'s reaction, when he tells the rest of the family about who I am. They're not going to like me much either. You know I care about you, but—"

She held up her hand. "Don't say it. I hate that word."

"Gianna—" He shook his head. "You want to make a life here. If you get hooked up with me that could get awkward and I'd do anything to keep you from being hurt."

"Really? You're actually saying that this town isn't big enough for both of you?"

"I know it sounds like something from a bad Western, but yeah, I am. And there's only one way to keep you out of it."

"You don't have to protect me."

"I can't help it where you're concerned."

He was talking about walking away. He was willing to give up a place that had touched his soul. But this wasn't a decision that just affected him and she should get a say in it.

"Look," she said, "It's not—"

"Shane?" His father was standing in the doorway and neither of them had noticed.

"Yeah, Dad?"

"There's someone at your front door. A young man. He says he'd like to speak with you."

Shane straightened away from the counter looking as surprised as she felt. "That's odd. I wasn't expecting anyone. Did he say what it's about or give you his name?"

Gavin shook his head. "He only said that he needed a few minutes of your time."

"Okay. I'll see what he wants."

Gianna had a bad feeling. This was like getting a phone call in the middle of the night. Someone stopping by unannounced this late on Christmas just felt weird. And that's why she walked to the door with Shane. He wasn't the only one who couldn't help going into protective mode. When she saw who was standing there, she slipped her hand into his.

"Hello, Dax. Merry Christmas."

"Shane. Same to you." If Dax Traub was surprised at the two of them together, he didn't show it.

"What can I do for you?"

"I have a favor to ask."

"What?" Shane's voice was neutral, but the rest of him tensed.

"I'd like to talk to you."

"My family is in from L.A."

"Sorry to interrupt your Christmas." Dax glanced into the room behind them. "Here isn't what I had in mind, anyway. Can you meet me at the Rib Shack? It won't take long."

The bad stuff didn't usually take very long to say. Shane's peace-on-earth expression disappeared, replaced by the intensity he'd worn like armor for the past six months. And Gianna couldn't blame him.

The two men stared at each other for several moments while Shane thought it over. Finally he said, "I'll meet you there. Is now okay?"

Dax nodded. "Thanks, Shane."

Gianna watched him walk down the hall to the elevator and her bad feeling got bigger. "Don't go, Shane. Whatever he has to say can wait until tomorrow when it's not Christmas."

"I want to get this over with. The sooner, the better."

Never would be better as far as Gianna was concerned.

Chapter Fifteen

On the short drive to the Rib Shack, Shane kept picturing Gianna's face, the stubborn tilt of her chin, the way her full mouth pulled tight with anger. He couldn't help thinking she was beautiful when she was angry. First, she'd been revving up to talk him out of leaving town, when he'd told her that things would be awkward with the Traubs.

They'd lived in Thunder Canyon for a long time. He was the newcomer who'd had ulterior motives and was the son of their enemy. It was a stigma that would stick; it would rub off on Gianna and her family. She'd found her way back and knew what she wanted. He wouldn't jeopardize that for her, which was why he had to do the right thing and go quietly.

He loved her too much to ruin her life by being in it.

Second, he'd had to talk her out of coming with him for this conversation with Dax. She would take his side against the Traubs. It's just the way she was and he couldn't let her do it. What finally convinced her to stay put was when he asked her to watch over his family. With her they were in good hands. And now it was time for the showdown.

The Rib Shack parking lot had a few cars, but it looked pretty quiet this late on Christmas. Holiday hours were posted inside for the guests staying at the resort, but he knew the restaurant was closed to the public now. He parked by the outside entrance; it would make for a quick exit.

"Best get this over with," he muttered.

"This" being the portion of the holiday entertainment where he was run out of town. He was stubborn enough to tell them to shove it, but for Gianna's sake he would listen politely then walk away. He wouldn't ask her to choose between the town and family she loved.

But, he'd learned something from his biological mother. Grace Smith Traub had shown him that the greatest love of all is letting someone go to give them a better life.

He walked through the parking lot as snowflakes started to fall and his breath made clouds in front of his face. As he opened the door and went inside the restaurant, the sounds of talking, laughter and children playing drifted to him. It pierced the loneliness that pressed heavily on his heart.

In the Rib Shack's main dining room, tables were pushed together to accommodate a large group—all of them Traubs as far as he could tell. He recognized Jason, who'd come from Texas to settle here. Clay, Antonia and their little ones were next to him. Forrest Traub and Angie Anderson sat so close together you couldn't see space between them. There were a couple more guys he didn't recognize, but they were Traubs, what with that strong family-resemblance thing.

As he moved farther into the room, conversation around the table stopped and everyone looked at him. When Dax angled his head, D.J. and Clay stood up, as if it was a strategy agreed on ahead of time. The three of them moved to meet him.

Dax slid his fingertips into the pockets of his jeans. "Thanks for coming, Shane."

"No problem. Looks like the gang's all here," he said.

"Not everyone could make it." Clay glanced over his shoulder at the group. "But there were too many to fit in anyone's house. D.J. volunteered the Shack for Christmas dinner."

Shane looked at the man in question who still hadn't said anything. The last time he'd been here, D.J. had thrown him out.

"We've got some things to say. Let's sit over there where it's quiet," Dax suggested, pointing to a far corner. "Otherwise the kids will drive you crazy."

That was a kind of crazy Shane wanted, but had given up hope he would ever have. Without a word, he followed the other men to the table all by itself in the big room. He had a feeling this wasn't so much about quiet as it was about protecting the women and children from the ugliness of the past, the flaw in him that was all about who his father was.

After the four of them took seats around the table, Dax looked at his cousin Clay, a look that said "get ready." "Some information has come to our attention."

Shane knew Clay was from Rust Creek where another branch of the family lived. He had the same Traub features—tall, muscular, dark hair and brown eyes. He was a little younger than the other two men and more boyish-looking. Although not now with intensity darkening his eyes and tension in his face.

Dax nodded at him. "Tell Shane what you told us."

"When I was a little kid…" Clay blew out a breath, then continued. "I overheard my parents arguing about Aunt Grace and Uncle Doug, Dax and D.J.'s parents. My mom just didn't understand how Grace could give away her own child then act as if he'd never existed. She was angry that

Uncle Doug didn't support her through it. Dad said that his brother would have had a hard time raising a child that wasn't his, but that ticked Mom off even more. She said Doug should have been man enough to put that aside for the sake of the baby, the child of the woman he loved." He shrugged at his cousins. "I only remembered recently. But when I was clear about the memory, I knew Dax and D.J. had a brother out there somewhere."

"Me." Shane looked at each man.

Dax nodded. "Clay wasn't sure whether or not to say anything to D.J. and me. Obviously that wasn't our father's finest hour."

"Or our mother's," D.J. added.

His brother nodded darkly. "We had a get-together last night for Christmas Eve and were talking about why the two sides of the family have been estranged all these years. Clay told us what he remembered. Then D.J. mentioned the conversation with you."

Shane looked at the man who looked so much like him. "The one where I told him about your mother and Arthur Swinton having an affair."

He waited for the explosion, but the two men didn't say a word. They looked shell-shocked and he realized the revelations were too recent. They needed time to take it all in.

"Look, I didn't come to Thunder Canyon to make trouble, just to find my birth parents. I did that. I'm sorry it involves your mother. I get that you don't want to believe it. But that doesn't change—"

Clay held up a hand. "D.J. told us what he said to you, but if you could cut him some slack… Just put yourself in his place. He had no reason to believe you. His mom died when he was a kid and his dad wasn't likely to bring up the subject." He rubbed a hand across the back of his neck. "But my parents knew Grace Smith had a baby and gave him up for adoption. They confirmed everything and it's why the two families had a falling out all those years ago."

"I didn't know any of this," D.J. confirmed. "Then you tell me my mother had a thing with Arthur Swinton. I thought you were lying and I couldn't figure out why you'd do that."

Shane figured he'd have felt the same if someone came to him with a wild story like this. All he could do now was reassure them. "I'm not looking for anything but the facts. If you want, we can do DNA tests to prove the truth once and for all."

"No." D.J. shook his head. "As soon as I calmed down, I realized all the evidence was right in front of me. Our personalities clicked. Similar sense of humor. I felt an almost instant connection."

"Then there was the strong resemblance that Allaire saw," Dax said.

His brother nodded. "We bonded right away, without even knowing the family link. It struck a chord that felt true. Then Clay tied everything together with what he remembered and we talked to Uncle Bob and Aunt Ellie, who confirmed his memory and everything else. We don't have any doubts."

Maybe not about being brothers, Shane realized. But there was still the fact of his father. He met their gazes, but this had to be said. "I know how you feel about Arthur Swinton."

The statement hung in the air and he knew they were filling in the blanks. His father was a criminal. But Gianna was right about him. "There's no reason you should believe this, but Arthur isn't a bad man. He loved our mother. Still does."

"You saw him in jail?" D.J. looked surprised.

"Yeah. He didn't know about me. She never said anything about being pregnant. No one should be too hard on her. Think about it. She was just a teenager. Scared. Under pressure from her family. I'm not judging and you shouldn't, either. No one's perfect and she was just doing what she thought was right for her family."

"I hear you," Dax said. "But it will take some time to work this through."

Shane nodded. "And I'm not saying Arthur deserves forgiveness, but he's a broken man. When she turned her back on him, he went off the deep end. He only saw that you all had her and he was left out in the cold."

"I'm not sure I can ever forgive him. He put me, my family and this town through a lot," D.J. said quietly.

Shane nodded. "I'd never tell you what to do, it's just that—"

"You're not like him," D.J. finished. "He couldn't handle what life threw at him, but it's not in the DNA."

"Pretty much." Shane was grateful he didn't have to make the case, that they got it. "I couldn't have said it better."

"It's a brother thing, I guess." D.J. stood and held out his hand. "I'm sorry for what I said."

"You mean the part where you threw me out of here?" Shane teased.

"That, too. I realized that in your shoes I'd have come looking for who I was. I'm sorry I was so hard on you."

"Forget it." Shane stood and took the other man's hand.

"Welcome to the family." D.J. pulled him into a quick bro hug.

Then it was Dax's turn. "Better late than never."

"Can't argue with that."

Shane remembered his dismissive comment to Gianna that you couldn't have too much family and knew now he was right about that. "This is a pretty good Christmas present."

"You're not getting mushy, are you?" D.J. joked.

"Of course not. You couldn't handle it."

And just like that they slipped into the teasing, macho banter thing that brothers did. It finally felt as if the last loose piece inside him clicked into place.

"Come on over and join the family," Dax said, indicating the gathering on the other side of the room.

"Can I get a rain check?" Shane asked. "Gianna is waiting for me—"

"I knew it," D.J. said. "There's something between you two, isn't there?"

"You're not matchmaking, are you?" Shane answered without answering.

"I don't have to. It's too late for that."

Shane just grinned at his brothers. The only thing that could keep him from joining the family group was Gianna. She'd been with him almost every step of the way. Even tonight she hadn't wanted him to be alone meeting his brothers and he wouldn't leave her alone any longer.

He had some things to say to her.

When she wasn't pacing, Gianna stood in front of the tall windows in Shane's living room, staring outside. It was a serene view most of the time, but not now. His family was watching a Christmas movie in the media room and had asked her to join them, but she couldn't sit still.

She shouldn't have let him go alone. D.J. was her friend. Maybe she could have been a bridge, helped the Traubs understand why he'd quietly gathered information instead of walking into their lives with guns blazing.

"Gianna?"

She turned and saw his mother. "Mrs. Roarke—"

"Please call me Christa. We're going to be seeing a lot of each other." There was a twinkle in her eyes.

Just a guess, but it seemed as if his mother was thinking there was something serious going on between her and Shane. It was serious, all right, but not in a good way. After learning that love had destroyed his father, it wasn't likely Shane would give it a try.

If Dax hadn't interrupted them, he would have told her he was leaving and they were over before even really getting started. Any second she expected Shane would come back and do just that. It was about protecting himself as well as her, but that didn't take the hurt away.

"Please tell me what's going on," Christa said.

"I'm not sure what you mean." That was lame and Gianna knew it. The woman was an attorney, for God's sake. Like she couldn't tell when someone was stalling?

"All right. I'll put a finer point on it. A man comes to see my son and he leaves. Now you're about to wear a hole in the floor from pacing." The woman's eyes narrowed on her. "Is he in some kind of trouble?"

"No." Probably not. She didn't think any punches were being thrown. All of them were too civilized for that, right? Except the information Shane had uncovered challenged all the Traubs' beliefs about their mother.

"Then why did he leave?" Christa asked.

Gianna didn't know what to do. This was Shane's journey, his story to tell, and should be done his way.

"He just went to the Rib Shack. It's a restaurant at Thunder Canyon Resort where they serve—ribs." She was babbling. And stalling.

"Imagine that." The woman gave her a "mom look," the expression specially designed to intimidate anyone under the age of forty.

"They're really good ribs," she said, all confidence leaking out of her voice. "A special sauce. Secret recipe."

"Uh-huh." Christa moved closer and there was understanding in her eyes. "Look, sweetheart, it's clear that you're trying to protect him and as his mother, I'm all for that. But if he needs help we need to go to him—"

At that moment the front door opened and closed, and Shane walked into the room. "Hi."

"You're back." Duh.

Gianna studied him and thank goodness he looked all right. No bruises or blood, but his expression gave no clue about what had happened.

"Shane, what's going on?" Christa asked. "Why did you disappear with that man?"

"Don't worry, Mom. Everything's fine. I'll tell you all about it later."

His mother studied him for several moments and seemed to see what she needed to. "You look all right. I'd know if you weren't. When you're ready to talk I'll be watching that hilarious Christmas movie about the little boy and the gun."

"Okay, Mom." When she started to walk away he said, "I love you."

She smiled. "I love you, too, son."

When she was gone, Shane said to Gianna, "We need to talk. Privately."

"Okay, but first—"

Without another word he took her arm and steered her to the French door. After opening it, he linked his fingers with hers, then led her outside.

"It's snowing," she said, blinking away the flakes that drifted into her eyes when she looked up at the sky.

"A white Christmas. That makes this an almost perfect day." He took off his jacket and dragged it around her shoulders. "There's just one more thing."

Perfect day? Not from her perspective. "What happened with Dax and D.J.?"

"I found my brothers," he said simply.

"That's not a news flash. What did they say?"

"That they're my brothers. If Ryan were here he'd say, 'What am I? Chopped liver?' The thing is, I love him, my whole family. I'd do anything for them."

"They feel the same about you." His mother had been this close to going to the Rib Shack to do battle with who-ever might be hurting him.

"That's what makes it so hard to explain why getting to know the brothers who share my blood was so important." He dragged his hand through his hair. "I feel as if I've found the missing part of myself. But that implies that Mom, Dad, Ryan and Maggie aren't enough. And that's just not true."

"I think they understand. After all, your mother started this search. She knew you needed to find yourself."

"And I did."

"So, I guess Dax and D.J. had a change of heart and be-lieved you?"

"Yeah. They're still reeling from the whole thing, but they welcomed me to the family."

"That means the Traubs and the Roarkes are all related, too."

"One big happy family. No one shut out," he said thought-fully. "Like Arthur."

"I know. Thinking about that makes me sad for him."

"That's his cross to bear, but I can't hate him for it. My mother was a good woman, only trying to do the right thing for everyone. I believe that she loved me and wanted me in a place where I'd have a fresh start, no black mark to start life with. As for Arthur…" He was thoughtful for a mo-ment. "He just loved too deeply a woman he could never have." He held the sides of his jacket together under her chin. "Now that I finally know who I am, I understand things about myself."

"Like what?"

"I've been running from life, but no more. When I

couldn't get on that plane it had nothing to do with the restaurant or a holiday plan. It was because of you. Through every important step on this journey of self-discovery I wasn't alone because you wouldn't let me be."

"It just wasn't right."

"Leaving you meant choosing to be alone and I couldn't do it."

He smiled down at her, then put his arm around her shoulders and held her close. Side by side they stared at the lights on the ski lift in the mountains.

"It was right here that I fell in love with Thunder Canyon." He met her gaze. "And right here where I fell in love with you."

She hadn't dared to hope and wasn't quite sure she'd heard right. "You fell in love with me? Right here?"

"Yes."

"But you didn't even kiss me that night," she reminded him.

"I was running then. How could I commit or ask you to when I didn't understand who I was? Now I know I'm a man who feels passionately, like my father. Except my story will have a happy ending because I don't intend to let you get away."

She rested her cheek on his chest, feeling the strong, steady beat of his heart, a rhythm that matched her own. "I assume you have a plan?"

"I do. First I want you to marry me."

She lifted her head and stared up at him. "I thought you were leaving Thunder Canyon."

"I want to put down roots here. Make this home base. I want you to be my partner in business and in life. With your experience and support, I believe together we can build a ridiculously successful restaurant empire and an even better marriage."

"Oh, Shane, I can't believe it—" Emotion choked off her words for a moment. "I didn't think it was possible to be so happy."

"I've never wanted anything as passionately as I want you, to have a family with you." He took her hands into his. "If I wasn't so dense I'd have bought you a ring, but we'll fix that as soon as the jewelry store opens tomorrow. Right now I just want you to say yes. I need to hear you say it because loving you is food to my soul."

"Yes. Yes. Yes. I love you so much." She threw her arms around his neck. "This is the best Christmas present ever. And you're right. This makes it an absolutely perfect day. Because 'tis the season of love."

He held her as if he'd never let her go. "That means every day for the rest of our lives will be like Christmas."

"And no mistletoe required. All I need is you."

* * * * *

THE MAVERICK'S HOLIDAY MASQUERADE

CARO CARSON

For my parents, Larry and Sue,
with gratitude for all the plays and ballets,
the Broadway musicals and the rock concerts,
and for setting the example by pursuing their
passion for the theatre. This theatre-loving
heroine had to be for you!

Chapter One

Fourth of July

"**D**o you see them?"

Kristen Dalton shaded her eyes with one hand as she looked up the road, but she couldn't see any hint of a horse-drawn carriage. "Sorry, sis. No sign of the bride and groom yet."

"I can't wait to see her wedding dress. The rumors have been all over the place. I've heard everything from country casual to Kardashian craziness."

Anything could be true. Although Kristen and her sister lived in a small town surrounded by ranches, technology made the world itself a small place. Even to the far northern edge of Montana, a gown from glittering Hollywood could be shipped overnight. Since the wedding dress possibilities were endless, the speculation around town had been, as well. For weeks, Kristen had been patiently listening to her twin, Kayla, list the pros and cons of every type of gown. Although today was the Fourth of July, her twin's excitement was closer to that of a kid on Christmas morning.

Kristen handed her sister her paper cup, then hopped up to perch on the top log of the split-rail fence that bordered the town park. She held out her hands for her cup and Kayla's. "Come sit with me. It could be a while. That photographer has to take pictures of a million Traub family members at the church."

Kayla climbed up to sit beside her on the railing, settling in for the wait. "What a beautiful day for their wedding."

Kristen thought it was a little too warm, nearly eighty degrees, which was as hot as things got this close to Glacier National Park. As she handed back Kayla's cup, Kristen took a healthy drink of her ice-cold wedding punch.

Thank goodness they'd decided to wear sundresses. They didn't match, of course. She and Kayla looked as identical as two peas in a pod, a phrase Kristen had been hearing for as long as she could remember, but they hadn't dressed like twins for as long as they'd been choosing their own clothes. From a distance, she supposed they looked like twins in blue dresses, but up close, they weren't alike at all.

Kayla's dress had an all-over print of tiny flowers. Her spaghetti straps were delicate, and she wore their grandmother's earrings. The shiny filigree drops were shown to their advantage on Kayla because she swept her hair up most of the time.

No one would ever see those earrings if Kristen wore them, because her hair was nearly always down.

And long. And wavy. And—*okay, I'll admit it, Mom*—always blowing in the Montana breeze and getting tangled. Their mother had despaired of keeping it neat and had given up trying somewhere around kindergarten, when Kristen had become quite adept at removing barrettes and bows.

Kristen could also admit that she'd deliberately worn blue because it made her eyes appear their bluest. Her denim halter dress always made her feel like she struck the right balance between sweet and sexy. She got smiles from the town's mavens and mavericks both. Rather than sandals, she wore her western boots. Not the solid, broken-in ones that she wore to do chores around the family ranch, but the ones with the hand-scrolled swirls in the leather. These were the boots she wore for two-stepping, waltzing and square dancing, all of which she hoped to do before, during and after tonight's fireworks.

All she needed was the right cowboy to dance with. *If only...*

If only there was a cowboy here in Rust Creek Falls that she didn't already know—and already know wasn't her type.

"I really admire Braden and Jennifer for thinking up this carriage ride," her sister said. "Their first experience as Mr. and Mrs. Traub will be private, just the two of them, as they start their journey together, figuratively, literally—"

"Briefly." Kristen nudged her in the shoulder. "The church is only two blocks away. Then we'll be right here, ready to say hi while we're really checking out the newest Mrs. Traub's gown."

Kayla shot her a look. "We're supposed to admire the bride's gown. It's expected."

"I know, I know. It'll be worth the wait, I'm sure."

"They say the best things in life are." Kayla sounded like she really meant that.

Kristen kicked the heels of her boots against the lower log railing. *Thunk, thunk.* She polished off the rest of her punch, then lifted her heavy hair from the back of her warm neck again. *Thunk, thunk.* "I hope this carriage looks amazing, because it certainly isn't a very fast way to travel."

Kayla nudged her shoulder. "I heard Sutter Traub located true white horses, and they went to someone's place south of Kalispell to borrow a two-seater surrey. Paige and Lindsay bought miles of white ribbon for it and were making bows all week."

"Wow," Kristen said, impressed at the wealth of details her sister knew. Kristen had only heard that the bride and groom were going to arrive at the park by carriage. "You've got wedding fever worse than anyone else in town, and that's saying something, considering the entire town is here for the reception."

Kristen stopped thudding her heels against the cross rail; even a twin might get annoyed at the rhythmic thumping, even an identical twin who understood Kristen's restless nature better than anyone else in the world. Squinting against the bright July sun, she joined Kayla in staring silently down Buckskin Road, past their old high school. Every kid in Rust Creek Falls had been educated there. Every kid still was. Some things in this small town never changed, and that was fine with Kristen.

She'd gone to the University of Montana, majored in theater and spent a summer as an unpaid intern in New

York City. Like Dorothy in a pair of ruby red slippers—a role she'd played onstage at the university—she'd realized there was no place like home. Cities were great fun to visit, but the tiny town of Rust Creek Falls under the big sky of Montana was home. It always had been. It always would be.

Small didn't mean boring. Things were always changing. Their local politics could make the national scene appear tame, but everyone had pulled together to rebuild after a flood had wiped out a substantial portion of the town just a couple of years ago. Old Bledsoe's Folly, an abandoned mountain retreat, was now an upscale resort that had the town buzzing with talk about developing the area's first ski slope.

But it was the people of Rust Creek Falls that were the most interesting. There must be something about Montana's famous Big Sky, because lots of folks who'd come to help with the flood recovery or to turn Bledsoe's Folly into Maverick Manor had ended up staying, partnered up after falling in love in Kristen's hometown.

She glanced up at that blue sky now, automatically scanning the horizon for planes—for a certain plane. It was a habit she'd formed earlier this year, when she'd thought the blue sky was bringing her true love to her. The handsome pilot of a commuter airline had turned out to be a heartbreaker of the lowest kind. Like a sailor with a girl in every port, he'd had a woman at every airport. Kristen still felt like an idiot for falling for him.

She got another shoulder nudge from her sister. "Does he fly into Kalispell on weekends now?"

Leave it up to quiet Kayla to never miss a detail, not even a glance at the sky.

Kristen wrinkled her nose. "I don't care what Captain Two-Timer does or where he flies or who he tells lies to after he lands."

"Or *to whom* he tells lies after he lands."

"You should be a writer, you know." Kristen resumed her rail-thumping. "I don't care 'to whom' he lies. It isn't to me, not anymore. 'Gee, I wish I didn't have to go. I won't be able to call you for a few days. You know I'd rather be with you, but this job is so demanding.' I was an idiot. I can't believe I couldn't see through him."

"You were in love."

"I'm not anymore." She tossed her hair back. "I'm in the mood to dance. I'm hoping for a handsome stranger or two to flirt with, but I'm not going to fall in love again."

"Not ever?"

"Not for a long while. Definitely not today."

Kayla didn't say anything for long seconds.

Kristen stopped looking for the carriage when she realized her sister was staring at her, not at the road. "What?"

"You shouldn't dare the universe to prove you wrong like that."

"Stop that. You're giving me goose bumps." Kristen jumped down from the fence, an easy drop of two feet at most, but somehow she stumbled and nearly fell. She was normally as nimble as a cat, and this sudden imbalance struck her as—funny? Yes, it was funny. It was good to giggle after that serious moment. "You stay here on carriage watch. I'll go get us some more punch. Give me your cup."

When Kayla reached down to hand her the cup, she slipped, too, and fell right into Kristen. They dissolved into giggles together, for no reason at all.

"What do you suppose is in that punch?" Kristen asked. "We only had one cup."

"I don't know, but stay here with me. Just look down that road and wait for true love to come our way."

Ryan Roarke parked his red Porsche in between two sturdy pickup trucks. The high-performance sports car belonged in Los Angeles, but this wasn't LA. In fact, Ryan had come to Montana to get away from Los Angeles. When he'd directed his assistant to reserve a luxury rental vehicle at the Glacier Park airport, he'd expected to be handed the keys to his usual Land Rover or an Audi fitted with a ski rack, the kind of rental he drove when he visited his brother in a different part of Montana, the upscale ski resort of Thunder Canyon.

This was July, however, and the roads were clear of snow, so the clerk had been enthusiastic when she'd handed him the keys to the Porsche. Ryan had attempted to return her smile when he wanted to grimace.

He grimaced now. Pulling into the packed dirt of the parking spaces at the edge of Rust Creek Falls' park in a Porsche was not what he'd had in mind for the weekend. The flashy car was so inappropriate for this rugged town, it made him look like he was having a midlife crisis. Ryan killed the powerful engine and got out, feeling like a giant at six-foot-one next to the low car. He returned the stares from a few cowboys with a hard look of his own.

Ryan knew what a midlife crisis looked like—too many of his fellow attorneys blew their children's inheritances on sports cars in an effort to replace their children's mothers with starlets—but he didn't know what one felt like. He was *not* having a midlife crisis.

He was only thirty-three, for starters, and a confirmed bachelor. He wasn't trying to appear more wealthy or powerful or attractive to women than he already was.

As the second generation of well-known attorneys in Los Angeles, Ryan already owned the sports cars, the Rolex, the hand-tailored suits. Physical intimidation had a subliminal effect even in a courtroom, and Ryan kept himself in fighting shape by boxing with exclusive trainers and surfing on exclusive beaches. When it came to young, blonde starlets finding him attractive, he didn't even have to try.

This was definitely not a midlife crisis.

So why am I standing in the smallest of towns in a landlocked state more than one thousand miles away from home?

He was supposed to be on a yacht, slowly getting sloshed with his fellow millionaires, drinking top-shelf mojitos while waiting for the sun to set over the Pacific and for the city of Los Angeles to blow an obscene amount of money on a fireworks display worthy of a Hollywood movie. One Laker Girl, in particular, was quite upset he'd canceled those plans. But the government had closed the courts of law on Friday for the holiday weekend, and for the past two years, whenever Ryan found himself with a chance to take a few days off, he'd found himself taking those days off in Montana.

The reason he'd first set foot in Big Sky Country was his brother. Shane Roarke had gained fame as a celebrity chef, a man whose dynamic personality and culinary skill had combined to give him the keys to the world. Shane had opened restaurants all over that world, but when it came to choosing one place to live, he'd chosen Montana.

Shane, like Ryan, was adopted. Shane had found his birth family in Thunder Canyon. He'd found a pair of half brothers, a baker's dozen of cousins—and the love of his life. She'd been working right under his nose at his own restaurant in the Thunder Canyon resort.

None of that would be happening for Ryan. Not in Montana, and not anywhere else on the planet. Unlike Shane, Ryan hadn't been adopted at birth. He'd been almost four years old, too young to have many memories of his birth mother, but old enough to have retained an image or two, impressions.

Feelings.

And that one clear moment in time: watching his mother voluntarily walk away from him, forever.

No, there would never be an embrace from a happy second family for him. He was loyal only to one family: the Roarkes. His parents, Christa and Gavin Roarke, his older brother Shane, his younger sister Maggie.

It was Maggie who lived here in Rust Creek Falls, some three hundred miles even farther north than Thunder Canyon. Maggie was married now, and she'd given birth to her first baby less than three months ago.

The Fourth of July wasn't a big family holiday, not like Thanksgiving or Christmas. Between the LA traffic to the airport, the security checks, and the need to change planes in order to cross one thousand miles, Montana was no weekend jaunt. No one was expected to travel for nine or ten hours to see family for a day in July. And yet, Maggie had mentioned over the phone that the whole town would be celebrating the wedding for a couple Ryan vaguely knew from a previous trip, and he'd booked a flight.

Another moment in time, another feeling: *A wedding in Rust Creek Falls? I should be there.*

He was acting irrationally, following a hunch. Was that any worse behavior than the attorneys who really were having midlife crises?

Maggie had told him the wedding would be in the church, a formal affair with five bridesmaids and men in tuxedos. Accordingly, Ryan was wearing a suit and tie. He owned a few tuxedos, of course, but since the wedding was in the afternoon and he was one of an entire town of guests, he'd assumed wearing black tie would be too much.

As Ryan made his way from the parking lot to the main part of the park, he returned a few curious but courteous nods from the locals. His assumption about the tux being overkill had clearly been correct, but even his suit was too much. The reception was also the town's Fourth of July community barbecue. Ryan felt exactly like what he was, an overdressed city slicker, standing in a grassy field that was dotted with picnic blankets and populated by cowboys in their jeans and cowgirls in their sundresses.

He stopped near the temporary stage and wooden dance floor. The bride and groom hadn't arrived yet, but the band was warming up and the drinks were being served. An old man came toward him, going out of his way just to offer Ryan a cup of wedding punch in a paper cup. Amused, Ryan thanked him, realizing the old-timer must have thought he looked like he needed a drink, standing alone as he was.

He was alone, but only because Maggie and her husband were back at their house, hoping their baby would take a nap so they could return for the fireworks later. Being alone didn't mean Ryan was lonely.

Ryan took a swig of the wedding punch, then immediately wished he hadn't. It was a god-awful sweet concoction with sparkling wine thrown in, something he'd never drink under almost any other circumstance. Worse, he couldn't just pour the stuff out on the grass. In a small town like this one, he was as likely to be standing near the person who made the punch as not. Some doting grandma or an earnest young lady had probably mixed the juice and wine, and the odds were good that if Ryan dumped it out, she'd see him do it. He'd break some proud punch maker's heart.

If there was one thing Ryan was not, it was a heartbreaker. His Laker Girl, for example, was irritated at losing a yacht outing, but she wasn't heartbroken. He kept his relationships painless, his connections surface-deep. In LA, it seemed right. Today, here in this park, it seemed...too little.

He polished off the punch, but on his way to the industrial-size trash can, he passed the punch table and found himself accosted by a trio of sweet little grannies.

"Well, don't you look nice?"

"Are you waiting on somebody? A handsome young man like you must have a date for this wedding."

"It's nearly eighty degrees. You must be ready to melt in that jacket, not that you don't look very fine."

He wasn't overheated. In Los Angeles, the temperature would easily reach one hundred, and he'd still wear a suit between his office and the courthouse. It took more than a reading on a thermometer to make him lose his cool.

Still, he appreciated their maternal concern. Their

faces were creased with laugh lines, and all three of them had sparkling blue eyes that had probably been passed down from the Norwegians and Germans who'd settled here centuries ago. It was like being fussed over by three kindly characters from one of Grimm's fairy tales.

"Here, son, let me refill your cup."

"No, thank you." Ryan waved off the punch bowl ladle.

All three women jerked to attention, then looked at him through narrowed eyes, their fairy-tale personas taking on the aura of determined villainesses.

"Don't be foolish, dear. The day is hot and this punch is cold."

This was Montana, land of grizzly bears as well as grannies. At the moment, it seemed like there might not be much difference between the two groups. When confronted by a bear, one should let it have its way. Ryan forced another smile as the punch pushers re-filled his cup.

"Thank you very much." He raised his paper cup in a toasting gesture, took a healthy swig to make them happy and continued on his way.

To where? Just where did he have to go?

To a trash can. He had nowhere else to be, nothing else to do, no one else to see.

His vision burst into stars, like he'd been hit in the boxing ring, a TKO. He put his hand out to steady himself, the wooden fence rough under his palm. He wasn't drunk. It wasn't possible on a cup of juice-diluted sparkling wine. And yet he felt…he felt…

Good God, he felt like garbage.

Useless.

Maggie was with her husband. Shane was with his wife. Even his parents were together back in California, planning their retirement, ready to travel and spend time together as Christa and Gavin after decades tirelessly fulfilling the roles of Mom and Dad.

Lonely.

One thousand miles he'd traveled, and for what? To be a stranger in a strange land? He looked around, keeping his grip on the split-rail fence. Everywhere, everyone had someone. Children had grandparents. Husbands had wives. Awkward teenagers had each other. The teen girls were toying with their hair, whispering and talking and looking at the boys. The boys stood with their arms crossed over their chests, testing their fledgling cowboy swagger, but they stood in a cluster with other boys with crossed arms, all being independent together.

All being independent, together. That was what this town was about. Ryan had first come here after a flood had decimated the southern half of the town. His sister had been helping process insurance claims in the town hall. Maggie was so efficient Ryan hadn't been needed the weekend he'd arrived to help. Instead, he'd picked up a spare pair of work gloves and started using his muscles instead of his brains, picking up the pieces, literally, of someone's broken dream.

Without a lot of conversation, he'd joined a cluster of men and women as they'd each picked up one brick, one board, one metal window frame to toss in a Dumpster before reaching for the next. One by one, each piece of debris had been cleared away. Independently but together, he and the others removed the remains of an entire house in a day, leaving the lot ready for a fresh building and a new dream.

With a few nods and handshakes, all the men and women had gone their separate ways after sunset, to eat and rest and do it all over again the next day. Ryan had never been part of something so profound.

He stared at the split-rail fence under his hand. That was why he kept coming back. For one day, he'd belonged. No one had cared which law firm he was with, which part of LA he could afford to live in, which clients had invited him onto their yachts. He'd been part of this community, no questions asked, and he'd liked it.

But now, they don't need me.

He rejected that thought, hearing in it the echo of a pitiful little boy whose mother had decided he was no longer needed in her life. Rejected that emotion as he had rejected it so many times before. He refused to be an unwanted child. He was a Roarke, a powerful attorney from a powerful family, and when he wanted something, no one could stop him from achieving it.

He just needed to know what he wanted.

The drunken, emotional craziness cleared from his mind as he kept staring at his hand, still gripping the solid wood railing. Slowly, he lifted his gaze, following the line of the fence as it stretched along the perimeter of the park. He could hardly believe the direction his own mind was taking, but his thoughts were heading straight toward one idea. What if he chose a new path in life? What if he came to Montana for more than a long weekend? Could he live here? Would he feel like he belonged, or would he always be skirting along the outside of the close-knit community?

His visual run along the length of the fence was interrupted a hundred yards away by two women in blue dresses who were sitting on the railing, their backs to the people of the town. The one with the loose, long hair threw her head back and laughed at something the other woman said, happy although she was on the outskirts of the party.

Happy, because she's not alone.

Shane and Maggie were happy in Montana, too, because they were not alone. Marriage and parenthood were sobering concepts for him. He didn't think he'd be very good at either one, and he didn't particularly have a burning desire to try, either. He let go of the fence and headed back toward the Porsche, loosening his tie as he went. Maybe he had come to Montana looking for something, but it hadn't been for love.

If he made such a drastic change, if he gave up LA for a life in a small town, he'd do so on his own terms. This was about a different standard of living, a different pace of life. There was only one way to find out if this town could meet his terms, and that was to try it on for size. Just for today, he was going to act like he belonged here. He'd eat some barbecue, dance with some local girls and decide if this community of extended families and battered pickup trucks was really richer than his moneyed life in LA.

If he decided it was, then he'd develop and execute a plan for responsibly resigning from Roarke and Associates in Los Angeles and moving permanently to Montana.

What if they don't like me here, now that they don't need me?

He shoved the boyishly insecure emotion aside as he opened the Porsche's trunk to get to his suitcase. The Porsche had its trunk in the front of the car and the engine in the back, making it just as unusual as

Ryan himself in this humble parking lot. The Porsche was doomed to always be different. But he, with a simple change of clothes, could make himself fit in. He'd brought the jeans he usually wore to ride ATVs in Thunder Canyon and the boots he'd worn when he'd helped out after the flood.

If the town rejected him this time, if he was treated like he was no longer wanted now that the flood was a receding memory, then no harm done. He'd lived through rejection before. He could take any heartache this town could dish out.

He took off his Rolex and tossed it into the trunk before slamming the red metal shut.

Chapter Two

"Well, it won't be long now. The band's tuning up."

Thank goodness. That giggly buzz from the powerful punch had started wearing off, giving way to a different sensation. After a few tipsy laughs with her sister, Kristen now felt more than sober. She felt almost somber, as she shifted her seat on the increasingly uncomfortable wood rail.

Her life needed to get on the right track. Things weren't right. Pieces were missing. She was twenty-five, a college graduate with a passion for the theater, yet she spent her days running to the feed store and performing the same ranch chores she'd been assigned in junior high. Not that she wanted to lose her roots—her family, the ranch, this town—but she wanted more. An outlet for her theatrical passion—something that was hard to find in her hometown. An outlet for real passion, too, someone to lose her head and her heart over—someone who wouldn't trample them this time.

This bad mood was probably just because a plane had flown overhead, reminding her that a good man was hard to find. Maybe she envied her pilot for having a home base but the freedom to fly and explore. If only he hadn't been exploring with other women in other towns...

Jeez, she was spiraling down into a full-blown pity party.

The band began playing its first song of the afternoon. Kristen looked over her shoulder toward the empty wooden dance floor in the distance. If no one else started dancing, she'd get the party started and be grateful for the chance. If there was one thing that could shake Kristen out of the blues, it was a party. And man, was she feeling blue.

Stupid airplane.

The wedding carriage appeared at the end of the block with a flutter of white ribbons and the tossing of a horse's snowy white mane. If Cinderella had been a cowgirl, this would have been her glass carriage.

"Oh, wow."

"Wow."

There were no other words between the sisters. As the surrey rolled steadily toward them, Kristen swallowed around a sudden but definite lump in her throat.

The closer the carriage came, the more clearly she saw the faces of the couple on the high bench. The groom, a man born and bred in Rust Creek Falls like Kristen herself, was transformed. Kristen felt she'd never seen Braden Traub before. Wearing a tuxedo and black cowboy hat, he held the reins loosely in his hands and kept his face turned toward his bride. Whatever she was saying, he found fascinating. He had eyes only for her and never looked at the horses, and yet, had those horses bolted, Kristen knew he would have had them back under his control within seconds, never allowing his bride to be in danger.

"I want what they have," her sister said, reverence in her quiet tone.

"Me, too."

With a love like that, she could branch out, she could fly, she could be fearless. A love like that would be her home base, the heartbeat at the center that made everything else come alive.

Kristen laid her head on Kayla's shoulder. Her sister was supposed to be the serious twin, but Kristen suddenly felt like crying, completely undone by the romance of the moment, by what was possible between a man and woman, by what she'd never experienced herself.

I want a cowboy, capable and strong, who has eyes only for me, who loves only me, 'til death do us part.

She loved her family. She loved her hometown. And someday, she silently vowed, she would love a cowboy who was honest and true. *If only...*

If only she could find the right cowboy.

"No more city slickers for me," Kristen whispered. "I'll have the real deal, or I'll stay single forever."

"To true love." Kayla raised her cup in a toast.

Kristen knew Kayla was trying to cheer her up, so she straightened and lifted her cup. "To true love. Too bad we're out of actual punch for this toast."

"It still counts."

The carriage had been noticed by other people as

it drew closer to the park entrance. Kristen and Kayla jumped down from the fence to join the growing crowd as they followed the carriage into the heart of the park. The bride and groom's tête-à-tête was over as Braden pulled the team to a stop amid applause, good-natured catcalls about what had taken so long and a flurry of activity as the bride gathered up her skirts and bouquet, preparing to get down from the high surrey bench.

"Looks like she went traditional with a sweetheart neckline. I'm going to the other side to get a better look at her dress, okay?"

"Have fun," Kristen said as Kayla slipped through the small crowd.

Braden tied off the reins and set the brake, but for added safety amid the noisy well-wishers, two cowboys held the bridles of the white horses as Braden jumped down from the surrey. One cowboy was Sutter Traub, the town's own horse whisperer, and the other was...

The Cowboy.

Kristen's heart thudded in her chest. Another one of those giddy waves of joy passed through her, even as the lump in her throat returned. The Cowboy! She'd wished for him and he was here, so soon after she'd made her personal vow, she could hardly believe he was real.

Yet there he was, a man she'd never seen before, holding the bridle and calming the lead horse as Braden handed his bride down from the surrey. The Cowboy— *her* cowboy—was the most physically appealing man she'd ever seen. Tall, dark and handsome barely began to describe him, inadequate to cover the physical confidence he possessed as he talked with the other men and kept the horse calm at the same time. The Cowboy had an air of authority that had surely come from a lifetime of handling anything that land or livestock could throw at a man.

Kristen stepped a little to one side, and the crowd parted just enough that she could check him out from his boots and jeans—check and check—to his white button-down shirt. It looked a little dressy for the picnic; he'd probably been at the church for the ceremony. He'd cuffed up the long sleeves, revealing strong forearms.

He was tan, but so were most of the ranchers who worked outdoors. Even the summer sun couldn't lighten his nearly black hair, which he wore short, but not shorn. It was long enough that she could see a bit of a wave in it, and she knew it would feel glorious when she could run her fingers through it. When he was hers, she'd have the right to touch him and casually brush his hair back from his forehead.

Her gaze traveled past his broad shoulders to the strong hands that held the bridle. When he was hers, she'd have the right to touch him anywhere. Everywhere.

Her fingers practically tingled in anticipation.

He wore no cowboy hat, but that wasn't unusual. Half the cowboys didn't wear one when they weren't working. A lot of the local guys wore ball caps with dumb fishing mottos on them, but not her cowboy. He looked too classy for that. He looked…

She couldn't put her tingling finger on it, but he didn't quite look like any of the cowboys from around Rust Creek Falls.

He's not from around here, that's why.

Kristen would have noticed him long ago if he were a local.

Who are you?

He looked right at her, as if he'd heard her ask the question. Over the nose of the white horse, across the dozen people who milled between them, their gazes met and held.

The people and the picnic and the party disappeared. Kristen felt only the heat in his dark brown eyes. He checked her out as thoroughly as she'd been checking him out, his gaze moving across her bare shoulders, down the V of her halter dress, taking in her boots with a brief quirk of his lips. She didn't miss it, because she hadn't looked away for a second. She was no shrinking violet. When he realized she was still watching him, he lifted a brow. She tossed her hair back and shrugged one bare shoulder.

Across the crowd, they shared a slow smile. If it was true that like attracted like, then she and this man sure were alike. When people said "two peas in a pod" to Kristen, they were invariably referring to her twin, but on this special summer day, Kristen knew that she and this man were a match, too. That smile said it all.

Without warning, the horse he was holding threw its head up. The Cowboy lost his grip on the bridle and took a head-butt to the jaw. Of course, he had the bridle back in hand and the horse steady in a second, but as his dark brown eyes met Kristen's once more, his mouth quirked again in a bit of a sheepish smile.

Kristen wanted to toss her head like the snowy white horse. *What do you know? I just made a cowboy lose control of a horse.*

With a self-satisfied smile, Kristen turned toward the pavilion and the punch table. It was time to get two fresh cups and introduce herself to the man of her dreams.

* * *

Ryan rubbed his jaw as he moved with the rest of the wedding party toward the stage.

That horse had hit him as hard as the best boxer he'd ever faced down in the ring. Ryan was grateful that he knew how to take a punch. He'd managed to stay on his feet, so he hadn't looked like a complete fool in front of the exquisite woman he'd been so thoroughly distracted by. He *hoped* he hadn't looked like a fool. She'd disappeared into the crowd.

He'd find her again. The crowd here wasn't big enough for someone to get lost permanently, a point definitely in favor of small towns at the moment. He scanned the people edging the dance floor, looking for her unusual blend of delicate features and a bold gaze.

The lead singer of the band spoke into the microphone. "Ladies and gentlemen, may I have your attention please? I'd like to turn the stage over to the mayor of Rust Creek Falls, Collin Traub."

Another Traub. Was everyone in the town related to the bride and groom? And, by birth and by blood, to Ryan's own brother?

As a man about Ryan's age took the mike amid a round of applause, everyone turned to face the stage. Ryan kept looking through the crowd, scanning the backs of the heads of the people in front of him, looking for one particular woman's long hair.

The attorney side of himself, which was practically the only side he had, yanked his attention back to the stage. If he was seriously considering a move to this town, he ought to be evaluating the mayor. Local government would have a huge impact on the growth of the town and the requirements for operating a business. He

couldn't prosper in a town that elected inflexible or un-
qualified people to office. Ryan focused on the mayor,
who still wore his tuxedo as part of the wedding party,
a tuxedo with a bolo tie instead of a bow tie, of course.
The men around here were never far from their cowboy
roots, even in their formal attire. The mayor's welcome
speech was sensible, friendly and, that most appreciated trait of all speeches, short.

Like Ryan's attention span. He couldn't focus on anything but seeing that woman again. The sun had highlighted her hair when he'd seen her, framing her in a
halo of light. He was looking for a shade of brown that
shone with gold, like caramel or honey or something
appealing he'd find in one of his brother's kitchens.

Unbelievable. He was turning into a poet. Beautiful, long hair was hardly a rarity where he came from,
but Ryan would bet a million dollars that he could bury
his hands in his mystery woman's hair and not have to
politely avoid the anchors of fake hair extensions. So
many women in Hollywood paid a fortune to look like
they had the kind of hair that his boot-wearing beauty
probably had gained through healthy living on a ranch.

In a flash, he saw himself burying his hands in her
hair, holding her reverently as she gazed up at him from
the pillow, her happiness a part of his pleasure as—

Get a grip, Ryan.

He needed to snap out of this. This day was turning strange, whether it was from the strain of work and
travel, the strangeness of ruminating over his siblings'
marriages or the sight of a bride and groom, he couldn't
say. Maybe it was the higher elevation or the cleaner air
or that damned syrupy wedding punch, but he felt off.

The mayor called the bride and groom to the stage for

the best man's toast. Ryan saw the three fairy-tale grannies circulating in the crowd, coming toward him with trays of paper cups, making sure everyone who didn't already have a drink in hand accepted one of theirs.

Absolutely not. Ryan Roarke, attorney at law, was not going to drink punch and spin ridiculous fantasies about a cowgirl he hadn't even met. He turned on his heel and headed away from the stage.

"Were you looking for this? I think you're going to need it."

Ryan stopped abruptly, face to face with the cowgirl herself. Had he been heading straight for her, or had she stepped into his path? Either way, she was right here, stunningly beautiful in denim and sunshine.

She held out a cup and nodded toward the stage behind him. "It's time for the toast."

From her, he'd take the punch. He'd probably stand here and drink water from the river Styx, as long as he could keep looking at her. She looked right back, her blue eyes and heart-shaped face framed by that hair he so keenly wanted to touch.

"I'm Kristen," she said with a smile.

He nodded gravely, aware that this was an introduction he'd remember.

"Ryan," he said, and he suddenly didn't care about Montana or Hollywood, about mayors and law firms. The only thing he cared about was getting to know the woman who smiled at him in a green park on the Fourth of July. She was worth traveling a thousand miles.

"You're not from around here, are you?" she asked.

"No, I'm not." Now that he'd decided what he wanted, he could relax. He found himself smiling at her—with her—without any effort at all. "But I could be."

The best man finished his toast. "To the new Mr. and Mrs. Braden Traub."

The crowd around them cheered and raised their drinks to toast the happy couple. Ryan tapped his cup to Kristen's, then watched her over the rim of his cup as they drank to the newlyweds' happiness.

The band struck up a song, a country-western ballad for the bride and groom's first dance, and the lovely Kristen turned to face the dance floor.

With the taste of that sweet punch lingering on his tongue, Ryan looked at the faces of the townspeople who were looking at the newlyweds, faces that were young and old and in between. He could practically feel the goodwill and best wishes being directed toward the center of the dance floor as the bride and groom danced alone. Where were the murmured whispers about the prenuptial agreement? The bets that this marriage wouldn't last longer than the bride's previous two or the groom's last three?

Ryan glanced down at the beautiful woman beside him. Her profile was not only pure physical perfection, but the expression on her face looked to him to be genuinely pure, as well, as open and honest as her friends' and neighbors' faces. He rubbed his still-aching jaw in disbelief. He'd had to see this to believe it, the possibility that an entire town could be truly wishing this couple a lifetime of happiness. If he wanted to fit in here, he'd have to leave some of his skepticism in LA.

The song came to an end, and Kristen bit the edge of her cup in her perfect white teeth so her hands were free to applaud with the rest of the crowd.

"Allow me." Ryan tugged the cup from her, charmed by her unselfconscious smile. He slid her empty cup inside his own, then turned to put them down on the nearest picnic table.

The lead singer of the band was doubling as the master of ceremonies. "Everyone is invited to join in for this next dance. For every couple who gets on the dance floor, the bride and groom will get another year of happiness, so don't be shy. Find your partners."

The fiddle player began the first notes of a country-western song in the clear one-two-three rhythm of a waltz.

Ryan didn't know how to two-step or boot-scoot or do any kind of country dancing, but a waltz was a waltz, whether it was danced under the chandeliers of a ballroom or on temporary wood planking in a park. He could fit in here, on the dance floor with the citizens of Rust Creek Falls, and he could waltz with the prettiest cowgirl of them all.

"May I have this dance?" he asked.

"You may." Kristen took her place in his arms with a graceful swirl of her denim dress. They began to move as one.

There was nothing that satisfied Ryan's sense of irony more than holding a beautiful woman in a ballroom dance. It seemed so civilized on the surface, when it was really a way to bring a man and a woman's bodies in sync. While they performed the prescribed moves of the centuries-old waltz, he could touch the smooth skin of her upper back, left bare by the halter dress. He could feel the incredible softness of her hair brushing his wrist as they turned in smooth circles. He could hold her so close that they stepped between each other's legs, graceful movements of her booted feet between his own.

"I love the waltz even more than the two-step," she

said, civilized small talk made while her thighs brushed against his.

"I do, too." Of course, he only knew the waltz, not the two-step, but he'd watch and learn the two-step in record time today. He intended to dance as much as possible with Kristen. This was where he wanted to be, but more importantly, this was the woman with whom he wanted to be. She moved with him effortlessly, lightly, wonderfully. The moment in time seemed perfect.

As if this dance were destined to be.

No. He didn't believe in things like destiny. Men and women had to carve their own lives out of the circumstances they were dealt. As beautiful as the woman in his arms was, as expressive as her eyes were and as easily as her smile came, it was still absurd to think she'd come into his life today because of destiny.

It was even more absurd that he was debating the possibility.

It had to be the wedding. The music. The damned effect of that punch. This was just an average town, a simple song, an average band. There was nothing special about this waltz, and the woman he shared it with was merely a pretty country girl. Those were facts, not fate.

He was an attorney, a man of letters. Like his parents, he believed in laws and rules, not in mystical interpretations of life.

But Mom, I'm not really a Roarke.

Oh, but you are. I think you were always meant to be my son, and I was always meant to be your mother.

The memory caught him by surprise. Did his analytical adoptive mother truly believe in fate, or had she said those words to comfort a boy who'd never forgotten being left behind?

"Are you okay?"

Kristen's soft question brought him back to reality. He gave her a polite, reassuring smile that was little more than a reflex.

"Yes, I'm fine."

How odd that she'd asked. He hadn't changed the rhythm of their dancing or the way he was holding her as he'd remembered his mother's words about destiny. On the surface, everything was the same, all smooth skin, smooth steps, synchronicity. And yet, Kristen had noticed his subtle change in mood.

She was more than a pretty country girl, and he couldn't fool himself otherwise. There was something special about her. This day had become so much more than a weekend away from the rat race. This town, this celebration, this woman all combined to make Ryan feel like he was standing at the brink of something new. Did she feel it, too?

He'd known her for minutes. He couldn't ask her if she believed in destiny, but he could hold her as the band played, so he lost himself in her blue eyes as they waltzed together under the big Montana sky.

The Cowboy didn't seem inclined to make small talk, and she loved dancing too much to want to chatter about nothing when she could be enjoying the music and the motion, so they danced in silence as one song led to the next.

Occasionally, though, she noticed someone on the dance floor would seem to recognize Ryan, and they'd exchanged a friendly nod.

Who are you? Where did you come from?

She was half-afraid to ask. He was too perfect for

her—he even wanted to dance every song, just like she did—so she could almost imagine she'd conjured him up. Like a figment of her imagination, he could disappear as easily as he'd arrived.

Sooner than she would have liked, the band stopped playing and the wedding cake was cut with the usual ceremony. It went without saying that after being so in tune with Ryan on the dance floor, they'd take their cake slices and walk in step toward one of the many card tables that had been set up under the park's shade trees.

Dancing had been all about communicating with movement, but Kristen had no desire to sit across from the man and eat wedding cake in silence.

"Will you be in town long?" she asked, jumping in with both feet and asking the most important question first. Her brothers would probably shake their heads and say she was being too bold again, but her sister would probably tell her she'd make a good journalist, getting right to the point.

"Just until tomorrow." Ryan set his plate aside and gave her his full attention, arms crossed on the table, gaze on her face.

Shivers ran down her spine. Hadn't she vowed to find a man who paid attention to her and only her?

Her sister had been so serious as they'd sat on the fence, telling Kristen she shouldn't dare the universe with her declaration about not falling in love today. If the universe had decided to prove Kristen wrong by setting the perfect man in front of her as a temptation— well, heck, that wasn't much of a punishment. She'd said she wouldn't fall in love, but a girl would be crazy not to reconsider after meeting a man like Ryan.

She flipped her hair back over her shoulder to keep

it out of the white icing. "What did you mean when I asked you if you were from around here, and you said you could be?"

"It's a thought I've been entertaining. It might be time to get out of the fast lane and settle down, somewhere away from the madding crowds. I like Montana."

She licked a little frosting off her finger as she listened. Not a lot of cowboys would describe their lives as being in the fast lane.

"I've visited a few places in Montana over the past couple of years," he said, "but right now, Rust Creek Falls looks just about perfect."

He was looking right at her. Another shiver went down her spine, and she decided the sensation was as delicious as the cake. She was already half in love with Ryan. He was handsome and humorous, with a cowboy's good manners and rock-hard body, and most of all, he seemed to be interested in everything she had to say. If he was considering a permanent move to Rust Creek Falls, the universe had won the dare. She'd fall in love today and be happy that the universe had known better than she had.

"Are you a Traub?" he asked.

"No, I'm a Dalton."

"Good. I was starting to think everyone was a Traub except me."

It could have been her overactive actress's imagination, but he'd said that line with a touch of wistfulness.

"Don't feel too left out. There are oodles of Daltons and Crawfords and Stricklands here, too. You don't have to be a Traub to live in Rust Creek Falls."

One of the Traubs in question passed near their table,

Collin Traub, the mayor, to be exact. He nodded at Ryan, who hesitated just a moment before nodding back.

"You know Collin?" Kristen asked. That was excellent. The more ties Ryan had to this town, the more reasons he had to stay.

"Collin who?"

"The man you just nodded at."

"No, not really." He looked away from her toward Collin, then glanced around the other tables, but his gaze didn't stop on anyone in particular.

He knew no one, then. That could be a lonely feeling. Kristen remembered feeling lost on campus when she'd first arrived at the University of Montana. The modest city of Missoula had seemed like a giant metropolis of heartless strangers.

She didn't want Ryan to feel that way, not in her town. She slid his discarded plate back in front of him, took his fork and scooped up a chunk from the best part of the slice, the corner between the top and side that had the most frosting. Maybe a little sugar would bring the smile back to his face.

She held the fork up. "Here, eat this. You can't let homemade cake go to waste."

He didn't smile. One brow lifted slightly at her impulsive gesture. She hadn't thought it through, but if she'd expected him to take the fork from her, she'd been wrong. Instead, with his intense gaze never leaving her face, he leaned forward and ate the bite off the fork as she held it.

It was a move for lovers. There was an intimacy to feeding someone. She could imagine that mouth on her skin, tasting her, taking his time, savoring the moment...

Kristen sat back in the metal chair and lifted the hair off the back of her neck. The heat of the day hadn't dissipated, although it was getting close to suppertime, but she knew the real reason she was warm, and it had to do with a man who was just a bit older, just a bit more self-possessed, just a bit more devilish, than the men she usually dated. The universe had outdone itself.

She leaned forward once more, determined to match Ryan's confidence. "Collin seemed to recognize you, even if you don't know him."

Ryan nodded once, a crisp acknowledgment of her observation. "I'm surprised. I didn't think anyone around here would recognize me."

The proverbial lightbulb went off over Kristen's head. What kind of cowboy talked about crowds and fast lanes? What kind of cowboy got recognized by people who were strangers to him?

A cowboy who starred in the rodeo, that was who. Collin Traub had once been a rodeo rider, and he recognized Ryan.

In ninth grade, Kristen had gone through her rodeo phase. She'd been able to name all the best cutting horses and recite the bloodlines of all the barrel-racing champions, but even then, she'd been more interested in boys than livestock. She'd been able to name the most handsome bull riders as well as the most noble horses. She'd begged her parents to drive her all the way to the Missoula Stampede. Afterward, she'd cut photos of her favorite cowboys out of the color program and taped them to the inside of her locker.

She'd outgrown that infatuation. Cowboy crushes had given way to movie star mania, and she'd left the ranch to taste life on the stage. Now everything seemed to be coming full circle. Here she was, eating wedding cake on the Fourth of July with a rodeo rider. The Cowboy. *Her* Cowboy.

Bravo, Universe. Bravo.

Since the professional rodeo circuit ran nearly all its events in July and August, she wasn't surprised Ryan had to leave town tomorrow. It was only surprising he'd been able to stop here today. He'd hoped Rust Creek Falls would give him a break from his everyday life in the fast lane. When people recognized Ryan, he returned all their nods politely, but he hadn't been striking up conversations or handing out autographs. He didn't want to play up his life on the professional circuit obviously.

She wasn't about to ask him about his life on the rodeo circuit, either. Her days as a fourteen-year-old fan were long behind her. Now she was the woman who'd fed a man cake while he'd devoured her with his eyes. That man was the person she wanted to get to know.

She only had today to do it. One day for him to decide if he'd ever come back to Rust Creek Falls—or rather, one day for her to decide if she ought to convince him.

One day that could decide the rest of their lives.

Chapter Three

Kristen missed the feel of having Ryan's arms around her, but even the most die-hard dancers had to take a break when the band stopped playing.

As the next band set up its equipment, Kristen got to know more about Ryan than the clean smell of his dress shirt and the way their bodies fit together in a slow dance. Sitting together on a corner of the stage, they discussed everything from favorite sports teams to favorite seasons. She loved the Green Bay Packers and Christmas. He preferred the New York Yankees and summer. He was the middle child of three; she was the baby of five—even if she was only separated from number four by a few minutes. His siblings didn't live in the same state as he did; her entire family lived in the same town.

"In other words," Kristen said, "we have everything in common."

"A perfectly logical conclusion." Ryan kept his expression perfectly serious, too, although she knew he was teasing her.

"It is." She polished off her punch and set her cup down, prepared to check off her conclusions one by one on her fingers. "We both enjoy watching professional sports. We each have one sister. We each have at least one older brother. We talk to our families all the time."

That made four. She wiggled her pinky finger, the last one she hadn't checked off. "And we both love to dance. Like I said, we've got everything in common."

His slow smile was just about the sexiest thing about him, and considering everything about him was sexy, that was saying something. "I have no objection to any of that. But for the sake of accuracy, and to give myself an excuse to keep watching a beautiful woman as she makes an animated argument, I have to point out that our preferred seasons are opposites."

"That is a fact." Kristen was never one to back down from a challenge. She lowered her voice. "Having one thing we don't agree on keeps it…interesting."

His gaze dropped to her mouth. He was interested, all right.

"Differences can be good. For example, you're a boy. I'm a girl." She pointed at his chest, then at hers, his gaze dropping farther, down to where she pressed her finger to her heart. "You're summer, I'm Christmas."

Just as their eyes had met over the head of that white horse, his gaze suddenly left her finger and focused right on her. He looked serious for real this time, no joke to it. "I believe if anyone could make Christmas better, it would be you."

Kristen leaned in a little closer. "If every Fourth of

July could be spent with you, I'd start to look forward to summer as soon as the first snow fell."

He was going to kiss her. Right here, sitting on the edge of the stage in the middle of the town's celebration, he was going to kiss her, and she felt her heart beating under her own fingertip in anticipation.

But he didn't. In silence, he looked at her for one second longer, then lifted his cup to her in a salute, and downed his punch.

"Hi, Kristen."

She looked up to see one of the guys from her high school drama club days standing over her with his guitar.

"My band's on for the next hour. Make sure you clap even if we suck, okay?"

"You'll be great." Kristen stood along with Ryan, and yielded the stage with a wave of her hand. "It's all yours. Break a leg."

The dance floor began filling up again. She spotted Kayla dancing with someone else Kristen hadn't seen in a while, one of their brothers' friends who'd been a few years ahead of them in high school.

High school. Again. She was twenty-five. She didn't want her life to revolve around high school. Hadn't she evolved since then?

Yes, of course she had. She was just overthinking everything.

There was something in the air today. The town seemed different somehow. Maybe because a police officer she didn't recognize had walked past her, heading toward the fountain and the sounds of a fight, although public brawls were rare in Rust Creek Falls. Maybe because a high-stakes poker game had kicked off at the Ace in the Hole bar, and lots of rowdier folk were drifting that way. Members of the wedding party were sneaking off, too, headed for the park exit, where the groom's truck was now parked in preparation for the getaway.

A getaway. It sounded appealing on one level, but she'd already been there, done that. She'd gotten a college degree, even lived in New York City one summer, and then returned to Rust Creek Falls by choice. She wasn't stuck here; she was happy here. People visited and ended up staying permanently, which was proof enough that the town was great. If the Cowboy settled down here, maybe she'd feel more settled herself.

"Where do you want to go?" Ryan asked.

Kristen almost laughed at the timing. "Is that a trick question? Do you mean where do I want to go in life or just in the next five minutes?"

"They say the journey of a lifetime starts with a single step." A smile teased the corners of his mouth. "I've always thought that put a lot of pressure on choosing where to step."

"Let's be daring and step this way, then." She stood shoulder to shoulder with him and deliberately raised her knee high, then took a giant step in the direction of the fence where she'd sat with her sister, waiting for true love to arrive.

Those moments with her sister seemed prophetic now. Her emotions seemed wild and free today, swinging from a kind of drunken silliness to intensely important. Through it all, she'd had Ryan's arm around her on the dance floor, Ryan sitting across from her at the table, Ryan walking beside her now, matching her stride for stride after that first silly step.

"I think the bride and groom are going to make a break for it," Kristen said. "We can wave goodbye from the fence." The fireworks wouldn't begin until after ten since the sun set so late in July, but Kristen had noticed the newest Traub couple saying goodbye to their bridesmaids and groomsmen.

"I guess they're not too worried about seeing fireworks tonight," she said. "Maybe they'll watch them from the balcony of Maverick Manor. That's where they're staying. They'll fly out tomorrow on their honeymoon."

"I'm sure they'll see fireworks tonight." Ryan kept his serious poker face in place as they reached the fence.

She did a little Groucho Marx imitation, wagging her eyebrows and pretending she held a cigar. "Fireworks? Is that what the kids are calling it these days?"

Ryan gave her a boost to sit on the top rail. His laughter was as warm and masculine as the brief touch of his hands on her waist. He stayed on the ground, leaning against the fence, and crossed his ankles as he settled in for the wait.

Kristen enjoyed the novel position of being able to look down on him. All that rich, dark hair, just waiting for her to mess up—and if she sat at just the right angle, she could see a bit of his chest below the unbuttoned V at his throat. He had no farmer's tan, just more yummy bronzed skin...

He looked up at her, catching her staring.

She was so busted, but she didn't bite her lip or blush or look away. She'd learned a long time ago to brazen out embarrassing situations.

"You were sitting right here when I first saw you," he said.

If he'd seen her sitting on the fence, then he'd seen

her before the carriage had arrived. She hadn't spotted him first, after all.

Why didn't you approach me right away? That was too bold even for her. She tried a different question. "What did you think about the girl on the fence?"

"That you were happy. You were laughing with your sister. I envied you."

"For having a sister?" She shook her head and answered her own question. "No, you have a sister of your own. You envied us for laughing. Are you not happy?"

"Is that a trick question? Do you mean for the next five minutes, or do you mean my life in general?"

She smiled at his light words, but her curiosity grew. "Let's start with at the moment."

He didn't answer her immediately, looking away to gaze calmly at the horizon and the first streaks of the sunset appearing over the mountain peaks.

She thunked her heels on the railing, stopped herself and smoothed her skirt over her knees. She'd rather be smoothing his dark hair.

"I met a wonderful woman today," he said, "and she's tolerating my company without complaint. I'm happy."

"Good answer, but that was a mighty long pause." She wanted to see his face, so she climbed down and leaned against the fence beside him, watching his profile as he watched the horizon. "I thought 'Are you happy?' would be an easy yes or no."

"I don't usually think in terms of being happy. It sounds frivolous."

She slipped her hand in his. It felt familiar, for they'd been holding hands in the traditional ballroom holds that went with the waltz and the two-step, but it also felt significant. There was no excuse of a dance this time.

He rubbed his thumb along the back of her hand, as if they often held hands while they talked.

"It's not frivolous, though," he said. "Happiness is serious. It's the driving force behind our lives. 'The pursuit of happiness' is a legal right. We all have the right to try to find it."

"To try." She echoed the words he'd emphasized. "Have you been successful in your attempt?"

He raised their joined hands and placed a light kiss on her knuckle.

"Today, yes."

She made him happy.

She sucked in a little breath at the compliment. But he'd said *today*, as if happiness were a rare occurrence.

"Isn't your life usually happy?"

"I'm working on it," he said with all the confidence of a man who was certain he'd solve a problem soon.

That kind of confidence must be nice to have. "How do you work on happiness?"

"My job isn't as fulfilling as it once was. I need to reevaluate. Refocus."

Kristen could imagine that even if he was born for the rodeo, it could easily be more stressful than happy. Rodeo careers were physically punishing and therefore short. He looked to be about thirty. He'd said he was considering a change of pace, getting out of the fast lane, but maybe he was being forced to by circumstances.

"It's more than my career, though. I find myself envying my brother and sister." He paused, and Kristen suspected that he was giving these thoughts voice for the first time. "Within a year of each other, they got married. My sister had a baby just a few months ago, and my brother is expecting his first."

"So now they're happy?"

"I wouldn't have said they were unhappy people before. They had great careers and a family they could rely on, but I can see that they have more now. Even though they weren't missing anything, they found something else, anyway, and now they are really living. Or more accurately, I should say they found some*one* else. Not a thing, a person."

A little distance away, the bride laughingly yelped as she and Braden were pelted with birdseed as they ran toward the opening in the fence. The groom's black truck was parked on the street beyond.

Ryan didn't move as the whole wedding party came closer. "I'm starting to believe it's not how much fame and fortune you have, but whether or not you have someone by your side."

As Braden and his bride ran past them, Kristen waved and shouted "good luck," but they already seemed incredibly lucky to her. She and her sister had started the afternoon by wishing they had what the newlyweds had. It hadn't occurred to Kristen that she ought to do something about it besides hope and wait. Ryan was right about pursuing happiness. It was sobering to realize that she'd been so passive about her life.

"I'm sorry," Ryan said quietly, and she realized he was studying her closely. "Here we are at a happy occasion, and I'm being too maudlin and reflective. Montana has that effect on me."

"Montana makes you sad?"

"Montana makes me think. I wish I didn't have to

leave tomorrow. I feel more at peace here than any-where else."

Then he'd be coming back.

She felt her buoyant mood returning. The truth was, no matter how much she admired Ryan's determination, hoping and wishing had worked for Kristen. Who was she to double-guess how the universe worked?

The groom opened the passenger door of his truck and began helping his bride gather up her full skirts so she could climb in. He knew which door to open for her because his friends had very helpfully used white shoe polish on the window to write the words *Bride Goes Here* with an arrow.

Kristen gave Ryan a gentle nudge with her shoulder. "The truck isn't as romantic as the carriage, but infi-nitely more practical. It wouldn't be too romantic to ride off into the sunset and then spend the first hours of your wedding night unhitching a team and stabling the horses, would it?"

"I would never argue with a cowgirl. If you say un-hitching horses would delay the fireworks, then I trust you."

"You're just humoring me now." He was doing that serious-joking thing again, implying she knew more about horses than he did.

"I'd bet the ranch that you live on a ranch. You must know horses."

The black truck drove off, the cluster of empty cans that were tied to its tailpipe clattering loudly behind it. Ryan gave their joined hands a tug and started leading her along the fence, away from the send-off crowd who were now milling about.

"I do live on a ranch, but what made you guess that?

Do I smell like I mucked the stables this morning? I'm not saying I did, but is there hay in my hair? Or do I just snicker like a horse when I laugh?"

He stopped walking once they reached a cluster of spruce trees. She moved a little closer into his personal space.

He didn't back up an inch. This close, in order for him to look down at her, his eyes got that heavy-lidded look. Bedroom eyes.

"Those aren't the clues that you live on a ranch."

"The boots, then?" She felt a little nervous, a little excited. Ryan had been willing to follow her playful lead all day, but the way he looked at her now left no doubt that he was a man who knew where the game was leading—and who'd know exactly what to do when they got there.

"You must be a cowgirl because you have incredible stamina," he murmured, "on the dance floor."

A shiver threatened to run down her spine.

"You practically glow with health. Your hair, your skin. You. Every single inch of you." They were so very close, bodies nearly touching in the quiet twilight, the sounds of the band and the crowd far in the background.

She wanted to kiss him. She could go up on tiptoe and taste his lips as she'd been dying to do forever, but she wanted him to initiate it. Good girls didn't steal the first kiss. How such an old-fashioned notion had been ingrained in her brain was beyond her, but there it was. She kept holding his hand, wanting so much more.

An evening breeze carried the crisp air from the distant mountains into the park, stirring the evergreen sent of the spruce trees, blowing a few strands of her loose hair over her cheeks. Ryan brushed them back, those bedroom eyes making the touch of his hand on her hair as sensual a feeling as she'd ever experienced.

As Ryan tamed her hair, she stayed still, wishing, wishing. His body was so much larger than hers, his muscles moving under the polished cotton of his shirt with the gentle motion of his hand.

Kiss me.

He let the last lock of her hair go, and his fingers brushed the bare skin of her shoulders, then higher, a smooth, light run up the length of her neck, a barely there brush of fingertips on her jaw.

Kiss me, kiss me.

The gentle touch of his fingertips was replaced by the sure warmth of his palm as he cupped her face in his hand. Her eyes closed.

Kiss me.

"Kristen Dalton." When he spoke her name, she felt the whisper of his breath on her lips. "Where have you been all my life?"

"Right here, waiting for you to find some happiness."

He kissed her, and, oh, it was a glorious feeling of soft lips and restraint, a tender you-may-kiss-the-bride moment. He ended it too soon, and she opened her eyes. Behind him, the sunset had come into its full colors over the snow-capped mountains that had defined the horizon her entire life.

Had she expected the kiss to make him happy? He wasn't smiling. His gaze was direct, his face so serious it was almost a frown.

Before she could say something, anything at all, he let go of her hand to hold her face between both of his palms. Words fled. He pulled her to him for a kiss that rocked her world. Rougher, more greedy. Possessive, more passionate.

Her fingers slid into the hair at the nape of his neck as he pulled her into him more tightly than any dance had allowed. She felt the hard planes of his body, and everything soft in her wanted to give in and melt in the safety of his arms.

She kissed him until his arms felt more sexy than safe. She kissed him until the only reason she was standing was that he held her up.

If he could have laid her down, if they hadn't been hiding in plain sight in a corner of the town park, she would have gone willingly. It would be madness, but finally, she understood the crazy things couples did. Love at first sight, undeniable desire, life-changing decisions made in a split second—it all made perfect sense.

He ended the kiss when she would not have, could not have. As they held tightly to each other, she could feel every breath that filled his chest. She panted softly herself, as if she'd run a mile. Run a mile, and won the race. The endorphin rush, the thrill of knowing that *this* had happened, that she'd found the one man with whom she connected more strongly than she'd known was possible, was almost frightening.

He placed gentle kisses on her temple and at the corner of her eye, little echoes of the passion that had just obliterated all her thoughts. "You smell fantastic, by the way."

It took her a second to remember what they'd been talking about before the kiss. "Not like a stable?"

"Like summer."

"Your favorite."

And then they were kissing again, hungry and intense. She wanted him with a desperation that threatened once more to make her shameless. He broke off the kiss but clutched her closer. His breath was harsh in her ear. "That was damned..."

"Scary?" she whispered.

"Powerful."

She pulled back a little bit. All the emotions overwhelming her were reflected in his expression, too. It made her feel even closer to him, to the one person who was weathering this unpredictable storm with her.

"I think..." She didn't have any clear thoughts, only feelings. Crazy, uninhibited feelings today, here in the town park. She looked up at him through her lashes, hoping to lighten the intensity. "I think we just found a great way to pursue happiness."

His smile was brief. "I still have to leave tomorrow. The fact that I'm falling for the most beautiful girl in the world doesn't change the fact that I have people depending on me."

Falling for her. He was falling for her, and everything was right in the world—except that he had to leave tomorrow. She didn't like it, but she understood it. The rodeo wasn't so different from the theater in many ways.

"The show must go on," she said.

"And on, and on. I get to enjoy the victories for about five seconds before the next challenge begins. But we still have tonight. How would you like to spend it?"

He had to ask?

She kissed him this time. He responded instantly, perfectly, opening his mouth to her demands, anchoring her to him with his hands. He kept the kiss from exploding into desperation this time, setting a slower pace, a more luxurious exploration. It was divine to kiss him, the sensation so perfect that it was like seeing a new color she'd never known existed or hearing a beautiful piece of music for the first time.

He broke off the kiss with a softly spoken *damn*.

"Ryan," she begged.

"I know." He tucked her securely against his chest. She breathed in the warm skin exposed at his throat. "I know."

Where are you staying? Let's leave the park now. The words wouldn't come, too many years of that good-girl upbringing preventing her from saying what she wanted.

"I have to leave tomorrow," he said, so quietly that she wondered if he was speaking to himself. "It would be…we should just…we shouldn't."

There was nothing else to say. A part of her wanted to plead childishly, *Don't you want to?* Or more importantly, *Don't you want me?*

She stayed silent, her cheek to his chest. He was older than she was and almost certainly more experienced, but she trusted herself to answer those questions. Yes, he wanted to. Yes, he wanted *her*. She could feel the muscle tension in his body. He was deliberately keeping himself under control. His breathing was steady only because he was requiring himself to breathe steadily.

He was being a true cowboy, one with all the courtesy and respect that a gentleman traditionally showed a lady. Hadn't she vowed she'd settle for nothing less?

Frankly, she wished the universe hadn't listened to her quite so thoroughly on that point. This man was hers, and they would be together sooner or later, and her body was certainly eager for sooner. With a sigh, she lifted her head and stepped back just a tiny bit, keeping her arms looped around his waist.

"I guess it's too early for fireworks," she said.

The corner of his mouth quirked in that hint of amusement she was coming to love. When the breeze blew her hair forward again, she tried to toss it back with a shake of her head, refusing to let go of Ryan.

He pushed her hair back for her and kept his hands on either side of her face. "I can hardly believe you're real."

"Wanna kiss me again to be sure?"

He laughed at that, a much needed break in the tension. "I know you're real. Amazingly, incredibly real. But today hasn't been. This isn't my real life." He let go of her face.

"But it could be. That's what you came here to decide."

He stepped back, and she let him go. Desire that could not be satisfied wasn't a desirable state to be in. But then he turned away from her—and from the sunset, the mountains, everything. He braced his hands on the fence and looked down at the railing.

As if the man hadn't already stirred up enough emotions in her, she now felt the tender tug of sympathy. There was some pain in the way he bowed his head as well as strength in the set of his jaw. It must be hard for a man's career to be ending when most people were just hitting their strides. The rodeo was unforgiving, and Ryan seemed determined to choose his next step in a purely objective manner. But any man who knew horses and victory and defeat, any man who appreciated music and summer and family, must have a heart.

She hoped he'd listen to his.

"Should I leave my current life and start a new one in

Rust Creek Falls? That's the essential question. I can't drop the commitments I've already made. Being impulsive would hurt too many people. Today was supposed to just be a first step. I only came to see the town and begin evaluating my options."

"That's perfectly logical." She said it with a straight face, the way he had over dinner.

He glanced sideways at her. "You don't think so?"

"I think you've already made up your mind. All this ponderous decision-making isn't necessary, but if it makes you feel better, ponder away."

Her attempts at humor were helping her regain some equilibrium, anyway. She turned around to lean back on the fence, resting her elbows on the top rail and hitching the heel of one boot on the bottom. She let her head drop back far enough so she could look up at the darkening sky.

She managed at least sixty seconds of silence before peeking at Ryan. He'd stopped brooding at the fence, at least, and was watching her. She supposed she bore some resemblance to the ranch dogs who flopped onto their backs when they wanted a belly rub.

"It would have been easier if I'd never kissed you." Judging from the deep bass in his voice, maybe she looked better than she thought.

"Then I'm glad you kissed me."

"Kristen Dalton, you are a serious complication."

"Nope." She pushed off the fence and mirrored his stance, arms crossed over her chest, standing solidly on her own two cowboy-booted feet. "I'm just a big, positive check mark on your balance sheet. You're determined to decide your next step very methodically, I can tell. When you make your official list of pluses and minuses, you'll put me on the plus side in bold letters."

"Kristen."

She waited as he tried to think of the right thing to say, but apparently she'd said something so logical, he couldn't refute it. It was almost as good as making him forget to hold the horse earlier in the day.

"In the meantime, we could stay here, alone, practically invisible to everyone else once darkness falls. Fireworks of one kind or another are bound to happen. That would surely go in the plus column."

He acted like he was giving the idea serious consideration. "Being arrested for public indecency would give me a chance to see the local jail cells firsthand. A well-run police force would go in the plus column."

"I'm sure the cells are lovely, but someone would have to catch us in the act first, and these spruce trees are mighty hard to see through. Did you notice they smell like Christmas?"

"Now that you mention it." He seemed faintly surprised at her words.

"It's the perfect blend for us, summer and Christmas."

Ryan moved to escort her out of their little corner of the world. "I think we need to keep ourselves busy while we wait for the fireworks. Should we head back to the dance floor?"

"You came here to see Rust Creek Falls. I just so happen to have known this town for twenty-five years. I'll give you a tour. You can rack up more check marks in the plus column."

Kristen pointed toward the gate that the bride and groom had used to leave on their honeymoon. "The first step is right this way. You're going to love everything you see."

She glanced up at him just as he said, "I think I already do."

He'd been looking at her, not at the town, when he'd said it.

If she could have blown a kiss to the universe, she would have.

Chapter Four

Ryan was losing his mind—but at least he was losing it while having one of the greatest days of his life with the most enchanting woman he'd ever met. He enjoyed every moment in Kristen's company, every teasing comment, every exuberant laugh, every country-western dance.

But that kiss had been a whole different world. The first taste of her mouth had rocketed into an intense need to make her his, desire going from zero to sixty in one second. It had been primal, almost frightening in its intensity. He was thirty-three years old, yet a kiss, a single kiss while fully clothed, had him rethinking everything he thought he knew about craving a woman's touch.

One particular woman's touch. Kristen Dalton, who somewhere between a waltz and a two-step had made a better life seem possible.

Kristen stopped outside the park and waited for one

lone pickup truck to pass them, then led him across the street. As they walked, he put his arm around her shoulders, left so thankfully bare by her summer dress. She slid her arm around his waist, a move as natural as if they'd been lovers forever. There was a rightness to it.

A rightness? There was that fate nonsense again. When had he ever thought or felt or wondered about the rightness of a casual touch?

Give up the analysis. Just enjoy the rest of the day.

"First stop on your tour. The local junior-senior high school. Go Grizzlies." She beamed at the brick structure, a plain two-story rectangle, government architecture at its most common.

"*The* school? There's only one?"

"There's an elementary school, but this is the one and only high school. It's very important to Rust Creek Falls. Whether you're a teenager or not, this is the hot place to be on a Friday night. It's our number one cure for cabin fever in the winter. When you can't stand seeing solid white out your window, come to the gym for the varsity basketball game. The whole town will be here, not to mention everyone from the opposing team's town. The clash of school colors will dazzle you after months of snow. There's pop and soft pretzels, and you can cheer the players and boo the referee. It'll get you through until spring."

He pretended to consider the building seriously. "It sounds like an item for the minus column. Solid white out your window that gives you cabin fever? Not so great."

"The snow isn't the town's fault, so you can't ding us for that. But to provide a cure for cabin fever?" She spread her hands out to encompass the school. "Definite plus."

It was ludicrous to think that he, Ryan Roarke, with his courtside seats at NBA playoffs, would count it as a *definite plus* to sit on gym bleachers and watch adolescents attempt to shoot hoops. He was accustomed to watching the best athletes in the world. He expected to be entertained by world-class professional cheerleaders. He knew how—

Professional cheerleader. He'd completely forgotten the Laker Girl he'd so recently left. She hadn't entered his thoughts for more than a moment after they'd parted ways, although they'd dated on and off for some time. And yet, had his sister not mentioned this town-wide wedding celebration, he would probably have been with that cheerleader right now, and she with him, simply for the convenience of having an appropriate "plus one" for a yachting weekend that was more about business than relaxation.

He knew other men envied him for never lacking in female companionship, but today—this crazy, emotional day—it seemed more pathetic than prestigious to waste time with a woman who meant nothing to him.

He looked down at Kristen. She was gesturing toward the distant baseball diamond as she told him about more school sporting events, her face radiant even as darkness settled around them. It had been easy for him to come to Montana and forget about a woman in LA, but Ryan knew he'd find it impossible to forget about Kristen when he left Montana. If he could take with him some of her zest for life, he would.

"You must have enjoyed being a student here. Or was it a torturous teenage experience?"

"Ah, another trick question. I want you to think I'm cool, so I should say high school was cool. But I don't want you to think I was too cool, so I should make sure you know I had my moments of angst. Honestly, I was always afraid I didn't fit in."

"You? Not fit in?" The idea was laughable.

"I was pretty insecure at sixteen, but I guess that's normal. Isn't it?"

Something in her voice, a trace of that insecurity, made him look at her more closely.

"Didn't you worry if you fit in?" she persisted.

He had, but it had been assumed by the adults in his life that it was a consequence of his early childhood. He'd been particularly withdrawn his sophomore year, and he'd overheard his parents debating whether or not they should take him to a psychologist. They'd wondered if it was normal teenage angst, as Kristen called it, or damage from being abandoned by his birth mother.

They'd concluded it was just a normal phase, but as he'd eavesdropped on their conversation, he'd concluded the opposite. He could remember the hem of his mother's dress as she'd walked away. No one else had a memory like that. Not his brother, not his sister, not his parents. There had to be something horribly wrong with him.

Thankfully, Kristen had never known that kind of pain. She'd introduced him to her twin on the dance floor. She'd waved at a man she'd told him was one of her brothers, although Ryan had already guessed as much from their resemblance. Kristen had been born into a close family, not adopted after being left behind. She'd been raised with love from the first day of her life.

It was incredible to hear her say that she'd worried

about fitting in. Kristen was outgoing and friendly in a natural way. She had to be welcome everywhere she went. If a woman like Kristen had spent her high school years wondering if she belonged, then maybe his parents had been right. Maybe his teenage years hadn't been anything out of the ordinary.

Kristen was looking up at him, patiently waiting for his answer.

"I worried, too."

But maybe that was normal. It was a radical thought.

She gave him a squeeze. "I told you we had so much in common."

He said nothing, thrown off-kilter by yet another loop on the day's emotional roller coaster, but then Kristen rested her head on his shoulder, and everything seemed to right itself again.

"I've been trying to get some after-school activities going here. The principal said the budget wouldn't allow for another student club. Maybe next semester. Always next semester. Anyway, are you ready for the next stop on your tour? There's a really great donut shop on the next block. It might be worth two pluses."

A teacher. Kristen didn't just live on a ranch and care for horses; she was a teacher. She spoke as if he'd already known it, but he'd missed it somehow—probably while he'd been tracing her curves, gliding his palms over the material of her dress.

He wanted to know more about her. He wasn't so blinded by lust that he'd overlooked her as a person. In fact, every detail about her out of bed contributed to how strongly he wanted her *in* his bed—but currently, his bed was in Los Angeles. Whether or not it should stay there was the question this little tour was supposed to help answer.

Kristen was more interesting to him than the town. He sat on the base of the high school sign and made room for her to sit with him. "What are you going to do if the principal puts you off until 'next semester' again?"

"I'll keep doing what I'm doing. There's always plenty of work at the ranch." She straightened out one leg and studied the toe of her boot. "The last time I interviewed with him, I hit the feed store on the way home. I remember thinking how odd it was to wear my nice professional pumps and carry chicken feed."

"It must be frustrating to have gotten that college degree and then not use it."

It was the wrong thing to say. Kristen stared at him, her blue eyes wide, and then she seemed to crumple a little, sagging against the school sign. "I hadn't thought of it that way. I just thought it would be good to have something to do outside of the ranch. Kayla does some copyediting for the local paper. I kind of envy her for having a little desk in an office in town. But wasting my degree? That sounds terrible."

Ryan wished he could take the words back. As an attorney, he knew that was impossible. They were out there now, on the record. For Kristen, though, he had to try.

"Forget I said that. You belong on that family ranch. You're lucky to be part of something like that."

"No, you made a good point. If I'm not going to use my degree, why did I bother getting it?"

"Pursuing an education is never a waste."

She wrinkled her nose.

He tried again. "Education is its own reward."

His irrepressible Kristen started to smile. "You're trying to make me feel better, aren't you?"

"I truly don't think it's a waste to have gotten an education." As always, her smile was infectious. He felt a little sheepish, but he smiled back. "And yes, I really wish I hadn't said that. I didn't mean to make you sad."

"No apology necessary. You said Montana didn't make you sad, it made you think. You're just making me think."

"And that's a good thing?"

"It's good, but it's not the best thing. The best thing is when you're making it impossible for me to think at all."

With a swish of denim, she stood and turned and then nestled on his lap. Everything he wanted in the world was suddenly in his arms, and it was all Kristen. The weight of her body, the feel of her skin, the smell of her hair and the taste of her mouth overwhelmed his senses. All his worries about normalcy were obliterated. This passion was far outside the boring bounds of normalcy, because the woman in his arms was extraordinary.

Ryan never wanted normal again.

Kristen continued the town tour under strict orders: no kissing.

She and Ryan couldn't seem to master a simple kiss. Outside the school, she'd wanted to be playful when she'd sat in his lap, but once the kissing started, it had gotten serious, fast.

Again.

Hard sidewalks had a way of imposing a limit on how far even consenting adults could go, however, so they'd eventually resumed their little tour, holding hands as they headed up the next street toward Daisy's Donuts.

"This building is one of the oldest ones, built in 1889. The rest of the brick ones on this side of the street are from the years the railroad was built. My mom remembers when this building was a five and dime, but now it's a boring old dentist office. It was built in 1909."

"Did they make you memorize this in school, or do you just have a good memory for that sort of thing?"

An unladylike snort of laughter escaped her. She'd been pulling the wool over Ryan's eyes for a full block of Victorian buildings.

"The only reason I know how old these buildings are is because almost all of them have the year they were built carved in stone. Look up there, at the very top of that building. It must have been a common thing to chisel the year into the keystone or the crenellation or whatever that's called."

"Trickery. Devious residents in this town. I think that has to go in the minus column."

"It's not a minus that a Rust Creek Falls native can read a date that is written in stone. If anything, it proves that the town has intelligent residents."

She stopped in front of the donut shop and faced Ryan. "They serve coffee and bear claws here that count as a plus. They get points for being extra cute, too. Bear claws in the home of the Grizzlies. Bears. Grizzlies. Why aren't you laughing?"

"Do we have any minuses yet? One?"

She stepped closer and wrapped her arms around his waist. "Considering how I want you to come back the first possible moment you can, it's not in my best interest to point out any downsides. You're looking pretty serious. Are you thinking of something negative?"

"Not when I'm looking at you."

She didn't know whether to melt into a puddle or squeeze him fiercely at those words. Her body kind of shivered in a mixture of the two. He broke his own rule with a swift kiss, then resumed their walk.

They didn't have far to go. Now that Kristen saw it through his eyes, the town really was small. At the end of the street, she turned to walk a block along the river that had overflowed its banks two years ago. Tonight, the river was as tame and steady as it had been most of her life. The town might be really small, but it was really perfect.

Kristen tried to imagine what was missing, what kind of thing would count as a minus when Ryan went through the pros and cons to make the decision she was certain his heart had already made.

When she'd moved away, finances had been in her minus column in New York. Ryan wasn't a broke college student, however. He must do very well on the rodeo circuit. His boots and belt were very fine leather. Even the buttons of his shirt were a quality she'd never seen on the shirts her father ordered from the Sears catalog.

Her father had missed her while she'd been at college, of course, and she'd missed him. Maybe family was an issue for Ryan.

"Would moving to Rust Creek Falls bring you closer to your parents, or farther away?"

He slowed his steps. "Much farther away, and you read my mind."

"Missing your parents would be a big minus, then. Will they be surprised if you choose Rust Creek Falls when you settle down?"

"Shocked, but if I decide to do this, they'll support

me. They've always been very goal-oriented people, but their main goal has always been to see their kids happy."

"Even if the pursuit of happiness leads away from home?"

"My brother and sister have already put them through that test. My brother most of all, when he decided to look for his birth mother. If that was what his pursuit of happiness required, then my parents supported him one hundred percent."

"Are you adopted, too?"

"All three of us, each adopted separately. We're not genetically siblings. Closed adoptions. It was a challenge for my brother to locate his birth family."

She felt her lips quirk in a Ryan-like half smile. "You sound like me, giving the answers to the frequently asked questions before anyone asks them. Mine goes, 'We're identical, not fraternal, there were no fertility drugs involved and twins do not run in the family.' Oh—and, 'Yes, I do believe my parents were surprised. Wouldn't you be?'"

He chuckled. "Should I admit that I didn't realize you were identical? In my defense, we only danced past your sister a few times. You are so uniquely you, though. I can't imagine mistaking you for anyone else. Does it happen a lot?"

"Sure. My parents have never been fooled, though."

"Parents are like that."

Kristen swung their hands a little and looked up at the stars. It was fully night and a little chilly, but she felt so content with the world at the moment she didn't mind a thing. "So, your brother found his birth family. Have you looked for your birth mother?"

"No." He rubbed his jaw, and she wondered if it still

hurt where the horse had hit him. "That is—no. I've got no need to."

Why not? The question was on the tip of her tongue, but his *no* had been so curt, she hesitated.

As the breeze from the river teased the ends of her hair, he frowned a bit. "The temperature has dropped. You must be freezing."

Despite the warm day, it usually dropped into the fifties at night, and she was in a halter dress that left a lot of her upper half bare. She'd jumped into her brother's truck to come to the wedding reception, and that was where she'd left her jacket and her phone, darn it.

"I'll be fine." Just to make her out as a liar, her body betrayed her by shivering. "You could put your arm around me."

He did, and they continued along the river, but he was silent and a little edgy beside her.

"This is Main Street." She wanted to lighten up the mood of their little tour. "It's one-stop shopping here for all your municipal needs."

"You've got goose bumps." He let go of her and started unbuttoning his shirt.

"Are you *literally* going to give me the shirt off your back? You can't walk around here undressed. I mean, I've never actually looked up the public indecency laws, but that can't be right. Not that the women of this town would mind a bunch of shirtless cowboys wandering around, but—"

"I'm *literally* wearing two shirts, and you've got none."

Sure enough, when he took off his dress shirt, he had a T-shirt on underneath. A tight, white, body-hugging T-shirt, tucked into his jeans. Good heavens, the universe was pulling out all the stops.

"Ryan…"

When she reached for him, he started dressing her in his shirt, tugging a sleeve over her outstretched hand. His moves were efficient, but it was undeniably sensual to feel his warm shirt on her arms and feel the tickle of his shirt collar on the back of her neck.

"Better?" he asked.

"Thanks." She pulled her long hair free from the collar as he tied the shirttails in a knot at her waist.

His hands lingered for a moment, before he put them on his own hips and squarely faced her. It occurred to her that he could hook his thumbs in his belt loops and yank off a pair of tear-away pants just like that. Not that she'd seen too many male stripper movies.

"I didn't mean to be so curt about my adoption. I'm not curious about my birth mother the way my brother was about his, because I remember her."

In a flash, all the sexual thoughts she'd been entertaining were banked, and concern for him took center stage.

"He was adopted as an infant, but I was almost four. That's still too young to remember much, but what I remember is… It's enough."

And it was enough to make him withdraw from her. The change was subtle, but his stance was tight, controlled. Like he was braced for a fight.

"Did she hurt you?" The idea of Ryan being abused as a toddler was enough to make her sick. All the wedding punch and picnic food churned in her stomach.

It must have showed on her face, because he took her hand again, his grip strong as he threaded his fingers through hers. "As far as anyone could tell, I hadn't been battered in any way. I've been told I was a little under-weight, but not significantly malnourished."

"Well, that's good." Such weak words, but she didn't know what else to say. The child he'd been had to be an important part of the man he'd become, but she couldn't pepper him with questions, not like she had over din-ner. Not on this topic.

Somewhere on a pop psychology blog, she'd read that men were more comfortable talking when they had something physical to do, so rather than stare at the dark river, she started walking. They turned onto Main Street, silently, together.

Kristen caught her breath at the scene. The street was completely deserted, not one car parked on the edge of the road. The streetlights were soft yellow globes, evenly spaced, drawing the eye down the dark road. The buildings flanked them on either side, standing like timeless brick sentinels in long rows that disappeared into the darkness a few blocks away. Beyond them, the snowcapped mountains marked the horizon, their white peaks lit by the full moon.

"I've never seen it like this," she whispered into the night. "It's like we're the only two people in the entire town. Just you and me."

They left the sidewalk to walk down the center of the deserted street. He must have felt the magic, too. They were the only two people in the world, safe and inti-mate in the open air. Where better to confide secrets?

As they walked, Ryan began to do just that. "She left me standing on the steps of a church."

"Do remember her face?"

"I remember the backs of her legs. I remember the hem of her dress as she walked away. She was irritated

with me, but I still wanted to follow her. I didn't have
anyone else to belong to. The only person I knew in the
whole world was walking away."

Kristen held tightly to his hand. He was so tall and
athletic, her cowboy, confident, too. It should have been
hard to imagine him as a vulnerable preschooler, but
the look in his eyes as he remembered that moment
touched her heart.

"I'm so sorry. That's a terrible memory."

"It's a useful memory. Without it, I would probably
be like my brother, wondering if I had a birth parent
out there, and wondering if they would be glad or horrified to hear from me. It's not easy to decide to start
that search. In my case, I don't have to go through that.
I already know. She didn't want me. She wasn't being
noble and giving an accidental baby a chance at a better life. She wasn't torn up inside because she couldn't
provide for a child. She just ditched me without any tenderness. Knowing that has saved me from wasting my
time and money searching for a woman who wouldn't
be glad to hear from me."

Kristen was afraid she'd sob if she spoke, if she
could have even thought of something appropriate to
say, which she couldn't. She also couldn't stand that remote coolness in his voice. She had to do something.

So she hugged him. She simply wrapped her arms
around him and rested her cheek on his chest and hugged
him.

His arms came around her immediately, reassuringly.
"It's okay, Kristen. It was thirty years ago. Are you crying?"

"Only a little." She sniffed in hard to stop the tears,

determined not to soak the cotton of his T-shirt. "Tell me that your adoptive parents were wonderful."

"My parents were wonderful. They are wonderful still. Why?"

"I just want your story to have a happy ending."

She didn't think he'd found it yet. Then again, they hadn't met before today. She hugged him harder, hoping he could see how much better their lives would be when they could pursue happiness together.

Ryan tried to get his emotions under control. Why in the hell had he shared the worst memory of his life?

He'd come here to see Maggie's new baby. That should have been enough for this trip far from Los Angeles. A pleasant wedding, a Montana-style wedding toast from a paper cup, and he should have been on his way.

Instead, Kristen had waltzed into his arms, and now he never wanted to leave.

He had to. If he didn't fly out tomorrow, a struggling screenwriter whose day in court had come would surely lose his challenge. His material had been stolen by a powerful studio. The man's life's work could go unrecognized and unrecompensed. Ryan was trying to stop a robbery in progress—and that was just Monday's case.

Los Angeles was his life. Today was just pretend, but Kristen's arms wrapped around him were real. Her tears were, too, and he'd unintentionally caused them. He never spoke about his birth mother. He shouldn't have started now. He and Kristen had precious little time left, and he didn't want to spend it making a lovely woman sad.

Her tour had been charming, her list of positive check marks all hopelessly naive and yet there was an undeniable truth that school spirit and homemade pastries were two of life's joys. He wanted the tour to continue.

I want her to show me something that will make me come back to stay. For real.

How could he possibly justify this move? Telling Kristen about his abandonment hadn't helped. It had only reinforced how much he owed to his parents. If he couldn't leave Roarke and Associates because clients needed him, then he absolutely couldn't leave the Roarkes themselves after all they'd done for him.

Convince me anyway, Kristen.

He ran his palm over her hair. She relaxed her grip and looked up at him, her blue eyes bright with unshed tears, her smile outshining them with her effervescent spirit.

Ryan lost his heart.

He wanted to believe something could come of it.

"Let's finish this tour. You were telling me about the wonders of Main Street." He turned to walk toward that faraway white-capped mountain, leaving the last Victorian facades as the buildings became more modern, with spacious stretches of grass between them. "I don't see a year on the keystone of this one. In fact, I don't see a keystone."

"The library. Built in, um…"

"No trickery."

"Well, I went to story hours there as a little girl, so I can guesstimate that the building is roughly twenty-five years old." She gestured to the other side of the street. "I know this one exactly. The community center is brand-spanking-new, built after the flood. The funds came in from an anonymous donor."

Ryan didn't stop her monologue, but he knew all

about the Grace Traub Community Center. Shane's birth father had contributed the money in honor of Shane's deceased birth mother.

"They built it in the perfect spot," she said, drawing him back onto the sidewalk as they continued past the community center. She stopped to point out the two-story town hall across the street, telling him about the monthly town meetings and how accessible he'd find the mayor when he moved here.

Looming at their backs was the church where the day's wedding had taken place, a traditional structure with a steeple that reached for the night stars. Wide, white steps led from the arched double doors down to the sidewalk. He ignored them.

"Living in a town this size is efficient. I'll give you the classic example, one every good Rust Creek Falls resident makes use of eventually, even though we all joke about it. You get your marriage license at the city hall." Kristen turned to look up at the church. "You walk across the street to the church and make your promises in front of the preacher, and then you head to the community center to cut your cake and have your first dance."

A bridal couple would have to pass the exact spot where they stood. Ryan had parked behind the church this afternoon and had entered through a side door. It hadn't been an intentional move to avoid church steps. He never did that—they were only concrete, after all. Tonight, they looked ominous, a ridiculous trick of the mind after an emotional day.

Kristen started up the steps ahead of him, taking them briskly, talking cheerfully. "Having the reception at the Fourth of July celebration today was a real departure from tradition."

It had been cold the day his mother left him. The church had been having some kind of Christmas festival, and he'd been given one of those cheap plastic snow globes. He could remember the hard feel of it in his hands as he'd watched his mother walk away.

"I've never seen a patriotic wedding like today's. The red, white and blue thing worked out great, didn't you think?"

Ryan put his boot on the first step and he saw, in his mind's eye, a shattered snow globe. He'd dropped the snow globe after his mother left. He'd forgotten that. For thirty years, he'd forgotten that, until now.

He saw the splattered water darkening the white steps. The shards of plastic. The bits of glitter that weren't as magical when they weren't clustered together. He didn't remember being sad in that moment, only resigned. He'd known before his fourth birthday that nothing good lasted very long.

Kristen's voice came down softly from above him. "Ah, church steps."

Her intuition was amazing to him. From the first moment they'd danced together, she'd been able to read the most subtle change in him.

She came down to the sidewalk. When he kept staring at his boot on the step, she slipped her hand into the bend of his elbow, as if he were escorting her to a formal affair. "Maybe if a man stood on a set of church steps with his bride beside him, it would give him a better memory to wipe that old one away."

She set her foot next to his, the fancy leather scrollwork of her boot obliterating the vision of the shattered snow globe. She was a bold one, this delicate-looking beauty raised in the land of glaciers and grizzlies.

"Maybe it would," he said quietly. "Maybe the ghost of young Ryan Michaels would finally disappear."

He wanted to believe so. Everything good didn't have to end. He'd just handled too many divorces and worked with too many people who were on their third and fourth marriages. In Rust Creek Falls, it seemed possible that two people could stick to one promise. Something good could last.

"I think young Ryan Michaels turned into a good man," Kristen said softly.

He lifted Kristen's hand to press a kiss in her palm. Everything seemed possible today, that the child Ryan Michaels and the man Ryan Roarke weren't so completely separate. That he, Ryan, could even meet the one perfect woman for him.

Kristen climbed the step to stand face-to-face with him. She rested her forehead against his, and he closed his eyes.

"Maybe," she said, "a man and a woman could decide to skip the church steps altogether. They could get their license and say their vows, too, in the town hall."

"But that's not how it's usually done in this town. If the bride had grown up here, she might feel like she missed out on her big day." *If she tied herself down to a man no one knew, a man who was a stranger to the local norms.* "People would talk."

"People would wonder why, but if it made the grown-up version of Ryan Michaels happier not to think about church steps at all, then she'd be happier if she could skip that part, too. They're promising to be a team from that day forward, and if it would make a less stressful wedding day for them as a team, that would be all that mattered."

"Kristen." He hadn't been looking for her; he hadn't thought a woman would ever understand him so well. Yet she'd been here in this tiny town in Montana, and he'd known, somehow, to come and find her today.

Fate. Destiny. Magic. He was ready to believe all of it.

He picked her up off the step and whirled her into the street. She landed lightly on her feet, laughing with him, gesturing toward the Traub Community Center. "Of course, they'd still have a grand reception. Everyone would come, but it would be just the two of them alone on the dance floor for their first dance."

"It wouldn't be a first dance for us." Ryan took her into his arms to waltz once more. In the middle of the street in their own private town, he led her in the elegant steps of the ballroom dance, thighs brushing in the dark as she hummed a country-western tune.

The fireworks were inevitable. The park was only two blocks away, so the fireworks were spectacularly close, their umbrella shapes forming shimmering willow trees over Ryan and Kristen as they continued to waltz, turning around and around on the solid yellow traffic lines that crossed the dark pavement under their boots.

It was just as inevitable that the fireworks would end, their last burst of thunder echoing off the buildings around them. Ryan and Kristen stopped, slightly out of breath from their dance, slightly breathless in their shared laughter. He had to kiss her, and he did, even knowing where that would lead. After long minutes of bliss and need, when the escalating desire made her whimper and he felt the sound in his soul, he broke off the kiss. "Let me take you home."

"Yes." Her fingers tightened in his hair, tugging in a way that was all the sexier because he was sure she hadn't done it consciously. She pressed herself closer to him, soft breasts against hard chest. "No—I mean, yes, but there are too many people at my house. Where are you staying?"

Maggie's.

Impossible. He would never bring a woman to his sister's guest bedroom, anyway, but with a ten-week-old in the house, either Maggie or her husband were up every three hours. Sleep was a precious commodity there, which was why he'd booked himself a hotel by the airport in Kalispell.

Yes. He'd forgotten for a second that he'd booked that hotel after staying with his sister the night before. He'd done it to be kind, wanting to make his predawn flight without waking Maggie and her family in the morning. Kindness was paying off. He could take Kristen to the hotel. They'd have a few hours of bliss, maybe catch an hour of sleep and then...

Damn it. It wouldn't work. He'd rise and pack his things, turn his rental car in at the airport and board the plane to begin ten hours of travel. He couldn't leave Kristen in a hotel room twenty-five miles away from Rust Creek Falls. It failed every test on every level.

The fantasy disappeared in a puff of imaginary smoke. The day was over. This was not his real life, and he couldn't make love to Kristen Dalton as if it were the start of something essential. He was leaving.

"What is it?" she asked. Headlights illuminated her face for a brief second as a car drove through the intersection beyond the church and town hall. Another followed close behind, driving away from the park now that the Fourth of July was over.

He let go of her shirt—his shirt—and walked her back to the sidewalk. "My flight is early out of Kalispell. God knows I don't want to go, but I have to. I've got commitments."

"We've still got tonight."

"To make love?"

"Nothing less."

His blunt question hadn't fazed her. *Nothing less* made him want her more fiercely than ever, but what he wanted was not what was best for her.

"And then what? I'll kiss you goodbye and leave you in a hotel bed by the airport, with no way to get home, and no promise that I'll ever come back."

She winced at that picture. A pickup truck turned onto Main Street and drove past them.

"Kristen, that's not going to happen. You're not the kind of woman who wants a one-night stand, but when I don't know what I'm going to do with my future, I can't promise you anything different."

"Like you said, that's not going to happen." Her soft hand rested on his jaw, so tenderly that it didn't cause him any pain despite taking that hit from the horse earlier. "You've got the heart of a true cowboy."

If today had shown him anything, it was that he wasn't a small-town rancher at all. "A true cowboy? What does that mean?"

"A true cowboy lives by a code that isn't so different from a knight's code of chivalry. You won't make a promise you can't keep. You're telling me that you won't sleep with me tonight because you can't stay the whole night and see me safely home? That's the most caring, romantic thing I've ever heard." She gave his chest a light smack and sighed with regret. "It's sexually frustrating at the moment, but romantic."

Her talk of cowboy hearts would only keep them both in this Montana fantasy. He needed to act like the lawyer he was and cut to the facts.

"We've found something amazing today, Ryan. This isn't going to disappear in the morning."

"But I am."

She flinched. If he'd ever needed proof that lawyers could be bastards, there it was. She withdrew her hand and looked at him with a little frown of reproach. "You don't need to drive that point home. I get it."

A passing car's headlights cast her shadow on the sidewalk and stretched it to the church steps beyond. Ryan didn't trust himself to speak.

"I understand that your job isn't the kind you can just leave on a moment's notice. I know it won't be easy for you to break away for a while, but once you've fulfilled all your commitments, you'll come back. I'll be waiting for you right here in Rust Creek Falls."

Her expression was open and honest and her words were full of promise. It was all too good to be true. Or rather, it was all too good. Nothing good lasted very long. He knew it, but judging by her hopeful blue eyes, she did not.

"I haven't made a decision. You shouldn't wait for me."

She bowed her head briefly, and his heart ached for hurting her.

"I'm sorry," he began, but she cut him off.

"Please don't. I don't want you to say anything that

will make you feel bad while we're apart." She looked over her shoulder at the cars and trucks that drove through the intersection, then nodded to herself a little sadly. "Here's what I think. This magic between you and me isn't going to disappear. I will still want you next week, and next month, and the month after that. You go and take care of whatever you need to take care of, then make your list and tally up your check marks. I have faith in you, Ryan. I'm going to leave now, while our day is still perfect and I can do it without falling apart."

She rose up on her toes and kissed him, hard and quick, on the mouth. "Hurry and come back. I miss you already." She turned and started walking away.

Ryan was so dumbfounded she was out of arm's reach before he called out, "Wait!"

She spun around, hope in her expression.

It was a hope he didn't feel. "I'll drive you to your ranch."

She plastered on a smile that looked almost genuine. "There's no need. At least a dozen people who are going my way will drive past me at the corner and give me a lift. It's a small town, remember? Being able to hitch a ride is a definite check in the plus column."

Then she turned around again, and this time, he let her go.

She'd be better off without some outsider from LA interfering with her secure life and her small-town dreams. Still wearing his shirt, she headed back to the life he'd interrupted today, a life that made her happy.

His gaze settled on the swish of her hem and the backs of her legs. *Woman Walking Away*, that was what he'd title it, if he could capture it in a photograph. He could paint it from memory, if he could stand the pain.

He was no artist. There was no way that losing Kristen after one perfect day could really hurt as much as watching his mother leave him while he'd held a snow globe in his hands. No way—but damn if it didn't feel close.

At the corner by the church, an SUV stopped and Kristen climbed in. She was gone.

A second of childish memory suddenly surfaced. He hadn't dropped that snow globe. He'd thrown it on the ground deliberately with all his three-year-old might, shattering it into a thousand pieces. This new bit of knowledge about Ryan Michaels fit Ryan Roarke. If he had a snow globe now, he'd hurl it at those church steps with all his might, too.

Ryan shoved his empty hands into his pockets and turned to walk in the opposite direction, heading toward the river that would lead him back to the park.

Back to the Porsche.

Back to reality.

Chapter Five

October

"I hate this stupid column."

Kristen let go of one side of the newspaper to flick the offensive page.

"Which one?" Kayla sat behind her on the bed, patiently working a wide-toothed comb through Kristen's hair.

"Rust Creek Ramblings. It's still going on and on about 'the power of the punch' and how many couples fell in love because of that Fourth of July reception. Ouch!"

"Sorry." Kayla was silent for a moment as she tugged a little harder at what must have been a particularly stubborn knot. "Maybe there is something to that poisoned punch theory. Don't you think it's awfully coincidental that people were acting so strangely? I mean, Will Clifton got married that night but didn't even realize it until the next morning. Our own cousin got arrested for dancing in a fountain and then fell in love with the police officer. That's a pretty crazy way to fall in love. Then Levi and Claire—"

"Levi and Claire were already married." Kristen snapped the paper shut and glowered at her sister's reflection in her dresser's mirror.

"Well, they're even more in love now."

If that stupid punch had made everyone realize who their true love was, then why hadn't Ryan come back yet? He'd drunk the punch with her. Kristen tossed the newspaper facedown onto her comforter.

"I need to get the bobby pins." Kayla went into the bathroom they shared in the sprawling log house on the Circle D, the same ranch house they'd lived in all their lives. The bathroom connected their individual bedrooms. It had double sinks and enough counter space for two women to keep all the cosmetics and accessories they could need. Their brothers had dubbed their mini suite "the girls' wing" years ago, and they'd kept away even after the fiercely pink *Keep Out* signs had been outgrown.

Kristen and each of her siblings had inherited land within the Circle D. Her brother Jonah, who had the advantage of being an architect, had designed and built a log cabin on his share, but Kristen and Kayla still lived in the girls' wing of the main ranch house. Owning land was not the same thing as having the money to build a house on the land.

Someday, she'd build her own house. Maybe someday would arrive when Ryan did.

"Okay, let's do this." Kayla returned to toss a card of bobby pins onto the newspaper. She plopped herself down behind Kristen and picked up the comb again.

Kristen moved the bobby pins to read the back page. An ad for next year's rodeo season taunted her. This year's season was already over. June, July and August were the touring months in the northwest for the professional rodeo, summer months that had come and gone.

Where was Ryan?

She wasn't surprised that he hadn't come knocking on her door in July. He'd told her that he had commitments to keep. He'd said it with regret, but people were relying on him. Rodeo riders signed contracts at the beginning of the season, after all, and contracts had to be honored.

The entire month of August, she'd hoped the tour would bring him back her way, close enough to visit her between rodeos. She'd looked up schedules and wondered which towns he was choosing to compete in, but no one named Ryan Michaels appeared in any of the events within a day's drive of Rust Creek Falls. Although she ached to see him again, she hadn't been too worried. The bigger rodeos with the bigger prize money were in the cities farther away. In September, when the season was over, he would come.

Every day in September, she'd dressed with care. Every single day, because every day had been the day Ryan might return.

But now, somehow, it was October.

Without warning, tears stung her eyes, an ambush she couldn't defend against, a sign that she was losing her faith in Ryan. She hated these odd moments where the voice of doubt would suddenly seem to be the voice of reason. *Face the facts: he's not coming back.*

She sniffed the tears back. She would pummel that voice into silence.

"Am I hurting you?" Kayla asked. "I'm so sorry. I'm just trying to get all these tangles out."

"It's okay," Kristen mumbled, too cowardly to admit the truth. Of all the people on the planet, Kayla was the last one who'd chastise her for holding on to her cowboy dream, but Kayla could look at a calendar and see what everyone else saw. Kristen liked to believe that Kayla looked at her with empathy…but that look was getting darned close to pity.

If Kayla looked at her with real pity, that would mean no one, not even Kristen's twin, believed that she'd mattered to Ryan as much as he'd mattered to her.

He's coming back. Even if he was too stubborn to see how many check marks were in the plus column, he wants me. He'll try to talk me into moving to wherever he chose to settle down. He's coming back.

In the meantime, she wasn't being entirely open and honest with Kayla, for the first time in their lives. She was acting, pretending that she wasn't eaten up with worry over Ryan, going entire weeks without mentioning his name, just to avoid that final, hope-killing look of pity.

"This is going to look so good on you." Kayla held up a picture of a beautiful ice skater from a Victorian Christmas card. Kayla's mission was to make Kristen's hair look just like the Victorian ideal of feminine beauty, because Kristen was auditioning for a role in Charles Dickens's *A Christmas Carol*. The play would open Thanksgiving weekend at one of the theaters in

Kalispell, and Kristen fervently hoped it would open with her in the role of Ebenezer Scrooge's former fiancée.

The thought of returning to the stage revived her sagging spirits. There were boards to be trod, greasepaint to be smelled and shows that had to go on. The theater was her passion, and although the principal at the high school wouldn't let her direct an after-school drama club, she wasn't going to give up something she loved any longer.

In July and August and September, as she'd relived every second of her time with Ryan, one moment that had nothing to do with love had kept running through her head. *It must be frustrating to have gotten that college degree and then not use it.* She'd majored in theater because she loved the theater. She had talent. She was trained. And most of all, she missed it. The lack of a theater in Rust Creek Falls might be her own check mark in the minus column, but the fact that the city of Kalispell was within commuting distance was a plus she intended to use.

Today, she was going to pursue something that made her happy. After Kayla finished making her look like a Victorian sweetheart, Kristen was going to drive the forty-five minutes to Kalispell and kill that audition. It was time to get a job doing what she loved.

She had Ryan to thank for inspiring her. She'd thank him in person, when he came to see her. It was October, so now he would come.

"Listen to this."

Kristen set down her half-empty cup and plopped her chin in her hand, prepared to listen to her sister.

"'Sunday, November first. The Power of the Punch has claimed another love match. During the fateful Fourth of July wedding of Braden and Jennifer Traub, Brad Crawford appeared to many to be impervious to the potent properties of the now-infamous punch, but the Rambler asserts that had he not partaken, or more to the point, if his fellow poker players had not partaken of the punch, then he would not have won the piece of property that included his prospective bride.'"

"How can you read that column?" Kristen asked. "It's torture."

Kayla frowned at her over the edge of the newspaper. "It is not. You just don't like it because you're never mentioned in it. You ought to be happy about that."

Of all the things Kristen felt, happiness was not one of them. Oh, sure, she'd been pursuing it. She'd landed that role in the play. She'd even managed to move out of her childhood home.

It wasn't enough.

She pushed her coffee cup away. At least she felt some pride that it was her own coffee cup, and she was sitting at her own kitchen table in her own house. Kayla had stopped in to share her first Sunday morning brunch in Kristen's new home.

Well, it was sort of her new home. Jonah had bought a block of five Victorian homes after the flood. They'd been dirt cheap, because no one else had dared to attempt to rehab century-old houses. Jonah had turned the home on the corner lot into his architectural firm's office. The other four houses were works in progress, and Kristen was going to be part of that progress.

She was proud of her new job in the Christmas play, but the commute from the ranch to Kalispell was over an hour and a half, round trip. The ranch was north of Rust Creek Falls, but Jonah's houses were on the south edge of town, close to the highway to Kalispell. Living here saved her hours and hours of driving every week.

She couldn't pay Jonah much rent. Regional theater was run mostly on donations and volunteers. She was lucky that her role paid anything at all, but it worked out to less than minimum wage when she counted up her hours. Living here was her second job. Instead of rent, she'd agreed to scrape and sand and repaint the interior of the house for Jonah while she lived in it.

Having her own place should have been exciting, and Kristen was certain she'd been performing her role of independent young woman admirably, fooling everyone. No one except Kayla suspected the truth she was masking: she was on the edge of a horrible heartbreak, clinging as best she could to her belief that she and Ryan belonged together. Her sister's empathy had evolved into concern this month. Concern was so very close to pity.

Kayla lowered the paper to peer at her once more. "I finished the rest of the column. It's not horrible, but I think the Rambler might have used the letter *p* just a bit too much, playing off the 'power of the punch.' Was that the part that tortured you?"

Kristen shook her head.

I can't do this. I can't pretend anymore.

"What part bothered you?" Her sister was waiting, no pity in her expression...yet.

"The part that said 'Sunday, November first.'" Kristen choked out her words. "He isn't ever coming back, is he?"

Then she put her head down on the kitchen table and cried.

* * *

The phone wouldn't stop ringing.

In the inner sanctum of Ryan's office, it was only a blinking light on the phone on his desk. Screening calls was his assistant's job, so Ryan could work without interruption. But his assistant was not here, and the incessant noise from the phone in the outer office had broken Ryan's concentration. He answered the damned phone.

"Roarke speaking."

"Roarke speaking here, too."

"Hey, Dad." Ryan tossed his pen onto his desk and sat back in his chair. "What can I do for you?"

"It's November first. You know what that means."

Ryan tried to recall which sporting events were nearby. "It means you're calling me from the PGA tournament at Newport Beach."

"It means it's Sunday. A day of rest. Part of the weekend. What are you doing in the office, son?"

Ryan rubbed his jaw. It had turned slightly black and blue the day after the horse had butted him in Montana. Everyone in LA had assumed he'd been hit by a model's jealous ex. In a nod to his boxing reputation, friends and acquaintances had been equally sure the other guy must look worse. Ryan the Player, everyone's favorite hero. Never would they have guessed he'd been hit by a pure white horse attached to a white-ribboned carriage.

That day had changed him. If he'd skated close to the edge of being a Casanova before Montana, then he'd been a monk ever since. No one noticed; men still clapped him on the back in approval and women competed for his attention in vain. People saw what they wanted to see.

Except his dad.

"You haven't taken a weekend off since when? July?"

Ryan had a feeling his dad knew exactly when. "Somewhere around then. I'm not putting in a full day here. Just a few hours."

"Then meet me at the club. It'll do you good."

Golf was his dad's thing, not Ryan's. Boxing, surfing, those were Ryan's preferred leisure activities. Actually, he hadn't been surfing since July, either. The boxing, though, he'd used like a drug for the past four months, throwing punches until his brain was numb, almost wishing for a hard hit to knock all the thoughts out of his head.

"Humor me. Come hit a bucket of balls with your old man."

Ryan supposed the fresh air would do him good. When he showed up at the club's driving range, he got much more than that.

"Your mother and I have been having some serious discussions about the future of the firm."

Thwack. Damn if his father couldn't make those balls sail. Ryan chose an iron from his golf bag and addressed the ball that had been teed up for him by a trendy automated machine.

"We want to retire earlier than our original timeline."

Ryan ignored the ball and turned to address his father instead. "Have you had some news I should be aware of?"

A week after Ryan's trip to Montana, his father had driven himself to the hospital with chest pain. He'd escaped any permanent damage beyond being chastised by his wife and son for not calling an ambulance, but the doctors had labeled it a wake-up call. It had been one for Ryan, as well. There was no way he could abandon his parents and their law firm for a Montana dream. The whole idea of living in a cowboy town had been a whim, anyway.

Kristen had been real.

Real, and out of his reach.

"I'm as healthy as a horse," his dad said. "But that's the point. I'd like to take my wife around the world while we're healthy enough and young enough to enjoy it. That's always been one of our goals."

Ryan felt the weight of the firm settle on his shoulders as he turned back to the tee. His parents deserved the good life, and to give it to them, Ryan would become the only Roarke in Roarke and Associates. They'd groomed him to take over someday, and he was ready. It didn't matter if that day came now or ten years from now.

I will still want you next month, and the month after that.

Kristen's words were never far from his mind. If Ryan followed in his father's footsteps and retired a few years early, he could move to Montana, guilt-free, in thirty years. That would be swell, if Kristen still wanted him thirty years from now.

Thwack. Ryan sent the ball on a long, hard drive.

His father approved. "Nice hit. We should think about beefing up the Associates part of Roarke and Associates before we retire. We're not trying to burden you any more than you already burden yourself. What do you think about offering partnership to Lori?"

The next ball had been teed up for him. Ryan knocked the holy hell out of it with his nine-iron. "We'd be smart to make Lori a partner whether you retire or not. We'll still need to hire an additional attorney. I'll start the headhunt."

"When? You're already working seven days a week."

Ryan readied himself for another swing, but his father reached across the low wall that partitioned the driving range and placed his hand on Ryan's shoulder.

"Let me tell you another one of my life's goals. I want my children to outlive me. That might make me a selfish old bastard, but I think I deserve to leave this earth without seeing you or Shane or Maggie leave it first. Every parent deserves that, whether they get it or not."

"What the—for God's sake, Dad. What kind of talk is this?"

"You're scaring me, Ryan. No one works as many hours as you've been doing and lives to tell the tale. Whatever demon you're trying to exorcise with work is winning. You need to try something else. Find a healthier way to forget whatever it is you're trying to forget."

Forgetting Montana and its breathtaking scenery, he could do. Forgetting the ideal of living in a small town, forgetting what it was like to belong to a community, all of that he could do. They'd been pipe dreams, Norman Rockwell pictures that were too perfect to be real.

Forgetting Kristen? He couldn't.

He'd been trying to adopt a brotherly attitude toward her. He was watching out for her best interests by staying away. She had a better chance at finding happiness in life and love with a cowboy who'd grown up where she had. She needed a man who understood ranches and horses and that pace of life. It was better for her if he stayed away. He'd learn to deal with it.

"I mean it, Ryan. You're working yourself into an early grave."

Ryan traded his nine-iron for his driver, a better club for beating the crap out of an inanimate object. "This is serious talk."

"It is. Now lighten up." His dad clapped him on the shoulder one last time and stepped back to his own tee. "Go home. Vegetate. Take a pretty girl out to dinner." Under his breath, he added, "Today."

Ryan looked in the direction his father was looking. He recognized the actress, and she recognized him. She changed direction immediately, walking toward him in her white golf skirt like she was walking down a fashion show runway. She had the legs and the attitude to pull it off.

"Ryan Roarke. It's been too long." Her hug enveloped him in perfume. Her civilized cheek kiss landed just a little too close to his ear, suggesting more of a lover's nibble on an earlobe than a meeting of friends. He got the message.

She'd sent him that message before. When word had leaked out that he may have done some work for a Tarantino or a DeNiro, rumors that he would never confirm or deny as part of his professional code, the constant stream of hopeful actresses had become a deluge. That was Hollywood. He wondered what rumor she'd heard this time.

Thwack.

"I've got a secret," she cooed. "I'm doing a screen test tomorrow. Isn't that exciting? It's all hush-hush, but you probably already know it's something for Century Films."

He said nothing. It wasn't necessary.

She placed her finger on her full, lower lip, pretending to be lost in thought. "Come to think of it, you introduced me to the man they've tapped to be the assistant director. He was in our little group when we took that trip to Carmel. Wasn't that a fun weekend?"

Thwack.

"You know, if you wanted to go back, I'm free this coming weekend. Who else was there last time? We could call around and get everyone together again."

"Especially the assistant director."

She perched on the bench that held his gear, crossing one long leg over the other and swinging her foot. "That would be such a boost for me. If you could arrange it, I wouldn't know how to thank you." The low purr of her voice and the come-be-naughty-with-me curve of her smile meant she knew exactly how she'd thank him.

Ryan looked at her, and wished for someone else. "I'm not available this weekend."

She didn't give up easily, but after some pointless banter, she did give up. Ryan had no doubt she'd find some other way to refresh her contacts with the assistant director and anyone else who could give her an inside edge to win the role.

"Not this time, then?"

Not ever.

She left him with another perfumed kiss, too smart to burn any bridges. As she sauntered away, Ryan's father continued working on his golf swing, as if he hadn't paid attention at all to what was happening on his son's side of the partition.

Ryan answered his unspoken question, anyway. "Not my idea of relaxation."

His father only grunted in a neutral way that could have meant anything.

Ryan began working his way through another dozen golf balls in silence. He wasn't interested in relationships that served careers any more than he was interested in the ones that were merely convenient. For the past four months of his life, he hadn't been interested in anything. Not in the golf or surfing that were the hallmarks of Southern California. Not in the endless summer of Los Angeles, and worst of all, not in running Roarke and Associates.

The pursuit of happiness, Ryan Roarke's personal pursuit of happiness, had led him to Montana. He'd fallen in love under the blue sky while looking into Kristen Dalton's blue eyes.

Fallen in love.

Thwack.

He'd fallen in love, and then he'd gone away and stayed away. Although Kristen had smiled and said she wasn't worried, he'd hurt her in those last few moments. If his father thought his son was leading a punishing life, Ryan saw some justice in it. He'd been treating himself badly because he'd treated someone else badly.

He didn't know if Kristen was hurting still. Perhaps she'd moved on.

Perhaps she hadn't.

He had no way to find out, short of making an ass of himself on the phone with his sister. Maggie worked in Rust Creek Falls's one law office for an attorney named Dalton. In a town that size, Dalton had to be related to Kristen somehow. If Kristen had been sad or depressed and told her family it was because Ryan had broken her heart, then Maggie would have heard about it. Kristen obviously hadn't been talking about him.

Brad Crawford, an acquaintance from the flood recovery days, had consulted him about land deeds last month. Ryan had resisted the temptation to ask about Kristen. Brad would have wondered why the heck Ryan Roarke was asking about one of the Dalton girls. Clearly, Rust Creek Falls wasn't buzzing with rumors that Kristen was brokenhearted over the man she'd spent the Fourth of July with, and Ryan would do nothing to stir up gossip where none currently existed.

No news was good news. It meant Kristen was fine without him.

Thwack. As fast as the automated range teed up the balls, he hit them, full force, full swing, full power. *Thwack. Thwack.*

"What's wrong, son?" His father was resting both arms on the wall, all pretense that he was doing anything but worry about his son completely dropped.

I miss her.

"Nothing, Dad."

Ryan needed to see Kristen again, if only to verify for himself that she was doing fine without him. He wanted what was best for her, so he'd have no peace until he was sure she was happy.

"I want to go back. To Montana."

His dad raised one brow, a move Ryan realized he'd adopted himself, long ago. "Your sister and Shane are bringing their families here for Thanksgiving in just a couple of weeks."

"I know. I need to see—I need the change of scene. I'll tie everything up this week and fly out Saturday.

One more document for Crawford came across my desk
this week. I'll handle it while I'm there."

His father didn't ask any questions or point out that
an overnight courier would be more efficient than an
attorney flying to another state.

"Have a good trip, son. Get done what you need to do."

Chapter Six

Date night.

Maggie Roarke Crawford had been looking forward to this all week. She'd even loaded her sweet little Madeline into the car this morning, driven all the way to Kalispell and gotten her hair done for the event. Seven months after having her baby, some of her most chic outfits fit again. Tonight, she felt a little blonder, a little sexier and more than a little ready to paint the town red. She and her husband, Jesse, had hired a babysitter and headed out to the hottest spot in town: the high school gym.

On Friday nights, when it wasn't basketball season, of course, the gym became the town movie theater. Maggie loved it. It was a little like watching a movie in one's living room with extended family, since a sizable portion of the town always showed up. Gossip abounded at the refreshment stand. At the end of the night, the moviegoers all helped stack the chairs.

Tonight's double feature had started with a romance that was replete with tear-worthy moments. Maggie was pretty sure her husband had started out hating it, but midway through, when the emotional scenes on the screen had made her sigh and cling to his hand with both of hers, he'd relaxed and settled in for the duration.

The second show was going to be the opposite, an action-adventure film full of explosions and cars. Maggie felt the need to stock up on chocolate in preparation. Apparently, so did most of the women of Rust Creek Falls, because the line for the concession stand was an almost exclusively female gathering. Everyone was talking about the romantic movie and its handsome leading man.

Her youngest sister-in-law, Natalie Crawford, was behind her in line, gushing about the movie's ending to Ben Dalton's twin nieces. Maggie turned around to join in the conversation.

"Omigosh, wasn't that the most romantic proposal at the end?" Natalie asked. "I think I'd be willing to go through the wringer just to have a proposal like that. Everything turned out all right."

"That proposal happened in the nick of time," said one of the twins. "If he'd done one more jerky thing, I don't think any kind of proposal could have convinced me to marry him."

Maggie wasn't sure which twin was Kristen and which was Kayla—they looked so much alike—but she agreed with the sentiment. "It was lucky for him that all his jerky things were done to save an orphanage. We can forgive a guy who's trying to save children."

"Plus, he had washboard abs," Natalie added with a wink.

"Yes, there's that," Maggie laughed. "Jerks should strive to at least have washboard abs."

Kristen-Kayla, the one who'd been talking, suddenly pressed the back of her hand to her mouth and made a distressed sound. For a second, Maggie thought she'd sneezed or choked, but no, that had been a sob.

"Ohmigosh, Kristen, are you okay?" Natalie asked.

The quiet twin put her arm around her sister's shoulders. "That movie was pretty sad. It had me in tears, too."

Maggie and Natalie and the one who must be Kayla instinctively clustered closer to Kristen, shielding her from public scrutiny.

"Let's scoot out of the way," Maggie suggested. "Here's a napkin."

Although Maggie didn't really know Kristen, there was an unwritten girl code that rallied them all to help. Maggie was just about to suggest they head for the ladies' room when the young woman shook her hair back and straightened her shoulders.

"I'll be fine. Really. I was just thinking that in real life, there's never an orphanage to explain things away, is there?"

Oh, dear. The poor thing had obviously had her heart broken. Maggie sympathized. "I'm afraid when real guys do jerky things, it usually just means they're jerks."

"Is this about the airline pilot?" Natalie asked Kayla, who gave a quick negative shake of her head.

But Kristen did one of those half laugh, half sobs. "It might as well be. I'm starting to think they're all the same. I was dumb enough to believe the pilot when he said he hated to leave. Now I know he was having a grand time seeing his other girlfriends. You'd think I would have wised up, but no. A handsome cowboy comes through town and I actually believe him when he says he hates to leave me, but he must. They always must go, simply must. I even believed that he was going to come back when the rodeo tour was over."

"A rodeo star?" Natalie was clearly dying for more details.

Maggie felt badly for Kristen, who was slowly shredding her napkin.

"I thought a cowboy would be different. He'd love his family more than anything else, and be loyal to his lady. He seemed to be a real gentleman, too."

Natalie frowned. "Yeah, but a rodeo star is a different kind of cowboy."

"He made it sound like this was his final season, because he was looking to settle down here in Rust Creek Falls. I'm such a sucker."

Kayla gave her twin a squeeze. "I would have fallen for the man, too. The stories he told you were so poignant, who wouldn't have?"

Maggie smiled to herself at the sister's show of loyalty. Shane and Ryan had always been loyal to her like that, too.

"He fed you more lies?" Natalie shook her head. "Men are pigs."

Maggie tried to temper that kind of blanket statement. It went against her mind-set as an attorney to accept a stereotype as a legitimate argument. "Let's just say if a man acts like a pig, there's almost never a justification. Kristen had it right. They're never protecting a secret orphanage in real life."

"Thanks, guys." Kristen kept tearing the napkin into pieces and crumpling the strips in her palm. "The thing is, I still don't think he lied. If he'd bragged that he owned a fancy sports car, that would be one thing, but what would be the point in telling me he was adopted? He remembered his first mother. She left him when he was three. Just walked away and left him."

That got Maggie's attention. One of her adopted brothers had been abandoned when he was three. What a strange coincidence for this rodeo rider to have been left like that, too.

"I'm sure he made it up to get pity points. What a scum bucket." Natalie gave Kristen a friendly bump, hip to hip. "Did he at least have washboard abs?"

Kristen laughed a little as she dabbed her nose with the crumbled napkin. "He did. I mean, I didn't take his shirt off, but he was rock hard when I hugged him."

This elicited some snickering from Natalie.

"He was a good dancer. Tall. Handsome. Nice voice, nice manners." The hint of a smile lit Kristen's face as she remembered the better traits of her rodeo star. The poor girl was still carrying a torch for this guy. Maggie was glad she had lots of support from a loving sister and from Natalie, too.

Maggie started looking around the gym for her husband, getting ready to graciously bow out of this circle now that the tears were under control. Natalie was settling in for the juicy details, and although Maggie was only a few years older than they were, she was starting to feel like the odd man out as an old married woman. These three were all single and had gone to school together.

Maggie craned her neck a bit, trying to spot her husband. Married women had benefits, and hers was Jesse Crawford.

"Where did you meet him?" Natalie asked. "Is he famous? Would I recognize his name?"

"I don't think so. It's Ryan Michaels. I met him here in town on the Fourth of July."

"The 'power of the punch,' eh?"

Maggie snapped her attention back to Kristen. Her brother was Roarke, not Michaels, but he'd been here for the Fourth of July. A man named Ryan, in town for the Fourth of July, who'd been abandoned at age three? It couldn't be.

"I don't know about the punch. I wish I had an excuse for being so gullible a second time." Kristen's hands doubled into fists. "I believed everything he said. He just about broke my heart with his story. He painted this whole picture about how she left him standing on the steps to a church—just *terrible*. It's over the top, right? I should have seen that, right? At the time, I felt so special that he was telling me something so personal, but it was just a line to make women want to comfort him. It worked."

Dear God, church steps. She was talking about Ryan. Her brother Ryan had broken this sweet girl's heart.

Frantically, Maggie thought back to the Fourth of July. They'd all gone to the wedding together, but Madeline had only been about ten weeks old, and she and Jesse had taken the baby home to nap. They'd all fallen asleep. Later, it had seemed like too much trouble to cart the stroller and diaper bag and the rest back to the park. She'd assumed Ryan had renewed an acquaintance from the flood recovery days, but he must have struck up a flirtation with Kristen. It all made sense, except why on earth had he told this poor girl he was in the rodeo? It was flabbergasting.

Maggie felt physically sick. Ryan had always been a lady-killer, but this wasn't LA, and Kristen wasn't a starlet. How could he? But he had, he clearly had, and now Kristen's spurt of anger was over and tears were welling up in her eyes again.

"The thing is, and please don't think I'm crazy or a complete idiot for thinking this, but the thing is, what if his story was real? He probably has a hard time trusting anyone. Maybe he does want to be with me, but his childhood affected him so that he doesn't believe a woman would love him. Or…oh, I don't know. What if he was injured, and he's been in a hospital this whole time? What do you think?"

I think I'm going to kill my brother.

But first, she needed to give Kristen some immediate advice. "Here's what I think you should do. You should get back in line and buy yourself a serious amount of chocolate, and you should avoid sad movies for a while. The next movie will be all car explosions and no plot. It's perfect." Impulsively, Maggie gave Kristen a hug and whispered in her ear. "Try not to drive yourself crazy with questions that have no answer."

Maggie left to find her husband. She had the rest of date night to salvage. First thing tomorrow morning, she would give Ryan a piece of her mind. Poor Kristen might not be able to get any answers, but Maggie would.

"Get your butt up here. Now. This minute."

"Good morning to you, too, Maggie. Nice of you to call."

Ryan clamped his phone between his shoulder and ear and hoisted his suitcase into the overhead bin. The noise of a couple of hundred people boarding the airplane gave him a certain amount of privacy to talk with Maggie before takeoff. She'd probably hear the background noise and guess where he was, but in the meantime, he could have some fun with her.

"Why would I come see you? Isn't it snowing there? Not to rub it in, but I was golfing with Dad this week. Scratch that. I am definitely rubbing it in."

Ryan took his first-class seat and waved away the flight attendant's offer of a drink. Strangers with backpacks and luggage and kids continued to file past.

"I'm not joking around, Ryan. You have to come up here."

Her tone of voice alarmed him. Ryan tuned out everything but his sister. "What's wrong? Are you at the hospital? Jesse or Madeline sick?"

"You're the sick one. You broke a girl's heart last time you were in Rust Creek Falls, you jerk."

He nearly dropped the phone.

"I was at the movies last night, talking to Kristen Dalton at the concession stand."

The name exploded in his brain. He hadn't heard anyone say her name, not once in all these months. She'd been only his own silent wish, his own secret memory. Hearing his sister speak about her was jarring, a sudden reminder that Kristen wasn't his private fantasy. She was a real woman with friends and family. A woman who lived a normal life and went to movies.

"She was in tears. The movie was sad, and it made her cry, and do you know why? Because you're extra sensitive when your heart's been broken. Kristen Dalton! Oh, Ryan, how could you?"

Kristen crying, brokenhearted—Ryan's own heart stopped beating for a moment. He tightened his grip on the phone.

"She asked you about me?"

"No, she didn't ask me about you. What kind of vain question is that?"

It hadn't been vain. It had been hopeful. He was on this plane because he'd needed to see for himself that Kristen was okay. That she'd moved on. That she was fine without him. *Closure.* He was having too hard of a time in California without it.

But now...

Ryan covered one ear and turned away from the aisle to better hear his sister. This flight connected to Kalispell through Las Vegas, and the passengers who boarded were boisterous, ready for vacation. Ryan concentrated to hear everything his sister said. Every word was crucial.

"If she didn't ask you about me, then how do you know I'm the reason she's heartbroken?" It was far more likely that she'd been dating someone else this fall. Just because Ryan couldn't stand the idea didn't mean it wasn't probable.

"Because I'm standing in line for some Twizzlers and Sno-Caps, and this really pretty woman starts pouring her heart out about a man who was adopted at age three. He's left her behind without a backward glance, that much is obvious to anyone who's listening, but she can't see that, because she's crazy about him. She's clinging to this idea that he's just afraid to believe in love after the way his mother abandoned him on church steps. And this paragon of a man that she's still hoping will come back is named Ryan."

A man that she's still hoping will come back.

The entire purpose of the flight changed in an instant. There was nothing of brotherly concern in his attitude toward Kristen. Screw closure. He wanted Kristen as he'd wanted her from the first: in his arms for a dance and a kiss. By his side for a laugh during a meal. He wanted her in his bed, and yes, he wanted to trust her with his heart.

If she wanted his heart. It had seemed unlikely after all these months, but suddenly, with his sister's words, everything he wanted and needed was possible. Everything could be his, if Kristen still wanted him. They could work out all the rest, somehow.

"You can't leave a girl hanging with her heart on her sleeve like that. She's really crazy about you, you moron. If you think you'll find a better woman down there in LA, you're wrong, but you at least owe it to Kristen to end things cleanly so she can move on."

"I don't want to end things."

"Well, you have to. It's just cruel, letting her carry a torch for you."

Hope was a painful emotion, forcing its way into a heart that hadn't allowed any room for it.

Maggie misinterpreted his silence. Of course, she only saw him as her brother, the player. It wouldn't occur to her that he'd been serious about Kristen. "I mean it, Ryan. If you don't get up here, I'll—I'll—I'll tell Mom."

Her threat cut the tension, and amazingly, Ryan found he could laugh despite the painful hope in his chest. "Don't do anything so drastic. I'm already on my way."

"Good. When you book your flight, let me know, and I'll pick you up at the airport."

"I said I'm already on my way. Listen." He held the phone away from his ear as the flight attendant repeated the announcement, which everyone ignored, about stepping out of the aisle to let others pass during boarding.

"Wait a minute. You'd already decided to come up here? Did Jesse call you last night?"

"I'd already decided last week to see Kristen. I told you I didn't want to end things, but you were too busy chewing me out to hear that."

"Wow. That's… I should get the guest room ready." She sounded a little faint.

"I'm staying at Maverick Manor. Between you, Jesse and the baby, that's three chaperones I don't need while I'm trying to woo a woman."

"Woo her? Not break up with her? Ryan, you can't do this. You can't keep letting her think you're some kind of rodeo star. The fake name, the whole cowboy masquerade—I just can't be a party to that. I'm not going to pretend I don't know you."

The flight attendant stopped directly by his seat and spoke loudly. "Excuse me, sir, but you're going to have to turn off your phone now."

"What are you talking about, Maggie?"

"Sir, I must insist. The doors have been closed."

"Sounds like you have to go," Maggie said. "I'll talk to you when you get here."

"What masquerade, damn it?"

"Sir."

"Kristen Dalton isn't in love with you. She's in love with a cowboy named Ryan Michaels. Hang up before you get kicked off that plane."

Chapter Seven

After ten agonizing hours of travel, Ryan hung up once more after talking to his sister. Numb, he sank onto the foot of the oversize bed in his room at Maverick Manor.

He hadn't done it on purpose. He'd worn cowboy boots and two-stepped to a country-western band, but he'd never said he was a cowboy. He hadn't specifically said he was an attorney from LA, either, but he'd never once talked about rodeos.

When he'd been standing by those church steps with Kristen, he'd accidentally let slip the name that he'd gone by as a preschooler. She'd apparently assumed he was still Michaels. That meant Kristen didn't know he was related to the Maggie Roarke Crawford who worked with her own uncle. She didn't know he was related to celebrity chef Shane Roarke. And she most certainly didn't know he, Ryan, defended contracts for movie studios and recording artists.

He'd wanted it that way. When they'd first met, he'd only said he was Ryan, not Ryan Roarke. He'd wanted to feel what it would be like to be a local.

The locals around here are all cowboys.

Maybe he should have foreseen that, but the locals weren't rodeo stars, damn it. He'd never been to a rodeo in his life. She'd been born and raised on a ranch. How had he fooled her so completely?

Ryan fell back onto the quilt-topped mattress.

He'd just have to level with her immediately. Like ripping off a bandage, he'd have to confess his missteps and mistakes. When he told Kristen that her humble cowboy who'd been considering a move to Rust Creek Falls was actually a high-powered Hollywood attorney who specialized in the entertainment industry, would she still want him?

He stared at the ceiling until the knots of the pine slats blurred into nothing. In their place, he saw the hem of a woman's dress, swishing with every step as she walked away.

The need to rip off a bandage was not a great motivator.

Although Ryan had spent a week rearranging his whole schedule specifically to see Kristen, he found himself stalling now that he was in Rust Creek Falls. He was dying to look into those blue eyes again, to feel her soft palm against his jaw, to run his hand down her soft hair. But first, he had to tell her that everything she thought she knew about him was wrong. She was going to be devastated. His first sight of her could be his last.

And so, after a restless night at the hotel, he spent Sunday morning doing everything except what he'd come to town to do. Instead of asking for directions to the Dalton family ranch, he located Brad Crawford and got his signature on that final piece of paperwork. Instead of knocking on Kristen's door, he stopped by Maggie's house to see the baby, who'd grown so much in four months it was astonishing.

He couldn't avoid the inevitable, but he told himself it was smart to delay it. This mistaken identity had caught him completely by surprise just twenty-four hours ago. He knew how to win a debate and he knew how to persuade a jury. Both of those things required careful preparation, and Ryan was not prepared to rip off any bandages without a plan. He needed time to think, and he needed to avoid Kristen until he was ready.

The hotel was too small for his restless pacing. He considered walking the perimeter of the park while he thought of the right words to say, but Maggie and her family were headed there. She'd become a true Montanan who thought forty degrees was perfectly balmy weather for a Sunday stroll. The park wouldn't provide any solitude.

He could retrace Kristen's tour. Walk along the river in broad daylight. Head up Main Street to that church where he'd said too much—or where he'd said too little. But revisiting the sights seemed too maudlin, too much like a scene from a sappy movie—and too risky. He might run into Kristen unprepared.

He got into the truck he'd rented and drove out of town. The highway led straight to Kalispell, right through the heart of town. Main Street was flanked by the same type of sturdy brick buildings that lined the streets of Rust Creek Falls. There, away from the Crawfords and Daltons, he parked his truck, got out and started walking.

* * *

"Let's try it again from the top of the scene. Old Scrooge and the Ghost of Christmas Past, I want you two to stand a little closer upstage." The assistant director looked over his shoulder toward the back of the theater. "Can we keep the spotlight on Old Scrooge if he moves upstage? Yes? Good."

Kristen stood motionless at center stage. This rehearsal was primarily meant to refine the blocking, deciding where every actor would move during the scene. The lighting director, the stage crew and the prop master needed to know where the actors delivered every line. It was tedious work, but part of being an actress was being patient.

Kristen hated blocking days. She got through them by using them as an acting exercise, in which she had to play the role of Patient Actress. Since Patient Actress would not tap her booted foot impatiently, Kristen stopped. She stuffed her hands in the back pockets of her jeans. They didn't wear costumes for most rehearsals, but Kristen wore a bright blue sweater with her jeans and boots, because her costume was a striking blue gown. She had her hair up in a messy bun to simulate the Victorian style she'd wear during performances. Her hair affected what angle she held her head, even which shadows the different stage lights cast on her face, so it was necessary.

"Belle, switch places with Young Ebenezer. I want Old Scrooge to be looking over his shoulder at you. He'll be seeing your face while you break his heart all over again."

Obediently, Kristen switched places with the actor who was playing Ebenezer in the prime of his life. The assistant director had one key point wrong, however.

"I'm not breaking Ebenezer's heart. He's already decided he loves money more than me. I'm the one who is brokenhearted."

She cut herself short. *I'm the one who is brokenhearted.* Saying those words out loud felt like a personal confession, although no one could know they were true for Kristen as well as Belle, the unwanted fiancée.

The assistant director flipped through the script in his hand, but he didn't stop on any page long enough to read a full line of dialogue. "We're not talking about motivation today. We're talking about lighting."

"Yes, but you want the audience to see Old Scrooge's face," Kristen persisted. "If his shoulder is to that half of the audience, they'll miss his expression. This is the moment where he realizes that letting Belle go was a mistake that ruined the rest of his life."

Again, she fell silent. She knew she was a fool for worrying about Ryan, but she wondered if he was happy now, after choosing a path that didn't include her. Last Friday, she'd said as much during movie night, but it had only earned her those terrible looks of pity from Natalie, Kayla and her uncle's partner, Maggie Crawford.

The actor playing Old Scrooge backed her up. "She's right. I'm the one who has to be devastated, not the younger me. Maybe if we stood this way—" he put his hand on Young Ebenezer's shoulders and the two of them shuffled clockwise for a few steps "—more of the house would be able to see both of our faces. There's a big contrast between what he felt then and how he feels now."

After more discussion, the assistant director left the stage to stand in the audience. He flipped through his script once more. "Okay, let's take it from, uh, Young

Ebenezer's line. 'Have I asked to be released from this promise?'"

Kristen took both of the actor's hands in hers, breathed in deeply to focus herself and then looked up at him with all the sadness of a woman who realizes her love is not returned. To become Belle, Kristen only had to admit to herself that she was unwanted. Ryan was never coming back.

Ebenezer looked at her coldly. "Have I asked to be released from this promise?"

"Not in words, no."

"How, then?"

"In the way you spend all hours in your counting house. In the way your smiles are only bestowed on the scales, when the balance of gold tilts them in your favor. Tell me truly, if you saw me today for the first time, would you make the effort to dance with me at Fezziwig's party? Would you ask your friends for an introduction to a girl who has no dowry?"

He lifted his chin sharply, his nostrils flaring in distaste at her question.

"You see?" She let the tears that welled in her eyes spill down her cheeks. "The man who loved me is only a memory. For his sake, I pray you will be happy upon your chosen path. You no longer want me to walk with you, no matter how much I wish it otherwise. Ebenezer Scrooge, I release you."

She bowed her head, and let go of Ebenezer's stiff hands.

"Okay, that's plenty." The assistant director made his way back to the stage. "That was great, by the way. Just do it twice every weekend from opening night through Christmas, okay?"

Kristen smiled obligingly, back in her role as Patient Actress, and used the cuff of her sweater to dry her cheeks.

"You make my job hard," Ebenezer said. "I'm supposed to look at you like you're as appealing as an empty wallet, but man, I just wanted to go down on my knees and beg you to stay."

"You made my job easy." Old Scrooge patted her on the shoulder with one hand and gave Ebenezer a good-natured shove with the other. "It'll be easy to call this guy out for being a fool. He really is a cold-hearted bastard if he can look in those teary blue eyes and not feel a thing. I was ready to deliver my line with gusto, if that pompous kid hadn't cut us off. When's the real director back again? Tuesday?"

"Thank you, Act Two," the assistant director called out in dismissal. "Act Three beginners, please. Act Three beginners, take your places."

Kristen made her escape into the wing. She couldn't decide if this was the worst role or best role she'd ever taken. The similarity of her situation to Belle's made for difficult rehearsals. The lines she had to speak came too close to her real feelings. She had to relive her dashed hopes over and over.

On the other hand, this role was a piece of cake for her as an actress. She had only to think of Ryan, and very little acting skill was required to give an authentic performance.

The bad news is, I got jilted. The good news is, I got great reviews.

She tried to laugh at her own joke, but the hitch in her breath was more like a sob. She felt a big, ugly cry coming on, nothing like Belle's gentle tears.

"I'm going out for some fresh air," she said to the stage manager. She threw her polka-dotted scarf around her neck and grabbed her red jacket from the folding chair where she'd thrown it three hours ago.

The stage manager checked the large clock over her station in the wings. "You might as well leave for the day. I can tell you right now we'll never make it to the final scene."

Kristen swallowed hard and faked a smile. "Thanks, Sue. See you Tuesday."

She all but ran for the stage door, barely making it outside before Patient Actress and Belle the Fiancée and every other role she'd been playing for the past four months gave way under the crushing weight of being Kristen Dalton, the girl who still wanted Ryan Michaels to come back for her.

The stores and shops of Kalispell were decked out for Christmas. Not one window or door seemed to have escaped the bonds of garland and ribbon. Despite this, Ryan could admire the brick buildings, sturdy brick squares that had withstood a century of Christmas seasons and could probably withstand a century more. He'd survive this Christmas, too. He always did, no matter what bad memories were associated with the holiday.

Ryan tucked his hands deeply in the pockets of his wool overcoat. It was double-breasted and sharply tailored, because he was not a cowboy and not pretending to be one. It was full-length, because he was from Los Angeles and the weather here was flirting with freezing, but it was also open in front because he'd been walking for block after block, building up heat. If the coat flared behind him like a cowboy's duster, he couldn't help it. Let people think what they wanted.

Except Kristen. What she *wanted* to think about him mattered. She wanted a cowboy. He kept running the scenarios in his mind, but no matter how he presented the basic facts, he couldn't imagine her face lighting up in one of her dazzling smiles. *Oh, you're actually living in a megalopolis over one thousand miles away? Fantastic!*

The cold November wind had cleared his mind and cooled his expectations. The truth was, she'd fallen in love with a rodeo rider because that was who she'd wanted to fall in love with. That was not him. He thought she was perfect as she was, a simple ranch girl, born and bred in a small town, but nothing good lasted for long. There was no real chance that he and Kristen could still be a couple after he told her the truth. Her feelings for him would be crushed in an instant, and all the glitter and magic would drain away.

Like a damned shattered snow globe.

He stopped walking, and stood on the cold sidewalk, letting the north wind blow away the childish vision— all gone, bye-bye. He turned on his heel to head back to his SUV. It was time to go face Kristen.

Kristen.

She stood on the sidewalk before him, perhaps twenty yards away, staring into a store window, a beautiful mirage for a man who hadn't realized just how much of a desert his life had become. He drank up the sight of her. How had he survived the deprivation?

She seemed tired, her shoulders low and her expression downcast. When the brisk wind pulled more tendrils loose from her pinned-up hair, she didn't seem to have the energy to turn her collar up.

He knew, somehow, he'd looked just as tired moments ago, before seeing her. He'd denied them both the chance to be happy. She had the right to be furious with him for causing her pain.

"Kristen." Her name was little more than a whisper, the apology he owed her too big for words.

She tucked a wisp of hair behind her ear and turned away, light and graceful in all her moves despite the sadness in her expression. When she turned her back on him and he lost sight of her face, something in him snapped. She had to go; he understood that. Nothing good lasted forever. But he couldn't let her walk away without telling her how grateful he was for the most perfect summer day of his life.

"Kristen!"

She looked over her shoulder. Their gazes met, and her blue eyes opened wide the moment she recognized him.

He took one step toward her, another, and then he realized she was smiling—smiling at *him*—and he was running. She came flying toward him, and he opened his arms wide and swooped her off her feet. Momentum carried them around and around as she laughed.

"You came back, you came back," she said, her arms tight around his neck.

He had her lifted high, so his face was buried in her playful scarf and loose hair for a long, blinding moment of reunion that needed no words. Then she slid down his body, until her cowboy boots touched the ground.

She kept his face in both her hands, smoothing her thumbs across his cheekbones. She was beaming at him, every bit as stunning as he'd remembered, yet ten times more vivid in person than a memory could ever be.

"You look amazing. Even more beautiful than I remembered, and I think of you every day as the most beautiful woman I know." He was babbling. He didn't care.

"I can't believe you're real," she said, exactly what he was feeling. "We never took a photo that day. Neither one of us brought a phone. You can't imagine how much I've wished I just had a picture of you—"

The catch in her voice made him catch her close again, holding her against his chest within the open folds of his coat. "I'm sorry. I'm so very sorry. I shouldn't have stayed away so long."

She nuzzled into the side of his throat. "You must have had a good reason."

Her faith in him was humbling. And misplaced.

You have to tell her the truth.

"I've been working." He rested his cheek on top of her head, regret in every syllable. "In California."

"California?" She picked her head up. Stepped back.

Ryan braced himself. The bandage ripping had begun. He'd known since Maggie's bombshell that it would come down to this. He'd never hated having to do something more.

"No wonder I couldn't find you." She bit her lip and looked up at him apologetically. "I kept checking the Montana papers for event results. Then it occurred to me to look at Wyoming. I might have gotten desperate enough to check out Idaho's results on the web a few times. Pretty bad, huh? But it never occurred to me to look at California."

He had to look away from those trusting blue eyes. "I didn't deserve to have you looking so hard for me."

"Did you come from California all the way back to Montana just to see me?"

"Yes, I did." She deserved to know the truth in this, as well. He wanted her to know he'd suffered, too, although it had been his own fault. "I was going crazy, wondering how you were. I missed you."

Kristen made a quick movement of her hands toward his face, and for a split second, he thought a slap was coming. He deserved a slap. Instead, with two hands in his hair, she pulled him to her, and kissed him. Hard. Hungry.

No memory could wake every cell in his body like this. He was alive, all sensation. The feel of Kristen in his arms, the smell of her skin, the very taste of her, each were their own small miracle. It didn't matter if he deserved her kiss; he was greedy for it and took what she gave him, savoring the connection that made him want to be closer still.

A passing truck honked a horn, whether in criticism or approval didn't matter. It was enough to bring Ryan back to the real world. He lifted his head to study Kristen's face and felt utterly satisfied with how thoroughly kissed her mouth looked and how perfectly pink her cheeks were. She rocked back on her heels—she'd been standing on tiptoe during the entire kiss—and gripped his arms for a moment as she regained her equilibrium.

She looked so feminine, so delicate, but then she smiled like a woman who knew a secret. "Someday, we are going to kiss when we are alone and indoors, somewhere very private, and things are going to burn so far out of control you won't be safe from me any longer."

He could've dropped to his knees on the sidewalk. She was so Kristen, so boldly herself. He wanted her.

Hell, he had her. She wasn't playing coy or shy or mysterious. She was thrilled to see him, as eager to pick up where they'd left off as he was.

But the hell of it was, he couldn't keep her. He wasn't the man she thought he was.

Rip off the bandage.

Not here. Not on a sidewalk in the center of town.

He tried to use humor to ease the sexual tension she'd just ratcheted into high gear. "There's a traditional order to these things. I think you're supposed to buy me a drink first. I passed a bakery not too far back. Maybe they sell coffee."

Her smile only deepened. "They do, but if you're daring enough to cut through the alley with me, there's a diner that serves amazing pie one street over. You'd be indoors with me for the first time, but I think you'll be safe if I have a nice slice of homemade pie competing for my attention."

She led the way through the alley. From behind, she made a colorful picture. Her caramel-colored hair was mostly twisted up. The hem of her red coat cut precisely across her jean-clad rear, and one end of her polka-dotted scarf fluttered among the loose tendrils of escaped hair as she took quick, decisive steps.

Another version of *Woman Walking Away*.

This was what he would see after he told her the truth, then.

He couldn't do it. He couldn't say the words that would shatter her feelings for him all at once. Those feelings were pure and sincere—yes, they were naive, but they were real, and their destruction could leave a permanent scar. For her own sake, he couldn't sit her down in front of a piece of pie and tell her everything she'd loved about him was a lie. It would break her heart.

It would shatter his.

They emerged from the alley onto a street nearly identical to Main, and then into a mom-and-pop restaurant that smelled of wholesome holiday baking. While gingerbread and pumpkin pie were topped with whipped cream for them, Ryan rapidly formed a new plan.

He didn't want to rip off any damned bandage, so he wouldn't. What if he could reveal pieces of the truth bit by bit, and slowly replace the image of Ryan Michaels with the reality of Ryan Roarke? He'd already told her he worked in California when she'd assumed Montana or Wyoming, and she'd accepted that piece of the truth easily enough. What if he could continue to do that this week? If she loved Ryan Michaels this Sunday, might she love Ryan Roarke by next Sunday?

Could she love him so strongly that she'd still want to be part of his life, even if that life had nothing to do with Montana and her cowgirl dreams?

He had one week to find out.

Chapter Eight

The last thing Kristen needed was more sugar. She was already bouncing off the diner's walls with excitement, because Ryan was here.

He's really here.

Just when she'd given up hope, he'd arrived, and gosh, what a reunion. He'd said everything she could have wanted to hear. He'd missed her. He'd come specifically to see her.

Then there was that kiss on the sidewalk. The memory of kissing Ryan and the reality of kissing Ryan were two entirely different things. Every second had been worth a month of missing him. Everything was okay now. Absolutely everything.

She took her gaze off Ryan just long enough to scoop the whipped cream off the top of her pie and eat it all in one bite, sugar be damned, and then she went back to devouring Ryan with her eyes.

Dear God, he looked good. He was dark-haired and dark-eyed, just like she remembered, and his tan hadn't faded despite the November weather. He still had that air about him that set him apart from the other cowboys in town. Something more sophisticated, maybe. A great haircut, a killer overcoat that even looked good hanging on the wall hook next to hers. The sweater he wore with his jeans almost looked like cashmere. If they ever put a rodeo man on the cover of *GQ*, her Ryan would be the perfect model. He had the strong jaw and an expression that didn't look like he laughed easily—but, oh, when he did, the camera must love him.

A camera. She jumped up to retrieve her phone from her coat's pocket and plopped back into the booth across from Ryan.

"I'm not making the same mistakes this time. Say cheese."

He didn't. Or rather, she didn't give him a chance to say cheese, but she got a wonderful shot of that one raised eyebrow and the quirk of his lips when he was going to smile, but hadn't started actually smiling yet.

She hit the symbols on her phone to make Ryan's image her wallpaper, setting it as her lock screen and home screen, both. "Much better. Sometimes, I was afraid I'd imagined you. Fortunately, the whole town seemed to have seen us sitting on that stage, eating barbecue, so I knew I wasn't crazy." Laughing, she looked up to find him watching her with a too-serious expression.

He laid his hand on the table, palm up, and she gave him her phone. He dialed a number, and within seconds, she heard a traditional, classic ring coming from the coat rack across the room. He disconnected the call and set her phone on the table. She felt relieved, knowing they had each other's numbers now.

"Much better," he said, gently echoing her words. "There was no one around me who knew you existed. I think it did make me a little crazy."

She put her hand in his and squeezed hard.

"I should have come sooner." The regret in his voice was painful to hear.

"You were working." She racked her brain for the California rodeos, information she hadn't thought of since freshman year of high school. "Where were you? Redding? Sacramento?"

"Not Northern California. I'm living in Southern California, believe it or not."

She'd been imagining that he was much closer all this time. It made it all the more understandable that he hadn't been able to steal away for a few days.

Southern California had major rodeos, but as a kid she'd known that she'd never be able to travel that far to see one. Kristen hadn't committed that information to memory, not like the events in Montana and Wyoming. Still, there was something about the serious tone the conversation was taking that made her uneasy. She wanted to keep riding the high of simply being in his presence again.

"Of course I believe you." This time, she winked at him. "It explains the tan."

That seemed to be the right thing to say. He relaxed against the back of his seat. She felt so happy she couldn't stay in hers. She got up and scooted into his side of the booth. His arm came around her immediately, and she snuggled against him like they were teenagers.

She couldn't see every nuance of his facial expressions now, but the trade-off was that her hand could rest on his thigh and her head on his shoulder. He was definitely not a teenager, but a man built for work. Thigh and shoulder, both, were hard-muscled. She was going to want to make love with the lights on.

He tapped her nose with one finger. "Is it the gingerbread or the pumpkin pie that's making you blush?" His voice was low, an intimate rumble for her ears only.

"It's you." She hated the blush, but she couldn't stop the direction her thoughts were going. "I should have guessed you were from Southern California. You don't have a farmer's tan like most of the guys around here."

He was silent for a long moment. "Exactly how do you know that?"

"Let's just say I had an opportunity on the Fourth of July to make use of a certain vantage point."

"Damn. I didn't look down your shirt."

"You're a gentleman. I'm not." She ran one finger down the soft sweater that covered his hard chest. "You're a gentleman who is tan all over. I don't suppose you Southern California cowboys go surfing after the chores are done?"

He shifted slightly. "I do surf, actually."

"You do?" The idea of a surfing cowboy was funny. "Do you wear a cowboy hat out on the waves?"

"Never, and that is the truth." With one finger under her chin, he lifted her face for a sweet kiss.

The diner made a good chaperone. The kiss stayed sweet.

It didn't have to stay sweet, not like the last time Ryan had been in town. She had her own place now. She'd never had a one-night stand. She'd never slept with a man on the first date. But last Fourth of July, she would have made an exception. She might even have blamed it on the punch, thanks to all the buzz in town about its having had a chemical effect in some way, but there was no punch in the picture now, and she wanted Ryan in a fiercely physical way.

Sitting beside him in public and eating a slice of pie set her senses on fire. She'd meant what she'd said on the sidewalk. If she got him alone, she'd seduce him.

He was hers. He'd come back to see her, and he'd come a very long way, too. She wasn't going to make the same mistake twice. If he had to leave the next day, she knew for certain she'd miss him whether they slept together or not, so they might as well—

Leave the next day. Those were chilling words.

"You don't have to fly out in the morning again, do you?"

He brushed her hair out of the way. "I arranged a week off work."

"A whole week. That sounds wonderful." It stretched before her like a huge chunk of time. Seven days. Seven nights.

The nights were on her mind. "Where are you staying while you're here?"

"Maverick Manor."

The name of the place triggered her family pride. "My brother designed that place. Jonah. He's an architect."

"It's one of the most striking hotels I've stayed in."

"Isn't it? It was a private house before he worked on it. I've started working for Jonah myself."

She paused, unsure how to proceed. She had no doubt that she'd know exactly what to do with Ryan if she had him alone in her new bedroom. She'd fantasized about the possibilities in detail, but she'd never considered the first step. How did one let a man know he should take her to her home, come inside and stay the night? She'd always had her parents and brothers under her roof before, so this was a new experience.

"You're working for an architect? That's got to be a huge change. I always imagine you working on your family's ranch."

"I still work there, too, four days a week. I couldn't leave my parents shorthanded." She tapped the edge of her pie plate with her fork. "It also gives me a chance to raid the kitchen and eat some of my mother's home cooking after I'm done in the stables."

"Do you mean you moved off your ranch?" He sounded absolutely stunned.

"I'm living in town. Jonah is renovating a block of gorgeous old Victorian houses. I'm living in one of them and working at the same time, a sort of sweat equity. Instead of paying my rent in cash, I'm paying it by doing some of the renovations. Are you going to eat your whipped cream?"

When he slid his plate toward her, she helped herself.

"To be honest, 'renovating' means I varnish stuff. There's lots and lots of varnishing to be done in a vintage Victorian. Lotsa wood in those babies, and Jonah is crazy about keeping every last piece of original trim. It's all curlicue gingerbread and a real pain in the neck. Pretty to look at, but trust me, you don't want to maintain it."

Ryan was listening to every word she said, and judging by that almost-curve of his mouth and the way his eyes were crinkling a bit at the corners, he liked listening to her. Kristen found that to be a total turn-on that had nothing to do with tanned chests and wash-board abs.

"Do you miss living on the ranch?"

"I probably would if I wasn't still showing up for breakfast four days a week. That's just enough to keep me from being so homesick that I want to move back in. I do miss Kayla, but it's fun to have her popping in for some sister time."

"Congratulations, then, on your first home."

Kristen sat sideways in the booth, tucking one leg under her so she could face him more squarely. "Thank you. Not just for saying that, but for being a big part of the reason I made a lot of changes this fall. Do you remember when we talked about the pursuit of happiness? You said you could be happier, that your work wasn't as rewarding as it had been, and I was so impressed that you were taking action to change things that weren't making you happy."

She hesitated at his slight frown. It probably wasn't realistic to expect him to remember every word they'd said, or even every topic they'd covered throughout the course of that day. She knew every word by heart, but that probably made her look like a lovesick little cowgirl. She wanted him to think of her as so much more.

Still frowning, he reached for one of her wayward curls and wrapped it around his finger. "I remember. Go ahead."

"You inspired me. I realized I was drifting along in a safe routine, but I hadn't stopped to examine what I really wanted. I don't know if you remember that I'd interviewed with the principal—"

"Every word, Kristen. I remember."

Her heart thudded hard, one solid thud, and she knew

it was the sound of a heart falling harder in love. "I decided that just because he'd said no, that didn't mean I had to wait on the ranch for an opportunity to open up. Now I've got my own house, and that was just the beginning."

"That's huge. There's more?"

There was the play, of course. He'd be so proud to know she was using her theater degree. But he was going to be here a full week, and that meant he'd be here on opening night. She was dying to brag about her return to the theater, but this could be a chance to really surprise him on Friday. If she could get him in the audience and then surprise him by appearing on stage, it would be dramatic.

She drew her knee up and hugged it with one arm, still facing him on the bench of the booth. "There might be one or two more things, but you can't expect a woman to divulge every secret at once. I might need to keep a little air of mystery about me."

He raised one eyebrow. "Considering I failed to tell you where I lived, I'm in no position to demand to know all your secrets."

"Here's the important part." She took a deep breath, focused and prepared to deliver her most important line. "You don't need to stay at Maverick Manor this week. I'd like to extend a formal invitation. Mr. Ryan Michaels, would you like to be my first guest in my first home?"

Of all the reactions she might have expected, the way he closed his eyes and turned his face away was not one. Her heart thudded into the silence.

"What's wrong?" she whispered.

The hand he'd rested on the table clenched into a fist. "For one thing, Ryan Michaels is not my name."

"More coffee, you two?"

The owner of the diner had apparently run out of things to do and had come over to chat, interrupting at the worst moment. Ryan needed to explain his name to Kristen. He couldn't sleep with a woman who didn't know his last name, no matter how important she was to him, and he couldn't explain the name confusion if this shop owner didn't leave them alone.

The woman gestured to the phone on the table. "Do you want me to take a picture?" She wiped her free hand on her apron in preparation.

"No, thank you." His curt tone made it clear that she should leave. It would have worked on any server in any city from Los Angeles to London.

Not this woman. She studied him more closely, looking him over. "I haven't seen you in here before. Did you come from the airport? Got a layover tonight?"

This was completely, utterly, not her concern. He glared at her, unwilling to give her a single syllable of *no*, but Kristen let go of the knee she'd been hugging and turned to face her. "He's an old friend of mine, Matilda. We were just catching up. Could you give us just a minute? The pumpkin pie was delicious, by the way."

Matilda kept her eye on Ryan, but she picked up the empty pie plate, took her coffeepot and left. For now.

Ryan had no problem dismissing unnecessary persons, but Kristen accomplished the same thing with a smile. His big-city impatience clashed with her small-town friendliness. He felt like a foreigner once more.

She turned all that sweetness on him. "Was she

standing behind me for long? Did she hear what I said to you? My face is turning ten shades of red now, I can feel it."

"She didn't hear anything."

Kristen had just asked him to spend a week in her home and in her bed. He'd told her she didn't even know his real name, yet she didn't seem hurt or suspicious. He didn't deserve her smile.

"Matilda brought up a good point, though. Did you just fly in today?"

"I landed last night." He hoped his expression was as neutral as he kept it during a trial. He was going to be forced to admit this meeting was a complete accident.

"And you came to Kalispell to find me today, which is...well, not so odd, I guess. Did you stop by the ranch? Maybe Kayla told you I'd be here today."

"No. I just came here because..." There was no hiding the truth in this case. "I had no idea what to say to you when I found you. I came here to walk, basically, and think. Then I planned to head to Rust Creek Falls to find you."

"So it was a total coincidence that you were on the same sidewalk at the same time?"

"It didn't seem so coincidental. I flew in to see you and I was thinking about you when I saw you, but it—"

"—is totally romantic, like you had a sixth sense where I'd be. I've got goose bumps."

Ryan couldn't help it; he had to grin at her relentless optimism. "I was going to say it was totally random."

"Seems more like destiny to me."

That word again. He wasn't ready to claim a belief in destiny, but it seemed better than dwelling on how nervous he'd been to see her again.

Kristen, completely at ease with the situation, helped herself to a bite of his gingerbread. "So, is Ryan Michaels like a stage name? You use it professionally?"

Back to the rodeo, then. She was too trusting. He wished he deserved that trust.

"When we met, I only told you my name was Ryan. It was intentional. I didn't want everyone in town to know who I was."

"You said Michaels much later that night, on the church steps."

"I was talking about the three-year-old version of me. Ryan Michaels was my birth name. It changed when I was adopted."

"Oh, of course. I'm sorry, I didn't think of that."

"Don't apologize. Please."

He had to tell her his real name now. It was the obvious thing to say next, but he hesitated. How well did she know everyone in Rust Creek Falls? His sister and cousin lived there. Maggie Roarke, Lissa Roarke. If for some reason Kristen knew their maiden names, then the bandage would be ripped off whether he liked it or not.

If the fates were kind, Kristen would only know his relatives by their married names. Maggie Crawford. Lissa Christensen.

"So what's your real name?" she asked.

He wouldn't have been surprised if his voice cracked like an adolescent. Thankfully, it did not. "My name is Ryan Roarke."

He waited, dreading the next spark of recognition, the inevitable *are you related to...?*

"Roarke," she repeated. "I like it." Then she took a sip of her coffee.

Incredible. Wonderful. He'd dodged the bullet. She didn't know Maggie and Lissa's maiden names.

Thankfully, neither his sister nor cousin had any business on the Dalton's family ranch, and he doubted Kristen had ever needed legal help from Maggie Crawford or hung out in the sheriff's office where Lissa Christensen's photo might have been on the sheriff's desk. His cowgirl wasn't the type to track down everyone's backgrounds—not like the owner of this diner—and for that, he was grateful.

"Ryan Roarke. It's a little catchier than Ryan Michaels, with the two *R*'s. Do a lot of rodeo performers use stage names?"

"I have no idea. Roarke is my real name." He felt the flash of guilt, although he was telling the truth. He *didn't* know if rodeo stars used stage names, although it seemed likely some would.

"It certainly explains why I didn't find you when I typed 'Ryan Michaels rodeo' in my internet search." She put her head back on his shoulder, and Ryan closed his eyes in both guilt and relief.

If she assumed he was still a rodeo star, well…they were getting closer to the truth. Bit by bit. Slow and steady, so that nothing would abruptly shatter beyond repair.

In his mind's eye, he saw the snow globe hit the church steps.

He opened his eyes, took in the sight of Kristen curved against him, the soft leather of the booth's high-backed bench sheltering them both. Nothing harsh. Nothing hard.

Beyond their booth, outside the wide glass panes of the storefront window, snow started falling in slow, fluffy flakes. He had the fleeting thought that he was inside the snow globe.

He hugged Kristen to him tightly. He didn't want anything to break. Not this time.

"That coffee has got to be cold by now." The woman in the apron reappeared, holding her coffeepot above their cooled cups, poised for action if he'd just say the word. "You might as well have it warm."

Ryan curtly nodded his permission.

Too harsh. Too hard.

He mustered up a smile as she poured the hot coffee. "Thank you. Everything here is warm. It's a nice place."

"Well." She produced a fresh spoon from her apron pocket and set it in front of Kristen. "Well, you just stay here and enjoy. It's only going to get colder out there."

"Oh, man," Kristen said in a stage whisper. "Somebody's going to get extra whipped cream from now on."

"I heard you," Matilda said over her shoulder. "You and your old friend just remember that we make wedding cakes here, too."

Chapter Nine

Ryan took her to dinner.

Kristen took him home.

Impatient with the slow burn of sexual tension that had been building all day, Kristen led the way back to Rust Creek Falls in her compact SUV and parallel parked on the street of vintage houses. She waited on the sidewalk while Ryan pulled his rented truck into the next closest spot. Her mind was still processing the incredible fact that today was the day that Ryan Michaels had come back.

No, it was Roarke. Ryan Roarke had come back.

But while her heart and mind kept feeling surprised—*today!*—her body was already well beyond that acceptance phase. Every inch of her craved the intimacy which every smoldering look over a candlelit dinner in Kalispell had promised. They were adults who wanted each other, who'd wanted each other since a waltz in July, and the time had come.

Ryan kept his hands in the pockets of his overcoat as he walked up to her, looking sexy and self-contained. Kristen felt a little shiver of nervous awareness. She might be an adult, but six feet of confident, controlled male wasn't something she invited into her bedroom. Ever. Her past lovers, which numbered exactly two, might as well have never existed, for all that her experience with them had prepared her for a night with this man. Ryan Roarke was in a league of his own.

"Which house is yours?" The bass in his voice struck just the right, delicious note.

She wanted this. Him. Them. So she lifted her chin with a confidence she didn't quite possess and held up her phone, acting as if she weren't dying to get him in the door and naked on the floor. "I'll give you a clue. I told you Jonah was a fanatic about keeping all the original wood. He doesn't feel that way about the electrical wiring. He's completely in love with high tech in his buildings. Ready?"

She punched a code into her phone, and like magic, the second house from the corner lit up. A rainbow of multicolored Christmas lights delineated the elegant lines of its arched front porch. "Isn't it wonderful?"

Ryan shook his head in amusement. "It's not even Thanksgiving yet."

"Less than two weeks away. Come with me. I have to light up the best thing myself."

She slid her phone into her pocket as she led the way up the newly installed wood stairs. Just last week, she'd sealed them against the coming winter weather. Today's flurries were already gone, but she had the satisfaction of knowing the wood had been protected against them.

On the wide porch, Kristen plugged an extension cord into an outlet near the front door. "Ta-da!"

Ryan turned to look at her most treasured garage sale find: a molded plastic Santa that was four feet tall and lit up from the inside by an old-fashioned, sixty-watt light bulb.

"Isn't he great? He should be in the yard, but I'm keeping him on the porch to protect him from the elements. He's the real deal from 1968."

Ryan had gone very quiet beside her, hands still in his pockets.

"He needs a Mrs. Claus, of course. He's half of a pair—you know, the kind where Mr. and Mrs. Claus are leaning forward to kiss each other?"

Ryan stepped behind her, very close.

"It's going to be a challenge to find her, but I've got alerts set on eBay."

Ryan pulled up the bottom edge of her coat and set his hands on her hips, his fingertips grazing her middle as he held her firmly to him. The street was empty, but her winter coat would have made it hard for anyone to see exactly what he was doing.

"Until I find a vintage Mrs. Claus, Santa will just have to blow kisses to the people on the sidewalk, even though I don't have any neighbors yet. Oh, Lord, I'm babbling, aren't I?"

Ryan bent to kiss her neck, nudging her scarf out of the way with his chin, replacing the material's warmth with the warmth of his mouth as he tasted the soft skin under her jaw. As her knees turned to jelly, he slid one hand across her stomach, wrapping his arm around her waist for support.

"My keys," she said, sounding as breathy as a vintage movie star. "Let me just…" She patted her pocket, felt her phone, pulled out her house keys.

Ryan turned her in his arms and kissed her full-on, capturing her gasp in that zero-to-sixty escalation of passion that she didn't want to slow down. He moved them farther away from the row of colored lights, pressing her back against the door's deep framing as he kissed her senseless, or nearly senseless. She kept just enough brain power going to fit the key in the lock and turn it.

She fumbled for the antique iron doorknob but his hand covered hers, his breath hot against her lips, his body hard against hers. "I'm not coming in," he murmured between tastes of her.

"You're—*what*?"

"Not tonight. I'm not coming in." Then he kissed her, hungry, making love to her mouth the way she wanted his body to make love to hers.

"Come in," she gasped. "Now. Please."

With a sharp sound of frustration, he jerked her coat up a little farther. Cold air chased his hot hand as he slid from her belly to her lacy, thin bra. He cupped one whole breast, shaping her softness to the contours of his hand. She melted at his touch, sliding down the frame an inch, grasping with her free hand for an anchor until she clutched his coat's lapel for support.

She tried to say *yes, more, don't stop*, but only whimpered deep in her throat. He stopped caressing her, and they stayed locked in that embrace, not moving, not kissing, just breathing.

"This is a bad idea," he said, panting in a way that made Kristen feel incredibly desirable.

"This is a great idea." She pressed her head back against the framing so that she could look him in the eye. "This is...powerful."

He sharpened his gaze, losing a little of that sexual haze. She knew he remembered using that word when they'd kissed in the summer.

"So come into the house."

"What's between you and me is not going to disappear," he said. "It will be powerful tomorrow, and the day after that, and after that."

Darn the man for using her own summer words against her.

He withdrew his hand and tugged her coat down. He still had her crowded against the door, but she felt that he was creating a deliberate distance all the same.

"If this feeling isn't going to change, then why not tonight?" Her hand jerked his lapel with her plea, a tiny motion that betrayed her huge frustration. They were so, so close.

He kissed her pouting lower lip, soothing her. Placating her.

She didn't want that. She wanted him, so she let go of the doorknob to grab his other lapel and pulled him to her with both fists. Her kiss wasn't soothing. It went from zero to sixty for both of them.

"Because," he said, a long minute later.

It took her a second to realize he was answering her question.

"Not tonight, because you don't know me. Not well enough for this."

"That's crazy. You're all I've thought about for four

months. I didn't believe in love at first sight, until I met you."

After a long moment, Ryan bowed his head. He nodded, even as he turned from her and took a step away, putting real physical distance between them.

She'd put the word out there. *Love.*

Her heart thudded, hard.

"Until a few hours ago, that love at first sight was for a rodeo star named Ryan Michaels. That's not me." His voice sounded harsh. The look in his eyes was…hurt.

So, he must have left the rodeo, something that had been a huge part of his life. He was no longer a rodeo star, and it bothered him. She didn't know how to help a man leave a career behind. To make it worse, she'd called him by the wrong name today, a name that reminded him of the worst time of his life. That, at least, she could fix.

"Your last name doesn't change my feelings. Ryan Michaels grew into the man Ryan Roarke is. You've been you all along."

He looked at her across three feet of porch planking as if he were looking at a woman who was far out of his reach. "Trust me on this. You should know me better before we make love. I do mean make love, because as powerful and crazy as this is, it's real. It would gut me if we made love and you came to regret it."

But there is a chance you might.

The implication was clear. So was Ryan's expression, his stance. Everything about him as he warned her off seemed straightforward and sincere.

What could she learn about him that would possibly cause her to regret having slept with him? She didn't regret sleeping with her college sweetheart, even though the relationship hadn't lasted. Then there was Captain Two-Timer—

She regretted that one. Ryan was right; there were a few possibilities that would be showstoppers for her.

"Okay, then. In the interest of avoiding any future regret, can I ask you a few questions?"

"Yes."

"Are you married?"

Surprise flickered across his face. "No."

"Involved with another woman? Is there another woman in another small town who thinks you are coming back for her?"

"No. I'm not using you to cheat on anyone else. It goes without saying that I'd never cheat on you."

"It goes without saying." She still felt like a fool for not having realized the truth about her pilot sooner. "But it's still better to have that one laid out as a ground rule."

"It sounds like there's a man out there, somewhere, who'd be better off not crossing your path again. Or mine." He crossed the gap he'd put between them, and brushed a few loose strands of hair away from her cheek. His fingers were cool in the night air. "No other women. An easy promise, one I've been keeping since the day I met you."

She shivered at his touch and his words, and let her eyes close.

Kiss me, kiss me.

He put his hand back in his pocket. "Did you have any other questions?"

She opened her eyes, disappointed. What else could cause her to regret sleeping with Ryan Roarke, whom she'd dreamed about for months, who'd traveled the length of the country just to see her again? "Do you have a disease?"

"Fair question. No. Do you?"

"Oh, you mean…no, not those kind of diseases. I mean, I've got nothing, uh, contagious. That wasn't what I was asking—but we should be asking, of course, I just wasn't, and…" She could beg him to make love to her without blushing, but everything else seemed to make her cheeks burn.

She took a deeper breath. "I meant, are you dying of any disease? Am I going to regret making love to you when I find out you have an inoperable brain tumor or something? Not that I wouldn't still care for you, though. If our time is short, I'd want to make love to you all the more, really."

"I see." His lips twitched into that almost-curve. "Nothing that I know of."

"Don't laugh at me. It would be horrible. Those are my least favorite movies. You can't drag me into a theater to watch heartbreak like that."

She was glad to see his sense of humor returning, anyway, his expression relaxing into a smile, although he maintained his stiff posture, hands in his pockets. As his chuckle made his breath puff out in little white clouds, it occurred to her that he might be cold. They'd had some flurries today, and he was used to the weather in Southern California, not at the Canadian border.

"We could go inside to talk. It's pretty cold out here. I promise not to seduce you."

"I can't make the same promise. Every minute we talk makes you more appealing."

She wrinkled her nose. "What turned you on? The talk about diseases or my sorry history of being cheated on?"

"It was the way you made yourself blush, and the way your past experience makes me feel so protective of your heart."

Thud. The man could stop her heart with his words.

She threw up her hands in frustration. "You know, Ryan, if you're going to talk like that, you have to take me to bed."

He smiled a bit, but he had those sad eyes again. "Let's give it a little time. Are there any other showstoppers you'd like to ask before I admit that I'm freezing and say good-night?"

"Showstoppers. That's exactly the word I was thinking. We're so alike." She looked around at her Christmas lights and her plastic Santa. "I'm drawing a blank here. I can't imagine what you're afraid I'll find out about you. Unless…"

"Unless?"

"You don't have any sexual fetishes I should know about? You're not into, like, Roman orgy reenactments or anything?"

Ryan crossed his arms over his chest and leaned one shoulder against the wall. "I'm not that cold, after all. Let's discuss this. Roman orgies are out, then? What other sexual fetishes are off the table? Or on?"

Kristen crossed her arms over her chest and leaned against the wall, too. "Describe yours for me, and I'll decide."

She'd managed to keep a straight face, but Ryan just about doubled over with sudden laughter. She was laughing, too, when he kissed her softly, then stepped back before she could test his willpower with a more passionate kiss. "On that note, I better leave. I'm already not going to be able to sleep tonight."

"Will I see you tomorrow?"

"What's the earliest possible time I can pick you up?"

It was so lovely to be with a man who was as eager to see her as she was to see him. "Actually, I have to work tomorrow at the Circle D. I'll be there by six."

"In the morning?"

"Of course. Why don't you come? You could check out our horses. I've got one who's an absolute nightmare to get trailered. You must know tons of good tricks about transporting animals."

Ryan's smile faded.

"Or maybe that's a really dumb idea. I'm sorry, I forgot this is your vacation. You probably don't want to muck out a stall on vacation."

He rubbed his jaw, then nodded as if he'd come to a decision. "The Circle D is a part of who you are. I'd like to see it. I'll pick you up and we can drive to the ranch together."

"Actually, if we showed up in the same rig before sunrise, my family might jump to some conclusions about how we'd spent the night. I wouldn't mind doing the time if I'd done the crime, so to speak, but why don't you just meet me there? Anytime after six will be fine."

"All right. I'm looking forward to seeing a genuine cowgirl in her natural habitat."

"Whatever you say, cowboy."

Ryan's smile didn't touch those sad eyes as he left without risking another kiss.

A *cowboy*.

Ryan threw his coat on the log bed of his hotel room. Throwing a well-tailored length of blended wool was a completely unsatisfying outlet for his frustration. A

punching bag or a sparring session in the boxing ring
would be better. Instead, he had to prepare to spend tomorrow with a bunch of horses.

He didn't know squat about horses, but Kristen was
going to expect him to give her advice. She'd talked
about love at first sight tonight, but she'd meant love at
the first sight of a cowboy.

He was no horse whisperer, but his brother-in-law
was. Ryan called Jesse.

Maggie answered, of course. Being both a lawyer
and his sister, she was doubly direct.

"Did you straighten things out with Kristen?"

Ryan yanked off one boot. "I'm working on it, Maggie. Let me talk to Jesse."

"Working on it? You didn't tell her the truth?"

"We're getting there. She knows I live in Southern
California now. She knows my name is Roarke."

"Roarke the rodeo star? Or Roarke the attorney?"

"Let me talk to Jesse."

"You've got to tell her. The longer you let this go
on, the more hurt she's going to be when she finds out
the truth."

He yanked off the other boot. "I never told her I was
a rodeo star."

"But you're letting her believe it. She's going to hate
you for that when she finds out the truth."

She's going to hate you...

He couldn't stand the thought. He hated the very
words. God, he wanted only for her to love him.

"Ryan?"

He set the boot down carefully, lining it up neatly
beside the rough-hewn leg of the rustic chair.

"Ask Jesse to call me when he gets a chance." His

voice sounded calm. His hand was steady when he tapped the button to end the call.

She's going to hate you...

He dropped his head in his hands and gave in to the shudder that racked his body.

Tonight, she'd said she loved him—or, at least, that she believed it was possible to have fallen in love with him at first sight. She didn't seem to resent him for being gone for months, and so far, she wasn't upset that at least two of her assumptions about him had been wrong. A name and a home state, those she could forgive—because she loved him?

Love should be unchangeable. He should be able to tell Kristen everything: Ryan Michaels, Ryan Roarke, cowboy, attorney. None of it should matter, but he had an old Christmas memory that proved otherwise.

Love was not unconditional, no matter what fairy tales others believed. A mother could decide she didn't love a little boy anymore. Nothing good lasted forever. He had to be careful with Kristen, and handle the possibility that she loved him with care.

He had a good plan. Kristen had pieced together one picture of him, and he was going to replace the wrong pieces, one at a time. Some day, Kristen might think his skills in a courtroom were impressive, but tomorrow, he'd be in a stable. He didn't want to look like an ass. When the phone rang, he knew what he had to do.

"Jesse. I've got a hypothetical situation for you. It's six in the morning, and you walk into a stable full of horses. What's the first thing you do?"

Chapter Ten

Ryan entered the stables with trepidation.

His brother-in-law had said the first thing he did was walk the entire length of the barn, once through. "You can get a feel right away if the horses as a group are calm. Then I look for any one horse who seems out of sorts."

According to Jesse, every barn had its own feed and care routine, so Ryan should follow Kristen's lead and respect the routine of the Circle D—as if Ryan might have a different routine in mind.

"You don't need special training to dump feed into a bucket or skim loose hay out of a water trough," Jesse had said.

"If she asks me to do anything more complex than that, what's your advice for a man who last touched a horse at eighth-grade summer camp?"

Jesse had laughed. "Generally speaking, horses are

patient creatures. They'll put up with a lot when they know you're trying."

"Generally speaking?"

"Good luck."

Ryan's first step into the barn startled a cat that bolted across his path and headed up a pile of hay bales to the safety of the rafters.

"I know how you feel," Ryan said under his breath. He wished he could dodge potential danger as effectively, but helping Kristen with her morning chores was a minefield he had to negotiate. He'd considered changing their plans. He could pick her up once she'd returned to her house and take her out for a nice lunch. Dinner and a movie. But he couldn't sleep in the plush bedding at Maverick Manor knowing Kristen was working hard in the cold November dawn. It offended some sense of chivalry or manhood deep down, concepts that were probably outdated, but he felt them nonetheless.

His first sight of Kristen Dalton in her natural element forced him to be more honest with himself. She looked like his most cherished Montana fantasy come true. This wasn't about helping a damsel in distress; this was about spending every possible moment with this woman, period. Full stop. If Kristen wanted to be with him, he wanted to be with her, wherever, whenever and doing whatever.

Her back was to him as she hung a pitchfork on a wall hook. Despite the barn's temperature being nearly the same as outside, Kristen wore only a faded pink sweatshirt and blue jeans. Her glorious hair, something that could easily become a fetish of his, hung in one long braid down her back, bouncing with each step as she pushed a wheelbarrow away from him, heading for the open door at the opposite end of the barn.

"Just cool your jets, tough guy. I'll get to you in a minute."

Ryan stopped in surprise, until a black horse stuck its head out of the stall she'd just passed and snorted at her, shaking its mane impatiently. Kristen continued out the wide door without stopping.

Ryan slowly walked down the center aisle of the barn, absorbing the feel of the place. It was spacious and organized, and smelled equally of animals and hay. Most of the stalls were empty, so he assumed they normally held the horses that he'd seen milling about in a fenced-in grassy area adjacent to the barn. As Ryan reached the door through which Kristen had taken her wheelbarrow, the black horse and three others stuck their massive heads over their half doors and looked at him with knowing, dark eyes.

He wondered if he should have brought carrots or some other bribe. He held his palm up to the brown beauty closest to him. "Sorry, I've got nothing."

The horse snuffled his palm, anyway. He petted its nose, the softness as surprising now as it had been in eighth grade. Ryan moved to the next stall and repeated the greeting with the next horse. He could see what Jesse had meant about being able to get a feel for the horses' attitude. Ryan could tell these animals were content and cared for. It didn't take a lifetime of ranch experience to recognize good health and a friendly disposition.

The black horse across the aisle bit at his door's latch and bobbed his head in a demanding way. The name plate over his stall identified him as Zorro. "Everyone's patient except you, son. You need to work on your attitude. You heard Kristen. Don't rush the woman."

"That's right, Zorro. I hope you're paying attention." Kristen's voice had a laugh in it. She let go of her empty wheelbarrow and came toward Ryan with her arms open for a hug, but she stopped short. "You look too nice. I'll get you all dirty."

Ryan took the final step toward her and scooped her against him. "You look fantastic."

"Oh, yes. Like a mucker of stalls."

"The braid and boots thing is definitely working for me." He lingered for a few dangerous seconds longer than he should have as he kissed the happy curve of her mouth, and set her down again.

"If braids and boots are your fetish, you'll be in heaven here in Rust Creek Falls. Put it in your plus column."

He couldn't resist touching the fine bones of her face, trailing his fingers over her cheekbone and along her jawline. Such delicate features for a woman as strong as she was. "The braid and boots only turn me on when your pretty face is part of the package."

Her gaze flickered over his shoulder. "I told you that you'd be in heaven. There are two women in Rust Creek Falls who meet your criteria."

Ryan turned to see a duplicate of Kristen walking toward them. It was disconcerting for a second, like seeing a special effect from a movie, although he'd known she had an identical twin. On the Fourth of July, they'd passed her sister a few times on the dance floor, but there'd been clear differences in their clothing and hair and the way they moved. Now, in jeans and boots and the braid he supposed was practical for working in a barn, they were startlingly identical.

"You must be Kayla," he said, extending his hand.

She dropped her gaze but took his hand, then looked up at him again with a shy duck of her chin. She was so unlike Kristen in her actions Ryan doubted he'd ever be fooled for more than a second.

"And you must be Ryan Michaels." Her voice was quiet in the cavernous barn.

Kristen jumped in. "It's Ryan Roarke, actually. My mistake. That's why I couldn't find him in any rodeo results."

"Roarke?" Kayla looked at him more directly. "Are you related to Lissa Roarke, then?"

Ryan released her hand, but not before she must have felt his little jolt of surprise. She knew maiden names, obviously. This was an unexpected mine that needed to be carefully defused.

"Lissa who?" Kristen asked.

"Lissa Christensen," her sister explained patiently. "The sheriff's wife. She was Lissa Roarke when she came here from New York and wrote that blog about the flood, remember?"

"Oh." Kristen turned to him and made a little gesture toward her sister. "If it has to do with writing or newspapers, she's into it. English major."

Ryan smiled, ignoring his racing heart. "Lissa is my cousin. She grew up in New York, though, while I was in..."

"California," Kristen finished for him, and she turned to her sister. "He's from California."

Ryan knew instinctively that Kristen was anxious to prove that she knew him well, although she hadn't made the connection with Lissa.

"Is that why you were here for the Fourth of July, then?" Kristen asked, phrasing her question like her sister. "You were visiting Lissa? That makes so much sense."

"Lissa was in New York because Gage was on duty for the whole holiday weekend." Ryan hadn't lied about his intention that day in the park, and he wasn't going to start now. "I came to look into relocating to Rust Creek Falls, remember?"

Kristen's expression brightened. "But now I know how you heard of Rust Creek Falls in the first place. A cousin has to go in the plus column. Being far from your parents is a bigger minus, but at least you'll have some family in town."

She was still so certain that the plus column would win. Whether or not Lissa lived in town didn't change the fact that the full responsibility for Roarke and Associates was being laid on his shoulders by his parents' impending retirement. Once he explained the situation fully, he hoped Kristen would understand. The dream he'd toyed with in July about living here couldn't become a reality. They'd have to be a long-distance couple, or she'd have to move to LA.

The black horse chose that moment to remind them all that he was not where he wanted to be.

"Okay, Zorro. Chill out. Let me check your feet before I turn you out." With efficient movements and a grace that Ryan was certain could only come from a lifetime of working with horses, Kristen put a halter on the black horse and led him out of his stall, then tied him to a railing in the aisle with some kind of knot that Ryan had probably failed at tying back in his scouting days. She grabbed a small tool from a bucket that hung on the wall, and crouched down to lift the massive animal's front hoof. With a series of soothing "good boys," she started working on Zorro's hoof.

Kayla picked up the handles of the wheelbarrow. "I'll be mucking stalls if you need me."

"I'll help." Ryan was confident he could master a pitchfork faster than the two-step, and he'd mastered that in less than one verse of a country-western song.

"You'll ruin your clothes," Kayla said. "That overcoat is just too nice for chores."

"It's all I brought on this trip. It can be cleaned."

Kristen looked up from her crouch on the floor. "Just put on another coat. I think Eli left that one here." She pointed with her pick to a beige canvas coat that hung on a wall with a cluster of leather straps and ropes.

Ryan hung his long overcoat in its place. The battered canvas coat was the same temperature as the crisp November air that filled the barn from the open doors. He'd barely shrugged into it when gentle Kayla took another tool out of the bucket and lobbed it not so gently at Ryan. He caught it by the wood handle, thankfully, because the rest of it looked like a loop made from a metal saw.

"Zorro has sensitive feet. If you brush him at the same time, he won't be so fussy for Kristen." She took the wheelbarrow and headed down the aisle to an empty stall.

Ryan thought the tool in his hand looked more likely to torture than soothe. He walked up to the horse, struck anew at just how large the beast was. He scraped the teeth of the metal loop lightly along Zorro's side. The horse didn't object, so he did it again, a little more firmly.

Kristen moved to the other front hoof, so Ryan kept running the brush along the horse, resting his free hand on the horse's neck as he worked, appreciating the heat and power contained in the muscles under the black coat. Although Zorro's hair had seemed to be too short to be brushed, the shades of black varied after each stroke as the nap of the hair reflected light at a new angle. Ryan kept the brush moving in a methodical pattern over the black gloss.

"I can see why he finds this soothing." Immediately, Ryan realized he'd said something that revealed this was a new experience for him. *Too soon, don't shatter*— but he couldn't cover the mistake without lying, and he couldn't lie to Kristen.

"Zorro's one of those that really love it. Of course, Snoopy over there really hates it. You know how it is. What works with one horse has the opposite effect on another." She moved to another hoof. "Good boy. You boys like to keep us guessing, don't you, Zorro?"

Ryan relaxed again. The sky outside the double doors began to lighten with the coming dawn. Incredibly, despite his blunder, Kristen assumed he knew horses. Then again, growing up on a ranch in Montana, maybe a person who *didn't* know horses was as foreign to her as an alien from a UFO.

He chose his words with care. "Kristen, I never told you I was in the rodeo. What makes you think I am?"

She stood up, finished with that hoof, and looked at him over Zorro's back. She rested her arm on the horse as she talked, like one would lean on a piece of furniture. She was completely comfortable around an animal that weighed one thousand pounds. Her unconscious confidence was sexy.

"Every once in a while, someone at the picnic would recognize you. I knew right away that you couldn't be just another hand making the rounds of the ranches, looking for work. You carry yourself like you are used to being in charge. Besides, and please don't think I'm materialistic or anything, you don't dress like the average ranch hand. You must be doing something that's a little more lucrative than a standard cowboy paycheck. I put two and two together."

She disappeared again, crouching down to pick up the last hoof.

Ryan kept brushing. It had been that simple, then. For a woman who only knew cowboys, there was only one kind of cowboy who would get recognized at the town picnic.

"Have you ever *not* dated a cowboy?"

The scraping sounds stopped for a moment.

"Once."

The scraping started again.

"He was from the city."

She said the word *city* like it was a curse. She referred to Kalispell as a city, with its population of how many? Twenty thousand? Los Angeles was a city of fifteen or sixteen million. If she thought a place like Kalispell was too big, she'd hate Ryan Roarke's reality.

"He was based in Denver."

A bigger city, then, but still small compared to Ryan's.

"A pilot."

The bitterness in that simple word snapped his attention from his own sorry worries back to Kristen. Bitterness was rare from her, but he'd heard it once before, during last night's conversation on the porch. Her one experience with a non-cowboy had been a bad one.

Ryan worked his way around to her side of the horse, brushing as he went, staying calm. "This was the guy who didn't understand that some things go without saying."

In her crouched position, her head was bowed, and her hands went still. "He was in the shower, getting ready to go back to work after his layover. His phone was right next to me on the nightstand. The screen lit up that he'd gotten a text, with a little preview of the message. There was this tiny thumbnail photo of a topless girl, and the first line said, See you at five. The current time was in big numbers, 10:16. That will be stuck in my brain for a long time."

Zorro threw his head up, objecting to the stroke of the brush. Ryan stopped until the first wave of jealousy and anger passed, then he crouched down next to Kristen.

"I told him off, of course," she said. "He put on his uniform and left me in the hotel. Seven hours after we'd been in bed together, I knew he was back in Denver, having sex with her. Breaking up with me didn't hurt him for half a day. I'm sure I was just some dumb cowgirl from Montana to him. Another variety to add to his menu."

Ryan kept his fury at the unknown pilot under control, mindful of his tone of voice around the horse. "I know that type. He'll never be faithful to anyone, ever, and it doesn't matter how wonderful the woman is."

It was rare for Kristen not to look him in the eye, but she toyed with the pick in her hand for a moment, then ran her hand down Zorro's leg, soothing the horse to soothe herself.

"Believe me, Kristen. It wasn't that you weren't a good enough girlfriend. The fault is all his."

She nodded. "I get that. I do. It's just that I'm ashamed of myself for believing his lies. I should have been able to see through them. I saw him every other week, and never questioned what he did or who he did it with between those times. He looked me right in the eye and lied to me, over and over, trip after trip."

She's going to hate you when she finds out the truth.

He couldn't tell her about himself today. He couldn't risk it. At that moment, he wanted, more than anything else in the world, to be a cowboy for Kristen, so she'd never doubt her own judgment again.

"I made a promise to myself," she said. "No more city slickers. I wished for a cowboy, and now here you are."

With regret, with tenderness, Ryan kissed her cheek. He hadn't lied, but he hadn't told her the complete truth. He stayed crouched beside her, wanting to tell her something true. "It goes without saying, I am with you and only you."

"I know. Cowboys get it."

"No. *I* get it. It's got nothing to do with cowboys, and everything to do with you. Because you're such an amazing person, there's no room in my head or my heart for another woman."

The wheelbarrow came to a halt beside them. Kayla crouched down. "What is it? Does Zorro have a cracked hoof again?"

Kristen barely glanced at her sister, but apparently, the look was enough between identical twins.

"Never mind." Kayla stood and pushed the wheelbarrow away.

Ryan stood and resumed his brushing, hoping the motion would help him center himself and bring back that calm feeling.

It didn't. It couldn't, because he hadn't clarified anything with Kristen except his desire for her, and she had to have known that already.

Kristen finished with whatever she'd been doing to the horse's feet and started loving on the horse, petting his nose and telling him sweet nothings. "You are being spoiled today, aren't you? Don't get any ideas about leaving me for Ryan. You can't run off to join the rodeo with him. No fame and fortune for you."

"Kristen."

He couldn't do this. He couldn't let her go on believing he was a rodeo star.

Don't risk it. Don't let it shatter.

He couldn't rip the bandage off, but he had to make one point perfectly clear. "My name won't ever be in your newspaper for winning a rodeo event. There will be no tour and no fame and glory. If that's what you're looking for in a relationship, I can't offer it to you."

She left the horse's side to walk up to him in that unhurried way ranchers seemed to move, but he didn't reach for her, nor she for him. They stood in the open door of the barn, the sunrise coloring the sky beyond them, the cold air between them.

"I didn't ask you to." Her blue-eyed gaze was unwavering. "It sounds like you haven't had a great love life in the past, either. Instead of a two-timing pilot, I'm guessing there's a woman who was more interested in getting close to fame than in getting close to you. Probably a lot of women over the years."

Every relationship. Some very intelligent women, some very talented, all of them beautiful and all of them, every single one, hoping to improve her Hollywood clout and connections. The up-and-coming actresses, the aging actresses, the models who wanted to be actresses. The pressure was constant in Hollywood; the game of who knew whom was crucial to landing parts. He didn't blame them, but he was weary. Kristen's complete lack of interest in Hollywood added to her small-town appeal.

"It's a career hazard. I've dated women like that too often."

"Was this what you were afraid I'd regret? That I would be sorry I'd slept with you if you weren't going to be on the rodeo tour next season? Because that would be insulting to me, and it would hurt to think you knew me so little. I realize you're used to women who want to travel with a celebrity, but I'm not that kind of woman."

"I know you're not." She was fresh-faced, makeup free, a naturally beautiful woman against the backdrop of a beautiful part of the country. Her braid had fallen forward and was lying over one breast. He wanted her fiercely. "You are too much a part of this ranch and this town to want to waste your life on the road."

"Well, that sounds nicer than saying I'm a homebody, I guess." Her smile was as irrepressible as the growing sunrise. Ryan wanted to hold her close and feel that warmth.

Reading his mind, she stepped into his willing arms and laid her head on his shoulder. He caught her close and kissed her hair, the corner of her eye, the bridge of her nose. She relaxed under his touch, the change in her muscle tension as obvious as Zorro's had been.

"I'm so glad you're here. After this week, will you be gone long?"

"I'm spending Thanksgiving with my parents. After that…"

He didn't know. He hadn't thought beyond this week, beyond satisfying that burning need he'd had to see Kristen once more, just once more. Standing in this barn, the differences in their lives were more obvious to him than ever.

So was his need to be with her. One week with her would not be enough.

"It may be a while, but…" He shook his head at his own idiocy. He wasn't kidding anyone, least of all himself. "I don't think I can go without you very long. I'll come back."

"I knew that last July." She shushed the impatient Zorro, then turned her sunny smile on Ryan once more. "But it's nice that you know it now, too. Four months was a long time for you to realize you should come back to the place you said makes you feel at peace. I hated knowing you were out there somewhere, not at peace."

"Montana doesn't give me peace. You do."

The sound of a very loud, very human yawn startled them both. Kayla was behind them, stretching her arms overhead as she sat on an overturned barrel. "I hate to bother you two, but if we could turn out these last four horses and clean the stalls…" She yawned again.

Kristen frowned a little. "Another late night? You've been tired a lot lately."

"I'm fine. I'm just trying to live without coffee."

Kristen looked horrified. "No coffee? Why would you do that?"

Kayla ducked her head, shy once more. "Caffeine is supposed to be bad for you. I read this blog that made me want to try going without it. Just for a little while."

"Sis, I love you, but that's nuts. Maybe you should get some breakfast. Ryan's here. He'll help me finish up."

Kayla left after a few more protests. Kristen picked up a pitchfork and sifted through the hay in Zorro's empty stall, coming up with a clump of manure and tossing it into the wheelbarrow. "Why don't you turn out the rest of the horses while I get started on the dirty work?"

Ryan took one look at the ropes and knots and bridles hanging on the wall and took the pitchfork out of Kristen's hands. "I'm sure your horses would rather say good morning to you." He was also certain he'd make a fool of himself trying to put a bridle on a horse for the first time. A pitchfork took no skill, only muscle, and that, thankfully, he had.

Kristen slipped a leather bridle around the brown horse's head, reaching up to guide its ears under a strap, all while keeping her gaze on Ryan. "We can get breakfast afterward."

Ryan stopped in midscoop. Here was another obstacle he hadn't planned on negotiating. If he met her parents, there would be the inevitable getting-to-know-you questions. He tossed the manure into the wheelbarrow. "I hadn't planned on meeting your parents this morning."

Before he could add an acceptable excuse, Kristen jumped in. "Oh, I didn't mean breakfast at the house.

It was too late last night to call and tell them you'd be here this morning. I know my mom. She'd kill me if I walked into the kitchen with you while she was in her bathrobe."

Kristen led Zorro and the brown horse around the wheelbarrow, stopping in front of him and tossing her braid back over her shoulder with a graceful movement of her head and shoulder. "My house in town is always an option."

Her hands were full and so were his, but their mouths met with a hunger that had nothing to do with breakfast.

"Wow. You weren't kidding about the braids and boots, were you?"

"Your house is not a safe option." He stepped back. "How about that donut shop from our tour?"

"Bear claws and coffee. Sounds perfect."

"Go Grizzlies."

"Spoken like a true Rust Creek Falls native."

He had no answer for that, either, as Kristen led the two horses out of the barn.

He wasn't a native, and no matter how content he felt in Montana, he couldn't leave his parents and their practice. It was clear that Kristen belonged here with her family just as strongly. He couldn't pull this sweet cowgirl out of Montana, and he couldn't hide from his responsibilities in California, either.

He jabbed the pitchfork into the hay. He'd be lucky to get away from work one weekend every few months. Her two-timing pilot had been able to spend more time with her than Ryan could. How long would he and Kristen keep these tender emotions and this burning attraction going? Through how many lonely months of separation between the occasional three-day weekend?

He dumped more waste into the wheelbarrow.

Nothing good lasted forever.

It couldn't be done.

Ryan stared at his laptop in defeat. The firm's calendar was no more flexible than a judge's gavel. There was no way Ryan could squeeze in a return visit to Montana between Thanksgiving and Christmas. When he left Kristen at the end of the week, he'd be leaving her until February, at the very earliest.

I'm in love with you, Kristen. I'll miss Thanksgiving, Christmas and New Year's, but I can make it back by Groundhog Day, and Memorial Day three months after that. Is that the relationship with a cowboy you've always dreamed of?

His reality sucked. He needed to tell her all of it, before someone else burst their private bubble. If he kept taking Kristen on dates in Rust Creek Falls, it was inevitable they'd run into Brad Crawford or Lissa or, God forbid, Maggie.

Disaster had been narrowly avoided this morning. After they'd mucked the last stalls and washed up, they'd headed for the donut shop. As Ryan had rounded the corner in his rented rig, the local term for any kind of vehicle, the sheriff's rig had been parked squarely in front of the donut shop. There was no way Lissa's husband, Sheriff Gage Christensen, wouldn't have sat with them. There was no way he wouldn't have asked Ryan how LA was treating him, and God knew what else. But the sheriff's truck had pulled out of its parking space just as they were pulling in, and Ryan had dodged yet another bullet.

After breakfast, he'd had the inspired idea to order sandwiches to go. A picnic at the actual waterfall that Rust Creek Falls had been named after had given him time alone with Kristen. He hadn't had to fear being unmasked at any moment by a friendly townsperson who might remember him from the flood cleanup. They'd seen no other humans on their afternoon hike. No grizzlies, either, and the placid but alarmingly large moose they'd spotted had been completely uninterested in meeting the new guy in town.

There'd been no dinner date.

Alone with his laptop was not how he'd hoped to end the night, but Kristen was at her mystery job in Kalispell. She'd given him one clue. Her job would help her become outrageously overqualified in the high school principal's eyes. Ryan had pretended not to guess the obvious, that she was teaching a night course.

He loved Kristen's determination. She'd win that teaching job sooner or later. Kristen as a cowgirl, home renovator and schoolteacher was an adorable combination. Kristen was perfect as she was, where she was. He couldn't ruin her life with his selfish desire to have her waiting for him in his beachfront high-rise at the end of his fourteen-hour days.

Sometimes the pursuit of happiness ended in a dead end.

It didn't have to end immediately, at least. Once she knew who he was and the limits of what he could offer, she might choose to be his long-distance lover. It couldn't last forever, but a few months of anticipating insanely heavenly weekends was as good as his life was going to get.

But if she said no when she found out how little he really had to offer her, he wouldn't be able to stop her walking away sooner rather than later.

One thing was inescapable: sooner or later, it was going to hurt like hell.

Chapter Eleven

"We never did go horseback riding yesterday. He wanted to go back out to the falls again. He thinks our falls are as pretty as Glacier National Park."

"Which you went to on Tuesday?"

"Right."

Kristen whispered the details of her week to her sister as they stood in the wings of the theater. Tonight was the final dress rehearsal, which meant she had to press down the hoop skirts of her blue Victorian gown to get close enough to her sister to whisper.

"And?" Kayla whispered. "Are you sleeping with him?"

"It was rated R, not X. But it was romantic, just the two of us." Kristen wriggled a little with the happiness of the memory. The motion added to her joy, because it was fun to make her skirt sway side to side.

"It's been just the two of you all the time. Awfully

private." Kayla was wearing regular clothes, all black from head to toe, the standard uniform of a stagehand. She had volunteered to serve as the prop master for half of the schedule.

"We don't always go off alone. You went to lunch with us today."

Ryan had driven her to Kalispell for buffalo burgers and sinful fries. It had been his suggestion to invite Kayla. Kristen had sworn Kayla to secrecy, though. She couldn't tell Ryan about tonight's dress rehearsal, only that she'd give Kristen a ride home after work.

"I want him all to myself. Kayla, I'm so happy when I'm with him. If he asked me to marry him today, I'd say yes."

"Silence on stage," the director called from his seat in the third row.

Kristen tried not to giggle like a disobedient child. She looked at Kayla, her partner in the crime of whispering, but Kayla was absentmindedly trailing her fingers over a bit of the black velvet trim on Kristen's gown, looking so sad that Kristen immediately felt sad, too. What had she said to put that look on her sister's face?

Marriage. It dawned on Kristen that she'd been taking giant steps since this summer, moving out, finding work, expanding her horizons. Most of all, falling in love. Maybe Kayla was feeling excluded.

Before Kristen could give her sister a squeeze and whisper that she shouldn't worry, that nothing could change the bond they shared as identical twins, Kayla yawned. She looked so tired. Come to think of it, she'd been sort of sad and tired for a while now, long before Ryan came back to town.

Without thinking further, Kristen put her hand on her sister's forehead.

"What are you doing?" Kayla whispered, jerking away in surprise.

"Do you feel okay? You seem kind of down."

"I'm fine."

"Maybe we should get you a chair."

"Really, I'm fine. I'm just a little…"

"A little what?"

Kayla squared her shoulders, and pulled Kristen deeper into the wings. "I'm worried about you. Everything seems pretty sudden with Ryan."

"I've known him for months."

"You've known *of* him for months, but you've really only known him for days. Are you sure you're in love with Ryan Roarke, or are you in love with the idea that this cowboy has come to town who fits your image of the perfect man?"

Suddenly, Kristen felt like she was the one who needed the chair. Hearing Kayla whisper doubts after she'd finally met Ryan was a horrible turn of events. She wanted her sister to say Ryan was wonderful. She wanted her sister to say that, having met him, she understood now why Kristen had kept such faith in him for all these months.

"Don't look like that," Kayla whispered. "I just want you to be sure you're paying attention to the real man, not the idea of being in love with a man. I don't want you to be hurt again."

Understanding dawned. "He's nothing like that stupid pilot. Ryan's like us. He worked with us in the stables twice this week. Didn't you think he loved all our twin stories over lunch today? He understands loyalty, and family, and—and love." But she hesitated over the last word, because Ryan hadn't said he loved her.

Really, she hadn't said she loved him, either. They hadn't talked about their future as a couple, only that he loved being with her and would come back as soon as he could. Maybe Kayla was right. Maybe she hadn't been paying enough attention to the real man.

The theater was plunged into darkness, her cue to take her place center stage before the lights went up on her big scene. It was time for Belle to make things perfectly clear with Ebenezer. Then she'd walk away and leave him alone in a spotlight as artificial snow began to fall.

Kristen picked up her fur muff and hurried to her mark. Belle needed to have a lot of courage to be so frank with Ebenezer about their relationship.

A little shiver ran down Kristen's back.

It's just a touch of stage fright.

But it wasn't. She couldn't stay in her happy fog much longer. She needed some of Belle's courage to ask Ryan exactly where their relationship stood. Tomorrow.

Kristen took her spot and waited for the curtain to rise. There was nothing to fear. She knew her part and she trusted her crew.

She had nothing to fear tomorrow, either. Ryan was no Ebenezer. Ryan would never place his career before her. In real life, she wouldn't be walking out of the spotlight and into his past.

"Oh, my gosh. It's my Mrs. Claus."

Kristen squeezed Ryan's hand in excitement, pulling him to a stop in front of the thrift shop. They'd had lunch in Kalispell again, and were window-shopping in the quaint part of town, the part that included Depot Park and the theater. Tonight was opening night. So thrilling—but so was finding Mrs. Claus.

"Do you think she's the right size? I don't think she's four feet. She might be the three-foot version. They made that in 1970. I've got the 1968 Santa. He's bigger."

"Maybe your Santa likes his women petite. I do."

Kristen bumped him with her shoulder, and he smiled his not-quite-a-smile.

Pay attention to the real man.

Her sister's words had been haunting Kristen all day. She looked at Ryan more closely as they stood outside the window. Its entire display was of Santas. Large ones, small ones, ugly atrocities from dime stores, all were mixed in with porcelain antiques. It was a dizzying array of red suits and white beards, but Ryan had already turned his back on it. That half smile said it all: he wasn't comfortable.

"Do dolls creep you out?" Kristen had gone to college with a girl who had a genuine phobia about dolls. To this day, Kristen felt bad about teasing her before she'd realized just how real the girl's aversion had been.

"Dolls?" Ryan looked at her with that brow raised in surprise. "Hardly. Did you want to watch a horror movie tonight or something?"

It was her turn to laugh uncomfortably. "No, I've got something else planned." His ticket to tonight's show was burning a hole in her pocket. She pointed at the store window, stretching the blue crochet of her mitten with her index finger. "So, it's Santa Claus, then. You don't care for Santa?"

He was about to say no, she knew it, but then he shook his head and looked at her like she was an unusual creature of some sort. "You really pick up on the strangest things. You're right. I don't care for Santa. I'm not a big fan of Christmas in general."

She remembered his words from the summer. "You said once if anyone could make Christmas better, it would be me."

"The decorations definitely look better when you're in front of them." His words were light and teasing, but Kristen knew she wasn't imagining the guarded look in his eyes.

"I thought you meant I'd make a good thing better, but you meant make a bad thing tolerable, didn't you?" She should have been paying attention. Tonight's play had scene after scene that included carolers and Christmas trees. "Just how averse are you to Christmas?"

Ryan turned to look at the street, with its red bells and green garland stretched between stores and giant candy canes tied to every pole. Then he looked back to the window full of Santas. "Most of this is fine. I hadn't really made the distinction, but you're right. It's Santa that particularly bothers me."

His attention was all on her. For once, it made her uncomfortable.

She tried for a nonchalant shrug.

"I don't believe in aggravating old injuries. You told me once about the church steps, and I think it's smart to just avoid them. There's a side entrance to the church, so why stand on the steps when you don't have to?"

Why go to a Christmas play when you don't have to?

She wouldn't give him the ticket. It was so disappointing, but really, she wouldn't make him do something unpleasant for the sake of her pride. She'd wanted him to see her onstage, but he'd love her just the same if he avoided a play that made him cringe.

He hasn't said he loves you. Pay attention.

Fine. Then he'd care for her just the same whether he saw her onstage or not.

She loved him, though, and she was concerned for his comfort. "Avoiding church steps or whatever else is unpleasant is simple enough, but avoiding Santa Claus... I don't think it's possible. December must be torture for you."

The sting of tears caught her by surprise. Disappointment, concern, love for a man who was leaving two days from now, her uncertain future—all of it added up. She puffed out a little breath and blinked back the tears quickly.

Not quickly enough. Ryan pulled her protectively into the alcove by the window. "Is that a showstopper? I didn't think that would make a woman consider walking away." The stiffness with which he asked the question was a sure sign that this was not a passing curiosity. This question mattered.

A woman walking away. Pay attention.

"What if you have children someday? Would you raise them without Santa?"

He was silent for an eternity.

She felt awful, keeping him by this window full of Santas. "We can keep walking. We don't even have to talk about this."

To her surprise, he enveloped her in a hug. "It's okay. I've never dated a woman who made me think about having children."

She hugged him back, grateful once more that he was leaving the rodeo forever. It sounded like a rotten life.

He let go of her and cleared his throat a little, a man prepared to make a formal statement. "I think children deserve to believe in the magic of it all."

Kristen let out the breath she'd been holding. If she'd had time to think up a right answer, that would have been it.

"I'd handle it." To her relief, Ryan winked at her. "You'll notice I'm standing in front of this window without going crazy at the moment. I didn't run screaming from the Santa on your porch. I'm a grown man, I can control my feelings. If I was with a child who wanted to sit in Santa's lap, I could stand in that line at the mall for as long as it took. Does that answer your question?"

She smiled and nodded and pretended she wasn't choked up by those tears once more. Poor Ryan. Her Ryan. The one she was paying attention to.

She started walking toward Depot Park and her theater. Ryan fell in step beside her, and she reached out to hold his hand, blue mitten to his black leather driving glove. Only one event in his childhood could have given him such an aversion to Christmas. "Did you see Santa before or after your birth mother walked away?"

He whistled softly. "Has anyone ever suggested the law to you as a career? You're so fearless in your questioning. I can just see you with a witness on the stand."

That surprised her, in a good way. She swung their hands a little bit. "I like that image. It makes me sound tough. Much more flattering than what my brothers would say. They say I'm like a bull in a china shop, always jumping in without thinking."

"No, it's an insightful question. Childhood memories are tricky, though."

"You were three, right? I'm trying to come up with a memory from when I was three. I don't think I have any."

"I was almost four, but I still only remember a couple of moments."

They'd come to an intersection with a traffic signal. Ryan pushed the button, and out of habit, Kristen shifted from foot to foot to stay warm while they waited for the signal to walk. She'd been doing that since she was a little girl.

"When I was three, my sister and I were taken to a preschool here in Kalispell once a week while my mother did the big shopping. I really only know that because my mom has pointed out the preschool to me and told me about it."

"The big shopping?"

"You know, the weekly grocery stock-up. My brothers went through boxes of cereal, so she bought them by the gross."

The light turned green, and they continued walking hand in hand, like grown-ups.

"Anyway, I suspect the preschool was a way for her to get her shopping done without hauling around two three-year-olds, but she insists that it was to improve our social skills. If you think about it, it would be easy for twins on a ranch to grow up without ever seeing other children their age. I don't remember the preschool at all, or at least I thought I didn't, but I remember this toy kitchen. It was made of wood, but it had a stove and sink, and the knobs were blue. I asked my mom once what happened to it, who had we given it away to, and she said we never had a toy kitchen. It had been at this preschool."

She slowed her steps, concentrating on that memory, and Ryan slowed down with her.

"That's it. I can't remember the classroom or any of the other kids or what the teacher looked like. I remember blue kitchen knobs. Isn't that weird?"

"I'm told that's normal. Below a certain age, you might remember something like the candles on a birthday cake, but you wouldn't remember the whole day, like who was at the party or what gifts you got. Just an image of a flaming cake."

"You were told that?"

"Part of the adoption process included counseling for my parents as well as me. I don't remember that, either, but to this day, my parents recommend it to other adopting parents. When I was old enough to ask questions, they always seemed to know what to expect. I asked about the church steps when I was in middle school. Before that, they weren't sure I had any memory of my birth mother at all."

His adoptive parents must have cared about their new son very much to have prepared themselves to answer all his questions in the future. She'd like to meet them some day.

"Is that all you remember? Church steps and the backs of her legs and the hem of her skirt?"

"It's like one of those six-second videos that you see on the internet. I'm looking down at my shoes, and I'm standing on cement steps. I know it's a church, and it's some kind of Christmas festival, because I'm holding a snow globe. It's brand-new to me, like I've just gotten this snow globe, and my shoes hurt, and my mother..."

He trailed off into silence.

"I'm sorry," Kristen said. "I shouldn't have asked you to relive that."

He looked almost surprised at her apology. "It's okay. I was just replaying that scene, and you were right. I would have said that Santa wasn't part of it, but he was. That snow globe had a little plastic Mr. and Mrs. Claus in it, puckered up for a kiss and bending toward each other with their eyes closed."

"Oh, no. Like the one on my porch?"

"It's a common scene. I dropped the snow globe when she walked away. There was water and glitter splattered everywhere, and those red figures were lying there in the open air, still straining toward each other, still trying to connect. They never get to kiss, do they?"

They reached the park, which was really just an open square. Soon, it would be filled with cocoa stands and craft stalls for the official start of the holiday season. Right now, in the sunny-cold afternoon, it was a still-green square by the railroad tracks, empty except for the plain evergreen in the center that awaited its holiday finery.

Kristen stopped walking and turned to face Ryan. "Why didn't you tell me? I would have retired Mr. Claus. I would have at least shut up about my quest for Mrs. Claus."

"Unnecessary, remember? I can handle it."

She felt the tears sting her eyes. "Right. Because you're a big, tough man and you can control your feelings."

"Is that so bad?"

She stepped into him, her boots fitting between his as she clutched his lapel in her mittens and looked up at him through lashes that were wet with tears. "I'm so very sorry. I'm sorry that Ryan Michaels had to learn to control feelings like those. And I'm sorry that Ryan Roarke has a girlfriend who is too curious. I shouldn't have been so nosy."

"Don't be sorry. I want you to know me." He lifted her chin with his leather-gloved hand and kissed away a tear. "You are so special because you want to know me. It's a gift to be with a woman who asks such real questions. Most women just want—"

He cut himself off abruptly.

"Women just want what?"

Long moments ticked by. At first, she was horrified that she'd brought up some other terrible memory, but when he wouldn't quite meet her gaze, she looked at him harder. What did women want from him?

"Oh, my gosh," she blurted. "You're blushing, aren't you?"

"Of course not."

"You are." She slapped the lapel of his overcoat with her palm. "That's what women want from you, huh? I guess I'm not very unique."

They both began to laugh, and it felt wonderful to be with him, laughing by an evergreen on a sunny day in the park.

"Kristen." Ryan pulled her to him. "You are the most perfect you. Never has a woman touched my heart the way you do."

Her heart soared at those words, and she looked up at him through lashes that were still dotted with tears. "With you, I'm crying one minute and laughing the next. I think that definitely means I love you."

"Are you sure you can love a man who is more of a Scrooge than a Santa?"

If only he knew. "Scrooge had his reasons for hating Christmas, and so do you. I'd have to have a heart of stone to hold it against either one of you. I've always had a soft spot for Scrooge."

"I've always liked Scrooge, too." His eyes narrowed the tiniest bit, and then he straightened and looked around the square. Red bells, candy canes, the tree awaiting its decorations—he looked critically at them all. "I've always thought I hated Christmas, but I don't. None of this bothers me. I watch at least one version of Scrooge every year."

"You do?" The ticket in her pocket might be a sweet surprise, after all.

"I do. I don't hate everything about Christmas."

"Just Santa?" she asked, wanting to be sure.

"Yeah, I'm not so crazy about him, but now I've pinpointed why. Thank you. I told you those questions were good ones."

"Being like Scrooge could be a good thing. He changes at the end of the play and ends up as the biggest Christmas fan of them all."

"That may be a bit ambitious, but I'll work on it."

"The day after Thanksgiving, there's a big parade through town that ends right here. The mayor lights the tree, and it stays lit all month. When you come back, I'm going to bring you here and kiss you until you have a great Christmas memory to start building on."

His smile dimmed a little at her words, but that was probably because a great Christmas was a new concept for him. "I told you when we met that if anyone could make Christmas better, it would be you."

She looped her arms around his neck. "And when I find my 1968 Mrs. Claus, I'm going to put her on the porch with her little mouth pushed right up to Santa's. It's too sad that they never make that connection. Mine are going to get to kiss all winter long."

He'd said her questions were like a gift to him, but she had something better to give: a promise. So while he was still chuckling, she spoke very seriously. "And, Ryan Roarke, whether it is Christmas or the Fourth of July or spring or autumn, I will never, ever walk away from you."

Kristen loved him.

Him, Ryan Roarke, who had once been Ryan Michaels, and who bore all the complications that came with his history. Miraculously, he'd come to Montana and found the one woman who had taken the time to get to know him inside and out, and she loved him.

They'd spent all week sharing their histories, their feelings, their desires. She knew nothing about the cars he owned or the clients he helped, but she knew his heart. She loved him, the real him, not an idealized image of a cowboy or a rodeo star. He could tell her about his law practice now, and it wouldn't change anything she loved about him, because she'd fallen in love without knowing about his Hollywood connections or his bank account. When he explained that he couldn't make it back in December, that there'd be no kiss by the town's tree, she'd be disappointed, but she'd still love him in January.

"Speaking of Scrooge," she said, "there's something you don't know about me. Close your eyes."

He closed them obediently. He heard the rustle of her bright red coat as she unbuttoned it. His own coat was unbuttoned despite the temperatures staying in the thirties. In only one week, his body had learned to tolerate the cold far better. If he lived in Montana, it would take no time to adjust.

"Now let me turn you so you're facing this way."

If only he could live in Montana. He couldn't let his parents down, but he needed to find a way to see Kristen more often. December was impossible, but perhaps he could fly Kristen to Los Angeles, if she could juggle her ranch, her renovations and her teaching job. She'd never want to live in LA, but she might find a visit interesting.

"Okay, open your eyes."

Kristen was beaming at him as she held a ticket in her mittened hand.

He took the ticket. "*A Christmas Carol*? We were just talking about it. You had this in your pocket the whole time?"

"I did, but I wasn't going to give it to you if it would make you sad. You have no idea how relieved I am to hear you say you like Scrooge. Tonight is opening night, right here at this theater." She gestured toward the sprawling brick building she'd turned him to face, a renovated train depot, by the looks of it.

She seemed overly excited about attending a local play, but he was game. "Great. We'll go. You've got the other ticket?"

"That's the surprise. You know that job I've been working at every day? This is where I've been."

His brain made a feeble effort to tie a teacher into the theater. She tutored children in the cast, perhaps. Dread started building, knotting his gut. He tried to connect a cowgirl to the theater, grasping at straws. Perhaps there were live animals in the play, and she wrangled them. But his heart knew what was coming, what came next.

What always came next, with every woman.

"After I met you, I knew that it was time to get serious about my passion, my career, my life. Everything. Because of you, I'm pursuing a little happiness here in this theater. I don't need a ticket, because I'll be onstage."

No. Don't say it, don't break it.

"I'm an actress!"

Good God. He staggered back a step. How could he have thought it would be any different with this woman?

He crumpled her ticket into his fist and shoved his hands in his pockets. "You knew. All along, you knew."

Her smile didn't falter, but the little wrinkle between her brows betrayed her concern at his reaction. She wasn't a good enough actress to hide her concern.

"I knew? Well, yes, I auditioned in October."

"An actress." He looked at her beloved face—yes, beloved, damn it—and felt like a fool.

"You knew I was an actress."

He couldn't speak he was so disgusted.

Her smile was completely gone now, as she so earnestly tried to make him believe this was a good thing. "You were the one who encouraged me to use my degree. You were the one who inspired me not to take no for an answer."

"From a principal. So you could teach."

"So I could create a drama club. I majored in theater, Ryan. I'd love to direct a play at the school. I love the theater."

"Of course you do."

She blinked at his mocking tone and even pulled that

trick with the tears again. He wanted to applaud her performance, shout *Brava!* for the way she'd so thoroughly performed her part this week, but he couldn't go that far. Not yet. Not while she looked like the innocent ranch girl of his dreams. Once she made it to Hollywood—and he had no doubt that a woman with her exquisite features could get noticed there—she'd be Botoxed for no reason, her lips augmented and her hair dyed blond, and then, when she didn't look so much like Kristen, he'd be able to harden his heart completely.

Right now, it hurt like hell.

"Well done, Kristen. Well played. A word of caution, though. You almost gave away your game at the beginning of the week. You accepted the fact that my name was Roarke too easily. You should have played it a little less cool that I was from California. You were supposed to think I was a rodeo star, remember? There are no cattle operations in LA."

"But... Bakersfield. Salinas." She sounded faint. Bewildered. Still beautiful.

He couldn't bear to look at her. For a week, he'd been denying himself the pleasure of her body, wanting her to know who he really was before he made love to her.

He had to laugh at his own naïveté. "I must've thrown you off by refusing to share your bed, but you compensated brilliantly. All those long talks, all that tender concern. It was a novelty to me, I admit. What were you hoping for, Kristen? Was I supposed to go to your little play tonight and be so besotted that I'd run to Scorsese and sing your praises? What are you earning at this theater, equity minimum? Did you think I'd negotiate a top contract for you?"

She'd deserve it. The way she was pressing her little mittens to her temples in confusion, the way her hair tangled with her polka-dot scarf and the November breeze pinkened her cheeks—oh, yeah. She was playing her role to perfection. He could get her top dollar.

"It backfired," he informed her coldly. "The sex would have been fine. No hard feelings. But to make me believe in love and family and goddamned Santa Claus? I just feel like a sucker. No one does favors for people who treat them like suckers."

Kristen held her palms out in a helpless gesture. The gentle shake of her head was just enough to make fat tears drop from her lashes to her cheeks.

"Who *are* you?" she whispered, the plea in her voice sounding so real his heart squeezed hard in his chest.

"Did you really think I was a cowboy? The rodeo star of your dreams? Please."

Finally, she dropped the innocent shock and moved on to something else, something angry. The stomp of her booted foot and the clenching of her fists were perfect touches. "Stop this. Stop. You're being hurtful, and I don't know why. You're from Los Angeles and you were never in the rodeo? What on earth do you do?"

"I'm an attorney." He crossed his arms over his chest, closing his jacket against the cold. "An attorney in the entertainment industry, and a damned successful one, as you well know."

"An attorney."

"A simple thing to search for on the internet. I honor my confidentiality agreements, but Hollywood studios do not, when they want to stir up publicity. My role in the Century Films controversy became common knowledge. How convenient for actresses who are ready to take their careers to the next level."

"I searched Ryan Michaels, the rodeo rider. You lied to me."

"I never claimed to be in the rodeo."

"But you knew I thought so. All week, you've been lying to me. You let me spill my heart out—oh! When I told you about that lying, cheating pilot, you should have told me you were just like him. Just toying with me while you were in town. Just playing a game until it was time to fly off to some other life."

And she hated him for it, judging by the look on her face. He steeled himself against the pain. Maggie had predicted it, but Maggie hadn't known that Kristen had been playing him for a fool all along. This was just an act.

Kristen took in a shuddering breath. "Were you lying from the beginning, even in the summer? Were you really considering moving to Rust Creek Falls? Did you care for me even a little?"

He'd be damned before he told Kristen any more about his feelings. She didn't need to know that his parents' need for him to take over the firm had ended his dream to move here, either. But as he looked into her blue eyes, wide with hurt and bright with tears, some piece of Ryan wanted to hold her and soothe her and reassure her.

He squelched the impulse. "I'm not the actor here, Kristen. You are."

Let her make of that what she wanted.

The cold air had dried the tears on her cheeks. "You shouldn't play with people's lives. You shouldn't have hurt mine. I only loved you."

Ryan hated himself for how badly he wished that were true.

"I think we've covered everything sufficiently," he said. "There's no need for a dramatic ending. You'll forgive me if I don't wish you luck in your acting career. Goodbye, Kristen."

She closed her eyes, a moment of misery, and started to turn away. But she only began the motion with her shoulders before she stopped herself and leveled her gaze on him once more. She said nothing, did nothing.

He raised one brow. "Go on. Your theater awaits. I've got nothing left to say."

"You're waiting for me to walk away. I made you a promise before I handed you that ticket. I told you I would never walk away from you. I'm standing right here, Ryan. If you want to leave me, if you want this to end, then you are going to have to be the one who walks. I won't do that to you. Not even now."

Now that you've broken everything.

Nothing good lasted forever. Finding out that Kristen's love had been a lie was really nothing more than he'd expected. Actresses were always ambitious, after all.

Ryan turned on his heel and began walking away. He shoved his hands in his coat pockets and felt the ticket. Without missing a step, he pulled the crumpled ticket from his pocket and dropped it onto the sidewalk.

I'm not this good of an actress.

Kristen could hardly hold herself together. Her hands were shaking as she tried to button the tight cuffs of her Victorian costume.

"Do you need help?" Kayla stopped to put down the bowl and spoon Scrooge would be using to eat his gruel.

In her shapeless black clothes, with her headset on her head, Kayla looked ready to make sure all the props made it onstage throughout the performance.

"Oh, Kayla. I'm so glad to see you. I had the most awful day with Ryan."

"Hold that thought. One second."

Kayla dashed off to one of the toilet stalls in the women's dressing area, cutting Kristen short just when she'd been about to spill all her misery.

She shouldn't give in to the misery, anyway. She should get through the show before she let her feelings out, because once she started crying, she was afraid she'd never stop.

She managed the buttons on her cuff, then the other cuff. Still, her sister stayed in the bathroom. Kayla hadn't been herself for weeks now, and Kristen was worried sick about her. She couldn't handle any more bad news, not on top of Ryan's betrayal.

Ryan. She couldn't stop thinking about him for a second. How could she have been so deceived? A Hollywood attorney, playing at being a cowboy. They'd never actually done any riding or training of the horses this week, she realized suddenly. That had been by design. *His* design.

But, dear God, the horses had loved him, and so had she.

He'd lied to her.

He'd left her.

She pressed her hand to her mouth, physically trying to hold her sobs in. She couldn't do this. She couldn't go out on that stage and say her heartbreaking lines while her heart was truly breaking.

"We've got a full house." The stage manager's voice came over the little speaker that was kept backstage. "Two minutes to curtain."

She was about to find out whether or not she could. The show must go on.

Chapter Twelve

Kristen's tears didn't wait for their cue.

From the wings, where she hovered anxiously near Kayla's prop station, she watched the first scenes of the play. The little boy playing the youngest version of Ebenezer was doing a good job. Too good for Kristen's state of mind.

The little boy had no one to love him, no place to spend the Christmas holiday. His classroom was barren. One by one, every other student left with a mother or father. The teacher gave him a book to read and threw one measly piece of coal into the stove, then walked out. Alone, rejected, unwanted, the boy huddled at his wood desk.

In the dark cocoon of the wings, Kristen's tears fell. If young Ebenezer had just dropped a snow globe on the floor...

Poor Ryan. He'd been even younger than this boy

when he'd been left alone in the world. Thank goodness he'd been adopted, but despite thirty years of being a Roarke, Ryan was still the little boy who'd learned to be so careful with his heart. Kristen had thought she could prove to him that her love was unbreakable, as solid and real as the love his adoptive parents had given him, but he wouldn't give her the chance.

Maybe a man who'd spent thirty years avoiding pain, a man who'd only very carefully chosen to return the love of those immediate family members who'd spent years loving him first, maybe that man would never change.

She would never know.

The tears started anew, and Kristen knew she would have to repair her stage makeup. Quickly. The Christmas party scene at the jovial Fezziwig home was about to begin.

While the stage was blacked out, the stagehands rushed antique toys onto the set, setting them under the tree. Kayla rolled a rocking horse onto the stage, then she zipped back to the wings with her arms full of schoolbooks from the classroom scene. She placed them in their assigned spot at her station, then she put her hand on her stomach and gave herself a pat.

Kristen's sobs hiccupped to an abrupt stop. That pat was the kind of thing a pregnant woman did to her growing belly.

Kayla was pregnant.

No. They were sisters. Twins. Kayla would never keep such a secret from her. She wasn't even dating anyone. But the months of fatigue, the nausea, even the decision to give up caffeine...

The lights onstage came up, bright white to make the

colorful party set pop. The audience applauded the set design before the first line of dialogue could be spoken, and Kristen watched her sister smile and take her hand away from her stomach to applaud, too. The white lights bounced off her black clothes, and Kristen wanted to cry all over again. Her sister had a definite baby bump. The first secret Kayla had ever kept from her was one of the most important ones of all.

It didn't seem possible that two people Kristen loved had so completely hidden their real selves from her. From Ryan's livelihood to Kayla's new life, Kristen had been oblivious to it all, a trusting, blind fool. Like the character of Belle, she only wanted to go back to the way things had been.

Belle was brave, though. When the man she loved changed, Belle faced the truth. In the face of Ryan's betrayal, Kristen had no choice but to do the same.

With a swirl of blue velvet, she hurried back to the makeup station, suddenly thankful for the chance to play Belle tonight. For the length of a few pages of script, Kristen would get to be brave.

And then, when the lights went out and the audience left, she would fall apart.

The Ghost of Christmas Past showed no mercy.

Old Scrooge wanted to enjoy the happiest memory of his life, but the figure in white and flame dragged him away as the curtain came down, obliterating the sight of Fezziwig's party and the lively dancing.

Ryan shifted his weight as he leaned against the very back wall of the theater. The happiest memory of his life was a dance, too. A waltz in the middle of an empty road. A sky lit by fireworks, a woman's voice humming the melody that guided them. Destiny.

The bitterness threatened to choke him. Her perfection had been an act, just as her performance tonight would be. Ryan had decided to buy a ticket at the last minute. He didn't bother taking his seat, because he'd be leaving soon. He only wanted to see Kristen onstage before he caught the last flight out. He needed to witness all her fake glory as an actress. When the happier memories swamped him, as they already had while he'd gone back to his hotel and packed, he wanted to be able to recall her on the stage, pursuing the career that she'd hoped he would boost.

The Ghost of Christmas Past pointed to the center of the dark stage. Scrooge begged her not to show him the inevitable, but of course he had to turn toward center stage, as well.

In contrast to the full set of the Christmas party, this scene opened on a simple park bench lit by a single spotlight. Standing in the center of the circle of light was Kristen, absolutely breathtaking in her winter velvet gown. Snow gently fell all around her.

Ryan heard a hiss of breath and realized it was his own. Kristen looked like a figurine in a snow globe. He'd come for a memory. He didn't want this one.

A young man in top hat and tails entered the circle of light. Kristen looked at Ebenezer with such longing, such regret, that Ryan was taken aback. With talent to match her looks, the sky would have been the limit if he'd wanted to launch her career.

Eventually the words of the play penetrated his thoughts. "Tell me truly, if you saw me today for the first time, would you make the effort to dance with me at Fezziwig's party?"

Yes. A waltz or a two-step, a wooden floor or asphalt, anything at all to feel her in his arms one more time.

"The man who loved me is only a memory. For his sake, I pray you will be happy upon your chosen path. You no longer want me to walk with you, no matter how much I wish it otherwise."

For God's sake, he couldn't stand here and listen to this. Either she was a world-class actress stuck in an obscure regional theater in a tiny town, or her heart was truly breaking as she spoke her lines. Either way, it was her misfortune. She was the one who'd been planning on using him. She'd said everything he wanted to hear in exchange for her shot at Hollywood.

Impatiently, Ryan picked up his coat and gloves and headed for the exit. The usher stopped him at the door. Ryan would have to wait until the end of the scene to open the door into the bright lobby. From the corner of his eye, he saw the hem of Kristen's long skirt as she walked out of the spotlight and was swallowed by the darkness.

"Go after her, you fool," Old Scrooge cried.

The usher held up his finger. One minute more.

Old Scrooge implored his younger self with an urgency born of grief. "Do you not see her caring heart? Lift your eyes from that cursed gold ring. Go after her! It's not too late for you."

But it was too late. The Ghost's flame was extinguished, the scene went dark, the audience erupted into applause and Ryan got the hell out of there.

An hour later, as he settled into his seat on the evening's only flight out of Kalispell, the voice of the pilot came over the speakers. "Ladies and gentleman, this is Captain Toomer speaking. Along with the rest of your Denver-based crew, we'd like to welcome you aboard Flight 89."

Ryan dropped his head back against the seat. A crew out of Denver. What were the odds? He could be leaving the woman who'd lied to him by taking a flight piloted by the man who'd cheated on her. Given destiny's warped timing, the odds were good.

The pilot who had *allegedly* cheated on her. Kristen could have invented the entire story to manipulate Ryan's emotions. That story had made her look good, really. She was the one who knew how to be faithful. She'd implied that the experience had negatively colored her opinion of men from big cities. Men like him.

Ryan lifted his head, a sudden jolt of adrenaline making him alert. She'd said she didn't like men from big cities. If her goal had been to attract Ryan, why would she say she avoided men like him? If her goal was to move to Los Angeles, why would she insist she didn't want to leave her hometown?

You fool...do you not see her caring heart?

It had been a trick. She'd used reverse psychology, saying she wanted the opposite of her goal to make herself seem all the more innocent. That had to have been it. She'd hidden her ambition, so he'd let down his guard. Ryan rested his head back once more, settling in for the first leg of his journey home.

You fool...

That had to be the explanation, because if it wasn't, then he'd just shattered something priceless.

* * *

"Another scotch, son?"

"Sure." Ryan turned with the decanter in his hand, ready to fill his father's glass.

His father had no glass. He merely stood on his own patio, his swimming pool sparkling in the sun beyond him, and slipped his hands into the pockets of his slacks.

"Ah. You meant, am I having another scotch?" Ryan tried not to sound too bitter as he laughed. Leave it to Dad to make his point so subtly. "Last I checked, I was over twenty-one, and I'm not driving anywhere."

Thanksgiving dinner was over at the Roarke home, but no one was leaving. Shane and a noticeably pregnant Gianna had flown in from Thunder Canyon, so they were spending the holiday weekend in one of the guest suites of their parents' home. Maggie and Jesse and baby Madeline had flown in from Rust Creek Falls and were staying for the weekend, too. Ryan was staying, as well, although he lived in the city. He wasn't going to leave this mini family reunion to spend the night alone in his exclusive, sterile penthouse. He didn't need more of his own company.

The sliding glass doors were open, and the sounds of football on TV spilled onto the patio. Sometime in the third quarter, the kitchen would be raided for a second piece of pumpkin pie or the first cold turkey sandwich of the weekend. Every year, he looked forward to that as much as he looked forward to the formal, hot dinner earlier in the day. This year, he'd also looked forward to finding relief from the loneliness that had been crippling him in the week since he'd left Kristen. Surely, surrounded by the family he trusted, Ryan's heart would be eased.

Instead, he was the seventh wheel. His parents, Christa and Gavin, were one couple. Shane and Gianna, another. Maggie and Jessie. That left Ryan feeling the absence of Kristen Dalton more acutely than ever. Thankfully, his father kept excellent scotch.

Shane joined them, carrying baby Madeline, practicing for his own impending fatherhood. "I can't get over the weather here. You forget how warm winter can be. It's already snowed at the resort. The ski bunnies are thrilled, but it means the main color we're going to see from now until Easter is white, white and more white."

"Go to one of the local high school's basketball games. There'll be lots of color."

Shane and his father both looked at him in surprise. Ryan shrugged, unwilling to explain where he'd gotten that advice.

Kristen's solution for a winter white-out had been so enthusiastic. Practical, too. Despite her secret agenda, he had to acknowledge that she really knew Rust Creek Falls inside and out. There'd been nothing fake about that tour. She'd had him seriously imagining himself trading in his penthouse for a luxury log home somewhere on the outskirts of town.

Which wouldn't have helped her get noticed in Hollywood.

Ryan stared into his scotch. Kristen must have known who he was that first day, of course. He'd been sitting with Maggie in the church during the wedding. Surely people knew Maggie was related to Shane Roarke, celebrity chef. It would have been a simple thing for Kristen to connect Roarkes with LA and show business.

Of course, she'd pretended not to know Maggie's maiden name later, but Kristen was a very good actress. She must have seen them together and realized that Ryan could be her chance to get out.

Then why had she invited him to come in? Had he moved to Rust Creek Falls, her plans would have been thwarted, yet that's exactly what she'd tried to get him to do.

The attorney side of him, which he'd once thought was his only side, picked another hole in his story. When, on that first day, could Kristen have seen him with Maggie? Kristen hadn't been at the church. Maggie hadn't been at the park.

Ryan set the scotch down, untouched.

"Are you in or not?" Shane asked, holding up a dollar bill.

"What?" Ryan couldn't think straight. His loneliness was rapidly morphing into a sick sort of dread. He may have screwed up. He may have made the biggest mistake of his life.

"Are you putting a dollar down on the Cowboys this year or not?"

"Sure." Ryan had been betting on the Dallas Cowboys to win the Thanksgiving football game since childhood, when losing a dollar had meant financial pain for the two brothers. "I don't have any cash on me. Spot me."

Shane sighed as if being asked for a dollar were a terrible imposition. "Here. Hold the baby."

Madeline let herself be handed from one uncle to the other without fussing. A series of mundane little family events followed. Shane took his wallet out of his back pocket as Maggie and Jesse joined them on the porch. When Maggie held her hands out for her daughter, Madeline stoutly refused the offer and clung to Ryan's neck.

There was laughter and Maggie pretended to be outraged at Madeline's preference for her uncle. Through it all, Ryan managed to stay on his feet and act sane. Inside, he was losing his mind.

Everything that had happened at the wedding had been real. Kristen hadn't been lying on the Fourth of July.

Ryan walked away from his family, carrying Madeline around the edge of the kidney-shaped pool to a lounge chair. He sat and stretched his legs out on the cushions. Madeline stretched herself out on his chest.

Away from the noise of his family, Ryan called upon his analytical side. Even if Kristen had started flirting with him innocently in July, this month had been a different story. On that late flight out of Montana, Ryan had decided it was entirely too coincidental for Kristen to have run into Maggie at the movies. She must have arranged it. Then she'd pulled off a performance as a lovesick woman that had been realistic enough to fool his sister into calling him back to Rust Creek Falls. He'd already been on his way, but Kristen hadn't known that. She'd had to use Maggie to be sure he returned.

The baby fussed a little, burrowing herself into a more comfortable sprawl on his chest. He patted the baby's back absently and stared at the blue water of the pool as she fell asleep. In the bright light of day, the scenario that had made sense on a midnight flight was full of holes so big, it didn't take an attorney to find them.

There was no movie theater in Rust Creek Falls. Movies were only shown on a certain Fridays in the gym. Most of the town turned out for the basketball games, Kristen had said, and he was sure that was true for the movies, as well. It was quite possible that Kristen and

Maggie had run into each other there without any nefarious plotting on Kristen's part. Ryan only knew a handful of people in town, yet he hadn't been able to take Kristen to a donut shop without running into Lissa's husband, the sheriff.

For the rest of his theory to work, Kristen had to have known not just that he was a Roarke, but that Maggie Crawford was, too. The biggest proof of Kristen's innocence was her sister. Kayla was Kristen's twin, her confidante, her biggest cheerleader. If Kristen had hatched a plan to hitch herself to Ryan for a Hollywood career, her twin would have known about it. Instead, when she'd learned that his last name was Roarke, her surprise had been genuine. *Are you related to Lissa Roarke, then?* Kayla was no actress. She and Kristen hadn't known he was a Roarke until he'd told them in the barn.

Case dismissed. Kristen was innocent, and he was a fool.

He'd shattered a snow globe once again. A thousand flakes of glitter and a hundred drops of water couldn't be put back together. Once upon a time, Christa Roarke had come and replaced the birth mother he'd lost. This time, no woman could replace Kristen Dalton. She was the only one he wanted. The only one he'd ever want.

Baby Madeline snuggled her soft head under his chin. Even a bachelor like Ryan knew that sleeping babies should not be messed with. His infant niece had him pinned to the chair when he wanted to pace restlessly. He wanted to hit a punching bag until he was too tired to think, but there'd be no escaping today. Ryan closed his eyes, remembering Kristen as he'd seen her last, a vision in Victorian blue, standing in a snow globe of a spotlight.

He had to try to fix this. He couldn't live the rest of his life alone like a bitter old Scrooge, angry at himself for not going after the woman with the caring heart. If putting a snow globe back together was impossible, then...

Then he'd be grateful that people weren't snow globes. He was going to fix this.

The baby wriggled. Ryan spread his hand across her back to calm her. Holding a baby, he realized, was even more soothing than brushing a horse. If he could win Kristen back, he'd give her all the horses she wanted, and as many babies as she desired.

Having babies meant getting married. It meant living together in one house as one family. He couldn't commute from Montana to LA and be a good husband and father. Ryan knew, without a doubt, that he'd want to raise his family in Rust Creek Falls, if he could find a way to make it happen. Unfortunately, he was a lawyer, not a cowboy, and there was barely enough legal work in Rust Creek Falls to keep Maggie busy four days a week.

Kalispell wasn't too far, and the town was easily four times the size of Rust Creek Falls. If he practiced law there, he'd never make as much money as he did here in LA, but he could make a good living. If he could win Kristen back, if he could fix the damage he'd caused, then he would never have to get on a plane and leave her behind again.

There was one thing he couldn't do if he moved to Montana. He couldn't run his parents' firm for them.

The sense of obligation was familiar. He wanted his parents to be happy. He wanted to help them out any way he could, but when any way meant he couldn't have a life with Kristen…

This was the point where he always got stuck, the point where he would give up and do something mind-numbingly physical. Not today. The baby breathed evenly, her little rib cage expanding gently under his hand, forcing him to stay still. Forcing him to find a solution.

He didn't have one.

The sound of his mother's laughter carried over the pool water. Ryan opened his eyes and took in the scene. Parents, siblings, their spouses. More babies on the way. His family. His foundation.

He didn't have a solution, but he did have a family. He hadn't trusted Kristen's love—a crucial mistake. But in many ways he hadn't trusted in his family's love, either. He'd once told Kristen that he knew his parents wanted him to be as happy as Shane and Maggie, but he'd been afraid to put it to the test.

It was time he stopped silently taking on problems alone. Tonight, over pumpkin pie and turkey sandwiches, he'd rely on the family he trusted to decide the future of Roarke and Associates together.

Then he'd get on the first plane back to Montana. Would a permanent move to Rust Creek Falls be enough to convince Kristen to give him a second chance? He'd shattered that snow globe in such a spectacularly awful way that he wanted something equally spectacular to prove he'd never lose his faith in her again. He needed some way to demonstrate that he would never again be the cold-hearted bastard he'd been when he'd left her.

Madeline's tiny fist gripped his shirt as she slept. He kissed the top of her head. Kristen's words came back to him. *What if you have children someday? Would you raise them without Santa?*

Ryan ran the tip of his finger over the dimples in the back of Madeline's hand. "You deserve a chance to believe in the magic, little one. For you, I could tolerate Santa."

The germ of an idea started to form.

Carefully, he got to his feet and carried his niece over to the family. "Maggie. Shane. I need your help. Who do you know in the mayor's office in Kalispell?"

Chapter Thirteen

There was no performance on the day after Thanksgiving.

Kristen should have been thankful for the respite. Tonight, she wouldn't have to relive the horrible feeling of losing the man she loved. Instead, she had to play a role that seemed even more daunting. She had to ride on a float in a Christmas parade, smiling and waving and throwing candy and generally acting like she was in a happy holiday mood.

The entire cast of *A Christmas Carol* was assembled on a flatbed truck that had been turned into a float. Kristen wore her full costume. In addition to the corset and hoops, the heavy skirt and tight bodice, she carried a faux fur muff and wore modern long johns under her dress, because tonight, the snowfall was real.

They waited at one end of Main Street near a high school band, a motorcycle club and a cluster of rodeo riders whose horses were dressed to the nines in silver saddles and fancy tack. Kristen looked away from the rodeo riders.

The last float featured Santa Claus himself, who would join the mayor in lighting the Christmas tree in Depot Park.

Santa Claus. The symbol of everything magical and wonderful about the holidays for her was a symbol of misery for Ryan. Was it any wonder that a man who didn't believe in Santa couldn't believe that her love was real, either?

It took every bit of acting skill she had to look happy through the entire parade. Two miles had never crawled by so slowly, but her ordeal wasn't over yet. Because of their picturesque costumes, the cast had been asked to wait by the Christmas tree until Santa's float arrived. When Santa lit the tree, the cast would add charm and holiday spirit to the town's official photos. They would be posted on websites and spread around social media. The exposure would have been nice if Kristen was trying to get jobs outside her hometown, but no matter what Ryan Roarke thought, she wasn't. The only things she'd get out of this photo session were frozen toes.

She stamped her feet and clutched her hands more tightly together inside her muff. The cast had been on the first float. Santa was on the last.

"Okay, let's have everyone line up now, half on each side of the tree." The Kalispell newspaper photographer also doubled as the wedding photographer for most of the couples in town, so he was pretty quick about getting everyone posed, ready and waiting.

Hurry, Santa. I want to go home. It's been at least five hours since I last cried. I'm overdue.

At last, the float with Santa's cardboard and plywood sleigh arrived. Kristen plastered on her smile when the cameras started to flash.

Santa dismounted his float with ease, moving in a way that was far more sprightly than his white beard would indicate he was capable of. This year's Santa was as tall as he was wide. He worked his way through the crowd, passing out candy canes to the children, who jumped excitedly at the sight of him. With every "ho, ho, ho," the children squealed in delight. Kristen's stiff smile relaxed into something more genuine, as well.

"Ho, ho, ho. Merry Christmas."

Kristen jerked her gaze away from the children to study Santa instead.

"Merry Christmas," Santa called again.

He sounded like Ryan.

Her mind was playing tricks on her. Ryan was in LA, where he belonged. Her sister had made some polite small talk with Lissa Christensen the day after Kristen and Ryan's fight, and Lissa had said that her cousin had left a day early, probably to put out a fire at his law firm.

Kristen knew he'd only wanted to get away from her as quickly as he could. He'd been so full of self-righteous anger—all of it directed so unfairly at her—that he'd wanted to put a thousand miles between them.

Kayla had also broken the mortifying news to her that if Lissa was Ryan's cousin, that meant Maggie Crawford was Ryan's sister. Apparently, she was Maggie *Roarke* Crawford. When Kristen remembered that meltdown at the movies, she didn't know how she'd ever look Maggie in the eye again.

"Smile, please. Keep smiling." The photographer

hadn't stopped snapping yet. Kristen obediently forced her face into a semblance of happiness.

"Ho, ho, ho."

Honestly, that man sounded just like Ryan. Impossible—even if Ryan had returned to town to visit his sister or cousin, he would never, ever be caught dead in a Santa suit.

With his sack of candy canes now empty, Santa walked to the tree and shook the mayor's hand. The switch was thrown, the lights came to life and the crowd went wild. So did the camera flashes.

Santa chose to stand right between the only two women, Kristen and the actress playing Mrs. Cratchit. It could have been Kristen's imagination, but Santa seemed to give her an extra warm squeeze. Was Mrs. Cratchit feeling such a strong arm around her waist?

"Ryan...?"

This man didn't seem to be angry at her at all. Considering how furious Ryan had been just days ago, it couldn't be him. Then again, Santa was an important role. Santa could never get angry in front of children—and Ryan would never ruin Christmas for a child, despite its having been ruined for him.

But Ryan also had no earthly reason to ever wear a Santa suit. Whoever this year's Santa was, it couldn't be the man who'd so recently broken her heart. It was pitiful that she missed Ryan badly enough to imagine it was him.

At last, the ceremony was over, the photographer was satisfied, and the cast was free to return to the theater to remove their costumes. Santa offered Kristen his arm as she headed across the green to the theater, and they each smiled and returned waves from the children and adults they passed.

They entered the theater through the stage door, which led almost directly to the black curtains of the wings. Santa looked all around, turning in a full three-sixty. "Are there any children here? No? Good. I'd hate to confuse the little kids."

He pulled off his hat with one hand and his white beard with the other, and turned to kiss Kristen, hard.

She hadn't seen his face, but it didn't matter. She recognized his kiss.

"Ryan." She murmured his name against his lips, but before she could begin to ask him the questions his presence raised, he spoke.

"I'm so sorry. Please forgive me for being a stubborn, pigheaded jerk."

"But…" She shook her head at his padded costume, just one more mystifying piece of the puzzle that was Ryan. "Why?"

"Because I hurt you. I jumped to all the wrong conclusions, and I refused to listen to you when you told me the truth. I don't deserve it, but please forgive me."

"I meant, why are you Santa Claus? This is like your worst nightmare."

"Not even close. Losing you is my worst nightmare."

Most of the actors had made their way back to the dressing rooms, but Ryan pulled her deeper into the wings, where the black curtains muffled their voices and gave them a sense of privacy.

"I'm wearing this suit so you'll know that I mean it when I promise you that I won't make the same mistakes twice."

"You won't assume I'm some kind of gold-digging, movie star wannabe?"

Well, that had rolled off her tongue a little too easily. She'd had a week to relive every painful word he'd said to her, though.

He dropped his head for a moment, chagrined, then looked at her again with such tenderness in his expression, it took her breath away. "For starters, yes. That kind of mistake. I'm so sorry. Do you know why I assumed the worst? Because those were the only type of women I'd known. They were the only type of women I dated, because they couldn't hurt me. They didn't matter. If they walked away, nothing inside me would shatter."

He touched her face with one hand, tentatively cupping her cheek, then stroking his thumb over her cheekbone. "But you, Kristen, you matter."

"Oh, Ryan." Kristen turned her face into his hand.

"I didn't know how to handle that. You are this wonderful, remarkable, beautiful woman who somehow fell into my hands, but I didn't know how to hold you. I was so afraid I'd lose something good, that I was paralyzed. I did nothing. That was a mistake, too.

"I was afraid to lie to you and afraid to tell you the truth at the same time. I told myself you couldn't handle too many corrections all at once, but the only real truth was that I was petrified I'd lose the best thing in my life. That's you. That will always be you.

"I learned when I was young that nothing good lasts forever, but I don't think that's true any longer, not after meeting you. I believe forever is possible, a good forever, as long as I can spend it with you. I'm wearing this Santa suit because I'm not going to avoid the good things in life anymore. I hope that, someday, you'll love me again. I hope that you'll trust me not to make the same mistakes again."

Kristen swallowed past the lump in her throat. Just seeing his face again, just being touched by him again, made her happier than she could have believed possible just a short time ago. She pressed her hand to heart, feeling out of breath from the emotions.

"If you can't forgive me tonight, I understand," Ryan said. "I screwed up badly, but I'll be here tomorrow. And next week. Next year. You promised me you'd never walk away from me, and I'm here to make the same promise back. I'm staying. Right here in Montana, right here with you, until you believe me when I say I love you."

"Oh, Ryan." Kristen tried to throw her arms around his neck, but his red suit's padding was completely in the way. Her hoops pushed gracefully behind her when she got close to him, but his stuffed belly stayed stuffed.

Ryan unbuttoned the coat and tossed it on a folding chair. Underneath, he was wearing a fitted black T-shirt with the baggy red velvet pants. He pulled her into his arms and held her against his strong chest almost as tightly as she'd dreamed for the past lonely week.

"I don't want you to settle for a Scrooge when you want a Santa," Ryan whispered. "I don't want you to settle for a lawyer when you want a cowboy."

"I don't want a lawyer or a cowboy. I want a Ryan."

"Michaels or Roarke?"

"Both, as long as he's happy with me."

"He couldn't be anything else with you in his life, and that's the whole truth."

Kristen kissed him almost as passionately as she knew she'd be kissing him tonight. In her house. Finally.

The cast of the play had begun filtering back out of the dressing rooms. A man in street clothes whistled at their embrace. Kristen tried to brazen it out, giving the crew a nonchalant shrug of one shoulder as she broke off the kiss she'd initiated. She smoothed her gown into place over her hoops.

"Some things go without saying, but this needs to be said. I love you, Kristen Dalton. It's been seven days since I've held you, and I never want to go seven days without holding you again."

Ryan dropped to one knee in front of her, and Kristen thought her heart stopped. Cast, crew, costume—all were forgotten as she focused on Ryan.

He patted his oversize pants pockets and got a little of that deer-in-the-headlights look, but then he slid on his knee to the discarded Santa coat and dug through it until he came up with a gray velvet box. The theater people gathered around them began to buzz with excitement.

"I wanted to wear the Santa suit to show you how precious you are to me." He opened the gray box and held it up. The diamond ring inside sparkled with every color of every Christmas light ever strung on a cozy house for two. "This is the other way I want to show you how precious you are to me. I love you with all my heart, Kristen Dalton. I will never deserve you, but I'm not going to let that stop me from being happy with you. Will you marry me?"

The photographer by the town Christmas tree was tireless in his effort to capture the happiness of the newly engaged couple.

Kristen had changed into her street clothes, including a chic white jacket with faux-fur trim and the most flattering nipped-in waist. She'd bought it this week in a futile attempt to use retail therapy to soothe her heartbreak, but now she was thrilled to have something fabulous to wear for her engagement photos. Ryan was looking handsome and sexy and cute all at once. That was possible when the fine tailoring of a man's coat contrasted with the bright red Santa's hat he wore.

"Wassail!" One of the street vendors came up to their little cluster of friends and family. "It's on the house. Wassail to toast the happy couple."

Kayla was standing next to Kristen, so Kristen took the chance to offer her some sisterly advice. As surreptitiously as she could, she gestured toward her sister's thickening middle. "If I were you, I'd pass on the mystery punch this time."

Kayla colored. "I don't know what you mean."

"I know your secret. I want you to be as happy as I am. We've got to talk."

"Soon. Don't worry about me right now. This is your special night."

On Kristen's other side, Ryan scrutinized the two cups he held. "Do you suppose this is safe to drink? They still haven't solved the case of the Power of the Punch."

"I was just saying the same thing to Kayla. You and I have so much in common."

"On the other hand, we just got engaged. Who cares if the wassail is a little too strong?" He grinned at her, looking more carefree than she'd ever seen him look.

"It is a very old Christmas tradition." She took one of the cups from him.

"You know, Christmas is rapidly becoming my favorite time of the year. If I'm going to be a changed man like Scrooge, I believe I need to fully support all the traditions."

Kristen tapped her cup to his. "In that case, down the hatch."

"In that case, Merry Christmas to the future Mrs. Roarke." They drank to their own happiness, and kissed under the lights of the tree.

"From now on," Kristen sighed, "I'm always going to love wassail-flavored kisses."

"From now on," Ryan said, "I'm always going to love you."

* * * * *

LET'S TALK
Romance

For exclusive extracts, competitions
and special offers, find us online:

- facebook.com/millsandboon
- @MillsandBoon
- @MillsandBoonUK

Get in touch on 01413 063232